"Snappy writing, a page-tu[ ]g [ ]
building make *Dying Bites* a satisfying meal of a book."
—Kelley Armstrong, *New York Times* bestselling author of
Men of the Otherworld and *The Awakening*

"*Dying Bites* is wacky, unpredictable, fresh, and amazing. I
would kill to write as well as DD Barant. Seriously."
—Nancy Holder, author of *Pretty Little Devils*

"This engrossing debut adds another captivating protago-
nist to the urban fantasy ranks . . . Barant's well-developed
world offers intriguing enhancements to mythology and history. Jace is remarkable, strong-willed, and smart, and she
sets an unstoppable pace. Look for the Bloodhound Files to
go far." —*Publishers Weekly* (starred review)

"A heroine with plenty of guts, moxie, and a sense of the
absurd. [A] fresh and original take on urban fantasy . . . Huge
kudos to Barant for spicing things up with a story that expertly
integrates detective work, kick-butt action, and a wacky
sense of humor. Make sure you get in early on the outstanding
new Bloodhound Files series." —*RT Book Reviews*

"DD Barant builds a strong world and fills it with fascinating
characters that will delight and entertain. *Dying Bites* is a
well-written urban fantasy with a gripping plot and a heroine who is quite believable with her very human flaws. I'm
looking forward to seeing more in this captivating world."
—*Darque Reviews* (starred read)

"Five stars. An exciting new series. It has humor, mystery,
and adventure. A great book!" —*Affair de Coeur*

"Barant does an excellent job introducing a whole new world
where vampires make up the majority of the population . . .
quick and engrossing . . . a great new series."—*Romance Reader*

Also by DD Barant

BACK FROM THE UNDEAD

DD Barant

St. Martin's Paperbacks

This is a work of fiction. All of the characters, organizations, and events portrayed in this novel are either products of the author's imagination or are used fictitiously.

BACK FROM THE UNDEAD

For information address St. Martin's Press, 175 Fifth Avenue, New York, NY 10010.

ISBN: 978-0-312-54506-2

Printed in the United States of America

St. Martin's Paperbacks edition / April 2012

St. Martin's Paperbacks are published by St. Martin's Press, 175 Fifth Avenue, New York, NY 10010.

10 9 8 7 6 5 4 3 2 1

ONE

One night. That's all I got, one lousy night.

Not that the night itself was lousy—no, no, no. That was pretty damn great. In fact, I'd have to say that of all the nights I've spent having amazing, mind-blowing sex with supernatural beings, this was the best. Okay, so I only have one other night to compare it with, and that was with a werewolf and not a vampire, and I was drunk on magicked-up booze on a Japanese bullet train, but still.

Maybe I should start over.

They say that office romances are always a bad idea. When your boss is a centuries-old vampire who runs the National Security Agency, and you're an FBI profiler from a parallel world who was dragged into this reality against her will, they say—well, they don't say anything, they just roll their eyes and shake their heads and wander away muttering underneath their breath.

Add in the fact that my boss, David Cassius, has what I can only call an endangered species fetish—human beings make up only 1 percent of the population here, the rest being vampires, werewolves, or golems—and that I'm an extremely strong-willed woman who doesn't want *anyone* to take care of her, and you have all the ingredients for a relationship H-bomb.

Did I mention how good the sex was?

But none of that matters, not now.

Because all I got was one lousy night.

"This is a bad idea," Charlie mutters.

Since we happen to be waiting for a bomb to go off, I can't really argue. "You got that right. But what other choice do I have?"

"Lots. You could read a book. Watch a movie. Buy new shoes. Walk in front of a moving bus—"

From behind my closed bedroom door, there's a hopeful whine from my dog. "Don't say the W word. You'll get Galahad all worked up."

"Sorry. *Jump* in front of a bus. *Leap* from the top of a skyscraper. *Throw* yourself in a live volcano—"

"I get the idea. Stop making suggestions and try to be a little supportive, will you?"

He turns and glares at me. When a golem with see-through plastic skin stuffed with three hundred pounds of black sand glares at you, it can be a little unnerving. Fortunately, I've built up an immunity over time. "Jace. This is as supportive as I can be while hiding behind someone's couch."

"You know, where I come from people hide *behind* sandbags when they're dealing with high explosives. You know, instead of beside them."

"Where you come from sandbags don't wear suits made of Italian silk." He has a point. His jacket is pale green, with just a hint of gold woven into the fabric. Matching fedora with a yellow hatband, of course.

I'm dressed in black sweatpants, sneakers, and a white T-shirt, but hey, it's my apartment and my day off, so I plan on being comfortable while possibly destroying my apartment. My partner, on the other hand, doesn't even know the definition of the word *casual*. I'd say he was born wearing a three-piece suit, but golems aren't so much born as manufactured. Charlie may be the most lethal person I've ever met, but his fashion sense is just as sharp as his killer instincts.

Needless to say, he's not thrilled with the prospect of crouching on my unvacuumed-for-three-weeks carpet while risking the possibility of severe wardrobe mal- function or even destruction.

I check my watch again. "Four minutes. I think the fuse must have gone out."

"I'll go check."

"No!" I yank on his arm and pull him back down. Char- lie doesn't take conventional explosives seriously—not be- cause he's invulnerable, but because of a global spell cast on this world back in the twelfth century. The enchant- ment is a subtle one; it doesn't make firearms or bombs impossible to create, it just makes everyone believe both concepts are ridiculous. Nobody's ever built a gun or a hand grenade or a nuclear weapon on Thropirelem—that's what I call this place, due to all the thropes, pires, and lems—because people have no faith in the ideas behind them. But then, when you're dealing with near-indestructible supernatural beings strong enough to pick up cars, your approach to warfare takes a very different direction. Charlie likes to pitch steel-cored silver ball bearings at just under the speed of sound, himself.

I, however, am the exception to the rule. I may not turn into a seven-foot-tall hairy monster, I might not drink blood and avoid sunlight—but that doesn't mean I'm helpless. I carry my own personal talisman, a heavy chunk of steel known as a Ruger Super Redhawk Alas- kan. It's one of the most powerful handguns ever created, and I brought it—and a crate of ammunition—with me when I crossed the dimensional divide to this world. Since then I've had the bullets specially modified, the lead replaced with hand-carved teakwood tipped with silver.

But I've only got so much gunpowder—and nobody here knows how to make the damn stuff.

I'm no chemist. I've tried taking samples to professionals to have it analyzed, but the spell blocks me every time; the lab results get lost or forgotten or thrown away, as if the material involved contains the distilled essence of incompetence. I've had more than one tech just stare at me skeptically and tell me he doesn't have time for pranks.

So I'm trying to make my own.

"You should learn how to use a bow," Charlie says for the hundredth time. "It's not hard. I'll teach you."

"Sorry, but I still don't have a supernatural's strength—the draw on those things is like trying to pull back the anchor chain for an aircraft carrier. I prefer a nice, simple trigger."

"We can have one custom-made. I know a guy."

I sigh. "It's not just strength, it's speed, okay? A thrope or pire archer can fire arrows so fast their bow basically becomes a semi-automatic weapon. Me, not so much—the first time I try to draw down on a suspect, I'm going to look like a pincushion."

"I doubt that."

"Thanks, but I lack your cheery optimism."

"No, I meant the pincushion thing. A broadhead shaft from a thrope bow would punch right through you. You'd just have a bunch of gaping holes in your body—the pincushion metaphor doesn't really work."

"I appreciate your tactful approach to accuracy."

"Not sure what does, though. A sponge? No . . . Swiss cheese, maybe?"

All right, so it's possible that mixing my own gunpowder and testing it by igniting some in my living room wasn't the most thought-out plan in the world. But I was feeling a little manic, a little paranoid, and more than a little sexually frustrated.

See, Cassius and I had finally had our moment. It was intense and epic and surreal, and since then—all of three days ago—I haven't spent a lot of time around him. I asked for a little space to process things, and he agreed far too quickly. I used the hours to do a lot of thinking and made a few important decisions, including setting up my own martial arts dojo—a twenty-four-hour whirlwind of renting a space, printing up flyers, driving around town dropping them off, and then hunting down some used equipment—which left me happy and exhausted and itchy to do something else so I wouldn't have to do any more thinking.

Because I was tired of thinking. I'm a smart person who spends way too much time inside her own head, and there are times when you just have to *do* something. "Too much knowledge numbs the will to action," my old sensei Duane Dunn used to say, and he was right on the money.

Because this was too big to wrap my head around, and the more I tried the more I got snarled by analysis paralysis. A centuries-old vampire was in love with me. I was having an affair with my boss, the director of the NSA. I was trapped on a parallel world full of supernatural beings. Any one of those things was enough to drive a sane person crazy if she spent too much thinking about it, and they were only the most obvious factors in the equation.

So, I gave up trying to understand, and decided to just go with the flow. Adopt, adapt, and improve, as John Cleese once said. Of course, he was playing an inept stickup man who was robbing a lingerie shop at the time, but the principle still holds.

I called Cassius up and told him I wanted us to get together. That night, at my place. I told him to bring his toothbrush, or whatever the pire equivalent was.

Then I decided to blow myself up. Because, you know, my subconscious is a lot better with metaphors than I am.

"It's not gonna implode," Charlie says.

"*Ex*plode."

"Whatever. How long are we supposed to wait? I got things to do." He stands up.

Whaboom!

When I was a kid, I had a cap gun. You threaded this roll of red paper through it, and when you pulled the trigger the hammer snapped down on one of the little dark dots of gunpowder embedded at regular intervals through the paper, making a satisfying *bang!*

I, however, being a spirited and inquisitive child, was *not* satisfied. So I took a whole roll of caps, placed it on a rock, and hit it with a much bigger hammer.

Did you know it's possible to hear the first two letters of the word *bang*? Yeah, a really loud *ba,* followed by a loud ringing where the *ng* should be. Went away in a few hours, though I'm lucky I didn't blow out an eardrum.

This is kind of like that. I don't go completely deaf this time, though; I can hear all sorts of other noises, like shattering glass and the dull impact of flying objects coming to a sudden stop.

My ears are sure ringing, though. I stand up slowly, and say, "Charlie?"

He turns his head to regard me. He's not wearing his fedora anymore. The front of his suit is blackened and shredded. I really should have moved that vase out of the way, too, because it's in about a hundred pieces—most of which are sticking out of Charlie's chest.

"Um," I say. "You really shouldn't have done that."

"*That* being what? Buying this suit—*yesterday*? Getting up this morning? Or agreeing to have a partner who's a brain-damaged pyromaniac in the first place?"

"I was going to go with standing up."

"What, and ruin a terrific punch line? Otherwise known as a *twelve-hundred-dollar suit*?"

"I'll pay for it, okay? Are *you* all right?"

He looks down at himself, where the neck of the vase is protruding from his belly like a rib with a wily escape plan. He grabs it and yanks it out, causing black sand to avalanche all over the floor. He slaps a hand over the hole and scowls at me. "I've been better."

"I'll get the duct tape."

And that was how I spent the evening while waiting for my new lover to finish work and come over for our first full night together.

One night.

One amazing, lousy night.

"Jace," he whispers.

I roll over, sleepily. He's lying on his side, propped up on one elbow, one leg bent at the knee. Classic pose for a classic body. I usually think of Cassius's looks in terms of surfer boy meets CEO, but the only suit he's wearing at the moment is the one he was born in, and the dim light softens his golden skin to something closer to honey. His blue eyes are a little less vivid, but still striking. Right now the rumor that he was the actual model for Michaelangelo's *David* is a lot easier to believe.

"Mmmm," I say. That's me, always a fountain of eloquence first thing in the morning.

"Sorry to wake you. I have to go in to the office."

"Awready? Whatime zit?"

"Early. Go back to sleep."

"*Was* asleep. You woke me up." That might sound a little cranky, but I say it around a yawn and a smile. Memories of last night are percolating through my brain—and other parts.

"I didn't want to leave without saying good-bye. Among other things."

I sit up. "Like what?" I'm not fully awake, but there's still a note of caution in my voice.

"Like how much last night meant to me." He says it simply, with no trace of sentimentality. A fact. Direct, honest. Beautiful.

"I . . . me, too."

"I know you don't do well with certain emotions, and I don't want something as ridiculous as embarrassment to come between us. Plus, we should maintain a certain amount of decorum at the office."

"I'm not following. Pre-coffee, brain no good."

He smiles. A knowing smile, the kind that somehow says he's appreciating me on a whole bunch of levels at once, with affection and wry humor and even a little impatience tempered by acceptance. The kind of smile you get from someone who really understands you—and loves you anyway.

"I'll keep my sentences short. You know how I feel about you." A statement, not a question.

I swallow with a suddenly dry mouth. "Yeah." For a little while during my last case I was actually *in* Cassius's head, and I got to see myself the way he sees me. I have no doubts, none at all, about his feelings for me. It's my own emotions I'm a little unclear on.

"It's a lot to get hit with, all at once. I understand that. But if we just ignore it, it'll become the elephant in the room—we'll always know it's there even though we never talk about it."

"So we need a way to talk about it *without* talking about it?"

"I suppose." He reaches out, puts one cool hand on my hip. "I don't want to overwhelm you, I don't want to drive you away . . . but I won't deny what you mean to me, either. I—*we* have to find a balance."

I nod. "No L word for now, okay? I mean, I know that you . . ." I stop. Damn it, why is this so hard? It's just a simple noun, after all.

No. I have no problem with it as a noun. It's when it becomes a verb that I start screwing up. Relationship grammar, as diagrammed by Jace Valchek, Professional Word Understander.

"Tell you what, Caligula," I say. "If you really need to express how you feel about me, let's be professional about it. We work in the intelligence field, right? So let's devise a code."

"What did you have in mind?"

"Well, it's the L word I have a problem with, and it's the elephant in the room . . . so let's go with that. El words: elevator, elemental, elegant."

"You want me to say I *elevator* you?"

I let my hand drift down from his hip. "Oh, I already know that. The question is, can I elevator *you* . . ."

"Going up or down?" he murmurs.

"Oh, hell. Let's just press *all* the buttons and see what happens . . ."

And then he disappears.

I don't hear from him all day. He's not in his office, and his cell number goes straight to voicemail.

I should make something perfectly clear. I am not a woman who defines herself by her relationship. I'm a stubborn, pushy, sarcastic, opinionated female with a fully functioning brain. I don't back down, I don't give up, and I sure as hell don't base my self-worth on whether or not a guy approves of what I do or who I am.

However.

I will admit to a certain amount of insecurity in the dating area. Not so much in what I think I have to offer; I know my own strengths and weaknesses, and they balance out into a challenging but damn fine package. No, it's my own judgment I'm suspicious of, largely because of a lying, manipulative fellow FBI agent that once not only persuaded me he was worth dating, but that he was in fact a regular human being and not a sociopath who would betray me and steal my promotion. Yeah. And when you consider that *identifying* such people is line one in my job description, it tends to shake my confidence a little.

So despite all the rock-solid evidence to the contrary, I start to second-guess myself about Cassius's intentions. Was this all a scam? He's a professional spook, after all, as adept at hiding his true agenda as a giant rabbit is at hiding eggs. Maybe I didn't *really* look into the depths of his soul; maybe I just got past the first few layers, into a cover story that he prepared years ago and planted inside his own head with sorcery.

Sure. Because I'm so irresistible that everything we've been through together has just been part of an elaborate scenario designed to get into my pants.

Okay, I may be a damn fine package, but I'm not Helen of freaking Troy. And Cassius isn't Lucifer, Prince of Lies, either. I give myself a kick in the mental butt and tell myself to grow up. Cassius is an important man in an important job—a job with global significance—and I can't get all antsy because he decided that putting out a brush fire in the Middle East was more important than returning my call.

That works for the rest of the day . . . but when the day ends and I go to bed alone, I start worrying again.

The next day, I get a call from Gretchen Petra, the head of the NSA's intel analysis unit, asking to see me in her

office. Gretch is a good friend, the mother of my god-
child, and a whip-smart pire who took her first sip of
blood in Victorian England. I walk through her open
door and say, "What's up?"

She looks up from the slim electronic tablet she's tapping at with one crimson-nailed finger, and smiles. She
seems tired, which is a first; usually, she's as steady and
unstoppable as a tank. "Jace. Good to see you. Have a
seat—but close the door first, will you?"

I ease the door shut, then sit down on the other side of
the large steel slab she calls a desk. There are no windows, just six large flatscreen monitors on the walls that
feed her a constant stream of text, video, and data from all
over the globe. Even with the overhead lights on, the screens
still project enough illumination to give the whole room
a subliminal, flickering glow.

"I've got some news about David." Gretch is one of the
few people I know who call him by his first name—even I
still think of him as Cassius. "He's on assignment."

"Assignment? I thought he was the assigner, not the
assignee."

"Yes. Well, this is a . . . special situation. And, needless
to say, a situation that calls for the personal involvement of
the director is not one I can divulge details about."

She's right, but it still feels like he's ditching me and
getting his secretary to call with a message that he'll be
working late. I push that thought angrily away—not only
is Gretch practically family, she'd never tolerate that sort
of behavior from Cassius. She's loyal to a fault, but she
also has a backbone that steel would envy.

I nod and force a smile in return. "I get it. In fact, you
probably shouldn't even be telling me this much, right?"

She leans back, brushing behind her ear a strand of
blond hair that's come loose from her normally tidy bun.
Yeah, her body language is definitely exhausted; slack

shoulders, bad posture. "Probably. But I have no choice; I'm operating under a direct order from Director Cassius himself. He said—and I quote—'Tell Jace I'm sorry about this but it couldn't be avoided. Don't worry, the solution is elementary.' "

The last word makes my smile tremble a little; not sure if it's trying to run away or metamorphose into a grin. "Direct quote, huh?"

And then Gretch does something I've never seen her do before: She *yawns*. Not that pires don't yawn—they sleep, after all—it's just that Gretch usually seems tireless.

"You okay?" I ask.

She nods. "Just a long night. Anna's teething."

I wince. "Ouch."

"Yes. I'm glad pire fangs can't pierce pire flesh—but that doesn't mean they don't hurt."

Anna is Gretch's child. A spell cast here at the end of World War II lets pires have kids, but there's a catch: Both parents have to age six months for every year their offspring does, until the parents judge that the child is an adult and call a halt to the aging process, locking the whole family back into immortality again. Gretch is a single mom, but Cassius offered to share the time-debt with her after Anna's father was killed. She's still as strong and hard to kill as all pires are, but it looks like even her stamina is being tested by a blood-drinking toddler with teeth issues.

"So. Any idea when the bossman will be back?"

"I'm afraid not. It could be days—but it might be weeks. He's appointed me acting director in his place."

I frown. Not that I disapprove of his choice—Gretch could run the entire world quite efficiently, given the chance—but because it's a bad sign. It means . . .

It means nothing, oh paranoid brain of mine. It doesn't matter if you're planning on being gone overnight or for a few months, you leave your best in charge. This is the NSA, not an advertising firm—you don't just call up a temp agency: *Yeah, I'm gonna need someone to fill in for me for a few days. Make sure they have some experience in running a national security agency, maybe a little background in black ops, some international diplomatic credentials . . . oh, and they have to be proficient in Word.*

"Thanks, Gretch. I appreciate the heads-up." I start to get to my feet.

She waves me back down. "That's not all. I have other information for you—information that's considerably more positive."

"You're giving me a muzzle for Charlie?"

"Funny, he asked me the same thing about you . . . no, this concerns an old acquaintance of ours."

She leans forward, her eyes intent. *"Aristotle Stoker."*

Now she's got my attention.

Aristotle Stoker. Descendant of the infamous Bram, who on Thropirelem gained fame not only for writing *Dracula* but also for the Whitechapel Vampire Murders— sometimes carving up prostitutes with a silver-edged blade, sometimes killing them with a wooden crucifix sharpened into a stake. On my world, Stoker never had children; here he did.

And a few generations later, Aristotle was born. He became a legend in the human underground, a killer of pires and thropes as elusive as a shadow and as a lethal as a silver guillotine. He racked up quite the body count before he used an internal political dispute to fake his own death and reinvent himself with an even scarier persona, that of the Impaler. The Impaler leapt from serial killing to mass murder, and hid so efficiently that for years no one knew for sure if he was even a real person or some kind of urban myth. I was the one who uncovered his real identity—well, he revealed it to me, actually—and I was the one who stopped his plan to turn a large percentage of Thropirelem's supernatural residents into immobile, living mummies.

We've run into each other since then. Despite the fact that he was a homicidal lunatic, I had a certain amount of grudging respect for him, at least at first; he was a human being on a planet full of monsters, doing his best to fight back against a status quo that had seen six million of his own kind sacrificed to an Elder God. It was hard not to see him as a heroic revolutionary—until I processed a few of the crime scenes he left behind.

He wasn't a revolutionary, he was a terrorist. His plan had nothing to do with righting wrongs or seeking freedom; it was about revenge, carried out indiscriminately. What was done to the human race here was horrible, but killing a bunch of innocent civilians decades later isn't the answer. I'm not sure what the answer is, or if there even is one, but I know Stoker's approach isn't going to solve anything.

He can help *me* solve something, though.

He can help me get back home.

TWO

"We have a confirmed sighting?" I ask.

"Yes. But there's both bad news and worse news attached to it," Gretch says.

"Lovely. What's the bad?"

"He's contacted us directly. Seems he wants our help—more specifically, he wants *your* help."

Uh-oh. Gretch is right, this can't be good. Stoker is every bit as cunning and manipulative as Cassius, with the added bonus of fanaticism. Whatever he wants from me, it won't be pretty.

But Stoker is the reason I was brought here in the first place. I signed a contract with the NSA—nothing satanic, just regular lawyer evil—stating that I would be returned to my own plane of existence when I captured or killed whoever was murdering thropes and pires in remote locations using bizarre yet ritual means.

That turned out to be Aristotle Stoker. He's my ticket home—and he knows it.

"What's the deal?"

"He claims he's uncovered a pire trafficking ring. Slave traders. Says he needs your help to eradicate it."

I scowl. I took down a ring just like that not long ago, a Mafioso operation that was smuggling pire women from Third World countries into the US to work as prostitutes and using the same network to send Gray Market lems from here to South America. "So he knows what I've been up to. Baiting the hook with something he thinks I'll chomp at."

"Perhaps. But this operation isn't trafficking in pire women, Jace; Stoker claims its stock-in-trade is pire *children*."

That stops me for a second. Just when you think the scum can't get any worse, you find another layer of filth below the last one. *If* he's being honest, and not just looking for a way to push my buttons. "Is he telling the truth?"

"Not necessarily. Pire children are highly valued, of course—one child is all that most pire couples ever have—but the NSA hasn't seen any rise in reported child disappearances."

"So he's lying."

"Perhaps not. Which brings us to the worse news: Stoker says he's in Vancouver. Canada, not Washington State."

I blink. I've been to Vancouver—on my world, not here—and it struck me as a perfectly lovely city. Gorgeous mountains that seem close enough to touch, great beaches, a huge park just off downtown full of ancient spruce and pine. Sort of a San Francisco vibe to the whole place, like all the hippie draft dodgers settled just over the border. "Yeah, so? Are we at war with Canada or something?"

"In a manner of speaking, yes. The so-called War on Drugs—Vancouver is a major center for the narcotics trade. We estimate there are thousands of Bane and Cloven labs and grow-ops scattered through the province of British Columbia." Bane is wolfsbane cut with PCP—popular with thrope street gangs—while Cloven is garlic-infused methamphetamine, used by pire meth-heads.

"They export it through the port, but they also smuggle a great deal into the US. The US–Canadian border is heavily barricaded and guarded, of course, but they keep finding ways across."

I get a little rush of that feeling that used to be a lot more prevalent when I first got to Thropirelem: the sudden impact of a piece of information letting me know just how alien this place truly is. On my world, the US–Canadian border is the longest undefended border in the world; here, it sounds like Checkpoint Charlie.

"Okay. How's our relationship with the Canadian cops?"

"Abysmal. The drug cartels dominate local politics, but they're not the only players in town; Vancouver's sort of a multicultural criminal melting pot. Zerkers control the waterfront. Chinese Triads and the Yakuza are prevalent in the downtown core, while the east side belongs largely to gangs from South America. Outlying areas like Burnaby, Surrey, and New Westminister are fought over by Vietnamese and Southeast Asian groups, notably the Death Dragons and the Sikh Warlords." She pauses. "And then, of course, there's the movie industry."

"Sure. Of course."

"Gangsters are always attracted to glamour. In Vancouver—much like in Las Vegas—they've decided to create their own. There's an entire studio system in place, heavily financed by racketeering money and largely modeled after Hong Kong. Battles between the studios can be just as epic and violent as struggles over the drug trade, and frequently involve the same players."

"On my world, people called Vancouver Hollywood North," I say. "Lots of American film and TV production based there." I shake my head. "This place sounds more like Juarez meets East LA."

"It's the homicide capital of the world, Jace. It's entirely possible that pire children *are* disappearing there;

that either the crime isn't being reported, or it's being covered up."

"And we have no official jurisdiction?"

"Very little. Canada *is* a signatory to the Transnational Supernatural Crimes and Activities Act, but that presupposes the cooperation of local law enforcement—and that's hard to come by. Should you decide to cross the border, the Agency won't be able to offer you much in the way of support."

"Which is probably exactly what Stoker wants. I have to say, Gretch, it doesn't sound promising. I mean, Stoker's a member of the Free Human Resistance—I find it hard to believe he cares about any supernatural, especially pire children. Pire children were why six million human beings were sacrificed to Shub-Niggurath, remember?"

Gretchen shrugs. "I know. It makes little sense—except as bait for a trap. Which suggests a rather darker possibility."

"Ahaseurus." It's the name of the sorcerer who brought me across the dimensional divide at the behest of the NSA, though it turned out he had his own agenda. Ahaseurus is much more than just a government shaman; he's a very old, very powerful wizard from yet another parallel world, and his hobby turned out to be killing me. Not me specifically; rather, all the different versions of me from all the different parallel worlds in the multiverse. The last time we'd met I'd thrown a very large monkey wrench into his plans, and he'd barely managed to escape with his life.

Thanks to Aristotle Stoker.

If they're still working together, it's another good news–bad news thing. Bad because, well, serial-killing immortal wizard with a Jace Valchek fixation. But good because I need to catch both of them in order to return home; my contract only specifies Stoker, but I need Ahaseurus for the actual spell. One way or another, I need to find both anyway.

"Stoker's promised to send evidence supporting his claims," Gretch says. "If and when such evidence arrives, my staff will analyze it thoroughly—if Ahaseurus is working with Stoker, we'll be able to detect any mystical tampering and identify his signature. But if the intel turns out to be good, how would you like to proceed?"

I lean back in my chair and think about it. The fact that Gretch is asking is really only a formality; as acting director, she has the power to order me to do whatever she thinks is appropriate. Not that Gretch would pull that kind of power play—she's much too smart. Which means she's already figured out what my answer will be and has begun preparing for it.

"I go," I say. "The proof will be good, or he wouldn't bother. He knows I have to go after him anyway; I predict his information will provide a reason to keep him alive when I do."

"It could still be a trap. He—or Ahaseurus—might be the ones taking the children."

"Maybe so. But Stoker's had the chance to kill me before, and hasn't taken it." Actually, it runs a little deeper than that—Stoker told me that killing me would be "a crime against humanity." I don't know about that, but I know he won't kill *any* human if he can help it. "And if he is telling the truth—well, we can't just ignore that, can we?"

"No. We cannot." There's no creature more bloodthirsty or savage than a mother protecting her young, and I've seen firsthand what Gretch is willing to do to protect hers. Even the prospect of children being threatened is enough to make my new boss's eyes a little redder and her incisors a little pointier.

A thought crosses my mind. "Hey, I won't have any trouble getting Charlie across the border, will I?"

"No, golems are fine. It's human beings that have to show caution—you could very well become a kidnapping target yourself."

"With Charlie around? Fat chance." I get to my feet. "Of course, in an environment like that he'll be breathing down my neck like a giant stone neck-breather . . ."

"I'll let you know when we hear from Stoker again."

"Do that," I say over my shoulder. "In the meantime, I'm going to go see if I can do something about my ammo problem."

"This—this is absolutely *weird*," Damon Eisfanger says. He sounds very happy, which makes me want to throttle him.

I'm in his lab, a few floors away from the intel division. Eisfanger's a forensics shaman, which means he combines sorcerous rituals and talismans with a scientific approach to pull data of all kinds from crime scenes. On my world, a good CSI can almost make a corpse talk; Eisfanger's specialty is removing the word *almost*.

Damon's a thrope from a mixed pit bull–Arctic wolf heritage, which gives him the stocky build of a linebacker; pale, ice-blue eyes; and hair like a polar bear's pelt. He's something of a geek, in that overly friendly, not-clear-on-the-concept-of-personal-space way, but he's got the IQ of a mad genius and the wide-eyed cheerfulness of a puppy. It's impossible to hate Damon, but extremely easy to be irritated by him.

He's perched on a stool, dressed in his usual white lab coat over a pair of jeans and a sweatshirt, peering into a comparison microscope. He looks into one eyepiece, then the other, chuckling gleefully to himself. "I don't believe it! I mean, I *literally* don't believe it. I don't think I *can!*"

"You do this *every time*," I say tiredly. "I give you the

sample. You take a look at it. You exclaim a few times about how bizarre it is. Then you wander away, get a sandwich, and completely forget about what you were doing."

"I do?"

"Yes. *Every time.*"

"Huh. Do I always get a sandwich, or is that just verbal shorthand for any random task?"

"Four out of five times, sandwich. Once you went to the bathroom. Maybe you had a sandwich while you were in there, I don't know."

He looks thoughtful. "I see. Interesting. Brief amnesiac episodes, triggering basal metabolism functions—that's mnemonic programming on a deep level . . ." He falls silent, an expression of intense concentration on his face.

"Damon."

"What?"

"This is the part where you forget everything you just said."

"Don't be ridiculous. We were just talking about—" He frowns. "Going to the bathroom?"

I sigh. "We were talking about *gunpowder*, Damon. You know, the chemical mixture that explodes when ignited, causing bullets to fly out of the barrel of my gun really, really fast?"

He looks skeptical. "You know, every time you tell me that I have the feeling you're pulling my leg."

"I know. The spell, remember?"

"Oh, right. So *what* do you want, again?"

"I want you to *analyze* it, Damon. Break the gunpowder down to its component elements, tell me what each one is and the proportion that they're mixed together in. Basic science. You can do that, right?"

"Hey, I'm kind of hungry. You want a sandwich?"

I am not going to shoot him. I'm *not*. I can't waste the ammo.

"Look, I'll make this simple. Just—just run a whole bunch of unmarked samples, okay? Like, two dozen. Don't even try to match a particular analysis to a particular sample, just run them all, print out the results, and stick them in a box. If we can't beat the spell, we'll try to fool it."

"I guess I can do that." He still looks doubtful, but I can't spend all day babysitting him while trying to outwit an ancient enchantment.

"I'll call you later."

"Uh, hang on," he says. "Speaking of forgetting, I almost forgot. Your blood work came back this morning."

Damon isn't a doctor, per se, but I trust him—that's why I had an analysis of my blood done by him instead of someone else. My immune system has just been through an epic battle with both the vampirism and lycanthropic viruses, and I want to verify that I'm still 100 percent human. "Yeah? Good news or bad news?"

"Good. You were infected by a thrope claw as opposed to a bite, right?"

Not to mention having my femoral artery sliced open at the same time. "Yeah. So?"

"So the virus that lives on thrope claws is slightly different from the one that lives on our teeth."

"I know, Cassius told me. He said the claw version was actually more virulent."

Damon nods. "It is. But having survived it, your immune system is now producing antibodies. I can't be completely certain, but I don't think you could be infected that way again."

"Wait. Are you trying to tell me that the next time I go toe-to-toe with an enraged, seven-foot werewolf I only have to worry about his *jaws*?"

"From a strictly infectious point of view, yes. Of course, you could still be disemboweled or decapitated or have your limbs torn off—"

"You're really not clear on how the good news–bad news thing works, are you?"

"—or get slashed to pieces or die by exsanguination. But you *don't* have to worry about being turned into a thrope from a simple claw wound." He pauses. "I'm pretty sure, anyway."

"Terrific," I say as I head for the door. "Do me a favor and try to stay away from the sandwiches, okay?" I check my watch as I step into the elevator; I should just be able to make my class.

When I first got to Thropirelem, I was more than a little overwhelmed. I hid that behind my usual combination of bloody-minded stubbornness and sarcasm, but one fact was inescapable: I was no longer the baddest badass in the room. Or in one *corner* of the room. Or even in that little supply closet just off the room, the one with the sawdust you're supposed to spread on vomit and the mop that smells like rotting spinach. In fact, that little old lady on the corner with the plastic supermarket bag could probably go half-were and rip my throat out in less time than it takes her to buy kitty litter.

I do have a few things that help balance the equation, of course. My gun—which nobody takes seriously until I actually put a very large hole in something, and sometimes not even then; my badge; a pair of modified *eskrima* sticks with snap-out blades that turn them into razor-sharp silver scythes. But really, one of my biggest assets has always been my martial arts training—I've been studying since I was ten. It's helped give me the self-confidence you need in a male-dominated profession, which unfortunately seems to be most of them.

That asset is all but worthless here. Pires and thropes are stronger, faster, and really hard to hurt. Not that hard to kill, if you know what you're doing, but lethal force is not always the best option. My knowledge of *kali*, Filippino stick fighting, helps a lot—but even with the scythes, I still have the speed and strength problems. Plus, it makes me far more reliant on my weapons than I'm comfortable with.

So I started my own dojo. Because, hey, those who can, do, and those who can't, teach.

I can practically feel my old sensei smack me in the back of the head for that remark, and I deserve it. I have nothing but the highest respect for the teachers I've had in my life; it's myself as a purveyor of knowledge I'm a little down on. It seemed like a brilliant idea at the time— make something here that was truly mine, create my own community—but the reality of the situation is proving a little less rosy.

"Okay, everyone, let's practice our palm strikes. Csilla, get your stance right—feet farther apart. Galahad, get *away* from the snacks."

My class consists of six wannabe kung fu masters: Xandra Adams, a teenage thrope; Vlad Varney, a thrope bouncer who likes to pretend he's a pire; Csilla Janos and Ludmilla Radzic, two illegal immigrants I rescued from an undead trafficking ring; Teresa McKeever from the Seattle Human Enclave, curator of the Archive of Human Works; and my dog.

Yes, I said my dog. Galahad's a dog were, one who spends his days as a St. Bernard and transforms into a large, potbellied man with a patchy brown-and-white haircut when the sun goes down. So far he's one of my best students, when he's not trying to snarf down everything on the refreshment table—though he has a distressing tendency to lick his opponent's face during grapples.

Teresa puts up her hand. She's a matronly woman in her fifties, in pretty good shape, currently dressed in a maroon tracksuit. "Jace?"

"Yes, Teresa?"

"I'm sorry, but my phone is vibrating." She sounds apologetic. "We're getting in a shipment from Paris, and I made them *promise* not to bother me unless it was urgent."

"Go ahead," I say. "Everybody else, back into position—"

Xandra puts up her hand. She's a sixteen-year-old thrope I met through her uncle when we worked together, and we somehow became friends. Xandra likes to experiment with body modification, which in a world filled with magic translates into things like corpsing—using charms to imitate the rotting flesh of a zombie—or blading, where razors are embedded into the skin edge-out like some sort of lethal fins. I forbid either one at class, which made her a little grouchy.

"What is it, Xandra?"

"Can I put my earbuds in while we're practicing? Listening to some tunage helps me get into a rhythm."

"This isn't aerobics, Xan. What are you going to do when you find yourself in a fight, ask the other guy to hang on a second while you make sure your iPod's charged?"

"But this is just *practice*."

"No, it's *programming*. That's what we're doing, programming your reflexes by repeating the same actions over and over. That way, when you find yourself in a dangerous situation, you won't have to think; your instincts will take over."

She frowns. "But I already *have* instincts. Thrope, remember? Fur, four feet, waggable butt extension?"

I sigh. She's got me there. "You already know how to use your fangs and claws, sure. I'm trying to give you some *new* instincts—ones that deal with leverage and pressure points and using your mass effectively. And that's not going to work if you need to have the latest top forty pop song blasting in the background to jog your memory—"

Now Csilla puts up her hand. She's a tall, strikingly beautiful pire, a refugee from a tiny war-torn country in Eastern Europe that I can't even pronounce the name of. She and Ludmilla Radzic were smuggled here by the Gray Wolves and forced to work as prostitutes until Charlie and I put a stop to it. She swore she'd never let anyone force her to do anything against her will ever again, and I believe her. "Csilla?"

"Yes. When do we learn how to kill?" Ah, these Slavic types. Blunt, practical, ruthless.

"I'll get to that, believe me. But you have to learn how to walk before you run—"

Which is when Gally tears to the front of the room and starts jumping up and down, yelling, "Walk! Walk! Walk!"

I decide now would be a good time for a short break.

As it turns out, Teresa isn't the only one who gets interrupted by a call. We're hardly getting warmed up when I get a call myself, from Gretch. Stoker's sent us another message.

I adjourn the class, tell everyone they're doing great, give them some homework to practice on their own, and say I'll see them next week. Then I take Gally home and get back to the office as quickly as I can.

"Our shaman's just finished checking it," Gretch says as I sit down opposite her desk. She taps the screen of her tablet a few times, and one of the flatscreens switches to a shot of Stoker's face. "No surprises, just a masking spell to make it impossible to backtrace."

I study the monitor. The best description I can give of Stoker is a brainiac caveman; his broad forehead and clear eyes radiate intelligence, but the heavy brow, square chin, and wide face look more Neanderthal than Nobel Prize winning. The hair's a long, shaggy brown mane.

Gretch taps her touchscreen again, and the image comes to life.

"Hello again, Jace." The familiar deep rumble of his voice, but sounding a little less self-assured than he usually does. The camera's in tight on his face, so I can't really make out much of the background. He looks off camera for a second, then quickly back. He blinks several times in quick succession, a visual clue that he's reining in his emotions. When he speaks again, his voice is a little flatter in tone.

"I know you don't have any reason to trust me. And I'm the last person in the world who should care about the welfare of pire children. But I've undergone some changes lately, and—" He breaks off, gives his head a little shake. "Never mind. That's the cry of every reformed criminal alive, isn't it? I've *changed, really* I have. I know you wouldn't believe it from the lips of a wife beater—and I've done things much worse than that. So I'll try to stick to the facts, and let you make up your own mind. You will anyway."

He pauses. "First of all, I've ended my partnership with Ahaseurus. When I realized what he was, what he wanted you for . . . let's just say we didn't part on friendly terms. I don't know if the NSA has any way to confirm that, though."

I glance at Gretch. She pauses the recording and says, "We can't track Ahaseurus with any deal of accuracy, but we collected a lot of mystic data about his abilities from the Nightshadow incident. Enough to alert us if he tries using similar spells. An NSA satellite got a spike of transdimensional energy out of Africa shortly after that, and nothing since."

I frown at her. "Two things. First of all, the NSA has magic satellites? And second—why didn't anyone *tell* me The Big A was in Africa?"

Gretch looks uncomfortable. "Because most likely he isn't. It's quite possible he's no longer in this dimension at all."

That's not—I hope—a euphemism for being dead; it means that Ahaseurus has jumped out of this reality and into a completely different one. And since there are literally an infinite number of these alternate worlds, hunting him down has just gone from difficult to impossible.

Gretch sees the look on my face. "It's not as bad as it seems, Jace. He's been here long enough to become mystically attuned to this world; a great deal of his power is here. He'll be back." She turns the recording on again before I can muster a properly indignant reply.

"The Free Human Resistance comes into contact with many underground groups," Stoker continues. "That doesn't mean we endorse all of them, or condone their actions. It just means that we're all hiding under the same rock, and no one can afford to blow the whistle on anyone else. If we don't hang together, we'll hang separately, right?

"But I can't stay quiet about this, Jace. I just can't."

He pauses again, staring just off center of the camera. Collecting his thoughts, or trying to build dramatic tension? I can't tell.

"Children are . . . everything. I don't mean that to sound sentimental, either; it's just that without a way to reproduce, a race dies. As monstrous as it was, I understand *why* the pires did what they did at the end of World War Two. It let their species survive. But that kind of global change, affecting that many people—there's no way to fully understand the consequences, not until they rise up and hit you in the face.

"For one thing, nobody thought about the orphans."

I glance over at Gretch. She flicks a glance back at me, but that's all. I know we're both thinking about Anna.

"The spell that lets pires have children has its dangers,

too; even a pire aging at half speed is more vulnerable than a full immortal. Some of those pire parents have died—through accidents or violence—and left their children behind. Stranded in childhood. No parents, no siblings, sometimes no relatives at all. There's no structure in place to take care of them. A thrope would just be absorbed into another pack, but pires are more solitary by nature.

"It gets worse. Not everyone is cut out to be a parent, and that includes pires. Some of them discover they don't want to be parents after all, some of them just can't handle aging after decades or centuries of immortality. Whatever the reason, they decide to rescind the spell—and abandon the child.

"Many of them wind up here, Jace. Vancouver is a dangerous place, a frontier city with little or no law. These children live on the streets, sleep under bridges, steal blood where they can or feed on urban wildlife: pigeons, rats, racoons. They prostitute themselves.

"And this is where they're stuck, Jace. *Forever*."

And now I see something else in his eyes. I've seen it before, usually on the faces of cops involved in really bad child-murder cases. *Haunted* is the only word for it; he's seen something he can't unsee, and he'd give just about anything to get it out of his head.

But he can't. He's going to have to live with it. There are a number of different methods, most of them unhealthy: booze, drugs, sex, adrenaline, suicide . . . or going the proactive route and deciding to *do* something. Get involved, try to change the world so you can prevent that terrible thing from happening again.

It doesn't surprise me that Stoker would choose the world-changing method. Monster or revolutionary, that's what he does.

"These children have been disappearing, Jace. The only

ones who've even noticed are the evil bastards that prey on them. And me. My comrades in the FHR certainly don't care—which is why I've quit."

"What?" I blurt.

"Intriguing," Gretch mutters.

"I don't know who's taking them, or why—not for sure, anyway. I have some leads, but I no longer have the resources to follow them up myself.

"I know what you're thinking, Jace. Where's the proof? How do I know this isn't just another of Stoker's elaborate plans?"

He shakes his head. "You can't, I guess. Who's to say I'm not the one responsible for this? I have every reason to lie, after all. So I guess I'll just have to see if you believe someone else."

He reaches out and grabs the camera, swings it around. It focuses on—

A child.

She looks about eight. Tangled, filthy hair that might be blond. Ragged clothes that don't fit right. No shoes. The clear green eyes of an angel in a face badly needing soap and water. She's perched in an armchair with her legs underneath her—not curled up comfortably, more like a wild animal ready to spring.

"Yeah, hi," she says. "I'm Gertrude. I live in 'Couver, I guess. Five of my friends—Teddy, Jill, Goldy, Big Fred, and Kitty—are missing." Her diction is clear and definite, with no hesitation. "Aristotle says you won't believe him, but maybe you'll believe me. I don't know. I guess I'm supposed to convince you." She frowns. "That's *hard*. I could show you their stuff, I guess—but that won't tell you much. Aristotle had a shaman try a locator spell, but it didn't work. So that means somebody's *hiding* them, right?"

She pauses, obviously thinking. "I guess you could get

a shaman to see if I'm telling the truth, but then you'd have to come here. I told Aristotle I could visit you, I don't mind, but he says I can't do that. The border's too hard to get across, he says. I knew that already—everybody knows *that*."

I didn't. But then, I've had a lot on my mind lately, like detonating my apartment and making my boss disappear into thin air.

"So I don't know if you believe me." She stares at the camera like she wishes she could reach right through it and yank us into the room. "But *you have to. Please.* Okay? They're my friends and I love them and miss them and they have to *come back* and be *all right*."

She stops then, glaring ferociously at me. If she'd burst into tears I would have felt manipulated, but it's her sheer determination that reaches into my chest and squeezes.

That's where the video ends, with her staring at me. I wonder how old she really is, and how good an actress she's had to become.

Gretch turns back to me. "There was a second file attached to it, with a mobile number in it and nothing else. To contact him once you're there, I assume. What do you think?"

"About what we just saw?" I shrug. "It's hard to believe Stoker would walk away from the Free Human Resistance—he's been a member his entire life. On the other hand, he's entirely capable of going it alone if he has to.

"As for Gertrude and what she told us? It didn't seem rehearsed, or like she was reading from a script. She appeared sincere—but one of the first skills the disenfranchised learn is how to lie effectively. It does dangle some fairly effective bait, though."

"Yes, I noticed that. If these children *are* being hidden using sorcerous means, a good forensics shaman would be able to detect the masking spell."

"But we'd have to investigate personally for that," I point out.

"So—despite what he originally claimed—he still hasn't provided us with any hard evidence. Just a story designed to tug at the heartstrings."

"It doesn't matter," I say. "He could say he desperately needs our help to hunt down a cowboy leprechaun riding the last living unicorn, and I'd still go. Whether he's telling the truth or not, one thing hasn't changed."

I get to my feet. "He's still my only ride home. And this time, I'm not leaving without him."

THREE

If I'm going, Charlie's going—I don't even have to ask. But if we're taking Stoker's claim seriously, we need to have a shaman along as well. Looks like Eisfanger's ammo project will have to wait—though I'm not sure how enthusiastic he'll be about the Wild West environment of Vancouver.

He surprises me by accepting my offer gladly, even eagerly. "Vancouver!" he chortles, sipping his hot chocolate. We're down in the NSA cafeteria, strategizing. "I've always wanted to go there!"

"Yeah?" I say, gulping down half my cappuccino. "Why haven't you? It's what, two, two and a half hours away?"

"Oh, I've tried. But the paperwork alone is daunting. Plus, US government employees in the security field are required to travel in pairs—it can be a real bitch to coordinate. But official clearance from upstairs will get us right through!"

"Not exactly," Charlie rumbles. He seems less than thrilled about our upcoming road trip. "Just up to the gate."

"Well, yes," Eisfanger admits. "But from there it's just a formality, right?"

"Uh-huh," Charlie says.

* * *

When we get there, I understand Charlie's attitude.

We can see the border long before we actually arrive. The spotlights are visible from miles away, and the sound of helicopters and the occasional fighter plane echoes through the air as we get closer. We're in Charlie's car, a lovingly rebuilt black 1947 DeSoto with whitewall tires, plush leather upholstery, and enough chrome to blind a hooker. Eisfanger's in the backseat, leaning forward like an excited kid on a holiday trip. Charlie's driving, of course.

"This is terrific," Eisfanger says. "I can't wait!"

"You been across many borders?" Charlie asks.

"Sure," he answers. "Well, a few. Okay, one. Japan counts, right?"

"This," Charlie says, "won't be much like Japan."

I don't need an explanation for that. Eisfanger was with us when we flew into Hokkaido, as part of an official NSA team investigating a crime under the terms of the TSCA Act. This time, we're traveling a lot farther under the radar.

The line we're in creeps another few feet. The fence ahead stretches to either side as far as the eye can see, and it's all the more impressive for how fragile it looks. I estimate it must be at least sixty feet high, and seems to be made of spiderwebs spun between tall steel posts with blinking red safety lights at their peaks. That has to be an illusion, of course; for one thing, a spider's web wouldn't be visible from this far away. And if it was, I'd hate to see the size of the spider . . .

"Tell me about the fence," I say.

Charlie grunts. "Created and charged by High Power Level Craft. Unbreakable. Anything smarter than a squirrel goes into a coma if it comes within a foot of it. Linked to a network of monitoring stations that run from Washington State to the East Coast. Goes subterranean, too, but nobody's sure how deep—that seems to vary."

HPLC is the kind of sorcery only governments have access to—scary, Elder Gods stuff. I wonder what the price was to have this fence erected, and who paid it. "That's a pretty massive expense just to keep a few thropes and pires from getting high."

"It's not just about the drugs," Eisfanger says. "It's cultural. In the United States, thropes are proud of how civilized we are. Across the border, they tend to embrace their animal nature with a lot more . . . enthusiasm. You'd be surprised how many people find that attitude frightening."

I think about my own world. "Yeah, not so much," I say. "Doesn't matter where you're from, people are always scared of taking too close a look in the mirror. When they do, they usually discover that the personality trait they hate the most in other people is the same one they hate in themselves."

"Huh," Eisfanger says. "So, deep down, a racist really hates—wait, that doesn't work."

"Racists don't hate personality traits, they hate *races*. What I mean is that somebody who can't stand, for instance, pompousness in others hates any trace of pompousness in himself—so much so that he tries to completely repress it. But that doesn't mean it isn't there."

"So," Charlie says, "a person who's always telling others to shut up thinks she talks too much herself?"

"Shut up."

"Thank you."

"You're welcome. Mouthy but generous, that's me."

I can see the actual checkpoint now. Big, blocky buildings on either side of multiple lanes with guards in booths. Lems in body armor carrying compound bows of matte-black carbon fiber stomp up and down the lanes at random, glaring into vehicles. They all look a lot like Charlie, glossy plastic skin stuffed with black volcanic sand.

I wonder if that means we'll be treated better—or worse.

Most border guards I've met have the attitude and authority of a heavily armed bouncer, in a job that's really a glorified version of the guy who sells tickets at the cineplex. It's like training a pit bull to kill giant rats and then chaining him up in the parking lot at Disney World; he *knows* there's something he should be stopping, but it's always just out of sight.

And in the meantime, he just has to clench his fangs and smile at all the clueless, idiot tourists that stream past day after day, asking the same questions, getting the same answers . . . no wonder these guys tend to go ballistic at the slightest provocation. They're ticking time bombs, getting wound tighter every day, and all they're waiting for is an excuse. Add in the usual territorial attitude of cops, a little nationalism, maybe some pack instincts, and you've got a recipe for an absolutely *outstanding* introduction to another country.

The car ahead of us is a thrope family, station wagon piled high with camping gear, three or four kids in the backseat that keep morphing from wolf cub to child and back, merrily bounding off the windows as they do so. One of them peers at me through the rear window, his little pink tongue lolling, ears perked up like a puppy. I smile and wave. He gives me the finger, and is promptly tackled by a sister who clearly feels this is an inappropriate response to a friendly overture.

"I have a cousin with a friend who works for the Border Patrol," Eisfanger says. "These guys are hard-core—they *have* to be. I heard a story about a woman going through a checkpoint with a baby—"

"Dead kid, body stuffed full of drugs and sewn back up," I say. "Right?"

"Uh, well, yeah—"

"Urban legend, never happened. Any others?"

"I've got one," Charlie says. "Not a legend, though. Wish it were."

I give him the quizzical eyebrow. Charlie likes to pull my leg, and took full advantage of my cultural clueless-ness when I first got here. He still likes to give it a yank now and then. "Go on."

"Guy I know. A lem. Big fella, one of those specially built heavy-duty laborers that stand about eight feet tall? Had this pire woman contact him, make him an offer. Seems she'd met her husband up in Canada, but they got into some trouble with the law and she wound up de-ported. She couldn't go there, he couldn't come here. What she wanted from this lem—let's call him Ricky— was some help getting across the border. She had this crazy idea that she swore would work, and she offered him a whole lot of money to give it a try.

"A lem's life force is embedded in the sand that makes up the inside of his body. You can replace the plastic con-tainer that holds it in, but lose too much of the sand itself and the spell animating the golem breaks and he keels over dead. But you can take out quite a bit and then put it back with no ill effects, especially if you keep it nearby. And this pire, she was a pretty small woman . . ."

"She wanted to be smuggled across the border *inside* the lem?" Eisfanger says.

"Sure. Why not? A pire doesn't need air. She'd stud-ied the idea, figured out how much sand she'd displace, learned how much you could temporarily remove from a lem and then replace . . . had it all figured out."

"I'm guessing it didn't go too well," I say.

"Everything went fine, at first. Cut a slit in his belly, scooped out just enough sand, wiggled inside and got herself good and buried. Ricky taped up the cut, made sure he kept the container with the sand right next to him. It's not unusual for a lem to travel with some extra for emergencies, and being a big guy gave him an excuse for a large amount. But they didn't figure on one thing."

Charlie shakes his head. "See, people try to smuggle stuff in lems all the time. The border uses metal detectors and body-imaging tech and spell alarms. The pire had a masking charm to make her spiritual signature kind of blend in with Ricky's, but neither of them thought to mask the extra sand. That was still giving off a lem signature, good and strong, one that *almost* matched Ricky's—almost but not quite."

"Because his was getting distorted by the pire hidden inside him," Eisfanger says, nodding. "Sure. I can see that."

"So could the border guard," Charlie says. "He put it together about as quickly as you did. Decided to have a little fun."

"He sweat the poor guy?" I ask.

"Oh, yeah. Dragged it out as long as he could, tightening the screws one at a time. Went on for hours. The guard was determined to break Ricky. Didn't have anything to do with the law or right or wrong by that point; it was just pure meanness."

"How'd it finally end?"

"Badly. The guard was going through Ricky's paperwork for the fifteenth time, asking him all kinds of inappropriate questions, just trying to push him over the edge. No dice. Finally, the guard tells him he's all finished, he can go as soon as he signs one more form. Hands Ricky a pen. Ricky takes it. Then the guard smiles and says, "Oh, hang on. That form has to be signed in *pencil*." He picks one up, leans forward—and punches it straight into Ricky's chest."

"Which means—oh, no."

"Yeah. This pire was a couple hundred years old. The

instant that yellow Number Two pierced her heart, she crumbled right to dust."

"That's—" Eisfanger shakes his head. "That's monstrous."

"Yeah, but it's not the end. They confiscated Ricky's vehicle, made him walk out on foot. Took him a while to get anyplace where a lem specialist could look at him. Enough time for the dust and sand to mix together real good."

"So he's what—half pire and half lem, now?" I ask.

"Technically. But what happened to Ricky was more in his attic. Thoughts, memories, emotions, they all got twisted around in his head. He gets cravings sometimes, even though lems don't eat or drink. He can't stand being out in the sun. Sometimes he talks about doing things or going places he's never been. Doesn't usually make a lot of sense."

Charlie falls silent. The punch line I was waiting for never arrives. A story is a journey, and sometimes that's how it is with a journey; you wind up in a completely different place than you expected.

"That's hard to believe," Eisfanger says. "I mean, you're telling me the guard committed murder—that he ended a centuries-long life, just for trying to sneak across a border? I can't see one pire doing that to another—"

"Never said the guard was a pire."

"Even so. Yes, there are a lot of thropes that don't get along with pires, but for one to go that far—"

"Never said he was a thrope, either."

That stops Eisfanger dead.

"You think thropes and pires have the market cornered on mean?" Charlie asks. His voice is cold. "There's a reason they use black sand for enforcement lems, and it ain't 'cause it's so easy to coordinate an outfit around. It's the color of our souls."

There's a charged silence in the car for a second after

he drops that one on us, and then he says, "Of course, it *does* simplify picking out accessories."

The car lurches ahead another few inches.

Finally, we're the next car. The vehicle ahead with the family in it takes twenty minutes to be processed, or at least that's how long it is between when they vanish behind a gigantic steel barrier that rises from the roadbed and when it lowers again.

Now it's our turn.

A metal wall rises up behind us with a grumble of hydraulic pistons. There's another one in front of us, blocking us in, and two grids of metal bars over one-way glass on either side. I feel a little like I'm in a cage, a little like I'm in a terrarium. Take a look at the exotic specimen from a parallel world, everybody—give her a cappuccino and she'll do a trick.

My brain is more than a little hyperactive, because it knows exactly where I am. This isn't a waiting room.

It's a killing box.

The barriers are there not only to hem us in, but to protect the guards on the other side of whatever lethal voodoo they have aimed at us right now. Something fast and fatal and capable of eliminating all three of us and our vehicle, I'm sure; when it comes to defending national borders, overkill is the only language the powers that be understand. Maybe we're parked over a portal to some other-dimensional Hell, and the push of a button will open a trapdoor and dump us into a demon-infested Infernal Pit; a place filled with those Eternally Damned by God, Devil, and Homeland Security.

The wall in front of us looks like it's been etched by some chemical process that left it full of tiny grooves and furrows, but that's an illusion, too; if I squint, I can make out the shape of runes, the entire surface covered with some sort of arcane script. I don't squint for long, though—even a few seconds spent examining those markings is enough to give me the beginnings of a queasy headache. A spell no doubt, something long and intricate crafted by government shamans deep in the bowels of the Pentagon.

And that's the truly weird thing: even though I'm about to enter Canada, this checkpoint isn't staffed by Canadians. It's an American facility, ostensibly there because the United States is generously offering to "help" with cross-border security; really, it's because the American government considers the local cops to be so hopelessly compromised by drug money that they can't be trusted. That, and it's a convenient excuse to spy on their own citizens—because, hey, anyone *leaving* the good old US of A must be up to no good, right?

The chamber fills with an eerie blue light. It doesn't seem to be radiating from anywhere in particular, it's just *there*. I know it's sorcery because I can literally feel it; like ants crawling all over my skin, probing, sniffing, *tasting*. It's a vile, invasive sensation, and Eisfanger doesn't look like he's enjoying it any more than I am. Charlie just stares straight ahead, his face impassive—but I notice he's gripping the steering wheel with both hands.

"Deep spirit scanning," Eisfanger says. His voice has a strange resonance to it, like I'm hearing him through a bad phone connection. "Don't worry, it's completely safe. Well, mostly."

"Mostly?"

"Side effects have been documented," he admits. "In a very small percentage of cases. Less than two percent."

"What *kind* of side effects?" Suddenly I'm feeling nauseous. Feels like the ants are crawling around *inside* me now, which is exactly as disturbing as it sounds.

"Memory loss. Synesthesia. And occasionally . . . vestigial growths."

"So I could forget my own name, start smelling purple everywhere and have an extra *nipple* sprout from my forehead?"

Eisfanger doesn't answer. On reflection, I decide I don't really want to know.

The blue light fades away, leaving me feeling like I just had a whole-body colonoscopy. A voice that sounds as if the speaker is about six inches away from my right ear intones, "You're going to need an interview. Park your vehicle in the lot to the right and wait for an escort."

"Terrific," I mutter.

At least we get to leave the box. I wonder about who's on the other side of those cage walls, and what the blue light let them see. And then I do my best to stop thinking about that, because I'm already ticked off and getting angry is only going to make things worse.

Charlie parks. There are already three other cars in the small lot, including the station wagon that was ahead of us. Eisfanger starts to open his door, but Charlie turns in the driver's seat and stops him with a hand on his shoulder.

"We wait for the escort," Charlie says.

And we do. Another twenty minutes passes. I do my best to stay calm, but I'm no good at waiting unless I'm on a stakeout. I try to get into that mind-set, but it's not easy when you feel like a suspect instead of a cop. What I'd really like to do is walk in and flash my badge—NSA trumps Border Patrol—but we're supposed to be travel-ing incognito. So I sell the concept to myself as a per-sonal challenge: If I can endure this without losing my temper, I win. After all, if Ricky the lem-pire can keep his cool, then so can I, right?

Our escort finally shows up. A big black sand enforce-ment lem, just like Charlie—and just like in Charlie's story. Even without guns, it's funny how much the cops in Thropirelem look like the cops in my world; this one's wearing body armor over his uniform, he's got a big leather belt loaded with every kind of gear except a pistol, he's even got a pair of mirrored sunglasses tucked in his pocket. His attitude is brisk but professional, and when he marches all three of us into the building, he politely holds the door open for us. I start to think we're going to be okay.

But then he parks us on the end of a long wooden bench facing a counter, and disappears through a door. More waiting ensues.

Five minutes go past until the door opens again. It's not our escort that comes through it, but the family from the station wagon. One of the kids is crying as quietly as she possibly can, while the mother tries to comfort her. The other kid looks stricken, like some essential part of his world was just smashed in front of him. And the father—

The father is an average-looking guy, short brown hair, a little paunchy. And at this moment, I doubt even Charlie would want to get in his way; he's got the rage of pure murder in his eyes, and it's being held back by the thinnest of leashes. The whole family stalks past us, and once they're gone I let out the breath I didn't know I'd been holding.

"So," I say brightly. "*We* shouldn't have any problems, right?"

A squat, yellow sand lem with a clipboard steps into the doorway. "Jace Valchek," he says.

We all stand up. "Just Valchek," the lem says. He turns and trudges back inside. I follow.

The room is small and windowless and has a table bolted to the center of the floor. He takes a seat on one side, I take the other. The chairs are bolted down, too.

"Miss Valchek," the lem says. He's got a brass name tag pinned to his white shirt that reads DELTA. He doesn't bother introducing himself, and I'm a little weirded out by the fact that he knows my name when I haven't shown anyone my ID yet. "I have a few questions."

"About what?"

"You're not in our database."

"But you know my name."

"It's how your possessions think of you."

Right. Animist magic, the basis of most sorcery in Thropirelem. Everything has a spirit, and some of them are apparently quite chatty. "I'm here on a government visa." I pull out the piece of paper Gretch gave me before we left. "All nice and legal."

He reads the paper, frowning all the while. "This doesn't say what your nationality is."

"I'm American."

"Then why do you need a visa?"

"Not *this* America. Parallel world. Doesn't the visa say that?"

He looks at me with flat lem eyes. "I'd like more information."

"I've been assured that piece of paper is all I require."

"Not by me."

And there it is. This guy doesn't care about what some *other* bureaucrat says; I'm on his turf now and he's going to make me play by his rules. Which, no doubt, will change depending on what his mood is.

"*This* is America," he says, thumping the end of one stubby finger against his desk. "Wherever you're from, whatever you call it, it's not *America*. Now—what is it you *do*, exactly?"

"I'm a psychiatric consultant."

"I don't know what that is."

"I'm a specialist in how people think."

He frowns harder. "There's nothing here about telepathic shamanism."

"I'm not a telepath. I study behavioral patterns."

"Why?"

To better understand morons like you leaps into my brain. It's successfully tackled by my common sense, who's been working out lately and eating right. "It's my job."

He grunts. "Sounds like a scam to me." Now he's being deliberately confrontational, so I let it pass. Common Sense beams and pats me on the back.

"What's your political affiliation?"

"I don't affiliate. Not before marriage, anyway." The Wiseass in my head slips that one past Common Sense, who wags her finger disapprovingly. Wiseass responds, using different finger.

"Are you refusing to answer?"

"I don't *have* any political affiliations, all right?"

"How do I know you're telling the truth?"

It's one of those blindingly stupid questions with no actual answer, designed to leave you sputtering in a combination of indignation, frustration, and fury. And while you're thrashing inarticulately in the throes of indigfrustury, they like to follow up with something even worse.

"How do I know you're not a criminal? Or a sexual deviant? You could even have some sort of communicable disease—I have no way to know. I have no way to verify any of this."

He's looking at me with open contempt. Not suspicion, contempt. I'm not guilty of a damn thing—except concealing the fact that I'm a cop—but in his mind I'm already a convict. I'm not a citizen he's trying to help, I'm a crook. Not because of the evidence—there isn't any—but because it's convenient for him to think of me that way. It gives him an excuse to exercise his power.

"Maybe I'm not any of those things," I say. "Maybe I'm a good person. Maybe I was brought here to *help* people." I try to keep the anger out of my voice, and pretty much screw that up.

He leans back. "Yeah, sure. I'll bet you're practically a saint. You want to know what I see? A human being. And you know what *I* am, right?"

A big, sandy asshole? the Wiseass tries to scream. Common Sense has her in a headlock, but it's a losing battle. "A lem."

"Golem," he snaps. "My race was *created* by yours. Created to be their *servants,* to build their *cities,* to die in their *wars.* But that was a long, long time ago. *Your* kind isn't doing so well now. Pretty soon, there won't be any of you left at all."

My kind.

I should have seen this coming. But I'm so used to Charlie that the idea of a lem that *resents* humanity never really occurred to me. And this angry little civil servant is going to dump a lifetime of that resentment on me.

"Look," I say. "I didn't have anything to do with that. The world I'm from, the culture I'm from, that didn't happen—"

He cuts me off with a wave of his hand. "Save it. Your world, your culture doesn't interest me. You're *here,* now, and your smart-mouthed attitude isn't going to get you anywhere. You understand me?"

Whatever sympathy I might have had for him vanishes. He doesn't want commiseration, he wants a target. "Yes."

"I need to verify this visa," he says, gets up, and stomps out of the room.

FOUR

Three hours pass before he returns.

Making you wait is the bureaucrat's most effective weapon. Paperwork is a close second, but it's really only waiting with the illusion of doing something.

I spend the time planning.

When he finally comes back, he just opens the door and motions me outside. Gives me my visa back and tells me I can go. I'm not surprised; it's more or less exactly what I was expecting. I smile at him sweetly and leave without a word, joining Charlie and Eisfanger in the car.

Charlie eyes me like he would a polar bear on PCP: cautiously. "Jace? You okay?"

"Fine," I say. "Let's go."

"Wow," Eisfanger says. "You were in there a really long time. They checked our ID, asked us a few questions, and then booted us out. We've been sitting here waiting for you ever since—"

"Let's. Go."

Charlie's radar is a lot better than Eisfanger's. Damon seems to suffer from the thrope equivalent of Asperger's syndrome—an inability to correctly read social cues and react accordingly—so Charlie tries his best to head off a

Jace meltdown by moving the conversation in another direction. "Vancouver. Last I heard, they had a pretty hot swing dance scene. Maybe we can find a little time to hit the floor." Charlie knows I love to swing dance, and he's not too shabby at it himself.

"That sounds like fun," Eisfanger says. "I mean, I don't dance myself, but it's fun to watch. Hey, maybe we'll even see some celebrities!"

"Could happen," Charlie says. "Plenty of them there, from what I hear. I don't know how many we'll find in swing spots, though. Stars tend to hang out in the really trendy clubs."

"True," Eisfanger admits. "And those are hard to get into. Long lines outside. We could be waiting a long, long time—"

He abruptly shuts up. There's a long silence, broken by Charlie sighing.

"Guys," I say. "It's fine. Don't worry about it. The pin of the Valchek Grenade is firmly in place."

"The what now?" Eisfanger says.

"I'm not going to lose it."

"Oh. Uh, good." Eisfanger still looks a little confused, but that's a expression I'm used to seeing on his face. I smile at him reassuringly.

I have a plan. Oh, yes, I have a plan.

"Sounds like half the celebrities in the city are movie stars and the other half gangsters," I say. "Interesting mix. On my world, a lot of movie and TV production happened in Vancouver because of a weak Canadian dollar and local tax breaks—plus it wasn't that far from LA, just up the coast. I'm guessing this kind of border security wouldn't have let that happen here."

"No," says Charlie. "The film industry in Van is pretty much homegrown, in more ways than one."

"How'd that come about?"

Charlie shrugs, one hand on the wheel. "Gangs with too much money. Started with porn, but that just generated more income. And you know gangbangers—it's all about ego. All it took was one guy making an action movie starring himself as the antihero, and pretty soon all the other warlords had to outdo him. Snowballed from there."

"Sounds a little like Hong Kong on my world, with Triads financing martial arts epics."

"Here, too. Lot of them got their start over in HK— but here's where the big money is."

We're driving through farmland now, cornfields lining the highway on either side. A hawk circles overhead in wide, lazy loops. Traffic is sparse, mainly big rigs hauling cargo to or from the port. I wonder how easy it is for them to get through customs.

Strangely enough, Charlie didn't have any problems getting his weapons across the border. They ignored my gun, of course—but they confiscated my scythes. Charlie wisely refrains from telling me this until we're at least ten miles away.

"Sorry," he says. "They could tell the scythes were yours. Apparently you didn't have the right permits."

A fact that Officer Delta refrained from mentioning. A final parting shot from Mr. Civil Servant. "That's *fine*," I say, and smile.

Charlie takes one look at me and shuts up for the rest of the trip.

Farmland gives way to urban sprawl interspersed with plenty of green space, stretches of tall fir or pine rising up next to gas stations or roadside restaurants. The highway becomes a freeway, which routes through a mostly industrial area called Richmond, over a bridge and then into the city of Vancouver proper. It looks a lot like Seattle at first, but that changes once we hit the downtown core.

Plenty of skyscrapers, but I don't spend much time looking up; it's what's at street level that's riveting, and not in a good way.

It's early evening. I see lems and thropes out and about, but none of the thropes are in human form; even the ones driving are in half-were mode. Those outside are almost all four-legged—packs of three or four roam together down the streets, darting and weaving through the traffic like suicidal bicycle couriers, bounding over and off cars. One slams into the DeSoto, claws screeching against the metal, and I can practically see the steam coming out of Charlie's ears.

We're on a street called Granville. Lots of neon, run-down hotels, bars, and sex shops, like Times Square before it was cleaned up. "No pires," I point out.

"They mostly stay indoors here, except at night," Charlie says.

"Why?"

"Because a popular gang initiation is to catch a pire outside during the day, and see how many times you can slash open his daysuit before he catches on fire."

"Ah."

We head for an area called Gastown, the oldest part of the city. When I'd visited Vancouver on my own world, I'd spent an afternoon there; like heritage districts in many cities, it had been spruced up into a tourist attraction, with old brick buildings now housing upscale restaurants and souvenir shops. Red cobblestone streets, an enormous steam-powered clock, and turn-of-the-century gaslit lamps completed the picture.

Well, the cobblestones are still there, as are some of

the buildings—though in much worse condition, and a lot filthier. The gas lamps have been replaced by the harsh orange glare of sodium vapor, and many of the lots are either weed-filled and fenced off with chain link, or hold only a burned-out husk of crumbling brick and charred wood. To my surprise the steam clock is still there, though obviously nonfunctional; as our car creeps past, I see that it's only a shell, the empty interior visible through a missing access panel. Even the hands on the clock face are gone.

It's no worse than many neighborhoods I've been to, but it hits me harder than I thought it would. It's because I've been here before—well, been to a version of it, anyway—and now it feels like visiting a place after a natural disaster has swept through, a hurricane or an earthquake. The landscape's familiar but everything's been damaged, torn down, swept away.

The disaster here, though, isn't a natural one. It's a wave of crime and drugs, of violence and corruption. Inner-city decay as bad as a case of gangrene, feeding on greed and poverty, desperation and indifference. I don't need to see the compounds the warlords live in to know they're just as opulent and decadent as this place is squalid and grim. That's how it always is.

Gastown was the original settlement that sprang up around the port, the place where the longshoremen and merchant marine would go to spend their hard-earned paychecks. Bordellos and speakeasies would have lined the streets in those days, maybe a few gambling parlors or opium dens. The oceanfront is visible through the buildings, only steps away, but there's a set of railroad tracks and at least two razor-topped fences between here and there.

The only people out and about seem to be the drunks, junkies, and hookers, all three of which seem to favor the non-hairy look. I remark on this, and Eisfanger informs me that the baseline human form burns fewer calories. I reply that we also look a helluva lot more attractive in fishnets, and he concedes the point.

The hotel we're booked into is called the Royal Arms, and the only thing royal about it is the castle-like security. No moat, but we have to buzz through two separate doors to get inside, both of which are heavily armored. There's also a big sign on the first one stating that illicit activities are not allowed and will not be tolerated, which I understand to mean the rooms are not available by the hour.

The lobby is old and dusty and features furniture that might actually qualify as antiques if they weren't held together with duct tape and baling wire. The clerk, a droopy-eyed pire who looks like he hasn't been outside in a few decades, signs us in and takes an imprint of my credit card. We've got three rooms on the top floor, the third. Charlie takes the car around to the underground parking, while Eisfanger and I grab some luggage and head upstairs.

The place isn't as bad as I thought it might be. Old, tired, and dingy, sure, but it's clean and doesn't stink. The rooms are larger than I would have expected—built when cubic footage was cheap—and the radiator in mine gives off a nice warm glow. Charlie shows up with the rest of our bags and announces that the parking lot is fairly secure, even has a lem guard.

"Haven't seen too many of those, either," I say. "Lems, I mean. Do the gangs do terrible things to them, too?"

"It's not that," Charlie says. "There are plenty of lems here, but you don't see them on the street much. No reason for them to be there."

"Guess not. They don't get high, drunk, or laid, and that's about all this place has to offer."

"Oh, I don't know. I hear the local ballet company is to die for."

"Wouldn't surprise me. Plenty of things here to die for . . ."

We get settled in, and then I call the number Stoker sent us and leave a message. I don't tell him where we are, just that we're in town and ready to meet.

And then we wait.

I clean my gun. Eisfanger leaves to grab some takeout, and Charlie goes with him for backup. They've been gone all of ten minutes when my cell phone rings.

It's coming up as a private call, number blocked. I answer.

"Jace," Stoker says. "You came."

"You knew I would."

"I did," he admits. "But I'm not playing you. I don't expect you to take that at face value—but try to remember what happened the last time we met."

"You did your best to kill everyone I know."

"Well, yes. But it was only a bargaining tactic."

Which, weirdly enough, is true. "Won't work again. I had that chronal spell thing nullified. And you know that sooner or later I'm going to take that damn sword away from you."

"True. Because it's already happened in the future and will have happened in the past. Don't you love time-travel magic?"

"Not even a little. What's your point?"

"That I promised not to kill any of your friends if you let me go, and I've kept that promise. Doesn't that get me a little credibility?"

"I'm here, aren't I?"

"And so is Mr. Aleph, I assume. How was the border?"

"Better than being force-fed rocks before being beaten to death with my own intestines. Theoretically."

"I'm sorry you had to go through that. But that's what it's like for human beings here—even when they work for the NSA."

Hang on. How does Stoker know I didn't just flash my badge and sail right on through—is he even better connected than I thought? Was the whole ordeal with Delta just another hoop he wanted me to jump through so I'd empathize with him as a fellow non-supernatural?

No, that's not it. I just forget how smart Stoker is, sometimes. Smart enough to deduce I might try to slip across the border incognito—which I've just confirmed. He knew what kind of reception I would get in that case, and that I wouldn't miss a chance to grouse about the experience. Now he knows that I'm here and that I have no official backup. God*damn* it.

"The real hassle was waiting for them to process the whole team," I say. "You'd think they could bypass a little paperwork for National Security, but cross-agency co-operation has a long way to go. You ever run into that in terrorist circles? One cell just *has* to prove its equipment is bigger than another's?" I hold my breath.

"Nice try. I know you brought a shaman along to verify my story, but other than Charlie that's all you have."

"Interesting theory. Doesn't make much sense, though. Why would I—"

"Jace, please. As much as you'd like to come after me with all the resources you could muster, it's politically unfeasible. And while my own resources aren't terribly robust at the moment, it's not hard to keep an eye on a single entry point for a day or two."

I curse silently. He *saw* us come across—or had someone else who did. Which means he knows exactly where I am *right now—*

"Calm down, Jace." He sounds amused. "Yes, I know where you are. But if we're going to be working together, sooner or later we have to establish a certain level of trust, don't we?"

"I suppose." I'd prefer a level that didn't involve him knowing where I sleep, though.

"Look, we should meet. I'll let you pick the spot, all right? The three of you and just me. Would that make you feel a little more secure?"

"I'll get back to you." I hang up on him, which might seem petty but in fact sends an important message: I can still walk away, anytime I choose.

But I won't. And Stoker knows that, too.

When Charlie and Eisfanger come back with the food I tell them about the call. Charlie nods as Eisfanger unpacks Styrofoam containers from a white plastic bag; he doesn't seem surprised that Stoker's one step ahead of us.

"I know a place," Charlie says. "Hard to set up an ambush there. We'll make sure we lose whatever eyes he has on us first, then go scope it out, let him know at the last minute."

Eisfanger hands me a pair of chopsticks and pops open a lid. He looks a lot more nervous than Charlie does. "So he knows where we are? Right now?"

"Sure," Charlie says. "We're on his turf."

"And that doesn't worry you?"

"Worrying is counterproductive. I prefer to direct my energies toward maintaining a state of caution instead."

I open the container Eisfanger hands me. Black bean chow mein, with the noodles nice and crispy. It smells heavenly.

"It might have a little chicken in it," Eisfanger says. "I told them I wanted it vegetarian, but I don't think they believed me."

"I'll pick it out," I say. "And Damon, you should relax.

The fact that he's letting us control the meet is a good sign—it lessens the chance of being set up."

Eisfanger nods, his mouth full of deep-fried something, but his eyes still hold some apprehension. "Maintain a state of caution," he mumbles around his food. "Right. Good advice . . ."

FIVE

Shaking whoever's tailing us is a good idea, but I decide to take it one step farther; after we're done eating, we leave the DeSoto parked and give the guy at the front desk some cash to have our luggage delivered to another hotel, then slip out a fire door, down an alley, and walk a few blocks before hailing a cab.

"We'll get the car later," I say. "For now, better if he thinks he knows where we are."

The new hotel, the Clarion, is even more run-down than the last one, but its security is just as good. Iron bars on the windows, too, though I'm not sure if that's to keep prowlers out or the residents in. I don't know if it's possible for thropes or pires to kill themselves by jumping off a tall building, but living in surroundings like these could tempt one to try.

The Clarion clearly has more long-term residents than the Royal did, and quite a few of them are lems. A group of four playing cards around a table in the lobby stare at us curiously as we check in. I can hear music playing somewhere upstairs, something jazzy with a lot of sax in it. The clerk, a lem wearing a faded brown suit, his fingers thick and heavy with peeling gray duct tape, tells us that pets aren't allowed and there's no cooking of food in the rooms. He puts us on the fourth floor, and then tells us that the elevator is "currently disabled." From the cracked and faded look of the sign taped to the doors, *permanently* seems a more accurate prognosis.

We haul our bags up to our respective rooms, which are smaller, dirtier, and more cheaply furnished than our previous ones. The bathroom is shared and at the end of the hall, but it seems in pretty good condition. Probably doesn't get that much use.

We unpack and reconvene in my room. There's only a single bed and one table with a chair; I take the chair, Eisfanger perches on the edge of the mattress, and Charlie stays on his feet. He tells us what he has in mind for the meet, and then we strategize.

When I feel we have a workable plan, I send Charlie back for the car. The Clarion has an underground lot, too, so we can stash it there without worrying about it being spotted from the street—but not right away. To add another level of security, Charlie's going to meet us at a different spot, away from our base of operations, and we'll proceed to the meet from there.

Eisfanger and I grab a cab. "Where to?" the driver grunts. He's a lem wearing a slouch cap, which seems to be a universal constant for cabbies no matter what world you're on.

"Someplace nice," I say. "Scenic, but not too far from downtown. A restaurant."

He thinks for a minute, then says, "You been to the Harbourview Tower? Helluva view, good restaurant. Little pricey."

"Sounds perfect," I say.

Harbourview Tower turns out to be the tall, Space-Needley thing I noticed on the way into town. It's got a glass elevator that crawls up the outside of the building and the obligatory rotating restuarant on top. It is, indeed, a little pricey, but I decide to splurge. We've already eaten, but coffee and dessert with a spectacular view sounds like just the thing to make me forget the grim little room I'll be sleeping in tonight.

One interesting thing, though: The security here makes the Clarion's look like a latched gate. A lem in a tuxedo—one of the white sand lems that seem designed for the service industry—runs two different wands over us, the first one obviously a metal detector, the second one more mystical looking. He finds my gun, of course, and politely asks me what it's for.

"Sex toy," I say with a straight face. "I go through a lot of batteries, too."

If a lem could blush, I'm sure he'd look like he was made out of brick. "Please don't take it out at the table" is all he says as he hands it back.

There's a fee just to ride the elevator, but they deduct it from your food bill. The view is as impressive as I thought it would be; we can't see the mountains now that it's dark, but the bay is dotted with the lights of ships and the city itself glitters beneath us. Pretty. Almost as pretty as our waiter, a young man with a charmingly shaggy mane and an engaging smile that tells me he's a pire, not a thrope—

Oh my God.

I'm so busy classifying him that I don't realize who he *is* for a full second. And then it's all I can do to keep from bursting out laughing. It gets worse when he introduces himself, which gets me a puzzled look. He does puzzled *very* well, which threatens to completely eradicate my last shred of self-control.

"Today's specials are beef Wellington and ling cod served with an apricot reduction. Our soup is an oxblood bisque. Would you like a drink to start?"

I try not to giggle. I know Eisfanger must be terminally

confused right about now, but he's used to not getting the joke—especially around me—and hides it reasonably well. "I think we'd like to see a dessert menu, actually. And bring us a couple of coffees."

He smiles. "I'll have the tray brought around." He takes our menus and turns to leave.

I can't resist. "One more thing," I add.

He turns back. "Yes?"

"Are you by chance an actor?"

His smile is modest, but still very familiar. Sigh. "Actually, yes, I am. Have you seen me in something?"

"Uh . . . no." That's a lie, but a long explanation doesn't seem worth it. "Your name seems familiar, though. I don't meet a Keanu every day."

He nods, glad for the attention but still a little disappointed. "Well, thanks for mentioning it. My agent must be doing something right . . . I'll be right back with those coffees."

When he's gone, Eisfanger leans forward and say, "What was *that* all about?"

"The multiverse's sense of humor. I wonder if I can get him to say, *I know kung fu . . .*"

Charlie calls when he's downstairs. We go down to meet him rather than have him come up; he says he isn't inclined to pay the elevator fee, but I get the feeling it's his weapons he's reluctant to part with rather than his money. We finish our coffees and I pay for them—and two slices of cheesecake—with a credit card. I could have used cash, but I can't resist scrawling something across the bottom of the receipt.

Eisfanger reads it over my shoulder. "Take the blue pill? What's that even *mean*?"

"Sorry. The Matrix can't be explained—only *experienced*."

"You are one weird date," Eisfanger mutters as we get in the elevator.

Charlie's in the DeSoto, idling at the curb. "Everything okay?" I ask, hopping in the front as Eisfanger gets in the back.

"No problems. Picked up our shadow, took him on a little tour of the east side. Lost him somewhere around Commercial Drive."

I pull out my phone and call Stoker. He answers on the first ring.

"Feel safer now?" he says.

"Loads. You ready?"

"I am."

He chuckles when I tell him where to meet us and what direction he should arrive from. "My, you *are* being cautious," he says. "How soon?"

"An hour."

"I'll do my best."

"You better. I won't wait there more than ten minutes."

"Then I better leave now." He hangs up. Again, not petty—he just wants to remind me that I don't hold all the cards. He has something he thinks I want, and he can walk away at any time, too.

There are three ways to set up a meet like this. One is the public option: Surround yourself with a crowd, making it unfeasible to start any sort of mayhem that could injure civilians and providing you with cover if you need to disappear quickly. Better for criminals than cops.

Another is the isolated location. Someplace you can control the entrances and exits, hide surveillance and snipers, keep a lid on the situation. Better for whoever gets there first—but only when you have the support personnel, prep time, and intel to back your play. We're a little thin on all three—Charlie's a great resource, but even he can't stand in for a federal agency.

So we go with option number three, a level playing field. And I do mean level—sea level to be exact. We're headed for Boundary Bay Regional Park, which sits on a spit of land extending into the bay itself. It's very close to the border—in fact, you can see the row of spiderwebbed poles in the distance, marching right off the beach and into the water. That's an additional bonus, one there to keep Stoker honest, but the real reason we picked this location was the tidal flats. At low tide—which is in about fifteen minutes—the flats stretch for mile after muddy mile, a vast, soggy expanse of nothing. Even if you have your own private submarine or aircraft, you'll be visible long before you arrive—and the proximity of the fence means you can't use any sort of magic unless you want a Black Hawk helicopter swooping down on you.

We arrive by boat, a flat-bottomed skiff we rent at a nearby marina. It takes us a little longer than the hour I gave Stoker, but I'm not worried he'll leave if we're not there when he shows up. It'll take him a while to walk across the flats, anyway, and I made sure he'd be the one slogging across them on foot.

We wait in the boat. It's a calm, cloudless night, the half-moon above us bright and strong. The surf laps against the beach, competing with the distant pulse of a chopper, and the smell of wet sand and exposed seaweed fills my nose. I can see a spot of light in the middle of the flats, flickering as it sweeps side-to-side, getting nearer. Good; he's not making any attempt to conceal himself.

Charlie and I get out of the boat. Eisfanger's not with us. We take a few steps up the beach, but stay near the shoreline.

Stoker trudges up. He's in jeans and a black T-shirt that stretches tightly across his massive chest. He's just as enormous as I remember, a giant of a man in peak physical shape. He's got the flashlight in one hand and nothing else.

"Jace," he says neutrally. "Charlie."

Charlie's been playing with a pair of steel-cored silver ball bearings ever since we came ashore, rolling them around in one hand. It makes a noise you can barely hear, but I know it well. Charlie can throw those ball bearings at just under the speed of sound, and he keeps an even dozen of them in spring-loaded holsters up either sleeve. His only response to Stoker's greeting is to click them together one-handed, the sound eerily like cocking a gun.

"We're here," I say. "Let's see your cards."

He shakes his head. "You haul me out to the middle of nowhere and expect me to make my case? I wish I could, but it's not going to be that easy."

"Oh? Exactly how hard is it going to be?"

"That depends. What will it take for you to trust me?"

"You in a federal prison and me back where I came from."

"I couldn't give you that if I wanted to. I told you, Ahaseurus and I are quits."

"So you say."

He sighs. "You are still the most difficult woman—no, human being—I have ever met."

"Thank you."

"You're welcome. Do you know why I'm here, Jace?"

"If it's for the clams, you should have brought a shovel."

In the moonlight, his smile is a broad white slash across his jaw. "Because I'm sick of death. It's all I've ever made, all I'm really good at. In your world, I could have been so many different things—but in your world, there wouldn't have been any need for me. Here, I'm a product of natural selection, an animal specifically evolved to fit a particular environmental niche. And I don't want to *be* that animal anymore."

It's a pretty speech, but I'm not exactly a dewy-eyed optimist when it comes to human nature. "So?"

"So when you reject death, what are you left with?"

"An undertaker with his hopes dashed?"

His laugh is the low rumble of an earthquake. "I really missed you, Jace. You're not going to like this next part, but if you want proof, there's only one way to get it."

Uh-oh. "So spit it out, already."

"Gertrude's disappeared. So have the few possessions the other kids left behind, which she was taking care of."

"How inconvenient," I say coldly.

"But I have another lead. A member of a Triad who says he has information and is willing to speak to us."

"So instead of a forensic examination of actual evidence you want us to take the word of a local criminal?"

Stoker shrugs. "Why don't we listen to what he has to say, first?"

I glare at him, but I'm not ready to shut this operation down just yet. "When and where?"

"I can take you to him right away. He's expecting us."

We take Stoker with us when we leave. Between his weight and Charlie's, I'm surprised the boat will still float. I operate the small electric outboard while Charlie keeps a baleful eye on Stoker.

"How are those swimming lessons going?" Stoker asks him. "You master the sinking-like-a-boulder stroke yet?" His tone is light, but it's a warning shot all the same; Charlie isn't built for an aquatic environment and Stoker knows it.

"Nah. These days, I just concentrate on finding a convenient flotation device and hanging on—you know, something like a big bag of meat. Doesn't work too well, though; even when I get a really good grip, I still tend to go straight down. Good thing I don't need to breathe, I guess."

Stoker smiles.

We take the skiff back to the marina, then get in the DeSoto—Charlie's forced to let me drive, while he sits in the back with Stoker. "Try not to completely destroy my clutch," Charlie growls as he hands me the keys.

"Please. I learned how to drive on a stick. The clutch is that thingie that signals lane changes, right?"

It's been a while since I drove a standard shift, but I only grind the gears a little and don't stall it out once. Both the steering and the brakes are manual, but it lunges like a tiger when I hit the gas and rumbles like a contented kitten on the highway.

"Nice car," Stoker says.

"Don't even," Charlie says. He can't decide if he should be more worried about the killer sitting beside him or the nut loose behind the wheel.

And then I'm driving, and no one's talking.

I'd like to have taken Eisfanger, had him sweep Stoker for anything sorcerous, but I couldn't put my entire team at risk; I needed to have at least one person in reserve in case things went off the rails. Stoker might have any kind of voodoo hidden up his sleeve, just waiting until we get far enough away from the border fence's alarms before he triggers a spell. If this is a setup, right now is the most dangerous time.

But nothing happens. We cruise back into Vancouver, park at the all-night restaurant where Eisfanger's waiting, and call him on his cell. He comes out to the parking lot carrying his shamanic tools in a brushed-aluminum case and does a thorough scan of Stoker in the backseat.

When he's finished, Eisfanger gets out and gives me the news. "Okay. He's got a few spells on him, but it's all self-defense and stealth stuff. The only heavy-duty magic is a healing enchantment, but it's one-use only. No tracking or eavesdropping bugs, no teleportation, nothing really lethal."

I feel a little of my tension go away. I don't bother saying good-bye, because it'll be back soon enough. "So he really is alone?"

Eisfanger shrugs. "Near as I can tell. Which means he's vulnerable—well, as vulnerable as a giant, genius-level psychopath with a lifetime of training can be."

"Thanks. Head back to the hotel—I still want you as backup for as long as possible."

"Sure." He hesitates. "Uh, okay if I finish my sandwich first?"

"Get it to go." I get back in the car.

"We ready to roll?" Stoker asks.

"As ready as we're going to be, I guess."

He gives me directions to our destination: Chinatown.

Being on the Pacific Rim, Vancouver gets a lot of Asian immigrants. Unfortunately, being the kind of town it is, it doesn't always attract the best and brightest; more like the bold and bloodthirsty. Chinese Tongs and Triads abound, mostly pires, many of their members professional soldiers that have been around since the Boxer Rebellion at the turn of the twentieth century or longer. On my world the Boxers were mystics and martial artists who wanted to get rid of Western influences in China; here it was much the same, only the mystics also drank blood and many of the Christian missionaries they wanted to get rid of howled at the moon after saying their bedtime prayers. Not that the whole dispute came down to thropes versus pires; there were plenty of Chinese peasants who preferred wolfhood to batkind, and more than one Western expat with an allergy to sunlight.

The uprising failed in both worlds, with the Imperial Court dithering over whether they should support the movement or repress it, and an alliance of Western powers finally stepping in to stop the slaughter of their own people. Lems fought on both sides, but in the end the rebels were outnumbered and put down—though the success the Boxers enjoyed for a while spurred the creation of other secret societies in their wake. Some of those groups had less altruistic motives than saving Chinese culture, and a century later the hardiest of those organizations are still around; they specialize in gambling, prostitution, the drug trade, and the occasional murder or extortion to keep things lively.

"But one of the biggest cash cows for them," Stoker says from the backseat, "is counterfeiting. Not just money, either—goods."

"I know," I say. "Designer clothing, name-brand electronics, furniture, toys—anything they can make cheaper and crappier."

"Lems, too," Charlie says.

"You're not serious."

"I am. Low-grade dirt mixed with the sand. Thinner skin, no quality control. Juice 'em up with the life force of a mouse, put 'em to work in factories. They have a life span of a few months, but half of them don't make it that long—they'll put too much stress on a seam and burst open. Spill whatever life they have left all over the floor, and the next lem in line will have to sweep up the remains. The leftovers get recycled, of course; wouldn't want to waste good dirt."

The car goes quiet for a second.

"Yeah," Stoker says, his voice hard. "That's exactly right. That's the value these . . . *predators* put on life. *Any* life."

"Unlike you," Charlie says. "What with your newfound respect for it and all."

"I never had a problem with lems," Stoker says. "I killed pires, I killed thropes. Never golems."

"You're a real saint," Charlie says. "How *lucky* I am to be in your presence—"

And then we're in the middle of a firefight.

Literally. Bolts of fire blaze through my line of sight, like a meteor shower at eye level. It takes my brain a second to process the fact that I'm seeing flaming arrows flash past, but by then I've locked up the brakes and thrown the car into a screaming sideways skid. The DeSoto screeches out of my lane and slams into the side of a bus, bringing it to an abrupt halt. The passenger-side window and windshield shatter on impact, showering me with safety glass.

I'm a little stunned, but unhurt. The side of the bus looks like a giant robot porcupine that someone set on fire. *Well, of course,* my dazed brain tells me. *An ordinary giant metal porcupine is far too mundane for the Jace Valchek lifestyle. Let's throw in a duck from Jupiter and a talking pickle, then we'll really have a party.*

Charlie has me out of my seat belt and out of the car before I can do more than blink a few times. "Stoker," I manage. "Where the hell is Stoker?"

Charlie's running with me in his arms. "I'll find him," he snarls, which isn't good. "First things first."

We're on Main Street, right beside a park. I can see an elevated transit system bridging the street, and three thropes with bows crouched on the roof of the station. Now I know where the arrows came from.

Charlie gets us behind a tree in the park, but it's not wide enough to provide good cover. "Archers," I say. "On the roof."

"I see them." He sets me down gently, then pops a ball bearing into each hand. "But they don't want us dead. They could have picked us off easily if they wanted to."

He's right. The arrows were designed to get our attention, make us stop. I draw my gun and look around for the second team I know has to be here.

But what I see makes no sense at all.

The roof of the burning bus erupts in a rending of metal as a figure at least twenty feet tall bursts out of it. It's almost as big as a military lem, but looks like it's made entirely from blue porcelain. Its face is the mask of a leering Chinese demon, the mouth huge and distorted and fangy. It's got a sword in one hand that could Ginsu a Volkswagen, and it seems seriously pissed.

But not at us. At the thrope archers that just shish-kebabed its ride, and are now sliding down ziplines to the street. And between them, standing in the middle of the street, is Stoker.

Who's grinning.

And when the archers touch down, execute three simultaneous tuck-and-rolls, and come out of them with bows drawn and arrows nocked—at the giant demon, not him—he begins to slowly applaud.

"Cut!" a voice bellows, and all three archers immediately relax their posture and their bowstrings. The demon lowers his sword, though his scowl is apparently permanent.

"You have *got* to be kidding," I manage.

Charlie's already striding toward Stoker, who puts his hands up defensively. "Slow down, big man. I had nothing to do with this."

And suddenly there's a film crew. The sides of three white panel trucks slide up, revealing cameras and personnel, the latter of which swarm out and start directing traffic and attending to the actors. A short Asian thrope in a turquoise silk shirt bounds out of one of the trucks and heads straight for us. He ignores me and Charlie and marches right up to Stoker. He glares up at him, hands on his hips.

"What do you think you're *doing,* ruining my shot like that?"

"Ruining your *shot*?" I yelp. I hate it when I yelp, but

I'm stressed and angry and off balance. "*You* shot at *us,* you Kurosawa wannabe! Where the hell do you get off turning a public street into—"

He dismisses me with an annoyed wave. "I have all the necessary permits for filming a *cinema verité* scene in a public venue. You'll be generously compensated for your participation and were never in any danger. But you, sir—" He draws himself up to his full five-and-a-half-foot height and glowers at Stoker. "You have spoiled a carefully choreographed action sequence by your rude carelessness. When threatened by the sudden appearance of an *Oni,* an innocent bystander isn't supposed to stand around and *applaud!*"

Stoker's still smiling, but his eyes have a hard gleam to them. "Well, that's always been my problem. I just don't do what I'm supposed to."

I take a deep breath and holster my gun, though naturally nobody's been paying it the slightest bit of attention. "Permits. You have *permits* to inflict this sort of random mayhem on citizens without any warning?"

"Warning? How am I supposed to get genuine emotion out of passersby if they know what's going to happen beforehand?" The director shakes his head, annoyed at himself for even talking to me. "I don't have time for this. Somebody pay this woman and get her out of here."

A flunky hurries up with a clipboard in her hand. "Ma'am, if you'll just come with me—"

"Yeah, no, I'm good. How about our *car?*"

"We're insured," the flunky—a thrope woman in her twenties, wearing a headset and dressed in jeans and a baggy sweatshirt—tells me. "I just need you to fill out a few forms—"

More paperwork, terrific. I look over at Charlie, worried that crashing his beloved DeSoto is going to make him go ballistic, but he seems surprisingly calm; in fact, he's wandered over to the bus—which is no longer on fire—and is looking up at the Chinese demon with his fedora pushed back on his head. The demon has taken off his mask, revealing a lem with a reddish orange hue to his skin and a gridwork of reinforcing wire just below the surface.

"Construction?" Charlie says.

"Used to be," the huge lem says. "This pays better, though the work ain't as steady."

Charlie nods. "Well, you take what comes along."

"Yeah, ain't it the truth."

A small crowd of thropes and pires has gathered in the park, clustering behind the barricades that have abruptly sprung up. Klieg lights flare to life on the tops of the trucks, turning night to day and making me wince.

A man strides forward. A tall, slender pire, Asian, dressed in an expensive and very well-tailored suit of deep scarlet. He walks up to the director and says, "I'll take it from here, Tommy."

"Hello, Zhang," Stoker says. "I didn't expect such an elaborate reception."

Tommy looks unhappy. "This is going to put us behind schedule! I'll have to redo the entire sequence—"

Zhang turns and looks at the director. His eyes are cold and very black. "Then you will. Now go away."

Tommy's skin tone gets a little paler, and he fades without another word. He may be the director, but Zhang is clearly the one in charge.

"My apologies," Zhang says. "When I asked you to meet me here, I neglected to think of tonight's shooting schedule. Unforgivable, I know. One should always consider the consequences of a plan most carefully."

Stoker nods. "Yes. I can see that."

It's clear what's going on now. This was no bizarre accident; this was a carefully calculated warning. Stoker plays in a dangerous league, and Zhang—whoever he is—wants Stoker to know he's somebody to be taken seriously.

Charlie rejoins us. "The car's a little banged up, but it's mostly cosmetic. Have to get the glass replaced, though."

"Allow me to take care of it," Zhang says. "It's the least I can do." He turns to me. "I am Mr. Zhang. And you are?"

"Jace Valchek." He doesn't offer his hand, and I don't offer mine. We nod at each other instead. "And this is my associate, Charlie Aleph."

"Greetings. I understand we have business to discuss."

I glance at Stoker, who gives me a barely perceptible nod.

"I suppose we do," I say.

"Then please, follow me—civilized persons do not discuss important matters in the street. Your vehicle is still operational?"

"She'll drive," Charlie says.

"I'm parked a short distance away. The black Mercedes." He nods again, then turns and walks away.

We return to the DeSoto. The outside still has a few white clumps of fire-suppressant foam clinging to it, but the broken glass has been swept away. The bus is in the process of being towed, the giant lem still sticking up through the top like a big blue jack-in-the-box. He taps the flat of his sword blade against the roof idly as he goes; *clang clang clang* went the trolley.

We get in the car, and this time I let Charlie drive. He doesn't argue, but he gives Stoker a long, hard look before sliding behind the wheel.

"So this is the guy?" I ask.

"This is the guy," Stoker says. "Mr. Zhang is the Four Thirty-eight for one of the biggest Triads on the West Coast."

"Four Thirty-eight?"

"They're big on numerology. Four Thirty-eight is his rank, which also translates into the title Incense Master. He's their chief shaman."

"And why is he willing to speak to you?"

"He owes me—more important, he owes the FHR. We negotiated some substantial weapons deals for him, and he doesn't want to risk losing us as go-betweens."

"Wait—I thought you'd left the Free Human Resistance?"

"Yeah, but he doesn't know that."

Charlie starts the car and follows the black Mercedes that's just pulling away from the curb up the street. It's a pire's car, so the windows are all heavily tinted.

Zhang turns left off Main, passing under a large Chinese arch, and we're in Chinatown proper. Stalls line the sidewalks, hawking everything from BBQ duck to imported rice cookers. Neon restaurant signs hum and flash overhead, reflecting off the conical bamboo hats that most of the bustling crowd seems to be wearing—even in half-were form. Steam wafts up from vendors' carts, and the air is rich with the smell of a hundred dishes cooking.

We creep slowly through the crowded streets, turning right, then left, then right again. The buildings are all old, brick or wooden structures crammed tightly together. A thick fog rolls in, cutting down visibility and reminding me how close we are to the ocean. Before too long all we can see are the two red taillights in front of us, glowing like demonic eyes.

I don't like this. I give Stoker a hard look, and he seems uneasy, too. "What's going on?" I snap. "Where the hell are we going?"

"Take it easy. Zhang wouldn't—"

A shudder passes through my body, making me gasp.

I can tell Stoker feels it, too, and Charlie slams on the brakes a second later.

I pull the Ruger out. The Mercedes's taillights have disappeared in the thick mist ahead of us. "Zhang wouldn't *what*?" I demand of Stoker.

"Lure us to Yomi," Stoker mutters. "Went there himself, and dragged us along on his tail."

"Yomi? Where the hell is Yomi?"

"You just answered your own question." I don't think I've ever seen Stoker look worried, but that's what's on his face now. "Jace, *Yomi* is the term for the Japanese underworld. In other words—Hell is exactly where we *are*."

SIX

"How about that," Charlie says. "After all those years of people telling you to go here, you finally went."

"Me?" I say. "*You're* the one who was driving. How can someone drive through the gates of Hell without *noticing*?"

"*What* gates? I didn't even see a sign."

Stoker starts to open his door. I grab his arm and stop him. "What are you, crazy? We're completely exposed— there could be anything lurking in that fog."

"If he wanted us dead, he wouldn't have taken us here," Stoker says. "And this car won't provide much protection anyway. Not against what lives here."

If we really are where Stoker claims, that's no doubt true. I let go of his arm and get out the other side. Charlie joins us.

The fog's a little less thick now. The buildings around us are run-down and abandoned, dark windows edged with teeth of broken glass, brick walls papered with torn, fading posters full of close-packed *kanji* script. The street we're on isn't paved, just smooth, hard-packed dirt. There are no streetlights, but the mist itself seems faintly luminous.

"What can we expect?" I ask Stoker tersely.

"Demons, unquiet ghosts, Kami spirits . . . and they

can come in just about any form. But they won't neccessarily be hostile. The Japanese version of Hell is surprisingly nonviolent."

"I'll keep that in mind when dealing with the locals," Charlie growls.

"So, no fire and brimstone?" I ask.

"No. Unchanging gloom and dreariness is about it. For eternity."

"As long as a giant horned demon isn't going to appear and try to eat my head."

"Oh, they have those here, too. But they have one very specific job."

"Which is?"

"Guarding the exits."

Of course. I look behind us at the way we came, and see nothing but the road blurring into the fog; if there's an exit back there, it's not visible. "So we're trapped in Hell. One where I don't even speak the language."

"Look on the bright side," Stoker says. "At least we're not dead."

"Oh, joy," Charlie says. "I may break into song."

"Nice to know things can always get worse," I say. "Being among the living means we have a shot at leaving, right?"

"Presumably," Stoker says.

I'm starting to get the whole "gloomy" thing. "What's Zhang's game? Why has he done this?"

"He must know I'm no longer with the Free Human Resistance. Whoever could deliver me to the authorities would be able to ask for a lot in return. Especially alive."

Brilliant. I'm not even the target here, I'm just collateral damage. "So we're in cold storage until he cuts a deal."

"Maybe not. I wanted to meet with Zhang because he claimed to know something about the missing pire children. Maybe he does; maybe he doesn't want me prying any further."

"We're stuck here either way," Charlie says. "Unless one of you has a 'get out of Hell free' card in their wallet?"

"We need to find one of those exits," I say. "Monsters or not, we can't leave without knowing where the door is. Stoker, any ideas?"

"Yomi's supposed to be located underground. Look for an entrance to a tunnel or maybe a staircase going up."

"We went under an overpass just before the fog got really heavy," Charlie says. "That must have been it."

"It probably won't look the same from this side," Stoker says. "Might be a bridge, an arch, even the door to a building."

"We'll try the obvious first," I say. "Head back the way we came. Maybe we can just drive over the guy guarding the tollgate."

We get in the car and Charlie gets it turned around. Down the road we go.

No magic overpass shows up. No bridge or tunnel, either. We drive until we hit a T-junction in the road, and then stop. The buildings on either side look much the same, and so does the road. There's no sign.

I sigh. "Terrific. Should we go left to Nowhere, or right to Nothing?"

I look out the window, tapping my fingers against the Ruger's barrel in frustration. I can see furtive movement behind tattered gray curtains in a window, an indication that we're not alone. I wonder how long it will be before the souls of the dead venture forth to check out the new residents, and if they'll send a formal representative or just kind of show up in a group. I wonder if they'll bring us a fruit basket as a gesture of goodwill, and if all the fruit will be dead and rotting. I wonder why my brain comes up with these things when it should be concentrating on the situation at hand.

And then the situation changes.

Zhang descends from the sky like a hanged man dropping through the trapdoor of a gallows. He jerks to a halt directly in front of the car, about six feet off the ground. He's dressed the same, but his eyes are burning a spectral white and I can see his skull glowing through his skin.

"Greetings, esteemed guests," he says. "Allow me to welcome the Bloodhound and the Impaler to the realm of Yomi."

"You forgot me," Charlie growls. He opens the door and gets out of the car, and I know why; he doesn't have enough room to pitch one of his ball bearings while he's in the driver's seat. I get out, too, taking aim at Zhang's midsection.

"You are hardly worth noticing, man of sand. But your mistress and her companion are well known to me, indeed—"

Charlie rifles a shot into his chest. It punches through Zhang's body like a bullet through smoke, leaving a fist-size hole in its wake. Zhang looks more irritated with the interruption than the assault, and the hole seals itself a second later. "That was most rude."

"No, that was medium rude. I got *most* right here." Charlie draws his short sword from inside his jacket.

I can already tell it's pointless, but I have to back my partner's play. I put a slug through Zhang's windpipe—the .454 round is big enough to more or less destroy his neck and spinal column, and decapitation is always a good fallback position when dealing with supernaturals.

But I'm not all that surprised when all I get for my trouble is a replay of Charlie's attack. Now Zhang looks more disappointed than annoyed, as if he were expecting better from me.

"I see," he says, and extends his right arm. The flesh melts away from his hand, leaving the glowing bones exposed, and it shoots forward, growing as it extends. By the time it seizes Charlie he looks like a doll in the grip of an immense skeleton.

I fire again, to zero effect. Charlie's managed to keep his sword arm free, and hacks at a metacarpal. The blade rings off the bone like it was made of granite.

"Foolish creature," Zhang says, and tightens his grip. He's going to pop Charlie like a balloon—

But then something crosses Zhang's face—it's what's called a micro expression, something most people would miss, and it's one of consternation.

"You are not worthy of death," Zhang says, and gestures with his other hand. A shimmering hole opens in midair, around twelve feet off the ground, and he tosses Charlie through it like someone throwing away an empty pop bottle. I can see what looks like a tile wall on the other side, and Charlie thumps into it none too softly.

Zhang gestures again, and the hole closes.

The sorcerer and I regard each other. I lower my gun, reluctantly. At least Charlie's safe—I'm pretty sure that was the real world Zhang just threw him into. Why he did that instead of just killing him, I'm not sure.

"As I was saying." Zhang's hand returns to its normal size and condition. "Both of you are well known to me. Mr. Stoker, will you not join us?"

Stoker opens his door and gets out of the car. "Thanks for all the help," I snarl.

"Combat was pointless," Stoker says. "*And* rude. My apologies, Mr. Zhang."

"You are most gracious." Zhang smiles, an extremely creepy thing to do when I can see his skull grinning behind his lips at the same time.

"I'm not," I say. "You can't keep us here, Zhang."

"I assure you that I can. While your hunting ability is renowned, even the infamous Bloodhound can be restrained behind a sturdy enough fence. The borders of Yomi are quite up to the task, I'm certain."

That's not what I expected. While it's true I've made some waves since I got to Thropirelem, I never thought of my rep as being something that traveled beyond the office. "So you know me?"

"Of course. You defeated a god, Bloodhound; that resonated through the mystical continuum. Every powerful shaman and sorcerer on this plane—and perhaps a few others—took notice. I'm surprised no one has tried to acquire you before this."

"Oh, it's been tried." I give him the coldest smile I can manage. "Didn't work out so well, though. Not for them."

"Perhaps I shall be more fortunate."

"Yeah, I doubt that."

He gives his head an acknowledging bow. "We shall see. In the meantime, consider yourselves my honored guests; while you are here, you are under my protection. Still, I would advise you not to wander far, or to eat anything but what I provide. To do so would doom you to dwell here for eternity."

"Damn. I was really looking forward to trying that zombie sushi place we passed a few blocks ago. Nothing like an undead California roll when you've got a craving, you know?"

Zhang just stares at me. Geez, tough realm.

"I shall return with provisions," he says, and zips up into the overhead fog like a corpse on a bungee cord.

"Well, that was interesting," I mutter.

"In a very Chinese sense," Stoker says. "You know the ancient curse, right?"

"May you live in interesting times? Yeah, that one popped up in my reality, too. Guess it's a universal sentiment." I holster my gun again. "I say we keep driving. If Zhang doesn't want us exploring, it might be because he's afraid we'll find an exit."

Stoker shrugs. "Or because he doesn't want something to eat his two hostages before he can sell them."

"There is that. In which case, I prefer to be a moving target. You coming?" I slide into the driver's seat.

He gets in beside me. "Where to?"

"Left. Let's start with that, and see what happens."

I check the gas gauge as we hit the road. Three-quarters of a tank. Wonder how long it'll last in the underworld—I have no idea what the rules are, other than Zhang's warning about not eating. If I fill up at a gas station in Hell, will the DeSoto be doomed to motor down these roads forever? And if so, will Charlie's insurance cover a fender bender with Beelzebub?

Shut up, brain.

More bland, deserted scenery. The buildings end and now there's only an empty plain on either side of the road. Then even the road ends, and we're just driving on flat ground. I stop and turn around, but I can't seem to find the road again. I stop and shut the engine off; no sense wasting gas if we don't have a destination.

"Something I can't figure out," I say. "Charlie. Why didn't Zhang kill him?"

"Because we're living beings in the land of spirits," Stoker says. "You kill us here, you release our life force. If that happens to you or me, it's just another human soul added to the local population. But in Charlie's case—"

I nod. "Ah. Guess Zhang could tell what's under Charlie's hood, huh?" Unlike most lems—who are animated by the spirit of a steer or other common animal—Charlie's charged up with the essence of a long-dead giant lizard. The last thing Zhang wanted was the pissed-off ghost of a *T. rex* to deal with. That's good news; it means the sorcerer is still vulnerable here. Too bad my partner's currently on another plane of existence.

"Yeah." Stoker leans back against the bench seat, propping one massive arm on it. "So. We need to strategize."

"We do. Got any ideas?"

"I do, but they all involve not being trapped in an other-dimensional limbo."

"Ah."

We fall silent. It's surprisingly easy to do, but not because Stoker and I are comfortable with each other; no, it's this place. The grayness outside seems to be seeping into the car, leaching away any sense of purpose, any hope. It takes a conscious effort of will to talk, and I realize that the longer we spend here, the worse our chances are for ever escaping. We need to stay engaged, stay alert—

Stoker reaches down and hits the PLAY button on the car stereo.

The sound of "The Boogie-Woogie Bugle Boy of Company B" fills the car. It's the perfect antidote, upbeat and cheerful and bouncy, as familiar as a favorite T-shirt and just as comforting. The grin that shows up on my face is a little slow in coming, but it's genuine.

"Good idea," I say. "I'm just glad Charlie wasn't in the mood for the blues."

"Yeah, let's try and accentuate the positive." Stoker sounds as if he's having a hard time doing that himself. "Because this is just going to get worse, Jace."

"You call that positive?" I shake my head. "We can't just sit here and listen to music until we run out of gas and the battery dies. We have to *do* something."

"Agreed. But what? We could wander forever in this fog and still never get anywhere."

"You're right. But I don't think this place follows the same rules we're used to. It's a . . . a *conceptual* place." I struggle to find the words to explain what I'm thinking. "Despair has an actual *weight* here, a physical presence. Other emotions might, too. The dead might not be able to feel much, but we still do. We can . . . we can . . ."

"We can what?" His voice is guarded.

"We can *fight.*"

"I'm not about to give up, Jace. But what are you *suggesting,* exactly?"

I slap him.

It's the first time I've ever slapped anyone. I've *hit* people plenty of times; with my closed fist, the heel of my palm, my elbow, my knee, even my forehead—but never with my open hand. Now I know why: It *hurts.*

"Ow!" we both say at the same time.

Stoker pulls back—when did he get so close?—and looks at me with both shock and guilt. "Okay, okay, I'm sorry!"

I cradle my poor hand. Slapping Stoker is like smacking a lamppost. "Sorry? For what? *I* hit *you,* you idiot!"

"I know! I was there!"

"Then why are you apologizing?"

"Because—wait." He rubs his cheek, which is turning a satisfying shade of red. "You hit me because . . ."

"When I said *we can fight,* I meant it literally. I thought I'd get the ball rolling, but apparently you don't *have* any." That's low, but we're not going to get anywhere by being nice here.

He blinks at me, then bursts into laughter. Okay, not the reaction I was going for, but any show of emotion at this point is a good thing. And it has the added effect of pissing me off, because I have no idea why me hitting him is so damn funny. Maybe I should have broken his nose, instead. *"What?"*

"I've been accused of many things, but never that. And considering what I *thought* you were proposing, it's even funnier."

It takes me a second to process that. And when I do, I get a very gratifying surge of anger in return. "*Proposing? With you? Here?* Are you out of your sociopathic Neanderthal *mind?*"

"No. But I could be out of my *pants.*"

I glare at him, and he stares steadily back. And I realize that what he's suggesting—what he thought *I* was suggesting—isn't that unthinkable. In fact, I did something similar to save Cassius's life, not too long ago; and as primal as that experience was, what could be more elemental than committing the ultimate life-affirming act in the land of the dead?

Sure. Because the only thing better than boffing your boss is waiting until he disappears so you can jump in the sack with the first psycho that comes along. "Sorry—we were in Hell, we needed a little cheering up, you know how it is."

"Not. Going. To happen," I growl.

He yawns. Deliberately. "Sure it isn't. You know that line, *Not if you were the last man on Earth?* Well, we may not be on Earth—but I *am* the only man here."

Now I'm sorry I didn't break his nose. "Listen, you arrogant, homicidal sack of testosterone—"

And that's when someone raps on my window.

"AHHH!" I spin around in my seat, scrabbling for my gun—

A gray face stares in at me. Her eyes look Asian, but it's the only distinguishing feature about her. She's dressed in some kind of formless gray shroud the exact color of her skin, and her hair is only slightly darker. She looks at me with the barest trace of interest on her colorless face.

We stare at each other. I feel like I've just been pulled over by a zombie traffic cop. "I'm going to need to see your license, registration, and brains, ma'am." I suppress the urge to stick my gun in her face—I really have to stop relying on the damn thing so much.

"I think she wants to talk to you," Stoker says.

"So? What if I roll down the window and she tries to eat my head?"

"She'll probably get food poisoning."

The woman continues to study me in a vague sort of way. I have to admit, I'm not exactly getting a hostile or dangerous vibe from her—and if she really wanted to attack me I doubt she'd announce herself beforehand or let a thin layer of glass slow her down. I sigh and roll down the window. "Uh, hi."

"Hi." Her voice is as dull and flat as an old butter knife. She doesn't offer anything further.

"Is there something you want?" I say. It seems as good a conversation gambit as any.

"No." More silence.

I try a different approach. "Why are you here?"

"Because I'm dead."

Progress, I guess—a whole three words. "How did you die?"

"I was old."

"Yeah, that'll happen." But not to pires, which means she was either a thrope or a baseline human. "How long have you been dead?"

"Ever since I got here."

"Were you a thrope?"

"Don't know what that is."

"Werewolf."

"What wolf?"

"No, *were*wolf."

"Oh." She pauses and straightens up, looking around. Then she raises one arm slowly and points to the swirling mist behind the car. "*There* wolf."

Stoker and I both swivel around and look out the rear window.

There's a figure back there, standing in the fog at the edge of visibility. Its silhouette is that of a thrope in half-were form, tall pointed ears jutting from a canine skull, but that shrinks down to a more human outline before my eyes. The figure takes a few steps forward, resolving into a redheaded man of indeterminate age. His features are narrow, with a slightly Asian cast to them, but nothing definite; he could pass for Hispanic or Caucasian or even Indian without much trouble. He's dressed in a tan trench coat over a dark olive suit.

"Hello, love," he says. His voice is self-assured, amused, and right off a London street.

I look at Stoker. "I think he's talking to you."

"Talking to both of you, actually." The man's red hair is darker than most, and slicked back with oil. "I mean, I hate to interrupt what seems a *fascinating* dialogue between you and Ms. Rest-In-Peace there, but when you're done discussing the relative merits of open versus closed caskets, I wouldn't mind a moment of your time."

I look at Stoker. He shrugs. "I think we can work it into our busy schedule, don't you?"

"Who are you?" I ask the stranger. "And what do you want?"

"You can call me Zevon, Agent Valchek. And as to what I want? Why, I want to provide you with a much-needed service."

"Let me guess," I say. "Protection?"

He gives a throaty chuckle. "Not at all. Transportation—which is to say, a way out of this place. Interested?"

"What did you have in mind?"

"A deal, of course. You provide something, I provide something in return." He gives me a grin, which is a little too feral for my liking. "What else did you expect?"

I sigh. "Something a little less cliché? Come on, guy with a fondness for red shows up in the underworld and offers to make a deal? Why don't you just pull out a contract and ask for a blood sample?"

Zevon looks slightly indignant. "Please. First of all, you have your cultural references all mixed up; this is Yomi, not Perdition. Second: I much prefer green to red, as you should be able to tell by what I've got on; and third, if you mean to suggest I'm after your soul, I should point out that you're already *here*. Honestly, if that's what I was after I'd just kill the both of you."

"You could try," I growl.

He shakes his head. "No, no, no. That's not my intention at all. I'm not Lucifer or Satan or anyone like that; I'm just a humble facilitator. Really."

"Uh-huh. So what's a humble facilitator charge for getting out of here?"

"Oh, it varies from customer to customer. Depending on the entertainment value."

I start to see where this is heading. "How about I hook you up with free cable? I know a guy."

His smile gets wider. "Oh, the reception in here is *terrible*. I know, I've tried. But you've got the right idea."

Yeah. In an endless gray blankness, anything new and stimulating would be invaluable. But what a demon—and no matter what this guy claims, that's what he must be—finds entertaining isn't going to be pleasant. On the other hand, the lack of traditional Judeo-Christian torments here means it may not involve red-hot pokers or bodily orifices. "So tell me, already. But I should warn you that my singing voice is terrible and I can't juggle."

"Oh, I think you're a *fine* juggler. Just think about how many balls you've got in the air right now—there's the dojo you just started, your friends, your dog, your new lover . . . and of course your job, which really counts as more than one. All those cases you get dragged into because of your expertise in profiling, when what you really should be doing is concentrating on the one that'll let you get back to your old life."

He pauses, obviously enjoying the grim look on my face as he effortlessly defines my current existence. "But look! The biggest ball of all has just landed in your hand! Aristotle Stoker, Fugitive Number One, right there beside you. Exactly one half of your ticket home—you should be overjoyed. Well, half overjoyed, anyway. Maybe just joyed."

"Get to the point."

"Which one? There are so many, all of them quite tasty; a point buffet, if you will. Let's start with a nice contradiction appetizer: the fact that you're collaborating with someone you really should be arresting."

"We have mutual concerns."

Zevon mock-frowns. "Oh? Well, I suppose there is the fact that you're both human. And single. And heterosexual. Which brings me to point number two . . ."

"You're just here to annoy us, aren't you?" I nod wearily. "Okay, go ahead. Beats us annoying each other."

"No, annoying you is just a bonus," Zevon says cheerfully. "Would you mind getting out of the car so we can talk face-to-face? More comfortable all round, I think."

Why not? I feel like I could use a little distance from Stoker right now, anyway. I get out on one side, Stoker on the other. I cross my arms and lean against the DeSoto with one shoulder. "So make your pitch, already."

"All right, here it is: I'll return both of you to the mortal realm—if you're willing to give up something near and dear to each of you."

I'm beginning to see how an eternity of vagueness could be considered Hell. "Which is *what,* exactly?"

"Well, that's the catch. You knew there was going to be one, right?" Zevon sighs. "That's the problem with this place. Nothing *surprising* ever happens . . . anyway, it's got be something you can both agree on, and acceptable to me. Let's get those lines of communication open, eh? Full and frank discussion, all options on the table." He beams at both of us.

"Not very subtle, is he?" Stoker says.

I shake my head. "Honestly? I'm a little disappointed."

Zevon blinks. "I beg your pardon?"

"Well, it beats all the artificial sexual tension we were trying to generate," Stoker admits.

"Maybe, but at least that was almost enjoyable."

"I thought the slap was a little cliché."

"Me, too. But hey, what about your leering redneck impression?"

"Over the top, I know. I was just trying to keep up."

Now Zevon looks a little miffed. "Artificial? Wait a minute—"

I cut him off. "We're not going to emotionally eviscerate ourselves while you watch, Zevon. Arguing back and forth over what really matters to us and what we're willing to give up? Not gonna happen."

"No," Stoker says. He takes a long, deliberate step toward Zevon, then another. It's that even, measured pace men use when they're being confrontational, accompanied by a steady gaze and an impassive expression. "But I'll tell you what will."

He stops a few feet from the thrope, who's looking at him more in curiosity than fear. Stoker leans forward—and says something too softly for me to hear.

Zevon grins. He throws an arm around Stoker's shoulders, and they stroll quickly away. The fog swallows them in a second.

"Hey!" I shout, and bolt forward.

But it's no use.

They're gone.

SEVEN

I know if I get lost in that fog I'll be even worse off than I am now, so I stay with the car. The car, and my new dead friend.

"I can't believe he did that," I fume. "Can you believe he *did* that?"

Ghost woman appears to think about it. "I'm not sure. Believing in things is *hard*."

"Well, it wasn't a request. Christ, I should have known he'd shaft me the first chance he got . . . what was I thinking, working with him? Did I leave my brain in my other pants?"

"I don't know. I don't have pants."

"Or much in the way of gray matter," I mutter. "Well, that makes two of us. Maybe we should team up—the Idiot Twins, Seventh and Eighth Wonders of the Underworld. Watch us perform amazing feats of stupidity without a neural net . . ."

"I'm not an idiot," the woman says. There's no trace of anger or any other emotion in her voice; she's simply stating a fact. "I'm just dead."

That shakes me up a little. The woman has so little presence that it's hard to think of her as a person—but even if she's no longer alive, there's still some kernel of humanity there, some self-awareness that makes her more than just an object. She was born, she had a life, she died; she deserves more than my offhanded glib insults—

"You really smell," the woman says.

"What?"

"No. That's not right." The woman pauses. "I mean you smell *real*." There's just the barest emphasis on the last word.

"Oh. I guess that's because I am. Real, I mean."

The woman nods. "Nothing here is. Not even me. We're just . . . moving pictures. Gray light through film."

That's more eloquent than I expected, and an unusual metaphor; a comparison to shadows seems more likely to me than a cinematography reference. "What's your name?" I ask, while doubting I'll get a useful answer.

She surprises me again, though. "Jinjing. Jinjing Wong."

"What did you do when you were alive, Jinjing? What was your job?"

"I was a cook. Many years. But only for my family the last ten. Retired."

"Retirement. That sounds good, right about now."

"Hated it at first. Always been useful. But found something else. Magic."

Now, *that* gets my interest. If Jinjing here was some sort of shaman, maybe her ghost still has a little mojo— enough to get me out of here maybe, or at least steer me in the right direction. "You were a shaman? Shinto?"

"No. Not that kind of magic. *Movies.*" This time, there's something approaching actual emotion in her voice. "So new. So wonderful. Light and shadow dancing, telling stories. I watched them all."

I blink. I'm not sure when Jinjing died, but apparently she became a film buff in her old age. "All?"

"Yes. I loved Buster Keaton. Very Chinese, in his way." A trace of a smile touches Jinjing's lips, but it's gone in an instant. "My friends didn't like them. Disrespectful of reality, they said. But I thought films were more than real, not less."

"I know what you mean. Life with all the exciting bits concentrated and the boring bits removed."

"Yes. Like a good stew." She pauses. "But now . . . nothing has flavor. There is only this . . ." She takes in the featureless landscape with one slow, all-encompassing look around. "Nothing."

I shiver, but the cold I feel isn't physical. I wonder if I'll sound like Jinjing after being trapped here for a few decades . . .

Which is when Stoker strides back out of the fog.

"Hey, Jace. Ready to go?"

I don't know whether to slug him or hug him. "What the *hell* was that all about?"

He reaches for the passenger-side door, but I block him. He sighs. "How about I tell you when we're out of here, huh? A door is about to open and we need to be ready to drive through it."

I give him a hard look, but if he's telling the truth my questions will have to wait. The fog in front of the DeSoto is swirling around, looking like the eye of a hurricane as seen from space; we both jump in and I start the engine. A yawning black hole opens before us. I have time to hope this isn't the proverbial from-frying-pan-to-fire routine, and stomp on the gas.

We roar into the darkness. My last glimpse of Jinjing Wong is through the rearview window, and she's already turning away.

Back to oblivion.

Leaving Hell, it turns out, is considerably rougher than entering it. I have enough time to yell "Close your eyes!" to Stoker, and then we're into the eye of the hurricane.

I've been across dimensional boundaries before. Sometimes the transition is hardly noticeable; other times it's disorienting and unpleasant. Guess what it's like this time?

The very first time I made a trip like this, the sorcerer who brought me across warned me to close my eyes, "for my own safety." I finally understand what he meant.

The darkness doesn't last long. It's replaced by madness.

I can't even properly describe it. An infinity of invisible eyes bleeding fire the color of pain. The smell of sideways hours. Gut-wrenching terror, overpowering déjà vu and hysterical nostalgia. Sharpness turned inside out and the taste of overcooked bleach. All of it pouring through my optic nerves, like my senses have narrowed down to one channel and everything's overlaid on top of it. I really wish I could close my eyes, but the rational part of my brain that's still working tells me that's not a good idea while I'm behind the wheel of a car. Okay, this isn't exactly driving, but I plunged into that portal at a pretty good clip and I'm probably going to come out the other end doing the same speed. I need to be ready.

It's over as abruptly as it began, leaving my abused central nervous system gasping and flopping around. The car is—

Indoors.

I slam on the brakes. We plow through what looks like a roulette wheel, then a craps table, then a few round tables covered in green felt. Poker chips explode into the air like a million tiny, brightly colored Frisbees. I wish I could say we didn't run anyone down, but at least four bodies thump off our fenders or grille. The last one hits the windshield face-first and sticks, an elderly Asian pire in a plaid cardigan who looks more offended than afraid.

We screech to a stop before we run out of casino—or gambling den, more likely.

"Can I open my eyes now?" Stoker says.

I look around at the room full of stunned gamblers. Some of them are starting to look a little upset, and the pire stuck to our windshield is shaking his fist at us and berating us in Cantonese.

"I wouldn't," I say.

Fortunately, that's when Charlie shows up. He makes his way past the wreckage and yanks open my door. "You okay?"

"Yeah, yeah. Sorry about the car."

"Don't worry about it. Little body work, is all. Bang out a few dents, she'll be good as new." He grabs the pire by the scruff of the neck and tosses him over his shoulder as casually as a gas-station attendant pulling a scrap of newspaper from under a wiper blade. "But you should really let me drive from here."

I don't argue, just slide over next to Stoker. Charlie climbs in, puts the car in gear. "Brace yourself," he says, and guns it.

Apparently the wall I stopped just short of is made of smoked glass—or was, anyway. Charlie smashes through it, into a thankfully deserted restaurant on the other side, through a dozen or so round tables with chairs stacked on them, into another large, smoked-glass window, over a sidewalk on the other side, and finally into the street.

"Nice," Stoker says. "Hope nobody's stuck to the under-carriage."

"Nah," Charlie says. "She'd be riding a lot rougher if that happened."

It looks like we're still in Chinatown—hopefully the right Chinatown in the right world. World-hopping always makes me nervous; what if I come back to the wrong one? What if it's so close I can't tell until years later, when some weird detail turns out to be different from the original—you know, like the French worshipping Jerry Lewis or something equally bizarre? Would the knowledge destroy me, or would I just shrug and go on about my life?

Of course, if I do wind up on an alternate version of Thropirelem I'll probably never find out, so I tell myself not to worry about it. And at the moment, I have more pressing problems.

"Doesn't look like we're being followed," I say. "Guess Zhang isn't quite as cocky in the non-metaphysical realm."

"He was just taking advantage of an opportunity," Stoker says. "I can't really blame him—I probably would have done the same."

"Yeah, I'll bet. Now *how* the upside-down seven seven three four did you get Zevon to open the exit door?"

"I can't tell you."

"Why not?" All the adrenaline in my system is being converted to pure frustration, and despite the fact that he just saved both of us, I'm about ready to throttle Stoker.

He shrugs. "That was the deal. I gave up something to gain *my* freedom . . . and got *yours* in return for keeping mine a secret."

"What? That's . . . that's . . ."

"Maddening? Sure. He knew that's how you'd react, which is why he went for it. Apparently Zevon likes his entertainment on the obnoxious side."

I take a deep breath and settle back in my seat. I am not going to let this get to me. Whatever Stoker traded, that's his business. I don't care what it is. I don't care at all.

I *don't.*

It's been a less-than-satisfying night. Stoker tells us that in light of Zhang's attempted abduction, there are certain things he has to attend to if he doesn't want every gang in Vancouver thinking he's now a target; not so much retaliation as sending a message. It's something he has to do on his own, not out of machismo but simply to reassert his position in the local underground heirarchy. It should have the added benefit of shaking loose a little more information about the missing children, too, or at least that's what Stoker claims. I'm guessing that the next time Zhang and Stoker talk it won't be quite as polite.

We drop him off on a street corner and he vanishes into the night. Charlie and I return to the hotel, where we give a worried-looking Eisfanger a quick rundown of what happened. Charlie, it turns out, was dumped in the bathroom of the gambling den. While surreptitiously checking out the operation, he overhead someone mention Zhang's name and decided to stick around to see if the sorcerer made an appearance—though he was just as happy to see us instead.

Then we collapse into our respective beds. I'm exhausted, more so emotionally than physically, and don't so much fall asleep as pass out.

And dream.

"Hello," Cassius says. "Nice dress."

I look down at myself. I'm wearing Nice Outfit #3, the one I wear on first dates when my hopes are still relatively high: green silk blouse, mid-length skirt, two-inch strappy heels.

Cassius, though, is considerably more upscale, if not exactly modern. He's dressed like medevial royalty, a gold-embroidered vest over a billowy shirt of deep purple, with heavy golden rings on his fingers and a spray of lace at his throat. Normally I'd mock him for such a getup, but dream logic tells me to simply accept it.

We're sitting at a café table on a patio under a sun umbrella. Cassius is in the shade, but he seems unconcerned at the closeness of the sun.

"Thank you," I say. "Bear with me, okay? I don't date much."

He smiles. It makes me a little light-headed, that smile, in all the right ways. "I've been known to go a few years between relationships myself. But let's not put too much pressure on ourselves, all right? I won't bite if you won't."

I laugh at that, because I know he's a vampire but he doesn't know I know, which puts me one up on him.

"So, what do you do?" I say, trying to keep a grin off my face.

"Well, let's see. I got my start in Rome. Lot of people think I was in on the bottom floor, but that's not strictly true. After that I kicked around Europe for a while, did some backpacking, helped found a few countries . . . you know, the typical young-guy stuff. How about you?"

"Got into a lot of trouble when I was a kid. Not because I was bad, exactly, more like I wouldn't back down from anyone and had the tendency to stick my nose where it didn't belong."

He nods. God, his eyes are so blue . . . I find myself thinking he *must* be a jerk. Anybody good looking gets so used to being handed everything on a silver platter, they can't help but turn into spoiled brats.

"Never back down, huh?" he says. "Wish I could say the same. But you know how it is: Once you start to compromise, your ideals begin to erode. Happens so slowly you hardly notice. By the time you do, decades have gone past and you're doing things you never dreamed you would. By then, it's too late; you can't undo the mistakes you've made. All you can do is atone . . ."

His voice is full of regret. Most jerks are defined by their selfishness; they just don't care about other people's pain. But listening to Cassius, I can tell he does.

"Sounds like you've led an interesting life," I offer.

"I suppose. Want to see some of it?"

"Sure."

He stands up and holds out his hand. Hesitantly, I take it.

We step away from the table and onto the ramparts of a castle, gray stone lit by torches. The moon is full, the sky full of stars. "Where are we?" I ask.

"Bavaria. Somewhere around 1550, I think. Lot going on back then; what eventually became Germany was divided into a patchwork of little kingdoms, and they were all at war with one another. I was in the thick of it."

"On whose side?"

He shakes his head ruefully. "Depended on the day of the week. So many different alliances, treaties, betrayals . . . honestly, I can't remember it in detail. But I do remember the countryside, and this view in particular. Lovely, isn't it?"

Beyond the castle's walls are rolling hills of green, shimmering gently like waves in the moonlight. "Very," I say. "You always bring women here on a first date?"

"No," he says, meeting my eyes. "Just you."

The night air is rich and heady, the smell of wild grass after a spring rain mixed with the tang of wood smoke. I feel like I'm about to be kissed for the first time ever, nervous and excited and a little impatient. He leans forward . . .

"Jace," he says softly. "The membrane is ripening."

"Yes," I murmur.

"Soon potential will maelstrom the lattices."

"I know, I know. Me, too."

There's something wrong with his face. It's—it's *spiraling,* eyes and mouth going into orbit around his slowly twisting nose.

"I need you," he says. "*Leapyear,* Jace. Leapyear for *me.*"

I step back, horrified. Now it's his whole body, spinning into a vortex of stretching, distorted limbs. "I will," I say, my voice shaking. "I *will,* I promise!"

The faster he swirls the smaller he gets, until there's only a blurred, whirling circle the size of my head hovering in front of me. I feel like I've just watched someone die.

And then I wake up.

EIGHT

"You look like hell," Charlie observes at breakfast.

"Didn't sleep well. Bad dreams."

Eisfanger looks up from the huge plate of food he's halfway through consuming: eggs, toast, bacon, sausages, pancakes, and hash browns, with a side order of ham. I'm sticking with coffee and a Danish, and so far the Danish is doing better than I am. "Well, no wonder, after what you guys went through—psychic trauma is practically a given."

"I slept fine," Charlie says. He's reading a local newspaper while we eat.

I give him a withering look. "You weren't there for very long."

Charlie has the grace to look wounded. "I'm sorry, okay? It's not like I left of my own free will."

"Yeah, yeah, don't worry about it." I drain my coffee cup and look around for the waiter, who bears absolutely no resemblance to a movie star.

"So—what did you dream about?" Eisfanger asks. He studies me with interest, as guileless as a puppy. For some reason, I just don't have the heart to smack him down.

"I dreamed about Cassius."

"*This* should be interesting," Charlie murmurs, going back to his paper.

"I dreamed . . ." I stop, and shake my head. "Most of the dream was pretty ordinary—a little non-linear, sure. But right at the end it turned into a real nightmare: Cassius transformed into some sort of vortex, and he was talking gibberish. Words that almost made sense but not quite."

"That doesn't sound too bad," Eisfanger says around a mouthful of eggs.

"It was how it *felt,* more than anything. I was terrified. There was this feeling of impending doom. I woke up covered in sweat and shaking."

"How I start every day," Charlie says. "You know, being your partner and all."

"Oh, you're in *great* form."

"Thanks. See what a good night's sleep will do?"

Eisfanger looks at me curiously, seems about to say something, then changes his mind and drains half a glass of orange juice in one gulp instead. "What's our next move?"

"We wait for Stoker to get back in touch," I say. "He got us down here, he's not going to just vanish now."

"Unless he gets himself killed," Charlie points out.

"Yeah, but with Stoker that's always a concern." I finally get the attention of our waiter and some more coffee. "And he's proven extremely hard to kill."

We finish breakfast. Charlie makes arrangements to have the car fixed, Eisfanger holes up in his room with some technical manuals, and I watch daytime TV.

By the time Stoker gets in touch it's late afternoon. He calls me on my cell and starts the conversation with, "How'd you like the chance to do a little target practice this evening?"

"On whom?"

"The bottom feeders who are holding the pire children."

I'm sprawled on the bed enduring an old rerun of *Gilligan's Island*—oddly unchanged even when done with pires and thropes—and now I sit up. "You've found them?"

"I have. Mr. Zhang was most cooperative. For a while."

Even though Zhang was a criminal lowlife who was perfectly willing to sell me to the highest bidder, Stoker's remark sends a chill through me. I have to keep reminding myself that he's still a sociopath, one who's murdered dozens of men and women because they weren't human in his eyes. That's often how serial killers view their prey.

"You're sure?" I ask.

"I do need to verify the information, but it'll have to be done quickly. You could help."

"How?"

"Meet me here at eleven o'clock." He rattles off some GPS coordinates and I jot them down. "Bring Charlie, wear something stealthy, and come armed."

"In other words, show up the same way I always do for our meetings."

He chuckles. "Meetings? Funny, that's not how I think of them." He hangs up. I frown at the phone, then put it down.

The car isn't back from the shop yet, though Charlie says it'll be done by tomorrow—he's only having the glass replaced, so it'll at least be drivable. We shouldn't need it, anyway; the address Stoker gave me isn't far from the downtown core, and we can easily walk there.

At just over a thousand acres, Stanley Park is bigger than Central, skirted by more than five miles of seawall and holding half a million trees. On my world, it was a beautiful, well-tended place to stroll beside the ocean or under conifers hundreds of years old.

In a world filled with lycanthropes, it's something else.

The seawall is nothing but jagged black coastline and a

few isolated stretches of rocky beach. The park itself is first-growth rain forest, deep and primeval. The only trails are those made by the residents, who are secretive and fiercely protective. It's considered untamed even by Vancouver's Wild West standards, a slice of wilderness populated by only the most solitary and vicious of packs. It's like a demilitarized zone, one where the only law is that of survival; the last time the city tried to bring it under control was almost thirty years ago, when they attempted to reopen the road that used to run along its eastern border. They gave up after fifteen days and thirty-two fatalities on the construction team.

And the coordinates Stoker gave us are right in the thick of it.

There's no fence around the park, just a wall of dense vegetation broken by the occasional opening of a trail. It edges right up to the city itself, but I note that all the buildings closest to the tree line are heavily fortified, more like bunkers than anything else. Despite the park's lushness there are few windows facing it, and the ones that do are barred and at least two floors up.

We're not stupid. Eisfanger has supplied us with NSA stealth charms, making Charlie and I nearly invisible to supernatural hearing or smell. We can still be seen, but we plan on staying out of sight as much as possible. Plenty of cover in the forest, after all.

While Eisfanger is having all kinds of trouble with my ammo, he had none with designing and building me a silencer for my Ruger. It looks much like a regular one—a long tube attached to the end of the barrel—but it's based on magic, not science, which in this case means it's a lot more efficient. I can take out a target while making less noise than a mouse clearing its throat.

We've also got a trap detector, a clever little sorcerous gadget that looks like a bundle of black feathers sticking out of a leather pouch. It isn't made to sense trip wires or deadfalls or anything like that—it operates on the assumption that any trap will have a spell attached to it preventing it from being accidentally tripped by the one who set it. I've got the pouch clutched in one hand, because if it finds itself in the presence of such a spell it'll silently pulse. The trails themselves are said to be reasonably trap-free, but once off them you have to navigate through any number of tribal territories.

Charlie and I are both wearing camo outfits to help us blend in. I bought mine an hour ago in a shop off Robson Street, while Charlie brought his own with him. I'm surprised his doesn't have double-wide lapels.

We step off the trail as soon as we're around the first bend. It's weird; I can still hear the noises of a major city—the traffic, the boats in the nearby harbor, the occasional plane overhead—but all my other senses are telling me I'm far, far from civilization. The air is rich and piney; the darkness is close to absolute. I let Charlie take the lead, on the assumption that his *T. rex* instincts, however buried they might be, are still sharper than my hairless monkey ones. Besides, he's got the GPS.

We travel slowly, carefully. Gradually my eyes adjust and I can at least make out the dim shapes of tree trunks, boulders, and fallen logs. We stop every now and then when we think we hear something, but I can't tell if it's just nerves on our part or someone else trying to be as quiet as we are.

We can tell when we cross a border from one territory to another. Not only is the smell of thrope urine strong enough for even my unenhanced nose to detect, there are also more visual markers.

A row of skulls stares at me, just above eye height. One nailed to each tree, facing the same direction, a procession of bony sentries extending as far as I can see in either direction. They've got some kind of symbol marked on them in bright red, an X with horns jutting from the top and fangs from the bottom.

The spell detector doesn't twitch. I hope Eisfanger remembered to charge its batteries.

We make our way deeper. Our objective, thankfully, isn't *actually* right in the middle—it's closer to the western edge. The park itself juts out into the bay, surrounded on all sides by water except a narrow bottleneck to the south, where we entered. We only have to cross two more tribal boundaries before we reach our destination, and luck seems to be with us; we don't run into any trouble.

We reach the exact coordinates Stoker gave us. It's a massive redwood stump, as thick around as a missile silo, its jagged top twenty or so feet above us; I'd hate to see the storm that brought this giant down. The fallen trunk is largely rotted away now, the moonlight shining down on it through the breaks in the canopy overhead making it look like the abandoned remains of some ancient, organic pipeline.

"Up here," a voice whispers. Stoker, perched on top of the stump like a predatory ape. He's dressed all in black, obviously preferring the ninja approach to the commando.

The trunk has plenty of handholds, saplings taking root in the redwood's corpse. We climb up and join Stoker. The top of the stump is only half jagged, the rest as smooth and even as a chain-saw cut.

"We're here," I say, keeping my voice low. "Where to now?"

"Like you said," Stoker replies. "We're here."

He taps out a complex rhythm on the surface of the stump. There's a noise like wet cardboard tearing, and a hole spreads out at Stoker's feet like a huge, empty eye opening. A dim green light glows inside.

Stoker climbs in, his feet apparently finding the rungs

of a ladder I can't see. I'd like a little more intel before I jump into the fray, but Stoker isn't leaving me much choice. I follow him, and Charlie brings up the rear.

It's like descending the conning tower of a submarine. The bottom is a good thirty or so feet down, definitely below ground level. The tube is machined steel, lit by small green lights, and bottoms out in a chamber around the size of a boxing ring. There's a large steel door in one wall, and nothing else.

"What—" I start to whisper, and then the steel door opens and an Asian pire steps through it. He's clearly a guard—dressed in night camouflage, a spidery compound bow slung over his back, a headset plugged into his ear. He's as startled to see us as we are to see him.

Me and Charlie, anyway. Stoker takes his head off with a single swipe of a machete I hadn't even noticed he had. The head hits the floor with a dull *thud,* the body collapsing beside it. It barely decomposes at all—our guard hasn't accumulated much of a time-debt in his undead life. He looks around eighteen.

Stoker doesn't hang around and offer an explanation. He ducks through the open door, pausing only long enough to snag the guard's headset, and we're forced to follow.

Long, narrow corridor, slightly better lit but still dim. The air is close and damp, like a musty basement. Poor ventilation, suggesting that this is a pire stronghold. Odd—Stanley Park is mostly home to thropes.

I grab Stoker by the arm and yank. It's not enough to force him to stop—he's a big man, all of it muscle—but he does anyway. "Sit-rep *now,*" I hiss. "Or Charlie and I are leaving."

"Bad idea. Protocol is to seal the operation if there's an incursion, which means kill anyone who isn't supposed to be here and send out sniper patrols to eliminate possible backup. You wouldn't get far."

"Far from *what*? Where *are* we?"

"A very bad place."

He shrugs off my arm and keeps going.

The corridor comes to a T-intersection. Stoker goes left, not hesitating—he knows where he's headed. We come to another door, also steel, more like the hatch of a ship.

The headset crackles to life. A few terse words, spoken in what sounds like Japanese. Stoker calmly replies in the same language, unsealing the door at the same time. The *"Hai"* he gets in response seems reassured.

We cross the threshold onto a gridded catwalk. Beyond the steel railing is a large chamber, three stories or so in height, spread out beneath us. It's filled with transparent cubicles stacked floor-to-ceiling along the walls and in several neat rows from one end of the room to the other.

The Japanese have something called capsule hotels. Small cubicles, stacked one on top of another just like this, each one containing a foam pad, a small TV, an inset light, and an Internet connection. They cater to people who need nothing more than a place to sleep for eight hours—often businessmen too drunk to go home. Minimum comforts, maximum efficiency, very Japanese. Sometimes, due to their size, they're called coffin hotels.

But these aren't coffins. They don't hold pires or corpses. Each one houses a human being, and the transparent tubes pulsing with crimson that trail from them make their purpose all too clear.

Stoker's taken us to a blood farm.

There are technicians in white hooded containment suits tending to several of the pods, fiddling with the controls that no doubt regulate how much product is being produced and the vital signs of the occupant. All very clinical and sterile, more like a high-tech winery than a blood factory. Mad science, sure . . . but mad science done with *pride*.

"I am going to kill every single person connected with this," I say calmly.

"That's why we're here," Stoker says, and unslings his bow. He nocks a sharpened wooden shaft, draws the bowstring, and puts the arrow through the heart of the nearest technician. The anti-contamination suit puffs out for a second as the pire's flesh turns to dust, then collapses to the floor.

Things get a little crazy after that.

Stoker gets two more before he's noticed. The remaining technicians find cover fast, and raise the alarm. Stoker's headset explodes with rapid-fire Japanese as their security forces try to figure out how many invaders there are and the best way to deal with us. I keep expecting to hear some kind of siren go off, but the only sound is the low-pitched humming of machinery and the excited chatter of the radio.

Stoker turns it off. "They've stopped broadcasting useful information, which means they've figured out we can hear them. They'll be flooding in here any second—we need to spread out and take them at the choke points: here, a door at the far end of the chamber, and another on the second tier of the catwalk system, halfway down and to the right."

There's no time to argue—but Stoker isn't giving me commands, he's giving me options. "Charlie, stay here and keep anyone from cutting off our retreat. Stoker, take the entry on the second tier. Both of you provide covering fire—I'm heading for the far door."

We move.

I go down the stairs quick as I can. I'm faster than Charlie but Stoker might have been a better choice; I have no idea what's going to pour out of that door on the other side of the room, and he does.

But I'm tired of being led around by the nose. Whatever lies beyond this room is no doubt important, and I want to get to it before Stoker does—no matter what's in my way.

I hit the base of the stairs and head for the center aisle of capsules. There's a white-suited technician crouching around the corner, and he throws his hands up in terrified surrender when he sees me.

"Stay down and you might live," I snap. The aisle is deserted except for Mr. Scaredy-Pants—

He jumps me.

Even though I've been here for a while, I still sometimes forget that people here have absolutely no fear of my gun. All the tech sees is a human woman carrying some kind of funny metal toy—why *wouldn't* he attack?

I slam into the wall of coffins with a grunt. The tech, naturally enough, is trying to get a forearm under my chin and against my throat. I can see a broad Asian face behind the faceplate of the white hood, and the beginnings of a smile.

I shoot him in the belly. The barrel's angled up, so it goes through his heart. Behind the plastic visor his features dissolve, leaving a skull with a much wider grin.

"Joke's on you," I mutter, and sprint for the end of the aisle. I can see the far left-hand edge of the door Stoker was talking about, but I don't have a clear view from this angle.

I'm halfway down the aisle when the door begins to open.

I immediately dodge as far to the right as I can, optimizing my field of fire, and squeeze off three quick rounds. They slam into the door with a shockingly loud noise, and kinetic force shoves it closed again. That gives me a few more precious seconds to lunge for the end of the aisle, where I can flatten myself against the left-hand stack of cubicles and shoot whatever comes through that doorway.

For a moment, nothing does. The door itself is large and metal and painted a flat white. It has no window. The bullets have made three very large dents in it, but carved teakwood with silver tips doesn't have a lot of penetrating power and tends to shatter on impact.

Something thumps against the coffin, right next to my ear. I whirl around, feeling horribly exposed, but see nothing behind me.

Another thump. I realize it's coming from inside the coffin.

They're made of some thick transparent polymer. The occupant is faceup, head toward me. I can't see the face, only the top of a skull shaved down to a bristly crew cut. The head lifts up, no more than an inch or two, and thumps down again. I suspect that's the total range of movement the entire body has.

Thump. Thump. Thump.

Charlie and Stoker are both wreaking destruction; I can hear the clash of metal on metal and the battle cries of the pire guards—but that soft, insistent thumping somehow seems louder than anything else.

And then it's joined by another.

And another.

And another.

It's a room full of telltale hearts, all quietly, urgently beating away. All of them tapping out the same message.

Let.

Me.

Out.

They know I'm here. I thought they'd be drugged or lobotomized or were under some kind of enchanted sedation, but they're *aware*. Locked in their coffins, blood draining out of them with every pulse, knowing they'll never see sunlight or breathe fresh air again.

The door still hasn't opened. There's a security camera over it, and it gives me a tiny bit of satisfaction to blow it to pieces. Then I march over to the door, try it—locked— and shoot the lock until it stops being one. I yank the door open.

Empty corridor. Fluorescent lighting, tasteful carpet, pastel walls. The hallway of a medical building, professional but trying not to be threatening, the architectural equivalent of a bedside manner. Doors down either side.

I go right to the end. There's a staircase leading up behind a fire door, and I suspect this is where all the medical technicians that weren't in the main room ran to when they realized they were under attack. I find an upright metal coatrack in one of the offices and use it to jam the fire door, staving off any possible reinforcements from outside. Then I do a thorough, careful sweep of every room, finding about what I expected: offices, labs, a locker room, all of them deserted.

It's the break room I find the most disturbing. Comfortable couches, a few low-slung tables, a large flatscreen TV, a shelf lined with cheap paperback manga. A large, plastic-lined garbage can half filled with little paper cups, all of them stained red on the bottom.

And a row of stainless-steel spigots over a metal trough that runs along one side of the room. Each one has a little plastic sign holder over it, with a paper slip labeled in Japanese.

I don't know why that detail sickens me so much. They're pires, they drink blood, getting to sample the product is obviously a perk of working here. It's just—it's something about the casualness of it, the fact that obviously the labels are temporary. I don't speak or write Japanese, but I'll bet that whoever writes those labels makes little jokes on them. You know, "a nice Caucasion Cabernet," something like that. Reducing the person whose life they're consuming into a chuckle for the benefit of their co-workers. *Boy, I sure hate Mondays, but did you see what Joe came up with for the new batch?*

Maybe I'm wrong. Maybe I'm just projecting my own perverse sense of humor onto a nasty situation. The labels could be completely factual: *Male, Asian, thirty-four.*

That's just as bad. A writer named Hannah Arendt coined the term *the banality of evil* for the matter-of-fact way the Nazis went about exterminating the Jews, and for the first time I think I truly understand what she meant.

By the time I return to the factory floor, Charlie and Stoker have taken down the rest of the guards. I'm not surprised; between the two of them, they're like half the Horsemen of the Apocalypse. I wonder if Famine and Pestilence are going to show up for the party, too—

Then I look around at the sick hunger all these coffins represent, and realize they're already here.

The only sound now is the soft, insistent thumping coming from the coffins. I'm staring at a wall of them when Stoker and Charlie join me.

"It's not what you think," Stoker says.

"What, you mean I'm not looking at a few hundred warehoused human beings who have been turned into *cattle*?"

"They're not human," Stoker says. "Not anymore."

That's not what I expected him to say. "What?"

"They aren't conscious. That noise you're hearing, it's not voluntary movement. Their nerves are being stimulated electrically to help maintain muscle tone. It makes them twitch. It's on a timer, cycles through every twenty minutes."

And sure enough, the thumping is dying down. Not all at once, but within a minute it's gone.

"They've been mind-wiped with sorcery," Stoker says. "No memory, no thought, no cognitive functions at all. All that's left is the hindbrain, which keeps them breathing."

I'm a trained psychologist; I know a little bit about how the brain works. "Limbic system?"

He hesitates. "Operational."

"So they still *feel*."

"I doubt that. If they do, it's on the most basic level: hunger, thirst, sleepiness."

"Fear. Rage. Arousal."

Stoker shakes his head. "Even if that's true, those are nothing but random hormonal surges in immobile slabs of meat. They aren't *people* anymore, Jace." His voice gets quieter. "And they never will be—the process is irreversible. I'm sorry."

"I hate to be the insensitive one," Charlie says, "but I had a little chat with one of the guys in the white suits and he told me there's a tunnel from this place to a house outside the park. A house usually containing a large number of well-armed gentleman who don't much care for trespassers. Whatever we came here to do, we should do it and leave."

I shake off the outrage, bury the horror in a bulging file inside my head marked ONLY TO BE OPENED IN THE PRESENCE OF SCOTCH, and put on my game face. "We're here for the kids, Stoker. I have no idea what a blood farm would want with pire children, but—"

"The kids aren't here, Jace." His voice is calm but unapologetic. "They never were."

I stare at him. "What?"

"I wasn't lying about the kids—pire children are disappearing off the streets, and the Yakuza that run this operation have something to do with it."

"If the kids aren't here," Charlie asks, "why are we?"

"Because this place had to be shut down," Stoker answers, "and I couldn't do it alone."

I should be angry. I should be *furious*.

But I'm not. I just feel sad, and very, very tired.

"Okay," I say. "You get a pass. But just so you know—if there's a next time, all you have to do is ask."

He nods. "Thank you. You should go back the way we entered—any reinforcements that show up won't chase you through the park."

"Us? What about you?"

"Every blood farm has a sterilization protocol. They won't use it except in extreme circumstances, like an otherdimensional incursion or a raid by law enforcement. I'm going to activate it before I leave."

I swallow. "You're going to . . . kill them. Everyone in these cubicles."

"That's right. And you know why?" He meets my eyes, holds them. "So you won't have to."

He pulls a scrap of paper out of his pocket and gives it to me. "Here. This is the name and address of a business that keeps turning up in connection with the missing children—any investigation should start there. I'll contact you with more information as I get it." He turns and strides away, toward the offices and labs. I stare after him.

"Jace," Charlie says. "Come on. Let's go."

And we do.

NINE

Charlie and I climb out of the stump and back down to the forest floor, where I stumble across the rotting remains of another pire guard—no doubt the one that was supposed to be guarding the secret entrance. We backtrack along our original trail, hoping our luck will hold.

"He was right," Charlie says, speaking so quietly I can barely hear him. "I've seen farms like that before. Those people were never coming back."

"He played us. Again."

"Yeah. Think the tip he gave you is more of the same?"

I sigh under my breath. "Maybe. It's worth taking a look at, I guess."

"Huh."

"What do you mean, *huh*?"

"Usually getting yanked around like this would set you off. Instead, you're considering letting him do it again."

I stop and stare at Charlie's outline in the shadows. "You know he's not going to just hit a switch and terminate all those prisoners. He's going to burn the whole place down so it can never be used again."

"That sounds about right."

"Yeah, it does. And that's why I'm not more pissed. I may not like being used, but Stoker and I are on the same page about this. It had to be done. So no matter how irritated I am, no matter how little I trust him, I'm still willing to look at the information Stoker's giving me. Because maybe there's another one of these horror shows out there that needs to be shut down."

"And what if that's what he's counting on? What if the next target is something else, something not quite so noble?"

"Then he's in for a serious disappointment."

We keep moving. There's no explosion behind us, no gout of flame, but Stoker may be using some kind of sorcery to demolish the place that melts the tech into a puddle or even sends it to another dimension. He's been known to use that kind of High Power Level Craft before.

Statistically, most mountaineering accidents happen during the descent, not the climb. It makes sense, not just from a physical but also from a psychological point of view; you're already tired, and you're subconsciously thinking the job's over. You've attained your goal, and now you're just going home. That's a recipe for mistakes, and a mistake on the side of a mountain can kill you.

The place we're traveling through is much more dangerous than the side of a mountain.

By the time we know they're there, they've already surrounded us. One second we're alone, the next we can hear little rustles and growls from every direction. We stop back-to-back, our weapons already out, and wait.

A light flares: a match, being struck. There's a man standing there, naked except for a leather tool belt slung around his waist and a pair of thick leather gloves. He uses the match to light a candle, which he then sticks in the crook of a tree.

"Hi there," he says affably. "Ready to die?"

He's wiry, with the kind of leathery tan only aboriginals and homeless people who live on nude beaches get.

His tool belt is crammed full of sharp objects, from knives and hatchets to things I can't identify. His face is long and lean, with a hawk-like nose and a pointed chin, his black hair lengthy and braided into a single plait.

"Not just yet," I answer. "I don't usually jump into a grave with someone I just met. I prefer a little conversation first, maybe a drink and some dancing."

He laughs, a low, throaty rumble. "Oh, I think I can provide that. We *love* to dance."

I glance around. The dim, flickering light of the candle reflects off at least a dozen pairs of yellow eyes in the shadows. "Me, too. Why don't we start with introductions? I'm Jace Valchek, and this is Charlie Aleph."

"The *Bloodhound*?" His eyes widen, not in surprise but delight. "No. You're not *serious*."

"Sometimes she is," Charlie says. "Not often, though."

"Thanks, Charlie. Yeah, that's me. So what?" It occurs to me that maybe revealing my identity is a mistake. If Zhang could auction me off, so could a pack of half-wild thropes.

"So *that's* the Splatter?" He points at my gun.

"The what?"

"You know, the thing you're so proud of, makes you think you're invincible?" He's grinning now.

"Yeah. That's it." Great. Bad enough no one who encounters my gun takes it seriously, now it's acquired its own absurd reputation. I don't care for magic, but some kinds I hate worse than others.

"Well, we wouldn't want you to use *that* on us," he says mockingly, and I hear the distinctive barking of thrope laughter from all around. "But don't worry, you won't have to. We're all big fans."

I blink. "You are?"

"Sure. Hey, you kicked Ghatanothoa's *ass*. Now that we know who you are, we wouldn't dream of hurting you."

I relax, ever so slightly. "That's good. Because we're just passing through, we're not looking for any trouble—"

"Oh, no trouble," he says casually. "No trouble at all. We'll take *real* good care of you until the ransom's paid."

Ah, crap. Here we go again . . .

Which is when the ninja drops out of the trees.

I like to think I'm adaptable, and that I know an opportunity when I see one. So I do my best to put a round into Mr. Toolbelt's chest while he's still gawking at the guy all dressed in black with a shiny katana in his hand.

Apparently I'm not the only one with good instincts, though, because the thrope handyman has already dived into the undergrowth. One of his pack lunges forward, trying to claw out my throat, and he makes just as good a target. I shoot him.

And then we're in the middle of another battle. This one doesn't go as smoothly as the last.

Facing a thrope in one-on-one combat is a nightmare. You've got an opponent who's bigger, stronger, and faster than you are, with razor-sharp claws on both hands and feet, plus jaws powerful enough to deform sheet metal. That's the floor model, bare basics. If you're facing a thrope that's prepared, he'll be armed—anything from close-up weaponry like a mace or ax to longer-range stuff like javelins or bows.

But we're not facing a single, well-armed thrope. We're facing a pack.

Thropes don't have to study the tactics of attacking in a group because it's already in their genes. Their instincts tell them the right way to encircle their prey, test its defenses, send in the best pack members to hamstring or cripple it before the others pile on for the kill. Those instincts may have been dulled a little by living in cities—but these thropes don't live in a city. They live in a savage little patch of urban jungle, and are well versed in fighting for their corner of it.

Arrows hit first. I'm between Charlie and the ninja, so they take the brunt of the attack. I hear the dull thunk of multiple strikes. I drop to the ground, stick my gun between Charlie's knees, and aim for the yellow eyes in the shadows.

I take out three of them before they figure out they can't just sit back and pick off my cover—plus, they actually want me alive and not with an arrow in my eye. So they charge.

Charlie stops the first one dead with a ball bearing through his windpipe, but that's all he has time for. Then they're on us.

The fight is fast and vicious. The ninja—who has as many arrows sticking out of him as Charlie—is very, very good with that katana. Charlie's Roman-style sword doesn't have the same reach, but Charlie is—well, Charlie. Fighting him is like sticking your head in a wood chipper: ill advised, messy, and over real soon.

Besides being sandwiched between two killing machines, I have the advantage that my gun, unlike a javelin or bow, works just fine in close quarters. I stay on the ground and blast away at anything with fur.

It's over as quickly as it started. I count at least a dozen bodies strewn around us, which I doubt is the whole pack—just a tally of the losses they were willing to take before they reconsidered and withdrew.

I scramble to my feet and reload as quickly as I can.

"I think that's it," Charlie says. He's got at least twenty arrows jutting from his chest, arms, and legs. He starts to snap the shafts off with one hand, leaving the heads buried. "For this group, anyway."

I've got the Ruger reloaded now, and the ninja has sheathed his sword. He's also bristling with arrows—

though not as many as Charlie—and now he begins to pull them out, one by one. They're simple wooden shafts sharpened to a point, no doubt used because they thought the swordsman was a pire. Apparently he isn't.

"That was a helluva risk to take, fighting in human form," I say. "Why didn't you go were?"

The ninja yanks the last arrow out and tosses it on the ground. He unwraps the black cloth from around his face as he answers.

"Silver is expensive. I knew that if they thought I were a pire, they would not risk losing stray shots in the forest. Besides—you do very well, fighting as a human. I thought I could do no less."

In the dim light of the guttering candle is a face I recognize.

It's Tanaka.

Kamakura Tanaka of the Nipponese Shinto Investigative Branch and I have history. Not all of it's good.

We met when I first arrived on Thropirelem. He was my liaison with the Japanese authorities while I was there hunting Stoker, and after an ill-advised night of drinking we wound up spending the night together. He's my first official ex in this reality, though one night hardly counts as a relationship. No, that was more embarrassing than anything else—where our shared history gets interesting is in the professional realm. And by interesting, I mean the part where he betrayed me, committed treason against the United States, and almost stranded me on a deserted atoll with an evil creature from another dimension.

"Tanaka," I say. "Huh. Never thought I'd see *you* again."

He looks ashamed, and a little sad. "Nor I you. You want an explanation—and I will give it to you. But not now. We should go, before we are attacked again."

"You okay?" I ask Charlie. "You took a lot of hits."

"I'm fine. This jacket has an internal layer with the same kind of self-sealing goo they use on tires. The whole damn thing is glued to me now, but it'll hold until I can do a proper repair job."

I consider our options. "Truce," I say to Tanaka. "Until we're out of the park."

"Then we'll see," Charlie growls. Charlie does *not* like Tanaka; I'm going to have about five seconds after we leave the forest to prevent him from performing a lethal lycanectomy.

"What he said," I say. "We're going *that* way. You can take point."

He bows his head in acquiescence, then covers the lower part of his face again and darts into the woods. We follow.

He obviously has a very similar route in mind; I only have to correct his course once. I hiss at him to stop, then creep nearer to tell him he needs to head more to his right.

"As you say." He starts to move, but I slow him with a hand on his arm and then fall into step beside him.

"You're stealthed too, right?" I ask.

"Of course."

"Then we can talk without worrying about being overheard."

"I thought you wanted to wait."

"No, that was you. It occurs to me that you might just vanish once we leave the trees. I've heard ninjas do that, you know?"

"You have seen too many movies."

"Probably. Have you seen the one where the giant monster rises from the bottom of the ocean and scares the hell out of the Japanese? Fortunately, the day is saved when one of their intelligence agents double-crosses the slutty American investigator and escapes with information vital to stopping its rampage—wait, no, that's not right. He winds up under arrest and has his ass deported back to Japan. I must be thinking of a different movie."

"I . . . am sorry, Jace. Deeply sorry."

His voice is sad yet composed, and he doesn't attempt to deny or justify what he did. I shouldn't be surprised—Tanaka always struck me as honorable in the extreme. I never doubted that he felt badly about his actions, any more than I blamed him for following the orders of his government. That was why I convinced Cassius to let him return to his country, rather than prosecuting him.

"I believe you," I say. "But you understand that I can't exactly trust you now."

"I know. I do not expect you to."

"What are you *doing* here, Tanaka?"

"I . . . am attempting to regain my honor."

"How? By leaping from the trees like a kung fu version of Tarzan and saving my life?" I pause. "Wait. That's not it, is it? You haven't been shadowing me and looking for excuses to play hero, have you?"

He sighs. "Yes, that's it. You know that woman you buy coffee from every day? That's me. The new receptionist at work? Also me. I am *very* cunning."

Good Lord, Tanaka's grown a sense of humor. "Okay, okay. So why *are* you here?"

"Isamu."

That stops me. Isamu is the name of the Yakuza *oyabun* who tried to turn me into the same kind of blood cow we found in that hemoglobin factory. Charlie and Tanaka disabused him of the idea, killing his prime assassin in the process. I was warned that Isamu would eventually come after me, but the last I heard he was embroiled in some kind of local turf war in Japan that was keeping him too busy to bother with petty things like revenge. Of course, I was also warned that centuries-old vampire crime lords tended to have extremely long memories . . .

"Isamu," I say. "What's he got to do with this?"

"The Yakuza supposedly has a blood farm in this park. I was attempting to locate it."

"So this is a coincidence?"

"Not exactly. I was conducting surveillance on a local thrope tribe that has an alliance with the Yakuza. When a scout reported the presence of a human woman and an enforcement lem, I knew who it must be. I trailed them to where they encountered you."

In the darkness, Tanaka is only a black blur beside me. I wish I could see his face. "Well . . . thanks for the assist."

"I am glad I could help."

"And that blood farm you were looking for? I can give you directions if you'd like—but after tonight it'll no longer be in operation. More like in pieces."

"I cannot say I am surprised. You have a knack for destruction."

I wonder if I should mention Stoker, then think better of it. I still don't know whether or not Tanaka deserves my trust, and I'm not about to give it to him just because he may have saved my life. Charlie and I could have taken that pack. Maybe. "So the NSIB is after Isamu, huh?"

"No. This is a personal mission."

I frown. "Sorry? What does that—"

"After the events of the Ghatanothoa affair, I felt it was my responsibility to neutralize the threat to your life posed by Isamu, as I knew he would not let it go. I attempted to persuade my employers of the rightness of this course of action, but they disagreed. I resigned."

"Wait. You're not a cop anymore?"

"I still serve the cause of justice, Jace. But I no longer answer to those whose political loyalties run deeper than their morality."

I'm not sure what to make of that. "So you quit your job because of *me*?"

"You saved our world, Jace, despite what it has done to your kind. In return, I betrayed you. I could not—will not—let an amoral monster like Isamu destroy you. You deserve our eternal thanks, while I—" He breaks off.

"You think you need to atone."

"My needs are irrelevant."

Ohhhh, boy. Nobody does the martyrdom-for-the-good-of-all bit better than the Japanese. If I told Tanaka, right now, to pull out his sword and fall on it for me, the only question he'd probably ask would be if I minded setting him on fire first. You know, if it wouldn't be too much trouble.

But I can't just tell him to stop, either. I have a psych degree—framed certificate and everything—and I know that someone like Tanaka won't just give up. He'll gladly throw himself under a train for me, but anything less noble and more rational won't do it for him. This is less about me and more about him; he *needs* to atone for what he's done, and eliminating the threat to my life may not be enough. He's convinced himself he needs to suffer, too . . . the only thing I'm not sure about is just how much. If I want to find out, I'm going to have to get him to talk.

"A debt of honor, then," I say. I nod. "I understand."

He glances toward me, then away. "I'm . . . thank you. I thought you would be angry."

"You don't know me as well as you think, Tanaka."

"Perhaps I do not. I have been mistaken about many things."

"No. You made a single error. One helluva big one, granted, but it was made honestly, in the interests of your country. Don't belittle yourself—you did the best you could. It wasn't a moral lapse."

"It is not a decision you would have made."

"Exactly. So you had a pretty good chance of being right."

I hear a low chuckle. "Now who's belittling herself?"

"Hey, I've practically turned self-denigration into an art."

"That's very Japanese of you."

It's my turn to laugh. "I guess. But even I would think twice about taking on the Yakuza on my own."

He holds up a hand for silence and we all freeze. A few seconds tiptoe past while Tanaka listens intently to something beyond the range of my merely human senses. When he motions that we can proceed again, it's another few minutes before I feel like it's safe to speak. "So how exactly are you planning on doing that?"

"I will find Isamu, and kill him."

"Sure. Because it's not like he'll have bodyguards or anything."

"He *will* be well protected."

"And easy to find. You can just look up a list of his public appearances on the Net."

"He will no doubt take pains to conceal himself from any possible attack. He will use sorcery as well as cunning."

"And being in charge of a criminal empire for hundreds of years, it's not like anyone has ever tried this before."

"He has buried *many* unsuccessful assassins—"

I snort in annoyance. "Will you *please* stop doing that?"

"What?"

"Agreeing with me. It's really getting on my nerves."

"I have considered all the possible obstacles, and prepared for them. They will not prevent me from completing my task."

"Uh-huh. You've got resolve, Tanaka, I'll give you that. But I'd feel better about your plans if you could provide me with something concrete, as opposed to steely-eyed determination."

He pauses, and turns around. "Very well. I don't want you needlessly worrying about me, Jace; I will do my best to allay your fears." He tugs down his mask so that I can see his face. "What do you know of the history of Imperial Japan?"

"Not much. Warlords, emperors, feuding clans of samurai—"

His eyebrows go up. "You know about samurai?"

"Only what I've learned from movies and TV."

He shakes his head. "Most curious . . . here, they have largely been forgotten. The samurai clans embraced the way of the wolf many centuries ago, valuing not only their strength and fierceness but also their loyalty. However, when vampires infiltrated the Imperial Court and turned the emperor, he saw the samurai as a threat, and tried to have them destroyed. He very nearly succeeded, though it took many years. But the undying can afford to be patient . . .

"It was called the War of the River Swallowing the Stone, a long, slow battle of attrition. Eventually, all the samurai clans were hunted down and killed—all except one. They went into hiding, surviving by posing as a roving nomad pack, never staying in one place too long. They kept the traditions and practices of their kind alive in secret, until the very idea of the samurai had passed into legend."

He meets my eyes, unblinking. "The name of that clan was Tanaka."

I study him. He's dead serious. "So you're telling me you're what, the last living samurai?"

"I did not say I was the last. But the members of my clan *are* the only samurai left—and I have learned their lessons well."

"That's very impressive, but—"

"It is not meant to impress you. It is simply a statement of fact. The Tanaka clan has survived for centuries, despite being ruthlessly hunted for many of them. We, quite simply, refuse to give in to circumstances. Isamu will die at my hand; I have sworn it. Can you not see this is the truth?"

What I see on his face is more than calm resolve; it's the complete and total focus of an obsessive. "Yes," I say. "I can see that."

"Then we need discuss it no more." He slips his mask back on and stalks into the shadows ahead, making no sound at all.

"That guy," Charlie says, "is going to be trouble."

"No kidding . . ."

We reach the edge of the park in another few minutes, but keep going until we're at least a block away. Tanaka turns to me as we stride down the sidewalk, pulling down his mask and hood. "I suppose our truce is concluded. Do you wish to take me into custody?"

"Don't see how I could. I don't have any jurisdiction here. But as far as I'm concerned, our truce is still active—I don't hold your past actions against you, all right?"

He gives me a slight bow as we walk along. "Thank you. Your forgiveness means a great deal to me."

"Look, we're staying at the Clarion hotel. Maybe we should think about pooling our resources."

He hesitates. "I will contact you if I obtain any information I think you might find useful."

"Fine—we'll do the same. Where are you—"

But I'm talking to myself. I only took my eyes off him for a second as we walked along, but he's vanished—probably slipped into that alley we just passed. I know it'll be empty if I bother to check, so I don't.

"Guy moves fast," Charlie notes. "You sure know how to scare 'em off."

"I wish that were true," I murmur. "But he's not going anywhere until he does what he came to do."

"Kill Isamu?"

"Or himself . . ."

Great. So now I have an obsessed, self-destructive thrope to worry about, too, one who's determined to regain his honor by killing an ancient Yakuza overlord. I also have to worry about said overlord, who holds a very definite grudge against yours truly. Maybe if I'm lucky they'll take each other out and I can ignore the whole thing.

Yeah, right.

Damn it, Tanaka. Why is it ex-lovers always pick the worst possible time to show up? I mean, yes, it is good that he has my back when it comes to Isamu, and yes, he's very capable, and I'll even admit that it's nice to have another friendly face around in a dangerous environment, but he's a distraction. I don't need to worry about his safety, I don't need to think about when or if he's going to call, I don't need to have those soulful brown eyes reminding me of that one night we spent together . . .

No. Oh, *hell* no.

TEN

When we get back to the hotel, I get on the phone to Gretch while Charlie fills Eisfanger in. I'm doing my best to plunge into full-on work mode, because the realization that I'm still attracted to Tanaka is almost as disconcerting as learning he's in town in the first place.

"Hemo," I tell Gretch. "That's the name of the business Stoker gave me. He says it's connected to the disappearance of the pire kids."

Gretch sounds concerned. "Do you think there's any credence to his story? Considering how he used you?"

"At this point I don't know what to think. He claims he isn't even working with the Free Human Resistance anymore, but clearly at least some of his goals haven't changed."

"Mmm. Well, shutting down an operation like that is a good thing, Jace. If nothing else, at least that's done."

"Yeah. But that's not the only surprise that popped up." I tell her about Tanaka, and why he's here.

"I'll try to confirm that with our Japanese counterparts, though they haven't been exactly forthcoming since the Ghatanothoa debacle. I'll let you know what I find out when I ring you back with the Hemo data."

She hangs up. I knock on Charlie's door, tell him and Eisfanger I'm going to have a long bath and go to bed.

Most people have baths to relax, but I find I can often do some good brainstorming while surrounded by hot water and suds. My bathroom holds stacks of water-stained notebooks as opposed to candles, and I prefer a nice cold scotch on the rocks to a glass of wine. I fill up the tub, ease myself in, close my eyes, and start to think.

The first question nagging at me is *What did Stoker give Zevon in return for our freedom?* Maybe he offered to kill someone—he's very good at that, after all.

Or maybe the whole thing was an elaborate con, designed to make me think I owe Stoker a favor. That doesn't really ring true, though—too much work for too little payoff. I mean, if he'd really gone to that much trouble to trap me in a Japanese Hell, I doubt he'd let me go that easily.

And what am I going to do about Tanaka? My imagination throws out a few interesting possibilities, which I hastily suppress. If there's one thing I can rely on, it's my own brain's ability to screw up my love life. I think it's in cahoots with a number of my glands, too.

With an effort, I push myself into a more business-like frame of mind. The pire kids. If they *are* disappearing, who's taking them, and why?

Maybe it has something to do with the whole time-debt issue. The kids aren't aging—but maybe they'd like to. That could make attractive bait for a childnapper.

Is it actually possible? I know another pire can volunteer to share the time-debt, like Cassius did with Anna after her father was killed, but who would do that for a stranger?

The solution, when it pops up, seems blindingly obvious. Another pire kid, of course. Normally the time-debt is shared between the parents, who each age at half speed, but it's entirely possible to do it with one taking on the whole load. I reach out, find my phone on the counter, and call Eisfanger. He answers on the third ring.

"Jace? What's up?"

I ask him about my theory. He disappoints me. "Sorry, but that wouldn't work. You need at least one parent in the loop—the debt can be shared, but not transferred entirely."

"Okay, thanks." I sigh and hang up.

Well, if it's being used as bait, it doesn't have to work—you just have to convince the kids it does. The real question is, what are the kids being used for?

I know it doesn't have to be anything sorcerous. It could be as simple and ugly as it appears, that the kids are being abused or killed or both. If they're being murdered, I'm probably hunting a pire; serial killers tend to stay within their own race. But if I'm after a child molester, that broadens my parameters by an order of magnitude; they can come from any walk of life, be any age, any race. About the only factor I could rely on was that they'd probably be male, and even that wasn't guaranteed.

The phone rings. I wipe my hand dry on a towel and answer it.

It's Gretch. "Mr. Tanaka has indeed left the employ of the NSIB. Hemo is the name of a corporation that specializes in blood products; specifically, they import and distribute a number of products from Japan—a popular drink called Gorilla Happiness Plus is their big seller. And yes, it does contain actual primate blood, though most of it comes from macaque or green monkeys."

"The Japanese blood trade. Interesting."

"My sources say they have definite ties to the Yakuza, though Hemo has never been directly implicated in any criminal activity. What *is* interesting, though, is the fact that a great deal of their annual budget goes into research and development."

"Trying to build a juicier monkey?"

"That would make sense—but no. They seem to spend it all on computer equipment and experts in machine code."

I frown. "What for?"

"I have no idea. Perhaps you could ask them, when you speak to their CEO."

"Who is?"

"Robert Mizagi. You have an appointment to see him today at four."

I groan. "I'm guessing that's AM?"

"He *is* a pire."

"Suppose I should try to get a few hours of sleep, then."

Yeah, that would be a good idea. Unfortunately—even after the bath and getting beneath the covers—I'm too wound up to find the offramp to dreamland. And if I had, the phone would have woken me up anyway.

The screen tells me it's an unknown caller. "Hello?"

"It's Stoker. Sorry if I woke you."

"Don't worry about it. You have another wild goose for me to chase, or is this call more about my chain and the method you're going to use to yank it?"

"I've got what you asked for. Sending you some pictures now."

And he does—half a dozen photos, it looks like. "Before I look at these, what are they?"

"Evidence. Have you checked out Hemo yet?"

"I have someone working on that, yes. They're a Yak front. So?"

"So I tracked down a homeless thrope kid who not only saw one of his pire friends get into a car, he snapped a few shots with his phone."

"He get a plate number?"

"Better. He went half-were and followed the vehicle until it pulled into the secured lot of a building. Guess which one?"

"The same one I'm visiting tomorrow?"

"Good luck." He hangs up.

I study the photos. None of them is very good—they're all either blurred, taken from a bad angle, or both—but I can plainly see what looks like a pre-adolescent girl getting into the back of a black sedan. Plates aren't visible in any of the shots, but I can't blame the cameraman for that—he was busy chasing a car through city traffic while running at full speed.

There's one photo that's better than the others, though. I can see a hand reaching out of the backseat, helping the child in, and on one finger is a very distinctive ring. Carved jade in a gold setting, looks like, though I can't make out much detail. I send the photos to Gretch—she'll do a much better job at analyzing them.

Now I'm thoroughly awake. I decide to clean my gun, a ritual I've used before to calm myself. I know it sounds a little weird, but there's a peaceful, Zen quality to doing something purely physical that you've done a thousand times before.

I get out the gun and my cleaning kit. I lay out a fresh, clean white cloth on the bed and start taking the Ruger apart. I fall into a familiar rhythm and it feels good.

At first.

But then something happens. Something that's never, ever happened before.

It starts as I'm cleaning and oiling each individual component: a feeling that something's wrong. That something's, I don't know, *missing*. I make sure there's nothing on the floor or under the bed, some little part I might have dropped. Nothing there.

But the feeling gets stronger. You know how you can forget something, and the only piece of information left in your brain is a little scrap of paper with the words YOU

FORGOT SOMETHING, DUMBASS written on it? It's like that, only stronger. Insistent, nagging. It's driving me crazy, but no matter how hard I try my memory just sits there with an idiot grin on its face, drooling and picking its nose. I finally give up and return to the task at hand, hoping the routine will relax me enough that whatever it is will surface on its own.

And that's when it hits me.

I have no idea how to put the Ruger back together again.

"Damon!" *Pound pound pound.* "WAKE UP!"

The door rips open. A snarling, snow-white, six-foot werewolf glares at me with ice-blue eyes. He's wearing pajama bottoms with little puppies on them.

"It's affecting me!" I blurt. "The spell!"

His snarl droops, then turns into a yawn. He signs *What spell?* with furry white hands.

I storm into his room as he shifts—a lot slower this time—back into human form. "You know, the spell! I took it apart and now I can't put it back together!"

"Can't put *what* back together?"

"My—my Splatter!"

"Your what now?"

I groan in exasperation. I'm having trouble even remembering what the damn thing is called. "That's what the Stanley Park pack called it. The Splatter. I guess because it makes things go splat."

"Oh. You mean your gun."

"Yes! Yes, my gun! Gun, gun, *gun!*"

"Just take it easy, okay?" He pads over to the bed in his bare feet and slips into a fluffy hotel robe like the one I've got on. Even the hair on his chest is white. "You took your gun apart? Why?"

"Maintenance. It's something I do on a regular basis. Dismantle, clean, oil, reassemble. But this time I got halfway through and just blanked."

Eisfanger blinks at me sleepily. "Sounds like a real crisis. Can we talk about this in the morning?"

"No! Don't you get it? I thought I was immune to the spell because I'm from another reality, but I've been here long enough that it's starting to take hold. Right now I'm all worked up, but by the morning I might not even be able to *care*. You know, I'll be all like *What did I ever see in that thing anyway?*"

"Well, now that you bring it up—"

"No! Don't you *dare* take its side! That's what it *wants* you to do!"

"Okay, okay, I won't. But I have to say, you're sounding a little paranoid."

"Of course I'm sounding paranoid! An ancient enchantment cast by an immortal serial killer is trying to *eat my brain*!"

"Oh. Well, when you put it that way . . ." He yawns again, then holds his hands up in self-defense when he sees the look on my face. "Sorry, sorry—I'm tired, not bored. I'm taking your problem *very* seriously, all right? What do you want me to do?"

"*Fix* it!"

"Umm. Right. Well, I'll try." He frowns. "Let's see. The spell doesn't let anyone take your gun seriously, me included. But I did manage to build a silencer for you."

"Yeah, you did. How'd you manage that, anyway?"

"I thought of it as a challenge in acoustic design. You know, isolated the engineering aspects of one specific effect and worked on that."

"Maybe you can do that again." I rub the palms of my hands against my forehead. "Ahh! This is going to be tricky. The spell is layered, and the second layer tells you to ignore any logical discrepancies the first layer might cause."

"What logical discrepancies?"

I glare at him, but he's not trying to be funny. "Never mind. Let's try to focus on one particular problem: how to reassemble my gun."

"I—no, that wouldn't work."

"Tell me!"

"No, it's *ridiculous* . . ."

I swallow. "Damon. Right now, I could really use a good laugh. *Really.* So please, *please* tell me your completely useless, stupid, *moronic* idea."

He looks hesitant, but then shrugs. "Well, this'll *never* work, but—we could look at some footage I have from when you first showed up. You remember? I took your gun apart, piece by piece, and recorded it."

I sigh. "What can I say? You're right. That *is* completely useless to me right now, seeing as how my gun is *already* in pieces."

"I know—but I was thinking maybe we could play the footage backward."

I goggle at him. Even though I know it's the spell screwing with my judgment, I can't believe I didn't think of that. "Yes. Get it, get it *now.*"

"Sure, I've got it archived on my laptop."

"Bring it to my room." I don't want to risk moving the disassembled gun, afraid I'll do something insane like throw the parts out a window.

Eisfanger grabs his laptop. A minute later, we're studying digital footage that's moving in reverse. I take a deep breath, grab the same two pieces that Damon's holding in the video, and fit them together. The *click* they make is the most reassuring sound I've heard all week.

I don't think about what I'm doing or why, I just focus on repeating the steps I'm watching on the laptop. It goes smoothly; once I've recaptured the rhythm my own muscle memory takes over. I even finish the last step on my own, without looking at the video.

I collapse backward on the bed, heaving a sigh of relief. "Okay. Don't want to go through *that* again."

"Glad I could help," Eisfanger says. He's perched on the room's single chair. "Though I still can't believe that worked." He gets up and reaches for his laptop.

I sit up abruptly and stop him. "Wait. We have to *do* something about this."

"Uh—we did. Just now. Remember?"

"We threw a bucket of water on a fire, Eisfanger. But it's not out. We need to find a way to get this damn spell out of my head. *Fast*."

He frowns and sits down on the bed next to his computer. "Yeah. Well, the problem with a spell like this—ancient, global, and self-masking—is that you need something equally old and powerful to counter it. I'm just a forensics shaman; I can't beat something like this on its own terms."

He sees the look of despair on my face and holds up one thick finger. "But. I don't *need* to fight it toe-to-toe; all I have to do is convince the spell that you're outside its parameters. That's why it didn't affect you when you first got here: it wasn't designed to work on natives of another reality."

But apparently now I've been here long enough to qualify—from illegal alien to landed immigrant, magic-wise. "So what do we do? Show it my passport? 'Hi, Jace Valchek. I'm here on business, not sure how long I'm staying, and I'm not bringing any fruits, nuts, or currency worth over ten thousand dollars with me.' "

"Actually, that's not far off. You've integrated pretty well into this reality, so we need to reverse that a little bit. Bring up your outsider vibe."

"How?"

"I've got an idea. Stay here, I'll be right back." He leaves his laptop on the bed and jogs out of the room. A minute later he's back, with his forensics kit in his hand. He sets it down on the bed, opens it, and pulls out a small, transparent bag with a scrap of pink cloth in it.

"What's that?"

"A piece of what you were wearing when you crossed the dimensional boundary."

Which was an oversize T-shirt sporting a picture of a panda, and nothing else. After I threw up on it and passed out, I woke up in a hospital bed and never thought about that shirt again. "*You* have it?"

Eisfanger looks uncomfortable. "Well, yes. It might seem mundane to you, but it *is* an artifact of another reality. We studied it purely for research reasons."

"And what did it tell you? Kmart sells a nice cotton blend in extra-large sizes?" My eyes narrow. "And why do you have a scrap of it with you, anyway?"

"It was in case you disappeared. I could use the psychic traces on the shirt to help pinpoint your location."

I guess that makes sense. "Well, look at that. It worked. Here I am."

He pulls the scrap out, selects a small pair of surgical scissors, and starts cutting the cloth into strips. "That's the problem. You're here, and the spell senses that. What we're going to do is use this cloth as a focus for transdimensional energy, and infuse your own aura with it. It wouldn't fool an actual shaman, but it might be enough to deflect the spell."

I nod. "Change my scent, throw it off the trail. Yeah, that might work. But—"

"What?"

"Tell me that piece came from the part of the shirt I *didn't* vomit on."

Eisfanger looks apologetic. "Sorry. This kind of thing works best with a maximum infusion of extradimensional material."

"Even if it's semi-digested french fries marinated in tequila? Don't answer that."

He's finished cutting the cloth into strips, and now he's braiding them together. "I'm weaving a simple radiant enchantment into this. All you have to do is tie it around your wrist."

"Huh. Well, what do you know. Where I come from, we call that a friendship bracelet." I lean over and take a sniff, then wrinkle my nose. "Though ours tend to be more colorful and less fragrant."

"The smell will fade—to your nose, anyway."

I sigh. "Thanks, Damon. Gee, maybe after this we could braid each other's hair and talk about boys."

He looks about as confused as he usually does when I'm trying to be funny, so I just pat him on the shoulder. "Never mind. I appreciate this."

"No problem."

He finishes, ties it around my wrist, and performs a short ritual. I feel a little twinge of nausea, which tells me it must be working. Once again, my body is informing me it's in a place it doesn't belong and never will. I tell Eisfanger good night and my body to shut up; it's always been terrible at important decisions, anyway. Before he leaves I let him know about my appointment with the corporate head of Hemo so he's up to speed.

It's almost 3 AM by now, so I have a shower—taking care not to get the bracelet wet, though I don't know if that makes any difference—get dressed, and go knock on Charlie's door. He tells me he'll be out in a minute and sounds as if he wasn't even asleep, though that's misleading; Charlie doesn't so much wake up as shift from inert to alert. He's also infuriatingly quick at getting ready, not needing to shower or shave or tend to any other tedious biological habits.

I grab a fast Danish to go and coffee from the hotel restaurant—one nice thing about Thropirelem, it's not hard to find places open all night. Charlie's car is back from the auto shop with new glass, and he drives while I talk, eat, and suck back caffeine.

"So that's the rundown on Hemo," I say between bites. "No idea what, if any, connection they have to the pire disappearances."

"Other than Stoker's word."

"Yeah. Vague accusations backed by no evidence. I'm just about done with that, Charlie. I'm glad we shut down that blood farm, but unless I get some genuine proof that pire kids are vanishing—and soon—we're out of here. Stoker can clean up his own messes."

"I figured. Maybe we should hit the streets, ask around ourselves. Might get better results than bracing a CEO."

"Good idea. I just wish I knew where to start."

"At the top. And the bottom. Then apply pressure in both directions."

I grin around a mouthful of Danish. "Mr. Aleph, I like the way you think. It beats the hell out of the way I've been thinking, anyway—or not thinking, as the case may be." I tell him about my middle-of-the-night panic attack and Eisfanger's fix.

Charlie grunts. "I always said that damn thing was more trouble than it's worth. And aren't you almost out of bullets, too?"

"I've got a box back in Seattle—but I'm down to six rounds here. After that, I'm going to have to rely on Eisfanger. Again."

"You really think he can duplicate that formula?"

"Sure. I mean, it should be simple—he just has to . . ."

I frown. My mind is filled to bursting with nothing at all. What was I just thinking about, again? "Oh, no . . ."

"What?"

"The bullets. They have this stuff in them that makes them *go*. And I—" I pound on the dash with a fist. "Damn it! Now I can't even remember what it's called! Goonpower? Funchowder? Happy Bullet Flying Snuff?"

"Gunpowder," Charlie says. "Calm down."

"Gunpowder! That's it!" I scrabble in my pocket for a pen. "Got to write it down. Can't forget." I find an old receipt and a pen and scribble the word in large block letters. "This is bad, Charlie. Eisfanger's bracelet isn't working."

"Just breathe, Jace. What's the full name of your weapon?"

"A Ruger Super Redhawk Alaskan."

"How does it work?"

"Like a camera. Point and shoot."

"And what happens when you use it?"

"It makes large, messy holes in things I'm angry at." I take a deep breath. "Whoooo. Okay, so I haven't completely lost it. I can still *use* the damn thing."

"Absolutely." Charlie pauses. "For another six shots, anyway."

"Just drive, sunshine."

The corporate headquarters of the Hemo company is in Yaletown, an upscale community of condos and apartment clusters on the shores of False Creek. The building is a sleek, mirrored monolith forty-five stories tall. We show our credentials to the guard at the entrance to the underground lot, receive passes, and park. The elevator takes us up, close to the top, and the doors open on a large foyer that's all black glass and chrome. An Asian receptionist who looks like she's slumming from her day job as a supermodel gives us a professional smile from behind her sleek, ultra-futuristic, and completely transparent desk. I can see that she's wearing a miniskirt, two-inch stilettos, and pink underwear. God, I hope that's underwear.

"Hello," she says. "Ms. Valchek? Mr. Mizagi is expecting you." She indicates we should go left with a graceful gesture of one immaculately manicured hand.

We do. The walls are tiled in glossy black stone with inset Chinese ideograms in gold leaf. Our shoes clack loudly on the polished cherrywood floor.

The door, a dark brown slab of intricately carved teak that probably cost more than my car, swings open silently as we approach. A handsome pire in his apparent forties, dressed in a conservative salaryman's black suit, stands in the doorway. He bows, enough to be polite but not deferential, and motions us inside.

The room is large and mostly empty. A large desk of the same teak is framed by a wall of glass that overlooks False Creek, with an excellent view of the two bridges and the ocean beyond. The walls are adorned with various certificates, mostly scientific doctorates and awards. One corner is dominated by an immense jade sculpture of a Chinese dragon curled around a sphere. No, not a sphere; a globe.

"Thank you for agreeing to talk to me, Mr. Mizagi," I say. "I have a few questions."

"Not at all," he says. There's a long, black leather couch along one wall and he motions for us to sit.

I don't, though. I'm staring at his hand.

And at the gold-and-jade ring on his finger.

ELEVEN

I decide to stay on my feet. Charlie, as always, follows my lead.

"That's a nice ring," I say. "Where'd you get it?"

Whatever he was expecting me to ask, that wasn't it. His eyes go blank as he comes up with an acceptable half-truth. "A gift, from an old colleague. To congratulate me on my promotion."

I smile. He's an embellisher. I *love* embellishers. They just can't leave well enough alone; they're convinced that unnecessary details added to a lie are like embroidery on a jacket, and that the prettier the lie, the more believable it is. The phrase *Give someone enough rope and they'll hang themselves* was created for embellishers, and with a little encouragement they'll weave a lie so big and intricate that pretty soon they'll be dangling from it themselves like a novice spider stuck in his own web.

(I probably should have stuck to one metaphor instead of mixing thread, rope, and webbing, but hey—once you start embellishing, it's hard to stop . . .)

"Your promotion here?" I ask innocently.

"Yes, as a matter of fact." Hmmm. Half-truth, I think. Just a little hesitation beforehand and a qualifier tacked on the end.

You have to keep the pace going with an embellisher or they'll try to change the subject, veer away from the lie. I quickly ask, "Where were you before this?"

"Japan. If you—"

"Is the ring Japanese?"

"Yes, it is. Very old. I was honored to have it bequeathed to me."

"From a colleague, you said. Your superior?"

"I—yes."

"I have contacts in Japan. What's his name?"

Mizagi stares at me and says nothing for a full second. Deer-in-the-headlights time. An innocent question, but if the gift was from someone in the Yakuza heiarchy, he doesn't want to disclose it. He needs a moment to come up with another name to give me, and when he finally does I know he's lying. "His name is Kamoto. Hondo Kamoto."

The lie is meaningless trivia, but it's enough to rattle him. A good start. "Mr. Kamoto, yes. I know him. I'll make sure to pass along your regards when I talk to him next."

Meeting his pointless lie with one of my own confuses him further. Now he's worried I'm going to verify what he's said, and it'll prove to be false. Already, in the back of his brain, paranoid fantasies about being caught and exposed are playing out. He doesn't have time to pay conscious attention to them, but they'll slowly grow in the background, destroying his confidence and raising his anxiety.

"Ah. Are you sure it's the same—"

"I was wondering about what you do here." I interrupt him smoothly, politely, as if he hasn't spoken at all.

He blinks, then grabs the opportunity like a starving man reaching for a drumstick. "Of course, of course. Our primary business when we began was hemovore supply, but we've branched out considerably since then. We have multinational interests and many different projects in development."

"Such as?"

"Real estate, banking, import–export, ranching . . . I can't list them all off the top of my head. But the area we're most excited about is TASS. I'm personally overseeing it." He gives me a self-important smile, the most honest reaction I've gotten from him yet.

"What's it stand for?"

"Technology Assisted Sorcerous Simulations."

"Sounds very high-tech."

"Oh, it is, it is! Our equipment costs are sky-high and so are the salaries I pay my programmers, but everything we have is bleeding-edge and top of the line. Considering what we're trying to accomplish, it has to be."

I hide the frown that's trying to escape. I was expecting him to bluff me, try to conceal what he's spending on computer R&D, but he seems almost pathetically eager to talk about it—the reaction of a geek who's intensely proud of what he's doing and oblivious to anyone else's lack of interest.

I, however, *am* interested, and show it by leaning forward ever so slightly, wetting my lips, and widening my eyes. Subtle cues that'll reinforce his ego and prompt more discussion. "You must be trying to accomplish something intriguing."

He beams. "Oh, we are. Normally I'd keep this under wraps, but I've been told it's all right for me to show you. In your *official* capacity, of course."

Gretch must have leaned on him, or maybe whoever pulls his strings did. One thing's for sure—the chief executive officer of a multinational corporation shouldn't have to be "told" what is or isn't okay to do with his own pet project. His role is clearly that of figurehead, with *scapegoat* standing in the wings and rehearsing its lines.

"Okay," I say. "Then show me."

The lab is on the thirty-third floor. Half the room is filled with stacks of computing towers, row after row of them, what's called a server farm. The other half holds desks with more mundane workstations perched on them, and there's an immense flatscreen monitor covering one wall that looks like they stole it from a drive-in on another planet. Various techs in white lab coats study monitors, tap away at keyboards, or murmur to one another in small, serious-looking clusters. A working environment, populated by professionals. Mizagi bustles in like an excited dad at bring-your-child-to-the-office day. "This is our nerve center," he announces proudly. "What we are doing here has never been attempted before."

"And what," I ask, "is that exactly?"

"We are building *shrinespace*."

I study the giant screen. It's outlined by an ornate, red-lacquered wooden framework with a pagoda-style peak, similar to the little Shinto shrines I've seen in people's homes. "And again—what is that, exactly?"

"You are familiar with Shinto? With Kami?"

"I know what they are, yes." Shinto is the national religion of Japan, as well as being a major source of magic in Thropirelem. It works through Kami, which are spirits—not just the spirits of living things or supernatural beings, but spirits that live in *everything*: rocks, trees, rivers, weather systems, kitchen stoves, your underwear. Shinto magic is largely a system of negotiation, whereby you communicate with various spirits and get them to do what you want. A Shinto priest explained to me once that all these Kami are organized into a vast bureaucracy, with every little spirit reporting to a superior. When I asked him who was at the very top of the pyramid, he just shrugged. "I don't know. Whoever it is, you have to get past a few million secretaries to talk to them, and I'm lucky if I can get the Kami in charge of properly working toilets to return my calls."

I nod. "So this is what? A virtual shrine?"

Mizagi chuckles. "It is much more than that. It is a *network* of shrines, within a shared virtual space. We hope to have one in every home that practices Shinto, eventually. Instead of one or two shrines in a dwelling, this will allow you to access *any* Kami, at any time."

It makes sense—like going from a primitive telephone system with a single dedicated line to a global, interconnected web. "Sounds like a good idea. Why hasn't anyone done it before?"

"The technology has only recently become viable. But the equipment is the least of it; the true challenge lies in negotiating the contracts."

I can just imagine. Take the world's biggest civil service, give every employee supernatural powers, then try to work out a deal with each and every department head, with all the attendant political infighting and maneuvering multiplied times immortality. Yeah, no problems there.

"Would you like a demonstration?"

I can tell by the way Mizagi asks that he's just bursting to show off his shiny toy, and I see no reason to disappoint him. "Sure," I say. "Dazzle me."

He trots over to a particularly serious-looking clump of technicians and speaks to them in Japanese. They disperse like a grease bubble in water touched by a soapy finger, coming to rest at various computer stations. Furious tapping and rapid-fire Japanese fill the room, and the immense screen flares to life.

It's hard to tell what I'm seeing at first. A swirling

golden mist with a disturbing amount of depth to it, like 3-D with an extra half-D tacked on.

"Now," says Mizagi, "who do we want to talk to?"

I'm tempted to put in a call to the god of Caffeine, but she already holds the mortgage to my soul . . . and then an idea blinks into existence and nudges me in the ribs.

"Actually, there is a little matter I wouldn't mind getting some help with. Is there a Kami of borders?"

"Oh, yes, certainly. Funado." Mizag smiles. "In fact, I've been dealing with him quite a bit—this project, after all, will have to cross many international boundaries." He nods at a technician. "Funado, if you please."

The technician nods back and taps away. The mist swirls away to the edges of the screen, revealing an Asian man of indeterminate age in a military-cut uniform with a peaked black cap and white gloves. He's standing at the center of a crossroads in the middle of nowhere, back stiff and arms at his sides, looking much like a crossing guard who's been the victim of a cruel prank and refuses to admit it. It's not like I'm staring at a three-and-a-half-D screen anymore; it's more like I'm looking through a window.

Mizagi bows formally. *"Ohayō gozaimasu, Funado-eu."*

Funado inclines his head and replies, *"Ohayō gozaimasu, Mizagi-san.* How may I assist you?"

Mizagi glances at me, a twinkle in his eyes. "I seek a boon for a friend. Agent Valchek?"

"Uh, yeah. Hi. I had a little trouble crossing from the United States into Canada, and something—two somethings, actually—that were rightfully mine were confiscated. I'd really like them back."

Funado frowns. "Describe these items, please."

"Two martial arts scythes. Silver-coated retractable blades. Ironwood handles. In a custom case."

His frown deepens. "Such matters are delicate. Normally I would suggest you first talk to the Kami of weapons or of personal combat."

"Sorry. I'm not that well versed in the etiquette here—"

One hand snaps up, like he's telling an oncoming bus to stop. "In this case, I will make an exception. I cannot see either Kami being happy with a warrior being deprived of her weapons. These items were taken by a border guardian?"

"Yes."

"For no legitimate reason?"

"No."

"Then I shall rectify the situation."

It's my turn to smile. I hope Funado "rectifies" Officer Delta good and hard, and doesn't use lubrication. "Thank you."

"I wish you well until we speak again." He waves his hand in a peremptory fashion and the golden mist swirls back, filling the window. A moment later that disappears and I'm looking at a blank screen again.

"Impressive," I admit. "You had him eating out of your hand. Can't be easy to tame a minor deity."

Mizagi waves away my compliment, but I can tell he's delighted. "Oh, I'm just the facilitator. Most of the actual negotiations are conducted by others with far superior skills."

That's not hard to believe. "Must be tricky, making deals with supernatural beings. I mean, people can be swayed by money, but what do you offer a spirit?" I raise my eyebrows, meet Mizagi's gaze, and hold it. A few seconds tick by.

"That's a complex process," Mizagi finally says. The first excuse of a professional who wants to deflect a question. "There are many, many—"

"Of course, I guess there is a sort of spiritual currency, isn't there?"

"I—yes, I mean if you're talking about energy as a medium, then in a sense—"

"Souls."

He stops in mid-sentence. The room has gone quiet, in that way that happens when people notice a confrontation. Doesn't matter whether or not you speak the language, when someone yells *"Fight!"* heads turn and ears perk up.

"Negotiating an agreement is like getting the gears of two different machines to mesh together," I say. "And nothing greases the cogs better than a little bribery applied here and there. Especially a deal as big and complicated as this one must be."

Mizagi bristles at the word *bribery,* right on cue. I've stepped over a line with that word, and now—according to the rules—he's entitled to generate a little indignation, some outrage and denial and *how dare you* as a defense.

But I'm not interested in a fair fight. While we've been talking I pulled up the photo Stoker sent me on my phone, and now I shove it in Mizagi's face. "How about the souls of pire children, Mr. Mizagi? Think they might be a tasty incentive to sign on the dotted line?"

He studies the picture. I see the flare of panic in his eyes as he spots the ring.

"You—this means nothing," he blurts. "I don't even know what that picture is supposed to be!"

"That's your hand, wearing *that* ring."

"That means nothing. It's a common design."

"Maybe. I can't prove it's you in this picture, not yet. *But I will.*"

He recovers a little of his composure. "This meeting is concluded. I must ask you to leave now."

"Fine. But this is only my first visit, Mr. Mizagi. I tend to get less and less polite every time I show up." I slip the phone back in my pocket. "Nice TV, though. *Much* better than the one you'll have in your cell."

We leave.

"Enjoy yourself?" Charlie asks as we drive back to the hotel.

"I did, yeah. Think we shook him up enough?"

He shrugs, one hand on the wheel. "What's enough? I would have been happy to pick him up by the ankles and give him a lecture on the operating principles of jack-hammers."

"Alas, the pleasures of subtlety are lost on me."

"You, hurricanes, and earthquakes."

"Well, we rattled his cage. Now we see how loud he howls, and who to."

Charlie sighs. "You know, the next time I get a new suit I'm just gonna have a bull's-eye sewn right on the back. It'll save time and reduce confusion."

"Good idea. Get me one, too, will you?"

I lean back in my seat and stretch. Too much tension in my shoulders and neck. Got to work more on teaching Galahad massage—right now he just kind of paws at my back in an enthusiastic but confused way.

I'm actually pretty happy with how things went. Between the photo Stoker sent me and Mizagi's reaction to it, this investigation has finally gotten off the ground. Something's going on at Hemo, and it's not kosher. It's not even Jewish. In fact, it's entirely unrelated to anything in the entire Judeo-Hebraic realm, and I'm not sure that's even a word. Plus, talking to Funado-san has given me an idea about how to deal with my ammunition problem—

And that's when something slams into the car.

"Not again," Charlie sighs. Which is an astonishing

amount of calm to display while our vehicle is executing a complete end-over-end somersault, but that's Charlie. I'm just grateful I'm wearing my seat belt and not holding a hot cup of coffee.

We smack down wheels-first, hard enough to bounce a couple of times—the DeSoto has great suspension.

"That was fast," I gasp. "We must have made quite the impression."

"Let's go make another one," Charlie growls.

We exit the car on either side, moving fast and low. I've got my gun out. We're on a side street a few blocks away from the hotel, bracketed by an on-ramp to a bridge on one side and a fenced-off impound lot on the other. No other traffic. Not a bad place for an ambush, really—unless you're ambushing us. Then it's a huge, huge mistake.

I spot them as soon as I'm out of the car. A flashy red convertible is skewed across the lane behind us, a young Asian pire with spiky black hair and a bright yellow leather jacket standing up in the passenger seat. He's got a cocky grin on his face and some kind of glowing green statue clutched in one hand. The driver of the car is slouched low, another Asian guy in wraparound shades.

"Hey! Bloodhound!" the guy with the statue yells. "My boss not happy with you! He want you say sorry!"

"Sorry!"

"Much better! We go away now, okay?"

He raises the idol and a shimmery green wave launches itself at us. I dive to the side, but the wave isn't aimed at me—it hits the trunk of the DeSoto, which promptly flips ass-over-teakettle once more, coming to rest on its wheels again about three car-lengths away.

Charlie and I stare at it, then at each other.

"A somersault ray," I say. "Well, there's something you don't see every day."

"Oops!" the guy calls out. "Sorry! My bad!"

"Kid," Charlie says, "Your bad is about to get a whole lot worse."

Charlie's arm blurs as he pitches one of his silver-coated ball bearings overhand. It smashes into the grille of the car, just below the hood ornament.

"Ha! Not even close!"

"Says you. Lets see how far you get with a cracked engine block."

The driver says something in Japanese. He doesn't sound happy.

"I guess we take your car," Mr. Cocky says. "No more throwing." He says something in a language that definitely isn't Japanese, and the idol's glow begins to pulse.

"Jace," Charlie says. "I can't move. You?"

I try. My legs feel like they're rooted to the ground. My arms are rigid, locked in place in front of me. "Pretty much immobile from the neck down," I report.

The guy—he must be a shaman—hops down from the car to the ground. He saunters toward us.

I really hate a guy who saunters.

TWELVE

"This is not good," Charlie says.

"Don't be so negative. I may have overreacted—I think I can wiggle my toes."

"Why didn't you say so? We're saved."

Mr. Cocky—now Mr. Casual—stops right in front of me. "Mr. Zhang *very* unhappy with you leaving. *Most* rude. Now we go back and he lock you up in much safer place. Maybe stick you in soul jar, bury you somewhere. Yomi not seem so bad, then."

"I'm glad you feel that way," I say, "since you're the one that's going there. Hey, Charlie?"

"Yeah?"

"Know what else I can wiggle?"

BLAM!

BLAM!

BLAM!

BLAM!

BLAM!

"I'm gonna go out on a limb, here," says Charlie, "and say the index finger on your right hand."

Mr. Casual is now Mr. Messy. He really shouldn't have stood right in front of my gun like that, but I'm in no position to complain. The driver takes one look at us and bolts from his car, going full-were in his panic and running right out of his clothes. I let him go.

"You all right?" I ask. My paralysis vanished as soon as the shaman went down.

"Peachy. Next time I'll take out the shaman first and the car second, though."

"Nah, it was the right move. He might not have lined himself up so nicely if you hadn't zeroed his ride."

I look down at my gun sadly. "But it's not all good news. I'm down to my last bullet."

"You didn't have to shoot him five times."

"Yeah, I did." I pause. "Well, maybe I could have gotten away with three. Or four." I pause again and think about it. "Mmm. Nope. I was right the first time. I *definitely* had to shoot him five times."

"As long as you're sure."

"Plus, all I could really do at that point was twitch, and once you start it's kinda hard to stop."

"I know. I've seen you drink too much coffee."

I arch an eyebrow. "Blasphemy. We shall speak no more of this."

"Uh-huh."

I walk over to the body of the pire-shaman-gangster. The idol he was holding is lying in the gutter, and it's no longer glowing. Ugly little thing, like a toad with too many eyes and an overbite. Carved from soapstone, looks like. "Think it's safe to touch?"

"Beats me. We should get Eisfanger to look at it."

"Yeah." I pull out my phone. "We're gonna have to fill out a ton of paperwork with the local cops, anyway. I just hope none of them is in Zhang's pocket."

Charlie looks at me. "Or the Yakuza's."

"Or are just corrupt and greedy and willing to sell me to the highest bidder."

Charlie keeps looking at me. I sigh and put the phone

back in my pocket. "Let's get the hell out of here before we hear sirens."

"Works for me."

Before I can stop him, Charlie leans down and grabs the idol.

"Don't!" I blurt. "It could—"

Charlie snaps upright. He turns his head toward me, moving stiffly. "Must . . . kill . . . Bloodhound," he rasps.

"Oh, hey, look at that. I still have one bullet left."

He relaxes his posture and tosses the idol from one hand to the other. "Urge . . . passing," he says. "Won't . . . call . . . bluff."

"Get in the car, zombie boy."

He does, dropping the idol in the backseat. "That wasn't even a real threat. I mean, it's a weapon that I'm incapable of taking seriously."

I get in beside him. "Hey, for a performance like that? You're lucky I bothered to threaten you at all."

"What? I was being menacing and mind-controlled."

"You know how they say a bad actor is wooden? A tree could give *you* acting lessons."

"You just don't appreciate nuance."

"A really *young* tree. A sapling."

"You probably can't even *spell* nuance."

"Just drive, okay?"

"So," Eisfanger says. He scratches the pale stubble of his crew cut and peers at the idol, now sitting on the hotel room table in front of him. "You just left? With a dead gangbanger and his car in the middle of the street?"

I shrug. "Nobody tried to stop us."

"I wouldn't, either, if you were carrying this." Eisfanger opens his forensics kit on his bed and starts rummaging around. "Early Babylonian, I think. Not HPLC level, but probably linked to one of the minor deities of that period who were trying to siphon off followers by pretending to be more powerful than they actually were. Some of them would even pose as Elder Gods, though that usually ended badly for them. And any civilization in the immediate vicinity."

"Wait," I say. "You're saying that the . . . *thing* this idol represents is only a *knockoff*?"

Charlie shakes his head. "What's the cosmos coming to? You just can't find an original Entity of Ancient Evil anymore."

"Not at reasonable prices, anyhow . . . so how dangerous is this chunk of rock, Damon?"

"I'll know after I run a few more tests. But at least it doesn't seem to have any tracking wards on it."

We leave Damon to his tests, going back to my room to reconsider our options. Charlie slumps into the room's single chair and I flop down on the bed on my back. "Ugh. So where's this leave us?"

Charlie tips his fedora back on his head. "I hate to say it, but I don't think Hemo was behind that attack."

"Yeah, that's what I was thinking. Too quick, for one thing. Mizagi would have had to report to whoever's really in charge, they'd have to make a decision, then the order would go out. The Yakuza's pretty anal about chain of command."

"So it was just Zhang, making another play?"

I sit up and shrug. "Maybe not even Zhang, just a couple of ambitious lieutenants. Those two saw an opportunity and went for it. Zhang might not have survived his little chat with Stoker."

"So we've got a Triad *and* the Yak after us now."

"Looks like. Isn't it nice to be popular?"

The dream is in black and white.

It used to be thought that the majority of dreams were in black and white. Then, in the 1960s, something interesting happened: color television arrived. And as it gained in popularity, the percentage of Technicolor dreams did, too. These days, only about 12 percent of people dream without color, and most of those people are over fifty-five. Black-and-white dreams are apparently largely a product of pop culture, a re-creation in the mind's eye of what it's seen on a screen, large or small.

In which case, I seem to be starring in a 1940s movie. One of those classic suspense and romance things, where the bad guys are always lurking in the shadows wearing trench coats and hats with the brim pulled way down low. In fact, that's how it opens: I'm on a corner, looking nervously across the street at the silhouette of a man just like that, standing at the entrance to an alley. Smoke curls lazily up around his face as he draws on a cigarette, but I can't make out his features.

I start to walk. It's late at night, no one else is around, and danger is in the air. The sound of my heels clacks loudly off the brick walls of deserted buildings. I look over my shoulder, but the man is gone. A wisp of smoke hangs in the air like an afterthought.

I have to get to the rendezvous. Not just my life, but the lives of others hang in the balance. I know this, just as I know that there are evil . . . *beings* trying to stop me. Was that man in the alley one of them?

Maybe. They're everywhere. There are so few of *us* left now.

There's a rumble of thunder, and it begins to rain. Hollywood rain, the heavy kind that falls straight down. I look around for somewhere to find shelter—

Someone reaches out from a doorway, grabs me by the arm. Yanks me into the shadows.

I open my mouth to scream, but a hand clamps over my lips. He's strong, inhumanly so, but I know he won't kill me—no, there are worse things in store for me.

And then I find myself staring at a miracle. Into the two
bluest eyes I've ever seen, so blue they're like holes into a
dimension of pure sky. His face is as monochromatic as
everything else, but those eyes belong to another reality
altogether.

"Ssssh," he says. "Okay?"

I nod, as best I can. He takes his hand away and slips
it around my waist.

"Oh, David," I whisper. "I was so *scared* . . ."

"Let's go. It's not safe on the streets, not now . . ."

He pulls me through an open door and inside. Leads
me up a rickety staircase and down a long hall to a room
with fading flowered wallpaper, a folding cot, and a bedside table that holds a bottle of whiskey and a cracked
glass.

He closes the door softly, never taking his eyes off me.
His blond hair is slicked back, and he wears a long gray
coat over an expensive double-breasted suit. He shrugs
off the coat, tosses it aside. I'm happy to see him but terrified at what he's going to say.

"Do . . . do you have them?" I ask.

Now he looks away. "I was only able to get four."

"But—but there are five of us! We *need* five!"

"I know. But they're starting to crack down—these
were the last four I could obtain. The shaman who was
supplying them has disappeared."

"Was he arrested?"

"Maybe. Maybe he just took a powder because things
are getting too hot. Give me some time. I'll try to find
another source."

"Time. Sure." I force a laugh. "Got plenty of that, don't
you? But us mere mortals aren't so lucky."

"Don't talk like that."

"How am I supposed to talk when you just sentenced

a member of my family to death? Hang a grin on my face, sing a happy little song?"

"I'll find you another." He sees my expression and adds, "Not another family. Another—"

"Yeah, sure."

"I'm sorry. I truly am."

"Thanks. That and a wooden nickel will get me twice what I got now: a big fat nothing with a bunch of zeros behind it."

That's not fair—or true—and I know it, but I'm angry and disappointed and scared to death about what I'm going to tell my folks, my kid sister, my big brother. I'm mad at the world, but the world has too many problems of its own to notice mine, and wouldn't care if it did. So I lash out at the man who's risking everything to help me, because he's here and so am I and both of us are trapped.

And because, despite everything he's done, he's one of them.

"The war was hard on everyone," he says. "I lost people, too. Good people. But it's over. Things will be better now—"

He's trying to get me to see the sunny side—which is a real side splitter, considering who he is—but his heart isn't in it.

"Better, huh? For who? Sure, the Allies won, but Hitler gets the last laugh. If nobody finds a way to stop the damn plague his sorcerers let loose before Berlin fell, pretty soon there won't *be* any human beings left to fight over. There'll just be thropes and pires—one breeds like rabbits and the other doesn't breed at all, not without humans to turn. Who do you think will come out on top then? In a few generations, your kind will be so badly outnumbered they'll be able to round all of *you* up and stick you in camps—but nobody'll come out again."

He turns away so I can't see his face. He doesn't speak for a moment, and I wonder if I've gone too far. It's true, every word of it, but pointing out what he already knows doesn't solve anything.

I'm suddenly ashamed of myself. David doesn't deserve my anger. This is an apocalypse for his race, too, just a slower one; and his immortality means he'll very likely be around when it comes to a head.

He's also gone to a great deal of trouble to obtain the charms that'll protect my family from the plague—they're almost impossible to create and nearly as difficult to get. The government has officially denied that any such charms even exist, and David refuses to tell me why.

But they work. Not a single human wearing one has gotten sick, while others around them collapse and sink into comas. They must use some kind of high-powered government sorcery, one the authorities want to keep under wraps; maybe even something they stole from a Nazi lab.

"I shouldn't have said that," I say. "I'm sorry. It's just—"

"I know," he says quietly. "Believe me, I know."

I've had no choice but to trust David, with my life and with my family's. I've set that trust against my anger, my fear, my sorrow, and my desperation, and when that wasn't enough to do the job I added more. A lot more.

It's my turn to grab his arm. I lift a hand behind his head and pull him down into a kiss. He's a lot stronger than I am, but he doesn't resist. He stopped resisting after the very first time, and I still don't know why. He says he loves me, but there's more regret than passion in his voice when he does. He's battling his own long list of feelings, and I don't know what he's using as ammunition.

I guess when it comes down to it, the only ammo we have against the darkness is life itself. So what is a man who hasn't been alive for hundreds of years supposed to do? What does he have to fight with?

Right now, he has me.

He pulls back from the kiss. "You don't have to do this," he says. "You never did. The charms are yours."

I slap him. It should hurt my hand, but doesn't. "Is *that* what you think I am?"

"No. Never." He raises a hand to his cheek, though I haven't left a mark. "It's what *I* am that I can't forgive . . ."

"Forget about forgiveness. Forget about everything, everything but me and you. Just for a little while . . ."

I kiss the corner of his mouth, tenderly. He doesn't react. I brush my lips softly against his, more a caress than a kiss. His lips part, but I don't give him time to protest. I lean in close, crushing my mouth to his, my body to his.

My coat slides off my shoulders and drops to the floor. I'm wearing a thin sheath dress underneath, and it joins the coat a second later. I'm already fumbling with his tie, pulling at his coat, neither of us willing to break the kiss. Somewhere, I hear a radio playing something slow and bluesy, a saxophone flirting with a bass while a piano dances in the background.

I finally pull back, breathing hard, to focus on unbuttoning his shirt. I don't know, there's just something about a man in a buttondown shirt . . . he watches me intently, letting me undress him, not saying a word. I have to kneel to pull off his socks and shoes.

I stay down there a while.

He stops me before I'm done—or before he is—and takes a step backward. He still isn't breathing hard, but his eyes aren't the only thing with some color now. I accept this in that way you do in dreams, but still find it fascinating; I wonder what else I can bring to vivid, colorful life.

I get to my feet slowly. I've kicked off my shoes, but I'm still wearing a camisole and underwear. He touches my breastbone with a single cool fingertip, then slides it to the right, to the camisole's strap. It slips off my shoulder. His finger traces its way across my skin to the other side, the other strap. The camisole falls away.

His other hand rises. Another cool fingertip touches my skin, just above my navel. I close my eyes and concentrate on the feeling as they trace their way along my body, two dots of sensation traveling to their inevitable destinations.

Ah. And ah.

His fingers move in slow, gentle circles. When they stop, I open my eyes and look down. Sure enough, I see two firm little nubs sticking out, and they're not just erect, they're pink. I wonder if David can see this or if it's just me . . . but before I can ask him he leans down and blocks my view of one of them.

Oh, my.

I arch my back and whimper. When he pulls away, his lips are pink. So is his tongue.

We find our way to the bed. He's never bitten me, he hasn't even asked, but tonight . . . tonight feels different. Tonight feels like an ending of some kind, like I'll never see him again.

Or maybe it's something else that's coming to an end.

He's normally a gentle lover, but not this time. This time is all about urgency and desperation and striving for something you know is just out of reach. We buck, writhe, twist. He can't seem to find a rhythm he's happy with, but I'm so revved up I'd be happy upside down, and a minute later I'm proven right.

It's ecstatic and maddening, frustrating and heavenly. All the other times, he must have been holding back, afraid of hurting me; now he's using his full strength, moving me from position to position like I weigh nothing at all; I'm on top, I'm on my back, I'm on my hands and knees. It feels like I'm having sex with an elemental force, making love to a hurricane or an avalanche or an earthquake. Something relentless and wild and powerful, so far beyond your control that you can only hang on and hope you survive the experience.

Every time I get close, he switches things up and does something else. It's driving me out of my mind. When I finally do orgasm, it's long and intense and loud.

I lay beside him, panting, covered in sweat. My whole body is flushed with a rosy glow, from head to toes and everywhere in between. So is his—but even though he's stopped, he hasn't reached the place I just arrived at. "You didn't—"

"No."

I reach for him. "Then we need to try *harder*."

He pushes my hand away, gently. "I don't think so."

I frown. "But—"

"It's not you. It's just . . . not that important."

"You're a much better lover than liar."

He smiles. "I wish that were true."

"So is that what I am to you? Just another way to punish yourself?"

"No." He props himself up on an elbow. "You're something special. Some*one* special. You mean a lot more to me than . . . this."

"This? Hey, we just lit up the sheets like the Fourth of July—I'm surprised the room didn't burn down. That's worth a little more than a single word, don't you think?"

"Of course it is. But there's a bigger picture here. And a lot more going on than you're aware of."

"So fill me in, Mr. Fireworks. As many times as it takes."

"Say that again. And *think* about it, this time."

I have no idea where he's going with this. "The offer stands. And from the look of things, so do you."

"That's not what I'm—" He stops. Tilts his head slightly in that way people do when they're listening intently to something very faint.

An instant later he's on his feet and pulling me to mine. "We have to get out of here. Now."

I don't argue, just grab for my clothes. "There's no time for that!" he snaps, and pulls me toward the door.

And then we're running down a hallway, naked, and something is chasing us.

Everything changes as we run, becoming more and more dream-like. The hallway stretches ahead of us to infinity, an uncountable number of doors lining either side, some of them ajar. We sprint past, but everything's going in slow motion now, and I catch unsettling glimpses through the doors that are cracked open: a jungle full of dinosaur-riding Aztecs, an eighteenth-century airship in low-earth orbit, a city populated by six-foot mantises. Everything's in full color now, almost oversaturated with it, and I have no idea where we're running to or what we're running from.

No, that's not true. I may not know where we're going, but I know what's chasing us. It's the man in the alley, the one whose face I couldn't see. He wants to devour our souls, and if he catches us we won't be able to stop him.

"The doors!" I say. "Maybe we can lose him if we go through one of the doors!"

"We can't," he says. "Can't dooooo thaaaaaaaaaaaattt . . ."

I look at him in horror. He's got a black, slimy-looking tentacle wrapped around his stomach, a tentacle that stretches back the way we came. It's not the only thing stretching, either; his whole body is being pulled like taffy, skull elongating, torso deforming, arms and legs getting longer as he's drawn backward. It's like seeing someone being grabbed by a living black hole, dragged down toward the event horizon by his belly.

He's still holding on to my hand, but now a ripple runs down the length of his arm, snapping his hand like the end of a bullwhip and hurling me away. We fall away from each other in opposite directions, his face distorted by the terrible gravity of the thing that's caught him, and I know that once it's finished consuming him I'm next . . .

THIRTEEN

I wake up screaming.

I stop as soon as I realize the dream's over and I'm awake—but it takes me a second to get my bearings, then another second to process what just happened and what the immediate consequences will be.

"Charlie! I'm—"

CRASH!

"—okay." I sigh. "Does our expense account cover hotel room doors?"

Charlie glares at me. The only thing he's wearing is his fedora, which actually makes him look a lot less naked than you'd think—golems have the same sex organs as a Ken doll, which is to say none. The door is on the floor, hinges and all. Charlie doesn't let a lot slow him down when he's in a hurry.

"You sure?" he growls, looking around like he expects to see an assassin hiding behind the drapes or under the bed.

"Yes. Bad dream, that's all. Go back to to bed."

"Can't." He looks down, then back at me. "Got a door to fix."

"Sorry."

"You got to stop with the sauerkraut and mushroom

pizza before bed," he mutters as he picks up the door and examines the damage. "I'm gonna need tools . . ."

"I'll call down to the front desk."

A terrific start to another great day . . .

I hole up in the bathroom and take a shower as Charlie waits out in the hall for maintenance to show up. I mull over the dream as I scrub, trying to figure out what it was trying to tell me.

A lot of it was actually close to reality: Cassius did smuggle anti-plague charms to the human population at the end of World War II. The plague was actually more of a curse, part of a deal the pires made with an Elder God named Shub-Niggurath to gain the ability to procreate. The deal required the sacrifice of millions of human souls, a price Cassius thought was too high. He'd done his best to help save those he could—though I don't know if he had a human lover while he did so. Knowing Cassius, it's entirely possible.

The black-and-white to color stuff was weird, too—in fact, as a psychologist I've never heard of that happening in a dream. It seemed like some kind of metaphor, beyond the obvious sexual one. But for what? The past and the present? Something simple becoming something complex?

And then there's how it ended. The thing chasing us down that endless hallway, all the doors and the bizarre things behind them. Were they supposed to represent memories? Choices? Emotions? I don't know.

What I *do* know is that the sense of menace was over-powering, so vivid and real that I can still feel echoes of it. Either my subconscious is scared to death of something and trying to send me a message—or this was more than just a dream.

It was a warning.

But from who? Cassius? If he's trying to communicate with me through dreams instead of just picking up a phone, does that mean he's in trouble? Or am I reading too much into having an ordinary nightmare under stressful conditions?

No easy answers pop up from the shower drain or magically appear in the soap dish. I lather, rinse, and repeat, not because I believe in following directions but because I need a little more time to ruminate.

Dream-Cassius was definitely trying to tell me something. He told me to think about what I'd just said. What was it again? Something about his lovemaking and comparing it to—

Fireworks.

I open my eyes in abrupt realization, and promptly get shampoo in them. I curse and turn my head into the shower spray to rinse them out.

Cassius's world has never *seen* fireworks. Fireworks were the crude precursor of firearms, which never evolved here. So what, right? It was a dream, it didn't have to make sense. But the thing is, Cassius not only noticed that discrepancy, but tried to point it out to me as well. Which means some part of my brain thought it was important enough to tap myself on my own mental shoulder through a surrogate.

Now that I think of it, there was another reference to guns in the dream—something about ammunition. So whatever the dream was really about, my gun—or maybe the global anti-gun spell—was involved.

I get out, dry off, get dressed with the clothes I brought in with me. Leave the bathroom and find a paunchy guy in jeans and a faded black T-shirt fixing my door with a cordless drill and a couple lengths of wood. Charlie's wrapped a white towel around himself, sarong-style, out of consideration for my delicate sensibilities. Together with the fedora, it's quite the outfit.

"Wow," I say. "You look like a hard-boiled . . . guy. In

a sauna. Like a guy who was really unclear on the whole hard-boiled thing, and tried to cook himself a little more. In a sauna."

Charlie gives me a look.

"Okay, not one of my best. Caffeine now, please."

"Just give a moment to slip into something a little less punch-line-oriented, all right?"

We rap on Eisfanger's door, tell him we'll be in the hotel restaurant. We get a sleepy but coherent acknowledgment and head downstairs.

Coffee. Gulp gulp gulp. Ahhhhh.

"Right," I say. "Brain function returning. Will to live at acceptable levels. Robot imitation program terminating—*now.*"

"I know I'm going to hate myself for asking this, but—in what way, shape, or form was that an imitation of a rowboat?"

"Robot. *Robot* imitation."

"What the hell's a robot?"

I squint at my partner suspiciously over the rim of my coffee cup. Charlie once got me to believe that lems prefer the term *Mineral American,* and he still makes the occasional outrageous claim with a straight face, relying on my relative inexperience with Thropirelem's history and culture.

After a moment's reflection, though, I realize that what he's saying makes perfect sense. Nobody ever came up with the idea of robots here, because a real version already existed: golems. They're mystical, not mechanical, but conceptually they're virtually the same thing; they're manufactured, they're inorganic, they're used mainly for repetitive labor or as weapons.

"Oh my God," I say, putting down my coffee. "You guys don't have robots. No R2-D2, no Gort, no Robby. No Data or Hymie or Optimus Prime. Wow."

"Yeah, it's a real tragedy. My grief is somewhat alleviated by not knowing what the hell you're talking about."

"I feel like I just discovered a whole branch of your family you didn't even suspect existed."

"Lems don't have families."

He says it bluntly, like it's a self-evident fact that he has no personal connection to. I'm not fooled. I can tell when he's trying to hide something.

"Well, now you do," I say. "Okay, they live a long distance away, and speak a different language, but just think of them as relatives from the old country. Part of your heritage."

"Heritage, huh? So these 'robots' have been around a long time? Longer than lems?"

"Oh, sure. C-3PO was built a *long* time ago. And far, far away, for that matter."

Charlie frowns. "Far away from what?"

"From, uh, here. I mean, all the robots I mentioned are from my reality, so they're *all* far, far away. Obviously."

"Obviously. So what, exactly, *is* a robot?"

"It's a machine. Usually humanoid, but not always. Some look like garbage cans on wheels."

"How inspiring."

"No, no." I finish my coffee and signal the waiter for a refill. "Most robots are *impressive*. Take the Transformers, for instance. We're talking fifty-foot-tall guys made out of steel and electronics and machinery. Walking engines of destruction."

"Like military lems. Grizzly units."

"Yeah, exactly! Except bigger and able to fly. And blow stuff up from a distance."

"Huh. That does sound kind of impressive. But I don't get the name: Transformers. What is it they transform into?"

I blink. "Um. All kinds of things."

"Like what?"

"It depends. They're all different."

"Give me an example."

I try to desperately come up with one that isn't ridiculous, but I can't remember any of their names except their leader. "Well, there's Optimus Prime. He turns into . . ."

"What?"

"A truck."

Charlies raises one hairless eyebrow. "A truck?"

"A really *big* truck."

"It'd have to be."

"A tractor-trailer rig, actually. You know, a semi? With a big trailer on the back?"

"Uh-huh." He's looking at me intently now. "So this fifty-foot, flying killer robot turns into a *truck.* Towing a *trailer.*"

"Well, yes."

"Why?"

I feel like I've been lured into an inquiry about Santa Claus by a six-year-old. "To fool people," I say weakly. "Because they aren't just robots. They're robots in *disguise.*"

Charlie leans back and considers this. "Yeah, I can see that," he murmurs.

I'm trying desperately to come up with a way to change the subject before Charlie decides to unravel my logic a little further when I'm saved by the unlikely appearance of a thrope dressed in the brown, short-pants uniform of a delivery guy. He comes straight over to our table and says, "Hi. Got a delivery for a Jace Valchek?"

I study him carefully. "How'd you know who I was?"

"I was gonna deliver it to your room, but the guy at the front desk said you were eating in here with a lem, and here you are. Sign here."

Charlie takes the package while I scrawl my signature

on one of those electronic clipboards. The guy thanks me and leaves.

"Seems legit," Charlie says. "Label says it's from Canada Customs."

The package is about two and a half feet long by a foot wide, and the weight is familiar. I grin and rip it open, revealing the polished wooden case I keep my scythes in. They're inside and seem none the worse for wear. "How about that. Funado is a god of his word."

"We should still have Eisfanger give them the once-over, make sure they haven't been messed with."

"Good thought. Paranoid, but good."

"Paranoia is just the bastard child of fear and good sense."

"Poor thing. Let's adopt it, give it a last name and raise it right."

"You want to get it a puppy, too?"

"Sure. We'll call it Panic. It and little Paranoia can play together at the park and scare the hell out of all the other kids."

My breakfast arrives at the same time Eisfanger does. He orders a huge meal himself, then scoops up the scythes and runs them back upstairs to check them out for any enchantments or spells that might be attached. He times it perfectly, strolling back into the restuarant just as his order shows up, by which time I'm halfway through my own. Charlie's hiding from the carnage behind a newspaper.

"Scythes are fine. So what was the yelling last night about?" Eisfanger asks as he digs in.

"Nothing much," I say. "Lucifer showed up, announced that Armageddon was starting, and apologized for all the confusion about the date. Apparently his prophecy department has been screwed up since he started outsourcing to another pantheon."

"Uh, is that your usual mix of sarcasm and bizarreness, or are you upset with me?"

"Not really. I just wondered why you didn't bother seeing for yourself. You know, what with all the screaming."

He chugs down half a glass of orange juice before answering. "Oh. I heard Charlie charge in, and then you two talking, so I figured everything was okay. I was ready to back you up if you needed it, but—"

"But I didn't. You're right, I'm sorry. False alarm, just a bad dream."

"Another one? About what?"

"Uh—just stuff."

"What kind of stuff?" Eisfanger has that combination of curiousity and cluelessness on his face, more interested in new information than picking up any pesky social cues of inappropriateness.

I sigh. "I had a dream that ended badly, with me being chased by some kind of nebulous, evil entity. Okay?"

Eisfanger frowns. He puts down his fork. "No. Not okay. Tell me the whole thing, start to finish, and don't leave out any details."

I raise my eyebrows. "Well, some of it was kind of personal, so I don't know if I feel comfortable with that—"

It's Eisfanger's turn to sigh. "Jace. You're not embarrassed about stripping down for a doctor, are you?"

"Depends on how drunk I am. And if he's a good tipper."

He pauses, then shakes his head and continues. "I'm asking in a professional capacity, all right? As a trained shaman, I'd like you to describe your dream so I can determine whether or not you were attacked on the astral plane."

Charlie lowers his newspaper. "Attacked?"

"Okay, okay," I say. I tell him the whole thing, glossing

over some of the more erotic parts. He listens attentively, not commenting until I'm completely done.

"Do you remember any distinctive odors?" he asks. "The smell of something burning, for instance?"

"No."

"How about pain? Could you feel pain in the dream?"

"I didn't feel anything like that, no."

He pauses, balancing his thick chin on two stubby thumbs. "Hmmm. What about unearthly sounds—any sort of whining or keening noises, something actively unpleasant to hear?"

"Nope."

"Okay, I don't think you were attacked. Those are all markers that usually accompany an astral incursion. But this is the second disturbing dream you've had involving Cassius, and this one doesn't sound normal."

"So, what? A premonition?"

He shakes his head. "No, I don't think so. More like someone was trying to contact you and having trouble doing it."

"Cassius, you mean?"

"Not necessarily. The Cassius character might have been a symbolic representation of someone or something else. It could even be a pun—the brain loves to interpret language in creative ways."

"So what's the message being sent?"

He shrugs. "A warning, obviously. But other than that, I can't say—there are just too many variables involved."

Terrific. A mysterious someone is trying to warn me about a mysterious something, and my own brain is playing games with me. I feel like I'm being punished for every pun I ever made. Including that one.

"This is good news," I say.

Charlie tosses his newspaper down on the table. "Absolutely."

"Why?" Eisfanger asks.

"Nobody tosses around warnings unless you're getting close to something they want you staying away from," I answer. "So we're definitely on the right track with Hemo."

"What's next?" Charlie asks.

"We ramp up the heat. I want you and Eisfanger to put in another appearance at Hemo, and this time I want the place checked out for masking spells. If those kids were really taken there, the place will be thoroughly masked, right?"

"That would make sense," Eisfanger says. "But a corporate HQ doing sensitive R and D is going to have all kinds of wards up anyway, and we don't have the warrants to peel them back and see what they're hiding."

"Doesn't matter. I just want them to stay nervous, and get a feel for their defenses. If they're trying to conceal something as specific as pire children there should be indications of it."

Eisfanger nods, but he looks troubled. "I'll see what I can find. How about you?"

"Thought I'd go to church."

Church isn't really accurate, but where I have in mind *is* a place of worship. A shrine, to be exact—to a piece of sushi. And no, it's not a restaurant, though my devotion to raw fish on rice does approach the religious. The sushi in question is called inari, which isn't fish at all but a piece of fried tofu. It's very common, kind of sweet, and named after a goddess: Inari, with a capital I.

Inari is kind of a big deal in the Shinto religion. Of all the thousands of Kami, she's in the top five—in fact, over a third of all household Shinto shrines are devoted to her. She started out as a humble rice goddess, but became more and more popular over time, largely as a protector.

After a few centuries, her responsibilities have grown considerably; she's now prayed to by actors and prostitutes, by fishermen, by people who want to prevent fires, by women who want to bear children. She's seen as a deity of desire, as the goddess you can go to when you need something.

But most of all, she's the patron saint of two very specific professions: warriors . . . and blacksmiths.

It was my encounter with Funado that got me thinking along these lines. On the surface my problem might seem purely physical, one of diminishing resources, but I can't see any way to resolve it except through the metaphysical. Even though it goes against my own stubborn sense of self-reliance to ask for help, I realize I'm fighting a losing battle on my own. When in Rome, do as the Romans do—and I've been stranded in Rome for a while now, with my supplies running low. Time to swallow my pride, slip into a gladiator outfit, and practice my Latin.

Besides—if I can't share a little girl-talk with someone who's fond of sashimi, ass-kicking, and a well-crafted piece of lethal steel, who else would I go to?

According to my laptop, the shrine is in an area next to the heritage district of Gastown, in a lane called Blood Alley. Not exactly welcoming, but in a world of pires it's really no more ominous a name than Bourbon Street. The neighborhood is obviously Japanese: corner stores with posters of cute anime animals in the windows, an average of two-point-five noodle shops per block, even pagoda-style roofs on the bus shelters.

Blood Alley is just that, an alley. It smells of rotting fish and rancid grease, it's got Dumpsters lined up at regular intervals, and even features a picturesque drunk snoring off his latest bender while slumped against an upended shopping cart. I can tell he's a thrope, because he's not wearing any shoes and his feet are large, hairy and clawed. I wonder if he howls in his sleep.

Most of the buildings that line the alley face the street, and from the rear it's difficult to tell much about them. What I mainly see are locked, featureless metal doors set into aging brick walls.

Until I get to the halfway point.

The shrine itself is in a narrow slice of land, flanked on either side by taller buildings. It's a three-story structure, an old, Victorian-style house with a steeply pitched roof, and it's set at the very front of the lot, as far from the alley as possible.

Not because it's trying to distance itself, though. It's to leave room for the arches—each one a classic Japanese *tori,* like an angular upside-down U with two beams across the top, the top one slightly bowed and the ends sticking out to either side. There are a long line of them, at least twenty, painted bright red and about ten feet high, placed directly next to one another so they form a kind of squared-off tunnel that leads all the way to the shrine itself.

I pause at the first one. It's flanked on either side by two white statues of some kind of animal; the sculptures are so stylized it's hard to tell what they're supposed to represent. Might be a wolf, might be a cat—hell, with that tail it could even be a squirrel. I shrug and walk under the first arch.

Either there's some kind of magic at work or the acoustics are cleverly designed, because by the time I've taken a dozen steps the noise of the city has faded away to nothing. I can smell the first faint tickle of incense, something that reminds me of cherry blossoms. Each of the *toris* has a line of intricate *kanji* symbols painted down the vertical beams.

The arches end at the foot of a staircase, an ordinary

set of wooden steps leading upward and onto a porch. More of the same statues on either side of the doorway, with incense burning on top of them. I go inside.

The interior is small and spare. White paper lanterns hang from the ceilings. The shrine itself looks like a dollhouse-size temple, a miniature pagoda with its own set of steps sitting on a waist-high platform of dark, polished wood. Vases with sprays of green foliage sit to either side, and *kanji*-covered banners hang down from the walls behind it. A tiny set of red *toris* like the ones I just walked under march up the miniature steps. I seem to be the only one here.

I stare at the shrine for a long time. I realize I have no idea how to do this, of what to say or even how to begin— and considering how important protocol is in Japanese culture, I'd better do it right the first time. There are times you can get away with being a wiseass and times you can't, and asking cosmically powerful beings to do you a favor is definitely in the *can't* column.

"You seem to be having trouble," a voice says behind me.

I turn. There's a monk standing there in a crimson robe, a pire with snow-white hair tied back and a little white beard. It's unusual to see pires that appear old, but I guess even the occasional senior citizen got turned back in the day. This one smiles at me and asks, "First time here?"

"Yes. Guess it shows, huh?"

"A little." His tone is gently amused. "Do not be nervous. Inari, for all her power, is a gentle spirit. She rarely turns away those in need."

"Well, that's good, because I'm definitely a gal in need."

"Perhaps I can help. What is it you require of her?"

"More of these." I hold up what I've been clutching in one hand ever since I walked through the door: my last bullet.

The monk bends forward slightly, studying it. "Most curious," he says. "What is it, a talisman?"

"I guess. A talisman of high velocity. Mainly, though, it's a weapon. Normally I have a bunch of these, but I'm down to my last one—and they're strictly one-use only."

"I see. You cannot obtain more?"

"No. I could make them myself—but there's a powerful spell preventing me. That's what I was hoping Inari could help me with."

"Ah. You require her assistance as the benefactor both of warriors and of those who work metal."

"Pretty much, yeah."

The monk frowns. "While Inari does offer her help to many—and her presence is most often felt in the heat of the forge or of battle—she does not involve herself with sorcery. That is the domain of other gods, and even gods must respect propriety."

"What? But—okay, I'm a little lost here. I thought sorcery was pretty much what all this was about."

Now the monk looks offended. "You are most assuredly mistaken. Prayers and spells are not the same thing. One is respectful; the other demands. Lower spirits may be compelled or bribed, but a goddess such as Inari is above such crudeness. She cannot help you in regard to a mere *enchantment*." He says the last word like it tastes bad and he wants it out of his mouth as soon as possible.

"Hey, there's nothing mere about this spell, okay? It's been around for centuries, it affects every single person on the planet, and most people didn't even know it *existed* until I showed up."

His white eyebrows go up. "That sounds most implausible."

"If you think *that's* implausible, take a look at this." I take my gun out of its holster and show it to him.

"What is this?"

"It's my weapon. It's extremely powerful. With the proper ammunition, it can kill a pire, a thrope, or a bull moose from a hundred yards away . . . but that's not the best part. The best part is that—despite how deadly it is—you won't take it seriously. You *can't.* I can demonstrate it to you right here and now, and you'll *still* think of it as some sort of unreliable gimmick. That's how the spell works."

He regards me seriously for several seconds. "You can prove what you claim?"

"Sure. Just follow me out to the alley."

"Very well." He motions me toward the door.

I choose one of the Dumpsters as my victim. This bullet isn't one of the special silver-tipped, carved teak bullets I normally carry; it's unaltered, a .454 round designed to deliver around sixteen hundred pounds of foot-pressure to its target.

I make sure the Dumpster doesn't hold any sleeping drunks first, then stride back to where the monk waits skeptically. I really hope this is worth using up my last shot.

"Okay," I say. "Let's be clear. Would you agree that a weapon that can put a large hole in that Dumpster from this far away is a force to be reckoned with?"

"I suppose I would."

"But once you see it, you won't. You'll think it's a fluke, or a trick, or just meaningless. You'll rationalize it away. No matter how hard you try, you won't be able to think of what I'm about to show you in anything but negative terms."

"Proceed."

I turn, raise the Ruger, and fire. I guess I should have warned the monk about the noise—the Super Redhawk roars like an angry grizzly when I don't have Eisfanger's magic silencer on it. The Dumpster bucks like it was kicked by an elephant and rolls back a good six feet. There's now a baseball-size hole in the side.

I lower the gun and glance at the monk. His eyes are open a little wider, but that's about the only sign of surprise. His eyebrows slowly lower as the expression on his face changes.

"That is . . ." He stops. I wait for it.

He tries again. "It is most . . ." He trails off.

It's all I can do to not blurt out *Ludicrous? Absurd? Stupid?* and every other synonym for *ridiculous* I can think of, but I don't want to influence him. I can tell the enchantment is doing that all on its own.

"Very interesting," he says at last. "It is as you said."

"I'm impressed. Most people get stuck in denial."

"I am more aware than most people."

Well, he's got me there. "So you see my problem? The reaction you're having is the same one *every person on Earth* has to my gun. It's so powerful it's even started to affect *me*. So who am I supposed to go to for help?"

He meets my eyes. "You," he says softly, "are not *of* this Earth. Are you?"

"Well . . . technically, no. But I'm not a supernatural creature, either. I'm from a parallel world, an alternate Earth. That's where my weapon came from, too."

"And you cannot return?"

"No. If I could, I wouldn't have to worry about ammo. Or a whole lot of other things."

He nods. "This spell. It is not sorcery—it is *kamiwaza,* the work of the gods."

"Well, great. That means Inari can help me out, right? This is on her level."

"I am afraid she cannot. As sorcery is beneath her, this is surely above. She will not interfere in the affairs of other gods—not at the request of a mortal."

"No, no—the spell wasn't cast by a god. It's this one guy. A shaman. A really powerful one, sure, but just a man—"

He cuts me off with a curt wave of his hand. "It matters not. Perhaps he is a god in mortal guise, or perhaps a god is working through him. Whatever the details, Inari will not involve herself, of this you can be sure."

I sigh and holster the Ruger. "Chain of command, right? Don't bother the brass with the problems of the troops. Thanks anyway."

I'm halfway down the alley when he calls out, "Wait."

I turn back. The monk motions me to return, and I do.

"Inari cannot help you," he says, his voice low, "but perhaps another can."

"Who?"

"As one shaman has caused your problems, would it not seem wise to call upon another to solve them?"

"I've been down that road. The spell screws with everyone's perceptions, shamans included. You can't fight a problem if your brain keeps insisting there isn't one."

"You most assuredly can, Agent Valchek. One can learn to fight anything—even the wind—with the right teacher. I know such a person. Should they agree to help you, this enchantment would simply be another opponent for them to face."

"And you think they could beat it?"

"They have never known defeat. It is more a question of whether or not they could be convinced that the challenge was worthy of their time."

Sounds like the monk is talking about some kind of martial artist shaman—which is a pretty good description of some Shinto priests I've met. Well, why not? Maybe it's possible to just pound a spell into submission. "So who is this person? How do I get in touch with them?"

The monk shakes his head. "You do not. They guard their privacy jealously. But I know of a place they can be found, at certain times; should you go there, they might be willing to speak to you. I will attempt to contact them in advance, to let them know of you and your quest. If they are agreeable, they will approach you and let you know."

"And if they aren't?"

"Then you will never see them."

I shrug. What do I have to lose? "Okay—where and when?"

He tells me. I do my best not to wince. He cautions me to come alone, and I assure him I will. Then he turns and goes inside the temple, and I walk back the way I came.

I'm a block away from my hotel before I abruptly realize I never told him my name.

But he knew it anyway.

FOURTEEN

Apparently, the favorite spot for this mysterious kick-ass shaman to hang out in is a graveyard. At three in the morning.

I'm sitting on a gravestone, kicking my heels against the polished granite and wondering if I'm even in the right area. The monk told me to come here but didn't specify any particular plot or mausoleum, and this place is huge. It's illuminated by a moon a little past half full, and the gently rolling terrain seems to go on forever. I've been passing the time by reading tombstones, trying to decipher if the grave holds a thrope, a human, or a pire.

MISSED AND CHERISHED BY HIS PACK. Definitely a thrope.

BELOVED CHILD OF THE MOON. Ditto.

TAKEN FROM US TOO SOON. Could be either, but the dates are an undead giveaway—thropes don't live for six hundred years. "Too soon?" I mutter. His relatives have either a black sense of humor or an overwhelming one of entitlement. I'm also surprised they even bothered with a plot—after six centuries, there couldn't have been much left of a pire but dust. Maybe they buried him in a vacuum cleaner bag instead of a coffin.

TOO GOOD FOR THE HORRORS OF THIS WORLD.

That one stops me. A woman named Caroline Meyer, only thirty-seven when she did the Last Tango. Human, almost certainly, and a little too close to my own age for comfort. I decide to take a little break from my reading and pay more attention to my surroundings.

Which are still as deserted as they were before. I can hear traffic in the background, though—there's a major street that runs along one border, just out of sight on the other side of a hill—but other than that it's . . . well, dead.

But not spooky, weirdly enough. In a world full of vampires, werewolves, and golems, a graveyard seems sort of mundane—like a campground, or a Motel 6. If something were to suddenly stagger from one of the tombs, my first thought would be, *What, the poor guy can't afford a place with central heating?*

But that doesn't happen. I'm starting to think I don't meet whatever standards this super-shaman has for taking on a challenge, or maybe that he—or she—just isn't interested in helping out a human being from a neighboring dimension.

I wonder again about the monk knowing my name. Did it mean something, or was it just some sort of minor magic trick guys like him use to seem impressive and all-knowing? Was the monk more than he appeared to be, or just a show-off?

The terms *monk* and *show-off* didn't really go together. And identifying me wasn't really a minor trick, either; knowing someone's name was a big deal in magic, even I recognize that. So what—

"Urrm," someone says beside me.

I snap my head around. There, one grave over, perched on a headstone much like I'm perched on mine, is a skeleton.

A rather strange-looking skeleton, actually. It seems a little lopsided somehow, like maybe it was taken apart by one person and put back together by a passing group of drunken stuntmen with a grudge against osteopaths. Its bones are different sizes and in different stages of decay: Some are a bright, polished white, while others are chipped and yellowing. Its eyeballs sit in their sockets like marbles guarding the entrance to two little caves. It cocks its head at me and grins in a completely involuntary way.

"Hallo," it says. It has a very strange accent, like a Swede doing a bad impression of a Russian.

"Uh—hello."

"I think that maybe perhaps you are waiting for me, yes?"

You've got to be kidding . . . "Uh, no, no. I'm just waiting for a bus. Do you know if the Number Eight runs past midnight?"

"Hah! You are making with the jokes, now! That is humorous and also being funny!" It points at me with a hand missing two of its fingers. There's something strange about its head that I can't quite put my finger on.

"Yeah, yeah, okay. The monk sent you, right?"

"Indeed! You are needing my help, is that not correct?"

I sigh. "I guess . . . wait. Are you just here to take me to someone else?"

"You mean like a guide, what with all the leading and pointing you in the right directions?"

"That's what I was getting at."

"And maybe even taking you someplace and not showing you how to be getting lost?"

"Yeah."

"Oh. Then, no." It indicates itself with a bony thumb. "Myself am the one, baby! I and me alone, with the else of nobody!"

"Oooookay . . . and what, exactly, *are* you?"

Who knew it was possible for a fleshless skull to look hurt? "Whaaaaat? How can you be not knowing of the glory of my being who I am? I am *Gashadokuro*."

"Right. What the hell's a Gashadokuro?"

"It is being a fearsome creature made of the bones. *Special* bones, only."

I nod. "Uh-huh. What kind of bones, the ones that didn't pass quality control? Bones you found at yard sales? Cheap off-brand bones made in Taiwanese sweatshops?"

He doesn't have eyelids, but I swear he blinks. "No. Is made from people who have died from the not eating."

I lean a little closer and squint. "Sure. Except they aren't all even *bones,* are they? That's the handle of a tennis racket in your thigh."

"What? No, is just deformed. From the nastiness of the starving to death."

"And your skull. It's made out of plastic."

"That is most scurrilous lie!"

"I can see the seam from the mold. And a little embossed merchandising symbol."

His shoulders droop. He heaves a sigh. "Is true. Is not easy finding bones of people who starve until they dead. Not now. Why can't Gashadokuro use bones of people with bad hygiene? Or bones of people who talk in movies? Then I could be being mighty fearsome, you bet. Instead, me is being stuck with anorexics and people who get lost in woods."

Probably not a lot of those, either, in a world full of pires and thropes—and lems don't even *have* bones. I feel obscurely sorry for the guy. "That sucks, it really does. But, uh . . . what about me?"

He perks up. "Are you planning on the starving and the dying?"

"What? No. I meant my problem—"

"Too bad. I am thinking you could be losing some of the weight."

"Excuse me?"

"Fasting! Is great idea! Easy, too—just to be *not eating*. Anyone can be doing, even fat cow like you!"

I can't believe I came out to a deserted graveyard at three in the morning in order to be insulted by a thrift-store skeleton. "Look, bonehead, I'm not fat. Not that you're much of a judge, anyway—to you, *everybody* must look overweight, right?"

He sighs, a long, reedy wheeze. "Is true. Fleshy, fleshy people, everywhere. I am thinking you are all disgusting, if truth being told. But that is being Gashadokuro's problem, not yours. Your problem very different, yes?"

"Yes. I need—"

He holds up a finger bone. "I am knowing already. You are needing Gashadokuro's specialty in one area of the particular."

He hops off his gravestone. One of his ribs is loose and clatters against another when he moves. "Not to be worrying. I will be helping, in most glorious and spectacular fashion!"

"Terrific. So you can tell me how to beat this spell and make more bullets?"

He glances at me with eyes that roll around like ball bearings in a shot glass. "What? No. I am to be biting your head off."

"You're going to *what* now?"

He shrugs apologetically. "Bite your head off—it's what Gashadokuro does. Aren't you knowing *anything*?"

I jump down off my own gravestone and take a step backward. "Hold on there, funnybones. First of all, I thought you were here to *help* me. And second—no offense, but you're not exactly terrifying."

"Oh, two-part question. Gashadokuro hates those, but

will be doing his best to answer. First part, with the help-ing? Yes, absolutely, but please to replace *help* with *bite*. Is easy."

He takes a step toward me. His posture straightens from a partial crouch to something more upright, making him seem taller. "Second part. This part is better *show-ing* than *telling,* I am most sure . . ."

He's definitely taller than I first thought. At least six foot two, maybe three . . .

Four. Six. *Ten.*

I scramble backward as he takes another lengthening step forward. Seven feet. Nine. Twelve. The truncated ten-nis racket replacing one of his thigh bones is now the size of an ax handle. He stares down at me with eyes the size of glassy baseballs—and he's still getting bigger.

"You see, Jace Valchek? Is all being a matter of pro-portion. Even tiniest mouse is being fearsome when size of lion, am I not honestly true?"

His voice is getting bigger, too, booming through the quiet of the graveyard like a drunk in a library.

"Yeah, yeah, okay," I say. "No need to get all shouty."

I draw my scythes. A single smooth, cross-handed ac-tion, practiced hundreds of times, from two specially designed holsters sewn into the lining of my jacket. Eigh-teen inches of solid ironwood in each hand, tipped with a steel cone sheathed in silver. Good for taking down pires, thropes, or even lems.

Giant talking skeletons, I'm not so sure.

I lunge forward. His knee is about level with my chest now. I smash his patella with a hard, right-handed swing, fragmenting his kneecap into dozens of yellowing shards. In a human opponent, that would be a crippling, agoniz-ing wound; the effect it has on Boney G is to make his lower leg fall off.

He doesn't fall down, though, just shifts his weight to

his other leg and balances on that. He puts his hands on his hips and glares down at me indignantly from a height of at least twenty feet.

"What did you be doing that for?" he demands. "Now I'm needing new knee!"

"Maybe you can get a deal on a pair," I say, and go for the other one—but he's ready for me this time. He kicks me with his stump, the end of the femur slamming into my chest and tossing me backward. I smack into a crypt, taking a hard shot to my skull and making the world go a little wobbly. I shake my head, trying to clear it, as an irate, Jurassic Park–size Halloween novelty takes an experimental hop toward me.

"Is no use trying for the escape. I am *Gashadokuro!* I am to be *biting* off your *head!*"

I struggle to my feet, feeling dizzy and leaning against the crypt for support. "Why?" I gasp.

"Why am I to be biting off your head? Well, is *trap,* I suppose. Gashadokuro not bother with details—am *big-picture* guy." He chuckles, a sound like gravel rattling in a tin can. "Pretty funny, yes? *Big* picture!"

"No, I mean . . . why bite *anyone's* head off?"

"Am not following."

"You don't have a stomach. You don't have a throat. You don't, as far as I can tell, even have a *tongue.* So what's the point in eating *anything*—including my head?"

He puts one hand on the roof of the crypt to steady himself and studies me. "Hmm. Is good point. Interesting conundrum is being for sure. Except, of courses, for one thing."

"What's that?"

"Is not so much about the *eating,* Jace Valchek. Is about the *biting.*"

He lunges for my head. I dive and roll to the left, hearing

those big teeth chomp together in the spot I just vacated. The sound is oddly muffled, but I don't have time to think about that now—I leap to my feet and run.

It's a decent plan. Sure, he's big—in the sense that water is wet—but he's down to one working leg. And really, how fast can a gigantic pile of bones hop?

As it turns out, he doesn't *have* to be fast. He covers so much ground in a single jump that he can take his time, aim carefully, then come crashing down right on top of me—or at least where I was a second ago. It's like being chased by an anorexic Godzilla on a pogo stick.

He hops, I scurry. Darting between tombstones, behind mausoleums, around statuary, trying to put anything I can between me and him. If I can just get out of his line of sight, maybe I can sneak away.

A moment later I see my chance. There's a stand of pine trees at the base of a low hill, and once I'm in it the branches will obscure me for a few vital seconds.

I run for it. Behind me, Gashadokuro bellows, "Ha! *And now for the biting!*"

I expect to feel a huge, bony foot stomp down on me any instant . . . but I make it to the trees. I immediately skid to a stop, then duck behind the largest trunk and wait, trying to quiet my breathing. He may not have ears, but that doesn't mean he can't hear.

I hear him thump down at the edge of the trees. They're too tightly spaced for him to fit easily between, so he'll probably hop around them. Whichever way he goes, I go the other way.

Except he doesn't do that. I hear the creak of bones, and then I hear his voice again, a lot closer. At the same level as my head.

"Jace Valchek?" He must be bending down, like a guy chasing a mouse peering under a bed. "I am knowing

you are in there, Jace Valchek. I am even seeing you—
that tree is being skinnier than you, you know."

I sigh. What I wouldn't give for a fully loaded handgun
right now. I'd blast that idiotic grin right off this overgrown, underfed zombie wannabe in about two seconds . . .

But that's not an option. What I have are my scythes
and my brains, and that'll have to be enough.

And then I see the enormous, floating albino spider.

It's his hand, of course. He knows where the mouse is
and figures he can just reach in and grab it. Well, there's
a reason that's generally a bad idea: Mice *bite*.

It's the hand with three fingers. I look for older, cracked
or yellowing bones, and find one proximal phalange on
the index and a metacarpal on the thumb. I step out from
behind the tree as he gropes for me, and deliver two precise and very hard blows, shattering both bones, then dart
behind another tree.

"Kind of hard to grab something without a thumb,"
I say. "Of course, you still have one left. Wanna try
again?"

"Why are you making of this so difficult?" he com-
plains. "Why not just be giving up? There is nothing
stopping you."

"Guess I'm just difficult that way."

I've bought a moment to think, anyway. Should I keep
running, hope that putting the stand of trees between us
will buy me enough time? Or would it be better to stay
put, hope he decides to cut his losses and leave?

"I am not doing the giving up, Jace Valchek!" he shouts.
"Gashadokuro is being very, very patient!"

Great.

So it's a standoff, me versus a giant, hopping skeleton
with bad grammar. I love my life, I really do . . . but I'm
a little short on patience myself. "Hey! Bone boy!"

"Yes, toothy morsel?"

"I don't have time for this. How about we—"

I don't finish my sentence. Instead, I dart out from behind my tree and take off at a dead run.

Straight toward my adversary.

Gash doesn't seem like the sharpest bone blade in the drawer, and it's considerably harder to maneuver on one leg than two. The element of surprise, better overall dexterity, and his lack of a lower leg means I can dash right under his dangling stump before he can effectively react. I snap the blades of the scythes out as I run, two gleaming, eighteen-inch-long razors that lock at a forty-five-degree angle.

"Whah—sneaky! But you are not doing the escaping—"

Wouldn't dream of it, Gashy old boy. I stop and spin around once I'm behind him. Now, let's see; the ankle-bone's connected to the . . . *knee* bone . . . which is about three feet above my head.

I jump and swing both scythes, but I'm not trying for impact this time; I hook one blade over the top of the fibula on his good leg, where the bone juts out a little before butting up against the femur, and the other around the joint and over the kneecap. I'm wearing good shoes with grippy soles, and I scale his tibia easily.

"What? That is not being of the fair, Jace Valchek!" He tries to brush me off with his stump, but misses. I climb higher, hooking the blades behind his femur and walking up the bone like a logger using a belt harness and spiked shoes to zip up a tree.

"Stop! You are girl, not squirrel!"

"That's good, because you're sadly lacking in nuts," I mutter, and swing a scythe right through where they'd be if he had any. I hook one blade through the obturator foramen, a round hole in the pelvic bone that muscles and nerves feed through, pull myself a little higher, and get the other on one of the lower vertebrae.

He's swatting at me now, trying to dislodge me without losing his balance, but I'm in an awkward spot. One bony hand does make contact, though, slamming into my thigh and knocking my feet loose. I hang on grimly, pulling myself up with my arms, getting my feet on top of the pelvic girdle.

"No! No! No!" Gash shouts. "Is being *all wrong,* Jace Valchek! You are making the nicks and scratches! You must be gettting down, nasty girl!"

Oh, I'll show you nasty. I've got him right where I want him now, and I clamber up his spine and rib cage as easily as using a ladder. He can't even reach me anymore—I'm at that precise spot you develop a burn when you go to the beach alone, because you can't quite get to it with the sunscreen.

"Hey, Gasho? What do you say we stop flailing around and have a conversation, yes? Or, you know, I could just chop your head off."

He stops trying to hit me and freezes in place.

"Yeah, I thought that might get your attention. See, while solid bone might be difficult to hack through, plastic is not. And that's what your enormous skull is still made of, right?"

"I . . . am guessing you wouldn't be believing me if I say no."

"Not so much. Now, a real skull is connected to the spine with all sorts of muscles and tendons and nerves, but a fake skull? Not only are all the fleshy parts missing, but the basic structure isn't even the same; I'm pretty sure your head is perched on top of your spinal column like an apple balanced on a fencepost, with the only thing holding that sucker on being magic. And magic doesn't tend to hold up to silvered blades real well, does it? I'm thinking one good swipe at the base of your noggin and the whole thing will pop right off. Want to see if I'm right?"

"No, no, that is not being neccesary."

It might seem like I've won, but this isn't over yet. I'm still perched far too high off the ground, and if Gashy figures out I can't decapitate him without dooming myself, he's not only going to call my bluff but probably just keel over backward and let gravity take care of me. I do *not* want my tombstone to read CRUSHED BY A GIANT PLASTIC SKULL.

"Let us everybody be calming down, Jace Valchek. There is no need for the violent behaving! We can being discussing this like the clever rationals we are."

"Okay. Let's sit down and hash this out, all right? And by sit down, I mean *slowly*."

I've got one blade hooked around a cervical vertebra and the other poised to strike if he tries anything. If I'm going down, it's going to be on top of a headless pile of bones—which actually sounds a lot worse than just hitting the ground.

But Gashy doesn't figure it out. He squats down carefully into a cross-legged position, making no attempt to shake me off. Guess he's not used to his prey biting back.

"Hokay. Am doing the sitting. Now please to be not knocking off my block, yes?"

"We'll see."

Well, at least I'm a lot closer to terra firma than I was a minute ago—a fall from here is definitely survivable. As long as I don't hit one of the gazillion headstones down there, of course. "What's the deal, Gash? Who was that monk, and why did he send you to kill me?"

"I am telling you for the last of time, Jace Valchek— was not for *killing*. Was for—"

"—the *biting*, yeah, yeah, I know. Answer the question."

He sighs. "It was . . ."

"Yes?"

"The fishies."

"The *fishies*."

"Yes. They are being *most* angry with you, Jace Valchek."

He sounds sincere, but I have no idea what the hell he's talking about. "*What* fishies? And why?"

"For the *murder,* Jace Valchek. For the murder, and all the *eating.*"

"What?"

"Salmon. Shrimp. Yellowtail. Mackeral. And *tuna,* Jace Valchek." His voice is still dead serious, almost mournful. "All the poor, slaughtered tuna . . . especially the *spicy* ones."

Sushi. He's trying to tell me this is about *sushi.*

"That's why they are coming to *me,* Jace Valchek. Because you are to be punished for your terrible, terrible hunger—and I am *knowing* about hunger. Gashadokuro is being *all about* the hunger."

"Yeah, sure, Big Bones. You're trying to tell me you were hired by what, a consortium of fish ghosts from all the sashimi I've every eaten? Do I have GULLIBLE tattooed on my forehead or something?"

"Do not be laughing, Jace Valchek. Is very, very serious. Spirits are being in everything—fish, also. And fish have gods, too . . ."

What he's saying—though still ludicrous—almost makes sense. The basic principle of animist magic is that everything *does* have a spirit inside it, and who's to say that some of those spirits wouldn't band together for a little revenge . . .

I shake my head. "Let's say there's some grain of truth to your story. How'd they contact you? What name did they refer to themselves as?"

"I can't be telling, Jace Valchek," he whispers. "Oh, no. Gashadokuro is being much, much too frightened of them. Worse things than having your head cut off, yes . . ."

He leans backward abruptly, twisting at the same time. He catches himself with his elbows at the last second before he hits the ground, but my scythe slides off his vertebrae and I'm thrown off.

I smack into earth a lot softer than I thought it was going to be, though it still knocks the breath out of me. I've been lucky enough to land on the fresh dirt of a recently filled-in grave—but with a giant skeleton about to use me as a breath mint, lucky is not how I feel.

Except Gash isn't pressing his advantage. He's scrambled to his feet—well, foot—and is hopping away as fast as he can go, shrinking at the same time. The combination makes it look like he's moving twice as fast as he actually is, receding into the distance at an amazing rate. Guess I put the fear of Jace into him.

Or maybe it was the fear of fishies.

I get up slowly. "Well, *that* was a fun evening," I wheeze. "I think I'll find a nice sharp stick to poke in my eye and then I'll call it a night."

Which is when I hear the sirens.

"You've *got* to be kidding," I say.

"Nope," the cop replies, and keeps filling out the ticket.

I'm in the back of a radio car. Not in cuffs, but still being detained. Neither of the two patrolmen—a blank-faced pire with freckles and a yellow sand lem—that pulled up in it seems terribly impressed with my NSA credentials. The lem even asked me what they stood for.

"It's illegal to be in a *graveyard*?" I repeat.

"It is when it's closed," the lem replies. I've never seen a lem with a gut before, but I think this one spends so much time sitting that he's started to spread out. "Posted hours are right on the gate. Not open at present."

"But—when are all the pires supposed to visit their dead relatives, high noon?"

The freckle-faced pire turns and looks at me with professional neutrality. "You're not a hemovore, ma'am."

"Thank you, Captain Obvious. But I really don't understand what the problem is here; I mean, it's not like any of the residents are going to complain that I was stomping around on their rooftops. Or am I mistaken? Is there some kind of back-to-basics movement I'm not aware of, with graves in style again? Pires trying to get closer to their roots, or maybe just closer to roots in general?"

The lem grunts. It's a noise he seems fond of, and makes often.

"No, no, I see what it is," I continue. "This is the pire version of camping, right? Go down to the local boneyard, sleep out under the freshly turned earth, sing a few songs around the old funeral pyre—"

"Pires don't camp in graveyards," Freckles says. He seems to have had his sense of humor surgically removed.

"Ah. Well, thanks for clearing that up."

A cell phone trills. The lem pulls his out of a shirt pocket and answers. "Yeah? Well, why didn't you just—oh. Yeah. That's right, Valchek. Uh-huh. Uh-huh. Well, you'll have to make it right with dispatch, because this is already—yeah? You can? No, no, I got no problem with that. Have to be quick, though. Yeah, he'll be all right with it. Yeah, I'm sure. Okay. Okay, we'll get right on it. Later."

He hangs up and leans over to his partner. Whispers something I can't hear. Freckle-face stops writing, glances back at me, then puts his ticket pad away.

"What?" I say. "You guys get a little yank from the chain of command? From somebody over your heads who's actually heard of the National Security Agency?"

The lem doesn't answer, just starts the patrol car. Freckle-face turns to look at me and actually smiles.

"Somebody's definitely heard of you," he says. "Matter of fact, we're bringing you to him right now. Can't guarantee how glad you'll be to see him, though . . ."

FIFTEEN

The cops bring me to what I assume is the ritzy part of town—if the carefully manicured hedges and tall metal gates blocking every driveway are any indication—and right up to the front door of a very large house with a red, pagoda-style roof. They don't take me inside, though, instead marching me around the side of the building and down a meandering, pebbled path lit by waist-high Japanese lanterns made of stone. They ignore all my attempts at finding out who I'm about to meet or why, though they do talk to each other:

"So," the lem says, "you been here before, right?"

"Once," the pire says. "Did a thing for them. Came here to get a pat on the head."

"What, you mean like a bonus?"

"Nah, this guy wouldn't hand a cop anything himself— too careful. This was more a whaddayacallit, expression of respect. Face-to-face. Cultural thing, I guess."

"Okay, I get that." The lem pauses. "So, no bonus, then."

"Not everything gets paid off in cash. There's favors, too. That's worth a lot."

"Right. You really think a guy like this is gonna do us a favor?"

"He might. Could be the favor is more like something he *doesn't* do."

The lem frowns. They've got me sandwiched between them in case I try to run. "I don't get it."

"You know. Maybe you screw up. Maybe you piss off the wrong person. Something like that happens, he could intervene, give you a pass."

"Oh." The lem considers that. "Think I'd rather have the bonus, myself."

"Corruption and stupidity," I say. "Back together for the first time. You're not even an enforcement lem—what, the police department couldn't afford the real thing?"

"Budget cutbacks," the pire says.

"Hey, that's racist," the lem says, sounding wounded. "The color of my skin doesn't define what I can do—"

"You're animated by the life force of a *cow,*" the pire says. "Not even a bull. A *dairy* cow."

"So?"

"So it's not like you have the instincts of a killer. You've got the instincts of something that eats grass and is used to being milked twice a day."

"That's not just racist, it's sexist."

"How can it be sexist? You don't have *that,* either."

This fascinating exchange is cut short by the path winding around a corner and into a more open area. I can see a still pool with a low waterfall trickling into it; a few fat, golden koi hover just under the surface. Mossy boulders loom artistically around the edge of the water, and a gray stone bench with a single occupant rests beside the path. He gets to his feet as we approach.

I recognize him instantly. It's Isamu.

I haven't seen him since our first meeting, at his estate in Japan. That was when my flippant attitude and smart mouth ticked him off enough that he decided to add me to his personal blood distillery; I disagreed with this decision, and demonstrated my feelings accordingly.

Things went downhill from there.

Isamu is a very old pire and member of the Yakuza, which makes him bloodthirsty twice over. He claims he's never tasted the blood of an animal, and I believe him.

He's wearing a simple black kimono, just like the first time we met. I doubt that's a coincidence. I can see hints of his tattoos peeking out from the edges of the robe, a design I remember vividly: layer after layer of faces, only the eyes visible, portraits of every human being he's ever drunk from. Trophies, etched into his immortal skin with magic and ink.

He smiles when he sees me. He's not terribly imposing, physically; a little over five feet tall, slight of build, balding on top. His remaining hair is jet black, worn long and tied back into a loose tail.

This is not a guy who needs to look scary. This is a guy who *is* scary, and knows it. Anyone who ever comes face-to-face with him knows it, too, or they don't live long enough to matter—with the exception of yours truly. I made all kinds of trouble, insulted him to his face, and got his best assassin turned into something you'd beat out of a rug.

But that was when I had Tanaka and Charlie at my back, and a fully loaded Super Redhawk Alaskan in my hand. Right now I don't even have my scythes; they're back in the police car, locked in the trunk. Yeah, this should be fun . . .

"Ms. Valchek," Isamu says. "How pleasant to see you again."

"Wish I could say the same, Isamu. What are you doing in Canada? Did your own country finally throw you out?"

"I have interests in many places, especially on the Pacific Rim. I'm merely here to sign off on a few business transactions before returning home." His tone is amused, almost gleeful, and why not? He's got me right where he wants me, and he intends to draw this out. With any luck, I'll expire of old age or boredom before he gets around to the actual revenge.

"Yeah, I paid a visit to one of your outlets," I say. "Nice little place, though a bit understaffed. Actually, by the time I left the place was practically abandoned."

His smile gets a little wider. "Yes, I'm sure it was. A pity. It was a most productive facility, and its output will be missed. I suppose the replacement will have to work even harder to make up for the lost revenue."

With yours truly as the star heifer, of course. I refuse to show fear—what I'm mainly feeling is anger. This monster is the one that deserves a slow, torturous sentence, not me. "Sorry, Isamu—I'm kind of busy these days. Tell you what—why don't I pencil you in for a lunch date, sometime soon? You and I can share a nice stake."

He chuckles. "Your empty bravado only heightens my pleasure, Ms. Valchek. But if my plans for you were as dire as you believe, we would not be having this conversation here. We would be conducting it in a sterile environment, with you strapped to a gurney."

"Imagine my relief. What do you want, Isamu?"

"I want to show you something." He turns, motioning me to follow him, and strolls down the path. Not having much of a choice, I do as he suggests. The cops stay where they are.

The path follows the edge of the pond, illuminated by paper lanterns hung from the trees. The patches of algae on the pond look to me like minature green continents.

We stop in front of an immense bell hanging amid four wooden posts, the surface patinaed with a subtler green and inscribed with many *kanji*. "Hey, this reminds me of a joke," I say. "There's this monk up in a bell tower—"

Isamu draw his hand back and makes a fist. He strikes the bell with it.

The sound that emerges is deep, sonorous, otherworldly. I feel it as much as hear it, as if it's resonating on exactly the same frequency as my bones.

It's getting louder.

I can't hear anything else. It's not just my bones that are vibrating in sympathy, it's my whole body. My vision is shaking along with everything else, and it feels like the whole world is coming apart.

Then it does.

Reality shatters, falling away in shards. Everything—the pond, the trees, the path—smashes to pieces. All that's left is me, Isamu, and the bell.

But there's another reality underneath, a swirling, blurry mass of color that gradually slows and comes into focus, resolving into a landscape of lush green. We're on the crest of a hill, thick with grass and dotted with wild-flowers. Below us is a valley, with a river gently mean-dering through it, and what looks like a small town. The sky is a vibrant, cloudless blue, the air full of the smells of high summer, from ripe fruit to sun-warmed meadow. I can hear birdsong, and distant laughter.

"What the *fuck*?" I say.

Despite the bright sunshine, Isamu stubbornly refuses to burst into flame. His smile is gone, though, as if the bucolic setting offends him on some deep, instinctual level. "Not what you expected, Ms. Valchek?"

"That's putting it mildly. What are you going to do now, try to sell me a time share in a condo?"

"In a manner of speaking. I have brought you here for a very specific reason, and it concerns an important deci-sion on your part."

"And what would that be?"

Isamu shakes his head. "Not yet, Ms. Valchek. You do not possess all the knowledge you need to make an informed choice. First, you need to examine your surroundings. Acquaint yourself with the locals. When you feel you know what you need to, then we shall talk."

I frown. "That's it? You want me to wander around, strike up a few conversations?"

"You will understand the purpose of this exercise soon enough."

"And what about you?"

"I will remain on this hilltop and wait. My movements here are somewhat restricted, but yours are not."

"Yeah? So what's to stop me from just taking off and not coming back?"

He smiles, ever so slightly. "The fact that the bell is the only way to leave."

I look around. Behind me is a mountain, and that's putting it mildly; it's the biggest mountain I've ever seen, one that makes Mount Fuji look like an anthill. It goes up and up until it literally fades out of sight behind some clouds at the edge of the stratosphere—you could probably jump from the peak onto a passing satellite, or maybe the moon. "I hope you don't expect me to climb *that*."

He chuckles. "No. That is beyond your reach. Go down to the village—you will be surprised at what you find."

Again, it doesn't look like I have much choice. I start hiking down the hill, and don't bother saying good-bye. I have no idea what's going on, or what's waiting for me down there.

But I don't think I'm going to like it.

The hill isn't steep, or very high. It only takes me a few minutes to reach the bottom, and when I stop and look back I can still see Isamu standing at the crest beside the bell. He doesn't wave, and neither do I.

The village sits right at the base of the hill. I'm not sure what to expect from it, but I doubt I'm going to encounter anything dangerous. This place just doesn't *feel* dangerous. In fact, it feels peaceful and homey and almost serene.

Which is a pretty good description of the village, too. Small structures in a variety of styles and materials: bamboo huts, adobe cubes, even animal-skin tepees. The inhabitants are a real mixture, too: Caucasian, Asian, African, Indian. The clothes are all simple and utilitarian, but again, there are examples of a dozen different cultures.

And everyone seems to be human.

Nobody acts as if my sudden appearance here is odd. I get a lot of smiles and nods, though nobody actually approaches me. I'm not quite sure what to do next; the unrelenting cheeriness of the place is starting to seriously creep me out, like I just wandered into some kind of supernatural Epcot Center full of idealized Real People in their native human costumes. Any second now one of them is going to try to sell me a pair of mouse ears, or maybe a few will start spewing smoke as their robot brains short-circuit.

Doesn't happen. What does is far, far stranger.

"Hey. Don't I know you?"

I know that voice.

I turn slowly, thinking I have to be wrong. I'm not.

Standing in front of me is FBI agent Roger Trent. The same Roger Trent I used to be engaged to, the same Roger Trent who betrayed me, stole my promotion, and in general revealed himself to be a complete scumbag. The Roger Trent who is, as far as I know, still working for the FBI back on the world I was born on and grew up in.

He walks forward, a puzzled smile on his face. Still tall, still good looking, still fit. He's dressed in a white T-shirt and faded blue jeans, well-worn sneakers on his feet. "I can't quite remember where from, but—"

I let him get about four feet away before I clock him.

It's not my best punch. My best punch would have broken his jaw, taken out a few teeth, and possibly given him a concussion. No, this is pure reflexive fury, pent-up frustration I've been carrying around so long I forgot it was even there. It feels unbelievably good to unload some of it.

It knocks him off his feet. He sprawls on his back in the dirt, looking dazed and not a little confused. No blood, though. I glance around, but everyone seems oblivious to the sudden violence. Interesting.

"*Now* I remember you," Roger says groggily, sitting up and gingerly feeling his chin. "You were there when I *died*."

Uh-oh . . .

Normally, I love the sensation when everything finally lines up and locks into place, that feeling of rock-solid certainty that you get when you figure out what's actually going on. Not this time.

This isn't my Roger. This is the Roger from Thropirelem, the one Stoker sacrificed as part of a ritual to wake up an Elder God.

This Roger is dead.

I know where I am.

I sigh, and take another look around. Nothing but gentle, smiling faces looking back. Damn. I was really hoping there'd be more scotch. And male strippers. And houses made out of chocolate, filled with male strippers who would bring me scotch. Ah, well, at least nobody seems to be carrying a harp . . .

I hold out my hand, which Roger 2.0 stares at for a moment before taking and letting me pull him to his feet.

"Sorry about that. Thought you were someone else."

"That's okay. Didn't actually hurt—nothing does, here. Just caught me by surprise is all."

I nod. "So. This is it, huh? The End of the Line, the Big Finish, the Final Reward?"

"The Afterlife, you mean?"

"That's where I was going, yeah."

He gives me a big, beatific smile. "Well, you don't have to worry about where you're going, not anymore. You're *here*. Welcome to Heaven . . ."

I just stare at him.

Game over. Apparently, I won.

Now what?

I wish I could say things aren't that simple. But—according to Roger, anyway—they really are.

He tells me as much as he can. Yes, he's exactly who and what he seems to be. Yes, there's a lot more to Heaven than what I see—this is just the part of it he and his fellow villagers prefer.

We're sitting on a bench in the center of the village. The longer he talks, the more I believe him—it's not so much what he says, it's everything around him. The air is too fresh, too clean. The smells are universally pleasant. The colors are slightly oversaturated, better than real, and every sound has this wonderful, crisp quality. Even the bench I'm sitting on somehow seems like the best bench ever, the smooth cool surface of the stone exactly right. It's like the whole place was run through a very fine conceptual mesh and had every little flaw removed.

"—so that was how I died," Roger says. "I don't mind talking about that. But some things I can't discuss . . . like the Powers in charge here. You understand that, right?"

"Not really. What, even in Paradise I need security clearance?"

"There are some things the living aren't ready to know."

"You mean I'm still alive?"

He grins. "Oh, yes. I didn't realize right away, but I've been . . . *advised* since then."

Sure. Angels whispering in his ear, no doubt. "So if I'm still alive, what am I *doing* here? You guys decide to explore the possibilities of tourism or something?"

Now Roger looks a little uncomfortable. "No, of course not. But this isn't exactly without precedent; living souls have been given glimpses of Heaven before."

Sure—prophets, usually. Not NSA agents who've been kidnapped by vampire Yakuza warlords. "*Why* am I here?"

"I don't know. How did you get here?"

"It wasn't my choice." I tell him about the bell, and what happened when Isamu struck it.

He nods. "Magic, then. Powerful sorcerers can visit other planes of existence—even this one—though they can't stay for long. This Isamu—he's waiting for you on the hill?"

"So he says."

"He can't go far from the bell. I'm surprised you can, actually."

"Maybe he's planning on stranding me here."

Rogers shakes his head. "Can't be done. When he goes back, you'll go with him."

He tilts his head abruptly, as if he's listening to something I can't hear, then smiles. "Oh. I see."

"What?"

"You're here to see *me*, of course."

"Why?"

"You'll have to figure that one out yourself."

My eyes narrow. My Roger had a tendency toward smugness that I never liked, and this one has it, too. Come to think of it, from what Stoker told me about this guy, he shared a few other traits with my version. "Don't take this the wrong way, but . . . you don't seem like you really belong here."

He looks back at me mildly. "Why would you say that?"

"Because I knew someone a lot like you—practically a twin, in fact. And he wouldn't make the cut for a place like this, not in a thousand years."

"Then I guess he and I aren't that much alike after all, are we?"

Hard to argue with that—but that's never stopped me. "Oh, I think you are. You were a car salesman, right? Liked to deal a little Bane on the side?"

He looks puzzled. "I worked for a car dealership, sure—but I never sold drugs. I was never in any trouble at all until those terrorists kidnapped me."

"That's not what I was told."

"Oh? And who told you, exactly? The guy who killed me?"

I open my mouth, then shut it again. Of course Stoker would have told me that his victim was a scumbag; he was trying to convince me to join him at the time. This Roger grew up in a very different world from the man who betrayed me—and maybe he grew up to be a better person, too. It all comes down to Nature versus Nurture, I guess, and which one has the greater effect.

I look around at where this Roger wound up, and I'm forced to admit that maybe—just maybe—he turned out to be a reasonably decent human being.

As if he's reading my mind, Roger says, "Okay, I was far from perfect. I probably got by a little too much on charm. I could be selfish. But I wasn't a monster—I was just *human*. Like you."

"And like everyone else here?"

He hesitates, just for a second. "Oh, no. Heaven isn't divided into *species,* Jace. This village is mostly human because we feel comfortable with one another, but there's nothing exclusionary about it. There are other villages—and towns, and cities, and islands, and forests . . . every environment you can think of. Everyone is free to come and go as they wish."

"So . . . what exactly do you *do* with all this freedom?"

"Whatever we want, Jace. Whatever we want."

I think about that. "Well, I can tell you one thing—given unlimited freedom, the Roger I knew wouldn't be spending it in an idyllic little village smelling wildflowers."

"I'm not the man you knew, Jace. But I think I understand why you're supposed to talk to me."

I shift on the bench to study him. "Why?"

"Incentive."

"Incentive to do what? Die? Now, *that's* a strategy I haven't seen before: Go ahead and get yourself killed, it's not so bad."

"I don't think that's it. I think maybe you just need to believe in redemption."

Maybe he's right. Maybe this Roger being here, now, is supposed to show me that people can change, that there's some good in all of us.

Yeah, sure. Except that the person who brought me here is not a good person, and never will be. In fact, I'm amazed he can come within a thousand dimensions of this place without bursting into flame, let alone be able to set foot here. I have no idea what Isamu is trying to pull—maybe it's some sort of bribe instead of a threat? If so, I'm still not getting it.

I guess I'd better go ask him.

It doesn't take me long to trudge back up the hill. Isamu's sitting cross-legged beside his bell like some kind of busker with the world's most inappropriate instrument.

"Okay, I've been to town and seen the sights. What's your point?"

He gets to his feet with one smooth, fluid motion. "You talked to Mr. Trent?"

"I did."

"You believe he is who he says he is? That this place is what he claims it to be?"

I sigh. "I grilled him pretty thoroughly on how he died. He had all the details right. And this place—well, if it's not Heaven, it's a damn good imitation."

"It is exactly what it seems to be, Ms. Valchek. I am a powerful man, but surely you do not believe that even I could create an entire plane of reality simply to fool you?"

"Okay, I'll grant that this seems to actually be some sort of . . . other-dimensional realm populated by spirits. So I'm going to say it again—*what* is your *point*?"

His answer is to turn and strike the bell again.

Once more, everything starts to vibrate. I'm a little more prepared this time, but it's still unpleasant and disorienting and goes on for far too long.

We're back where we started, beside the pond. I shake my head, trying to clear it, feeling slightly nauseous.

"Here is my point, Ms. Valchek. You are interfering in matters that do not concern you, and this is complicating things that should remain simple. I can forgive the attack on my blood farm, because you were obviously duped into it by Aristotle Stoker. What I cannot countenance is your meddling in the affairs of the Hemo Corporation. It is simply a business, one poised to become quite profitable through entirely legitimate methods, and your blundering about has the potential to disrupt delicate negotiations now under way. I will not have this."

He turns to me, his hands clasped behind his back. "You will leave this city, this province, this country. You will abandon your investigation. Or I will bar you from Heaven for eternity."

I have to hand it to him; as far as overreaching, grandiose threats go, this has to be near the very top. "And how do you plan to do that? You expect me to believe you have some kind of deal with—"

"It is not a question of any sort of 'deal.' I used the principle of Cosmic Harmonics to bring you to Heaven, and I used the same method to bring you back. But the return trip was not quite the same, was it?"

I don't answer. But he's right—it felt different, subtly wrong, like hearing an instrument that's out of tune. I can still feel it, actually, a kind of subliminal vibration in my body and brain.

"I altered your essential being," Isamu says. "On an extremely basic level. Your spirit cannot return to that place, not ever—it will reject your very soul. Your own shamans will verify your condition. It is one that will last for the rest of your life and even beyond . . . unless, of course, you do exactly as I say."

SIXTEEN

The cops drive me back to the downtown core. They even give my scythes back. I don't say much during the trip, and neither do they—not until the very end, after they've let me out of the car. Before he gets back into the passenger seat, the pire says, "Word of advice? Whatever he wants, let him have it. Nobody crosses this guy and lives to talk about it."

That almost makes me laugh. Almost. "Funny. It's not the living part I'm worried about."

The pire gets back in the patrol car, and they drive off. Guess I can't count on backup from local law enforcement.

I have a lot to think about on my walk back to the hotel. I call Charlie and Eisfanger on the way, tell them I'm all right and that I need Damon to do a thorough check on the status of my soul. He says he'll have everything set up by the time I get there.

It's still dark, but dawn's not far off. It's probably stupid of me to even be on the street at this time, but I don't want to take a cab. I need to keep moving. And frankly, I feel sorry for anyone foolish enough to try to mug me right now.

Heaven. No Jace Valcheks allowed. What does that even *mean*? Do I go straight to the other place, or does my condition keep me out of there, too? Do I spend eternity pin-balling back and forth, or do I wind up like a metaphysical bug squashed against God's windshield or Satan's grille? Is there some kind of bargain-basement afterlife I could get into instead, maybe a place with harmonicas and roller skates instead of harps and wings?

Maybe there's an appeal process. I mean, how does an evil piece of crap pire get away with dictating terms to the Almighty, anyway? Can't I lodge a formal complaint? Or just march into a church and demand to speak to a supervisor?

Oy.

This is too big to wrap my brain around. I don't even know if Isamu's telling the truth yet; I'll have to see what Damon says. In the meantime, I'm determined to treat it the same way I treat any threat to my personal safety—ignore it, put my head down, and charge straight ahead.

When I get to the hotel, I go right to Eisfanger's room. He and Charlie are waiting for me; Damon's already got the bed shoved against the wall and a warded circle set up on the floor.

"That's it," Charlie says. "I'm getting a pair of bracelets with a nice thick chain, and one of 'em is going around your wrist."

"Do me a favor and lock the other one to an angry wolverine, would you? I could use the peace and quiet."

Eisfanger tells me to sit inside the circle. He holds a small metal bowl level with my breastbone and runs a stubby finger steadily around the rim. An eerie tone rises up from the bowl, then starts to pulse. Eisfanger stops what he's doing. He looks worried.

"That's—not good," he says.

"So Isamu was telling the truth?"

"I need to do more tests."

Which he does. He draws blood, he chants, he taps away

on his laptop. He raps a tuning fork in the vicinity of my chakras and listens carefully to the result. He burns some herbs, rubs the soot into my spine, and makes me spit in a copper goblet.

Charlie watches all this with his arms crossed, leaning against the wall. I can't tell if he's angry at me, at Isamu, or himself. Probably all three.

"It's not your fault, Charlie. It was a total fluke that I wound up in the hands of two corrupt cops."

"Uh-huh. So how'd your middle-of-the-night meeting in the graveyard go?"

"Um . . . fine."

"Get your little ammunition problem cleared up?"

"Well, not really. Turned out to be sort of a dead end."

"Much like the fate of your immortal soul?"

"Maybe. Ask Eisfanger."

Eisfanger looks up from his laptop. "I can tell you this much for sure: Yes, you've had your harmonic balance altered. I can't reverse the situation, and I doubt anyone but Isamu can. And yes, the spell seems to be keyed to a particular dimensional frequency, and structured to resonate just out of sync with it. Wherever he took you, you're not going back."

"That much I figured. The real question is, was that Heaven or not?"

Eisfanger looks deeply troubled. "I don't know."

"What do you mean, you don't know? You're a shaman *and* a scientist—you took readings, you measured things, you studied the data. How can you know the dimensional frequency of someplace and *not* know whether or not it has Pearly Gates at the entrance?"

Eisfanger shakes his head. "For one thing, because there are a *lot* of spiritual realms. For another, information on any sort of afterlife tends to be contradictory, incomplete, and impossible to quantify. It's nothing but a collection of personal experiences that rarely mesh with one another. Most people agree there's some kind of existence after death, but exactly what kind is highly subjective. About the only thing that's anywhere near consistent is cultural influence—people from the same ethnic background tend to have the same kind of experience."

"So I went to Heaven, but not the *only* Heaven?"

Eisfanger hesitates. "Yes, but—"

"But what?"

"There's a good chance it was, in fact, *your* Heaven."

"Why?"

"The way you were brought there. I can't be sure without examining the bell itself, but considering the principles involved, he most likely focused the bell's vibrations through you. He was driving, but it was your essence that told him where to go. That's how I would have done it, anyway." He frowns. "Did you see anything familiar there? Somebody you know, maybe?"

I let out a long, slow breath. "Just a guy I watched die once."

"Oh."

"Wait. I'm not *from* here, right?" I say. "Shouldn't I go to whatever afterlife exists in my *own* reality?"

"Actually, no," Eisfanger says. "Souls don't automatically cross the dimensional divide on death. You'd stay in this universe—it's just a question of which sub-dimension."

First time I've ever heard of Heaven and Hell referred to as sub-dimensions. Kind of like the suburbs, only with a longer commute.

Nobody says anything for a long moment.

"Well," says Charlie. "Guess it's a good thing Heaven was never really an option for you in the first place, right?"

I give him the best smile I can muster. It's not very good.

"Don't take it so hard," Charlie says gruffly. "You're not gonna die for a long, long time. I guarantee it."

I almost believe him.

I lie in the darkness, staring at the ceiling, and think.

What's really interesting is that Isamu didn't just kill me. The only reason for that is because he can't, and that means that killing me would cause more trouble than scaring me off. Whatever he's up to, he wants me out of the way with the minimum of fuss—which means no investigation into the murder of an NSA agent.

Gashadokuro certainly seemed to be doing his best to kill me, but he didn't strike me as a professional assassin. And the two cops who took me to Isamu didn't seem like they were there specifically to target me; more like they were part of a larger effort and just happened to get lucky. That means there's another player in all this—and somehow, I don't think it's "the fishies."

Isamu mentioned delicate negotiations. With who? Potential investors? Possible, but the Yakuza has plenty of cash; if it's trying to woo financial partners, an enormous amount of money must be at stake. Government-level funds, or at the very least multinational corporations.

Or maybe the negotiations aren't strictly about economic considerations. Maybe they have to do with alliances, agreements. Hemo is in the midst of brokering deals with an uncountable number of Kami, and those are exactly the kind of talks that can easily break down—trying to hammer out a contract with, say, the Spirit of Thunderstorms might mean dealing with abrupt flashes of anger and/or bouts of weeping. So it could be that Isamu doesn't want to risk ticking off a particular spirit by simply eliminating me—though I have no idea which one would be put out by me meeting an intimely end. Is there a Kami of Unreasonable Stubbornness?

I turn the facts over and over in my mind, looking for the thread that links them all, the pattern I know is there. I can feel it, but it won't materialize. Something else is there, blocking the way, distracting me. I know what it is, but I don't want to admit it.

I'm scared.

Fear is nothing new to me, or any cop. We just find ways to deal with it, live with it, acknowledge its presence without letting it interfere with our work.

But this is different.

For all his threats, Isamu never really scared me. I don't care how long he's lived or how many terrible things he's done, in the end he's just another bad guy who thinks he can beat the system. He's wrong—they always are. They make a mistake and then I get them. It's really that simple.

But this situation has me spooked. It's easier to risk death when you don't know what's on the other side, and now I do: a big sign reading DO NOT PASS GO, DO NOT COLLECT YOUR ETERNAL REWARD. Suddenly, I have a real, genuine reason to not want to die.

Okay, that sounds a little nuts. What, before this happened I didn't *care* if I lived or died? No, of course not.

It's just that now, I care *more*.

It's a brilliant strategy. Guaranteed to make me nervous, insecure, prone to second-guessing myself. Even if I don't knuckle under, Isamu's got me at a definite disadvantage. Forget menacing my life, or even my friends and family— here's a nice existential crisis to slow me down.

There's a knock at my door. "Jace? You still awake?" It's Eisfanger.

I get up, throw on a robe, open the door. "What's up?"

"With all the excitement, I forgot to tell you—Stoker had this delivered to the front desk." Damon's holding a cardboard box with a folded piece of paper on top. "I've already examined it, but I thought you'd want to, too."

I take the box and step back into my room, motioning Damon in with a jerk of my head. "What is it?"

He steps inside and closes the door. "Possessions of one of the pire kids that disappeared—that's what the note said, anyway."

I unfold the note and read it. *Jace: This belonged to one of the missing children, a pire named Wendell—I managed to track it down in a pawnshop. Don't know if your shaman can pull any psychic traces off it, but thought you should have the chance.*

I put the box down on the bed, open it, and peer at what's inside.

It's a baseball glove.

"I've run all the tests I can think of," Eisfanger says. "Couldn't find anything that will help us locate the owner, but I can verify it belonged to a pire boy named Wendell."

I pull the glove out. It's a soft, faded brown, the gilt lettering of the brand name almost completely worn away. It smells like old rawhide and linseed oil. This was a glove that was well used. And well treated, rubbed with oil to keep it supple. An outfielder's glove, it looks like.

"How long did he own it?" I ask, turning it over in my hands.

"Thirty-four years," Eisfanger says quietly.

Thirty-four years. Three and a half decades of playing catch, laughing with friends, snagging pop flies out of the air. "The boys of summer," I murmur. "Except this little boy didn't play in the sun, did he? Nothing but night games for him."

"He played center field, if it makes any difference."

"It did to him," I say. "Any idea how it wound up in the pawnshop?"

"I talked to the spirit of the glove, and all it remembers is how long it's been since Wendell picked it up—a few weeks." Eisfanger pauses "It . . . misses him."

"I'll bet you do," I say to the glove. "Thirty-four years. That's not a possession, that's a marriage—ending in a very sudden and unexpected divorce."

I toss the glove back in the box. "Well, no way Wendell sells this glove or leaves it behind on purpose. He's either dust or a captive."

"Kind of what I thought. But it still doesn't prove Stoker's telling the truth."

"No. It doesn't."

I give the box back to Eisfanger, thank him, and tell him good night. Then I go back to bed and resume not sleeping.

I haven't really thought about the victims in this case. I've been so focused on Stoker that I haven't connected with the reason I'm here. My own drama is getting in the way—and that has to stop.

A profiler needs to know the victim of a crime as well as the criminal. The victim tells you many important things, from why they were picked to where the perp will strike again.

But there's more to it than cold, hard facts. Knowing the victim connects you to the case in a very intimate way. It gives you resolve. It gives you motivation.

It gives you anger.

I lie in the dark and forget all about my hypothetical problems with some presumed afterlife. I focus on what I know for sure.

I focus on Wendell. And his glove.

What seems like years later, I finally fall asleep. Except I don't, quite. I'm in that zone where dreams and reality collide, where you think you're still awake but you're really not. I keep coming back to something Isamu said. Something he asked me.

Surely you do not believe that even I could create an entire plane of reality simply to fool you?

My eyes snap open. I sit bolt upright.

An entire plane of reality, no.

But an entire *virtual* reality?

Hell, yeah. Heaven, too.

I get up and throw open the curtains. The sun is just starting to peek over the horizon. It's going to be a good day, after all.

But not for everyone.

If you're going to break into a business run by pires, the best time to do so is high noon; even the ones that work late and always pack a protective daysuit in their brief-case tend to be home and asleep in a very dark room by then.

"You want to tell me again why this is a good idea?" Charlie says in a low voice. A fair question, since we're currently inside an elevator shaft, without the benefit of any actual elevator.

"Sure. Because security inside elevator shafts is notoriously lax, the locks on doors to elevator machine rooms are a joke, and even gaining roof access to a building with an elevator machine room on top of it isn't that hard."

We're climbing down a maintenance ladder, Charlie below me. Somebody's helpfully scrawled the floor number in chalk beside each set of doors, so I know where we are and how far we have to go.

"That's not what I meant. I meant why are we burglarizing the headquarters of a multinational corporation in the first place?"

"Because this is where the answers are."

"Really? Because all I've seen so far is a lot of grease and dirt."

"You're lucky I didn't go with my first idea."

"Which was?"

"Gaining entry through the sewer."

"This is mostly a pire building. Probably only one toilet in the whole joint."

"That's why I went with the roof."

Thirty-third floor. Charlie pries open the doors, then gives me a hand across. We're right outside the lab where Mizagi so proudly showed off his TASS project.

But that's not the only thing in there—that much I'm sure of.

The door is locked, with a keypad beside it. I pull out the fetish Eisfanger gave me, a knotted piece of hair, wire, twine, and bone, and drape it carefully over the lock. It's not a key, though; it's a gag.

"Go ahead," I say.

Charlie kicks the door in. Sometimes it's handy to have your own personal battering ram for a partner.

If the fetish is doing its job properly, the alarm system is currently stuck in a feedback loop, screaming into its own ear but nobody else's.

Charlie stalks inside. I follow.

The lab looks pretty much the way I remember, only a lot dimmer; the room's mainly lit by the hundreds of small telltales on the equipment, glowing a steady red or green. The large screen at the front is dark. The server farm hums and whirs to itself in the far half of the room.

"Answers, huh?" Charlie says. "Do we look for a filing cabinet with a big A on the front, or d'you figure they store 'em in a separate room?"

"We need to check the computer system, genius."

"Oh, these are *computers*. I thought they just liked watching TV while getting in a little typewriter practice."

I sit down at a workstation and tap a key at random. The monitor switches from screensaver mode to active—doesn't look like the system is encrypted. I start looking around.

Most of the files relate to shrinespace, a cross-indexed

list of thousands of Kami. But that's not what I'm interested in.

I find it in a file marked HEREAFTER 2.0.

There's a lot in there, mostly files jammed with machine code. But there are a few text files, too, and the one marked OVERVIEW provides me with a pretty good idea of what's going on—not the technical aspects, but the real purpose behind this project. I whistle, long and low.

"So you're impressed?" Charlie asks.

"Was that my *I'm impressed* whistle?"

"I believe it was."

"That's because I'm impressed." I shake my head. "What these guys are up to . . . well, it's impressive."

"I'm getting that. You want to say it again, or are you done?"

"Done? I'm just getting started. Charlie, we have to go in there."

"In *where,* exactly? The computer-generated Paradise you say these guys built? I thought Isamu locked you out of there forever."

"He did—which is fine by me. I don't care if I never see Roger Trent again, in any version: dead, alive, or alternate."

"You forgot computer-generated."

"That's just it, Charlie—he wasn't a program. He was the real thing, a spirit. It was his surroundings that were man-made."

Charlie tilts his fedora back on his head. "And you know this how?"

"Because of this." I point to the screen and the file I just pulled up. "Heaven won't have me, Charlie. So I'm going to pay a visit to the other place."

"Not without me, you're not."

"Wouldn't dream of it. Which, apparently, is kind of how we're going to get there."

The protocol is fairly simple. Charlie and I go over the process together—the only equipment required is an intricately braided platinum-and-gold necklace with a single crystal embedded in the weave and the exposed tip of a fine silver wire embedded in that. The wire, sheathed in black plastic, ends in a jack that plugs into the keyboard. Every workstation has one in a drawer under the monitor, though I don't remember seeing any in use during Mizagi's demonstration.

"That's it, huh?" Charlie says, dangling the necklace from one finger like a dead snake. "Put this noose around our necks and jump?"

"I'll have to hit a key, actually—but jumping is more or less accurate. We'll leave our bodies and enter what they're calling the Interface Zone—kind of a holding area. From there we choose one of two bridges. We want the one that isn't all bright and shiny."

"And we can't bring weapons?"

I shrug. "Not physical ones, no. We'll only be there in astral form. Fortunately, I have my razor-sharp wit to rely on—you're kind of out of luck."

"Uh-huh." He frowns. "Not ideal. We go in together, there's nobody here to guard our bodies. You go in alone, I can't protect you from whatever's inside. I don't like it."

"Relax. This place is deserted, and we'll have a code word that'll yank us out of there if we get into trouble. If a bunch of computer techs can handle this place, I'm sure we can, too."

He doesn't look happy. "I guess."

He pulls up a rolling chair and sits down next to me. He's got to take off his hat to put the necklace on, which makes him look oddly vulnerable.

I slip my necklace on. The crystal, slightly warm, snugs into the hollow of my throat. We're both jacked in, ready to go.

I hit the key—

Cerulean light surges upward, flooding my vision from bottom to top with a tsunami of brilliant blue. It recedes just as fast, draining away and revealing a new landscape spread out before me, an infinite plain of glossy black marble under a vast white sky. There's a single dot of green in the exact center of the horizon, getting larger each second, an immense jade missile hurtling toward us at thousands of miles per hour. It stops no more than a foot away, revealing itself to be a garden that stretches to either side as far as I can see.

I give my head a shake. It's still there, attached to my neck, which is a relief. I inhale through my nose, and smell—nothing. Guess they haven't gotten around to programming that in yet. A moment ago I was sitting but now I'm on my feet, and the ground feels solid beneath them.

I turn to look at Charlie, and get a surprise.

He's bigger than he usually is, now standing around twelve feet tall. He's still wearing the same sharp, pinstriped suit, but it's now a dark green as opposed to dark blue. His skin has a scale-like quality to it as opposed to its normal smooth plastic sheen, and his eyes have vertical, reptilian irises.

And he has a tail.

"You turned into a midget?" he says, staring down at me.

"Not so much," I say with a grin. "More like you got in touch with your inner dinosaur."

He shifts his balance, notices something different, turns his head to look over his shoulder. "Huh. How about that."

"Never seen one of those in pinstripes before. You must have one helluva *tail*or."

"Haw. Haw. Haw." When he talks, I realize his teeth are all very pointy. Guess I shouldn't really be all that surprised; Charlie, after all, is animated by the life essence of a long-dead *Tyrannosaurus rex*.

I check myself out, but I seem to be dressed in my usual work clothes: black slacks, white blouse, black jacket. Shoes I can fight in. My scythes didn't come with me, but the holsters did.

"You good to go?" I ask Charlie.

"Yeah," he rumbles. His voice is even deeper than usual.

We step into the garden.

The plain immediately vanishes as the garden folds around us seamlessly. Charlie's face is impassive, but his tail thrashes nervously.

The garden is wild and overgrown, flowers and weeds and tall grass crowding the gravel path. Willow trees slouch in the riot like green, slope-shouldered giants. Shaggy hedges run haphazardly through it all like the abandoned foundations of a gigantic forest mansion.

"Not what I expected," I murmur as we walk. "Seems chaotic. Out of control."

"Yeah, magic can do that. Anything complex has a tendency to creep, spill over its borders. Needs constant attention."

"Like a garden." I get it—they set the place up this way as a reminder. A physical metaphor using metaphorical physics, a way to keep in mind how easily the forces they were dealing with could get away from them. Creeping sorcery . . . much like the anti-firearms spell that's slowly growing in my own brain.

The path doesn't go far before it forks, a bridge to either side. Both spans are gentle wooden arches with railings, and both arc over a river. But the river flowing beneath one bridge is gentle and calm; the one that flows out from beneath the other is a raging torrent. The sky over one bridge is peaceful and blue, while the other is dominated by a dark gray thunderhead, lit with the occasional flash of ominous lightning.

Between the two bridges there is no river at all, just a dried-out gully with a cracked, dry-mud bottom, like the pattern on the inside of an old china cup. There's a log wedged in the mud, and a hulking figure sitting on it.

The figure gets to its feet as we approach. It's all muscle, about fifteen feet of it, covered with rough skin the industrial gray of a batttleship. Its hairless skull is horned, two white conical spikes jutting up at least three feet from either temple. It's got a face made for the word *ugly,* and teeth a British dentist would be ashamed of. No nose, just two oval slits. Pointed ears, long black talons on its fingers and toes. Dressed in what looks like a loincloth made from a family of four, skinned and stitched together with twine.

Funny. I don't remember the online manual saying anything about this . . .

SEVENTEEN

The monster stares at us. We stare at it.

"Hey," the monster says. "How ya doin'?"

"Okay," I say.

"Good," the monster says. There's a pause.

"So," I say. "What are you, some kind of AI?"

The monster scratches his chin with a long black talon. "Don't know what that is."

"It's a kind of computer program. Stands for Artificial Intelligence."

"Oh. Nope. I'm an *Oni.*"

"A what now?"

"*Oni.* Type of demon. Stands for . . ." He frowns. "Maiming, I guess."

"You stand for *maiming*?"

"You ever try to maim someone when you're sitting down? Not as easy as it sounds."

Charlie clears his throat. "Yeah. 'Scuse me. You're some kind of guard, right? I mean, you're not just hanging around waiting to maim people at random, are you?"

The *Oni* shakes his head. "Nah. That'd be kinda rude, wouldn't it?"

"A tad," I say. "So you're here to guard the bridge?"

"Guard it? Nah. What's the point of that?"

"Well, if you're not guarding the bridge, then what—"

"I mean, come on," the *Oni* interrupts. "When's the last time you heard of someone stealing a bridge? Doesn't make any sense."

"What if someone tried to burn one of them?" Charlie says. He unbuttons his jacket.

"Burning bridges? I always thought that was just a figure of speech . . . anyway, these are *magic* bridges. Don't think they *can* burn. Why, is that why you're here?"

Charlie slips his jacket off and hangs it from a nearby branch. "Nope. Just want to use one of them, is all." He undoes the top button of his shirt, loosens his tie.

"Oh. Well, in that case we have a problem. See, it's my job—"

"To stop people from *using* the bridges," Charlie says. He takes his fedora off, hangs it next to his jacket. "Sure. I apologize for being unclear."

"Unless you know the password. You don't, right?" He sounds hopeful.

"Not a clue," Charlie says. He unbuttons his shirtsleeves, then rolls both of them up past the elbow.

"Glad to hear it," the demon says, and stalks forward.

I decide to stay out of the way and enjoy the show.

I don't get a chance to see Charlie really cut loose very often. He gets by a lot of the time on menacing looks and the occasional threat—but that doesn't mean he's all bark and no bite. The reason those threats work so well is that he's able to back them up, and most people get that.

But every now and then, someone's dumb enough to test him.

The demon's bigger. He's got claws, and those horns. This is his home turf, and he's doing exactly what he was put here to do.

I give him a minute, tops. Longer if Charlie's having fun.

They stop, just out of each other's reach. Charlie's got

his fists up and cocked, ready to unload. The demon flexes his claws, his arms back and to the side, ready to swipe.

"You gonna pull some kinda demony trick?" Charlie asks. "Blast me with magic eye beams or something?"

"Nah. You?"

"Well, I do have this one thing I use my tail for."

"What's that?"

Charlie's tail flicks to the right. The demon's eyes follow it.

Charlie lunges forward, swinging a hard left to the demon's gut. The *Oni* grunts and staggers backward a step.

"Distraction," Charlie says.

He follows it with an uppercut, hard enough to lift the *Oni* right off the ground. Most opponents would come down in a boneless heap, but the demon's tougher than that; he lands solidly, and retaliates with a slash that rips Charlie's shirt half off and shreds his tie. Back in the real world those claws probably would have torn right through the plastic skin of Charlie's chest, but here his hide seems closer to reptile than beach toy.

I really wish I could stick around to see the rest, but I'm not much use as a spectator. While Charlie keeps Big Ugly busy, the best thing to do is capitalize on the fact that the gatekeeper is occupied.

So I slip around the fight and cross the bridge over the raging river, beneath the thunderstorm.

If I'd tried that with the other bridge, the one with the tranquil water and blue skies, I wouldn't have gotten far. The vibrational whammy Isamu put on me would have stopped me dead in my tracks—but what I'm looking for isn't in the Yakuza's happy little artificial afterlife. The files I scanned told me that much.

So I find myself, once again, in the gloomy underworld of Yomi.

* * *

I have to admit that Isamu's plan—or Mizagi's plan, or possibly some anonymous programmer's plan—is pretty slick. Maybe it started with shrinespace or maybe that was introduced afterward as a cover, but the idea that eventually evolved is much more ambitious. It hinges on the existence of multiple afterlives, and the fact that these realms are generally based around cultural preconceptions. A Christian Hell, for example, would be full of fire and torment, populated by leering, sadistic demons. Not a nice place to visit—or to have angry at you.

The Asian Hell, by contrast, is simply *boring*.

Now, that's a very Eastern approach, and no doubt a room full of philosophers could spend an eternity arguing about which fate was worse: everlasting agony or never-ending dullness (or possibly being locked in a room full of arguing philosophers). But there are three very important, salient facts that the Yakuza gleaned from this situation.

One: There aren't nearly as many demons in Yomi as in other Hells, just the ones there to keep souls from getting out. And of these, most of them—like the one Charlie is currently tussling with—are just as bored as the rest of the inmates.

Two: In a universe full of afterlives, there is always room for one more.

And three: Bored people make good customers, as long as what you're selling is entertaining.

What the Yakuza have done is to outsource Heaven. They've created an alternative, bribed the guards at the prison next door, and populated it with the souls of the damned. The damned bored, in this case.

It couldn't have been easy. Afterlives might be inhabited by the dead and run by demons—or angels, I guess—but ultimately they're the domain of gods. To pull this off, the Yakuza have to be in bed with someone big. Those kinds of beings always demand a high price for their services, and that price is always paid in blood.

I know whose blood, too.

When it comes to sacrifices, innocence is the preferred currency. Younger is always better. So how about those stuck in childhood forever—would their immortality preserve their attraction, or would the gradual corruption of life on the street taint the flavor of their souls? Would their supernatural nature render them less desirable? Or would the salty tang of painful experience provide an intriguing counterpoint to the sweetness of youth, one a god might find irresistible?

I don't know the answer to that. I don't even know that the kidnapped pire kids are still in one piece. All I have are suspicions—that they're being used to power the spell that keeps the bridge between Yomi and Hereafter 2.0 open, and that they're being held here in Yomi. Eisfanger rigged up a pire-detector charm for me, which he says will glow if I get anywhere near the kids.

I look around. The bridge is still there behind me, but a gray fog swirls around it at the midway point, obscuring the other side. The river is gone, too—there's nothing here but mist and a featureless gray plain, blurring together in the distance.

And unlike last time, I'm alone. No car, no Stoker, not even my own body—I'm just like any other spirit here, except for the fact that I'm not dead. Yet.

Maybe I can use that to my advantage. What can a living spirit do that a dead one can't?

I think about it. Think about how quiet this place is, how its defining aspect is that nothing ever happens.

I smile. And then I throw back my head and *yell*.

"HEY! YOU! YEAH, *YOU*! YOU GOTTA SEE THIS!

IT'S—IT'S CRAZY! I MEAN, YOU WOULD *NOT* BELIEVE YOUR EYES! THIS IS SOME SERIOUSLY INSANE STUFF!"

I pause. No takers yet, but I'm just getting started.

"I HAVE NEVER, EVER SEEN A CHIHUHUA THAT BIG—OR WEARING A HAT LIKE THAT! OR RIDING AN ELECTRIC MOOSE! *WOW!*"

Deep breath. "AND WHO'S THAT WITH HIM? IS IT? IT CAN'T BE! NOT HIM—AND HER—AND *THEM*! BUT IT IS! AND LOOK AT WHAT THEY'RE CARRYING! I CAN'T BELIEVE THEY LET THEM IN HERE WITH THOSE! IT'S TOO MUCH!"

I pause again, longer this time. You have to build up a little suspense.

"OH MY GOD, THAT'S AMAZING! IT'S THE MOST BEAUTIFUL THING I'VE EVER SEEN! IT MAKES MY EYEBALLS WANT TO EXPLODE WITH HAPPINESS! NO, EYEBALLS, DON'T DO THAT! I WANT TO SEE MORE! I WANT TO SEE IT UP CLOSE, RIGHT HERE, WHERE IT IS HAPPENING RIGHT NOW!"

Apparently the stamina of my vocal cords in spirit form is pretty impressive, because I don't feel even a little bit hoarse. I resume bellowing.

"THANK YOU! THANK YOU, EYEBALLS! I'M SO GLAD I SAW THAT! NOTHING WILL EVER BE SO—AAAAAAH! NO *WAY*! I WAS WRONG! THAT IS *SO* MUCH BETTER! THAT NEW THING MAKES THE OTHER THING LOOK LIKE CRAP! BROKEN CRAP! CHEAP, MASS-PRODUCED BROKEN-DOWN OLD CRAP THAT IS GOING TO DIE ALONE AND HAVE CATS EAT ITS FACE!"

Whoops. Getting a little off message. Time to bring it back.

"BUT IT'S OKAY, THE NEW THING TOTALLY

MAKES UP FOR IT! WOW, LOOK AT IT GO! I
DIDN'T KNOW IT COULD DO *THAT*! THAT IS
HIGHLY IMPROBABLE BUT VERY ENJOYABLE
TO WATCH!"

Still no takers? Time to switch tactics.

"I COULD WATCH THAT ALL DAY! TOO BAD
IT'S SLOWING DOWN AND WILL SOON STOP! I
BET IT WILL VANISH AND NEVER APPEAR
AGAIN! I AM SO GLAD I WAS HERE AND MY
EYEBALLS DIDN'T EXPLODE! BUT WAIT! WHAT
IS HAPPENING NOW? IT IS THE FIRST THING!
THAT CHIHUAHUA LOOKS ANGRY! THE MOOSE
ISN'T HAPPY, EITHER! I THINK THEY MUST BE
JEALOUS OF THE WONDERFUL NEW THING! NO,
NO, NO! DON'T DO THAT, CHIHUAHUA! STOP
THAT, MOOSE! IT'S HORRIBLE! I CAN'T WATCH!
SOMEBODY STOP THIS SENSELESS ATROCITY!"

One last pause, one more deep breath.

"OH, THE HORROR! THE INHUMANITY! THE
WEASELS! FOR GOD'S SAKE, WILL SOMEBODY
THINK OF THE WEASELS! I CAN'T TAKE THIS
ANYMORE—*EEEEEEEEEEE!* MY EYEBALLS!
THEY JUST EXPLODED! I NO LONGER HAVE ANY
IDEA WHAT IS GOING ON AND WILL HAVE TO
STOP YELLING!"

I stop. I don't have long to wait.

"You're very loud."

The voice comes from directly behind me, so close
that I almost jump out of my astral skin. I spin around
and see—

Jinjing Wong. Looking exactly the same as the last
time I saw her, of course. Just as colorless. Just as dead.

"Oh! Yeah, sorry about that. I was just trying to attract
somebody's attention."

Jinjing looks to my left, then to my right, her gaze

sweeping slowly over me as emotionlessly as the beam from a lighthouse. "I don't see any weasels."

"There aren't any weasels."

"Your eyeballs seem intact."

"That they are."

She pauses. I wait, because I'm genuinely curious as to what she'll say next.

"Did they leave?" she asks.

"Who?"

"The moose. And the Chihuahua."

I consider my answer carefully. "Yesssss. They left. But *I'm* still here."

She looks at me blankly. "I would have preferred the moose."

"Yeah, I get that a lot. Look, I could really use some directions."

"Directions? You are in Yomi. Whichever way you go, you will still be in Yomi."

"I know. I get that. But see, what I'm looking for is *in* Yomi but relatively new."

"A new thing? In Yomi?"

"Yes. I know this place doesn't change much, so it should really stand out."

"Oh. You mean The Place."

"The Place? What's The Place?"

"The new thing in Yomi."

I take a deep breath. "Of course. Can you show me this place? Is it far?"

"It is not far. I will show you."

She turns without another word and trudges off. I follow, staying close, not wanting to get lost in the mist.

So far, this is going better than I hoped. I figured most of the real badasses in Yomi stampeded across the bridge to Disney Yakuza as soon as they could, so whoever showed up to investigate my little ruckus would probably turn out to be harmless. The fact that it's Jinjing is a stroke of luck—I think.

"Jinjing, do you remember me?"

"Yes. I told you before, I'm not an idiot."

"You're just dead. Yeah, sorry. So . . . Yomi's a lot emptier now, huh? Lot of souls emigrating?"

"Some have left. But Yomi holds many. Still many souls here."

"Okay, but the ones that have left—what *sort* of souls were they? And please don't say dead ones."

"Bad souls. Evil. Violent. They could do no harm in Yomi, but they did much when alive."

"How do you know?"

"We talk. That is all there is to do."

Yeah, and Jinjing is such a fascinating conversationalist. "So let's talk. Tell me about The Place."

"It is new. Demons came and built it. It houses seven who are neither alive nor dead."

"You mean pires? Seven pires?"

"Yes. Small ones."

Children. Seven pire children. If I had a pulse right now, it'd be speeding up. I'm trying to think of what to ask Jinjing next when she stops and says, "We are here."

The building that rises out of the gray fog is four stories tall and vaguely pyramidal, in that each successive floor is smaller than the one below it. It's as gray as its surroundings, and appears to be made of old, cracked concrete. There are no doors or windows. Tall iron poles tipped with spheres of dark metal jut from the cornices of each floor. What looks like black lightning crackles around them, occasionally arcing up into the sky without a sound. The architecture reminds me more of an industrial structure than a temple, the kind of building you'd find housing a generator substation or an electrical routing hub.

I pull the charm out of my pocket—or the astral equivalent of it, anyway—and check it. It's a little piece of folded silk, and right now it's got seven little blood-stains on it.

I stare at it, then up at the building. I've found them. Problem is, I have no idea how to get inside, or what to do when I get there. I need some serious mystical help—Eisfanger would be a good start, but I suspect he'd find himself out of his depth pretty quickly. This is going to require a high-level NSA shaman, which means getting out of here and in touch with Gretch as soon as possible.

Which raises all sorts of other interesting questions—like, can I find my way back here again? And if I do, do I even have the legal right to enter the premises? Who do you go to when you need a search warrant for another plane of existence?

I fold the cloth and put it back in my pocket. Then something occurs to me, a question I haven't asked yet. "Jinjing—why haven't *you* left?"

"Don't want to be a soldier."

A *soldier*?

That opens an entirely new and unpleasant can of worms. Big, ugly, supernatural worms.

Soldiers mean an army. An army means a war. And a military force comprised of spirits implies a war so far out of my jurisdiction I can barely see it with the Hubble telescope.

But a war waged on who? For that matter, who's in charge of this hypothetical army? Am I looking at an invasion of mundane reality, a campaign against another afterlife, or some kind of large-scale mercenary operation with the Yakuza farming out combat units to the highest bidder?

This is all a bit much. A case involving kidnapped kids has abruptly mushroomed into some kind of multiversal military conflict. I really wish I had a chair so I could sink into it, but since I don't I opt for lowering myself slowly to the ground and hugging my knees. After a moment, Jinjing joins me.

"Ah," she says. "Sitting. I did that once. Something to do."

Well, in Yomi you take your pastimes where you can get them. Which, for some spirits, apparently includes enlisting in the Astral Marines. "Yeah? How'd that go?"

"Didn't go. Sat."

"Right. For how long?"

"Hard to say. Not long. Few years."

"Sounds relaxing. I could use some of that."

"Not as good as it sounds."

"Nothing ever is . . ." I stare up at the blocky concrete. I can hear an almost subliminal hum coming from it now, if I really concentrate. It's soothing, calming. Hypnotic. I really have no desire to do anything but just sit here and listen to it.

And I'm not the only one.

I didn't notice them before, but there are figures in the mist surrounding the structure. Just out of sight, but becoming more and more visible every second. Is the mist drawing back?

No. I can just see farther into it. My senses are acclimating, getting more in tune with their surroundings. I realize, in some distant part of my mind, that this is what those who dwell in Yomi see all the time. There is no mist for them; they see the endless blankness broken only by the occasional empty, abandoned building and the shuffling dead.

Whom I'm becoming one of. I try to move and find I can't.

Stupid. Of course an installation like this is going to have defenses. Not obvious ones like the guard Charlie took on, but subtler things. Like some sort of field that amplifies the natural effect of this place and turns anybody nosing around into a mindless, immobile captive.

It's getting harder and harder to think. I need to get out of here, but I can't even turn my head anymore—I'm stuck staring at the side of the building, a blank gray space that's becoming a better and better description of my brain.

And then I hear the voice.

"Jace." It's muffled, unrecognizable as anything but male. Charlie? I try to respond and can't.

"Yog-Sothoth," the voice says. The word means nothing to me—is it a name, a place, a thing?

"Yog-Sothoth," the voice repeats. What am I supposed to do now, say *Gesundheit*?

I feel a hand on my shoulder. With its touch, I can move again. I stand up and turn around.

It's Cassius.

EIGHTEEN

"Ugh, soy sauce," Cassius says.

"What? Yog soy thoth?"

"Don't talk with your mouth full."

I blink. Cassius drops his hand from my shoulder and turns back to the—barbecue?

I look down at the bottle of soy sauce in my hand, then at the piece of sushi in my other hand. I look up again, feeling very confused. I was just thinking about something important, I know I was—but now it's gone. Oh, well. Probably wasn't important.

"I don't know how you can use that stuff," Cassius says. He's turning over steaks on the grill, a big black propane-powered thing set up on our deck. He's dressed casually in shorts, sandals, and a tight-fitting T-shirt, protected from the sun by the overhead canopy and UV-resistant plastic sheeting that lets in light without turning him into a cinder. "It's mostly salt."

"Says the guy who sucks down nothing but AB negative for lunch," I fire back, but there's a playful note in my voice. "You know the rules, sweetie—no bugging me about my health until *after* my first heart attack."

"As opposed to the ones you give me on a regular basis."

"Those are due to your delicate nature and sensitive constitution. I told you when you married me you wouldn't be able to keep up."

"I should have listened."

"Too late. Now you're stuck with me." I pop the sushi in my mouth and give him a quick kiss on the cheek. He pretends to make a face. "Fish breath," he says.

"Bloodsucker."

I throw my arms around him from behind and press my face against his back. He's wearing the cologne I got him for Christmas the first year we were together—just the tiniest amount—and after ten years I don't even think of it as artificial. It smells like him.

"Dad! Is my steak ready yet?"

I mock-frown at my son. Only nine, but as smart as his father and outspoken as his mother. Charles looks up at me, plate held in one impatient hand. He's as blond as Cassius, with my big dark eyes.

I sigh. "How did we wind up with a carnivorous offspring again?"

"I stand by my theory that he was switched at birth."

Charles rolls his eyes. He's a champion eye roller, and I guess I know where that particular trait came from. "Oh, please. I'm half human, so I can eat whatever I want."

"Half human and all stomach," I say. "You've got one parent who's a vegetarian and another who's on a strictly liquid diet, so what do you choose to chow down on? Meat, meat, and more meat. You're going to sprout fur at the next full moon, I know it."

"*I'm* not going to," his sister says from the door to the kitchen. Only seven, but Lucinda's already bossing her older brother around. She squints at me from behind mirrored sunglasses—she favors her father's side of the family and is especially sensitive to sunlight. *"I'm* going to keep on drinking blood. Food is *yucky."*

"Well, at least you're easy to buy groceries for," I tell her. "Wouldn't hurt either of you to have a salad now and then, though—"

"EEWWW!" they say simultaneously, and then burst into laughter. Cassius grins at me over his shoulder in that way only one parent can to another: it's a combination of *Kids—what are you gonna do?* and *I love them so much it hurts* and *How did we ever get so lucky?*

"Right back atcha, Caligula," I say softly.

So we have supper and the kids tell us about their day. My husband listens intently to every word they say and asks them questions that range from the thoughtful— "Why do you think he said that to you at that particular moment?"—to the absurd—"When *is* it appropriate to wear a duck as a hat?" I tease him and them and they tease me right back. Just another meal in the Valchek/Cassius household.

After we've cleaned up, Charles goes upstairs to do some homework and Lucinda plays in the basement. Cassius and I snuggle up on the couch together and argue about what kind of movie to watch.

"Death Wish Seventeen," I say. "Come on. I've never seen it."

"You know they replaced Bronson with a giant puppet three movies ago, don't you? One that's a better actor."

"You just don't appreciate the genre. If you had your way, all we'd ever watch would be Shakespearean productions and period pieces."

"I lived through a lot of those periods."

"No, you didn't. You *unlived* through them."

"Exactly. So seeing those same scenes in daylight intrigues me."

I sigh. "Great. So it's a combination of nostalgia and archaeology for you, and a snorefest for me."

"You'd rather see an urban vigilante find new and interesting ways to decapitate people?"

"Hey, it's research. I might pick up an interesting new technique. Maybe even one that'll save my life."

He gives me a look. "Not fair. And besides, after sixteen sequels they've used up every plausible method known to pire- or thropekind. The last one had someone killed with an industrial washing machine."

"Oooh, that's one of my favorites. Especially what Bronson says as he's loading the machine up with quarters: 'The only constant . . . is change.' Menacing *and* philosophical."

"But extremely improbable. Where did he find all those silver razor blades he dumped in?"

"Weren't you paying attention? That evil Bane dealer used them to torture people who owed him money."

"I must have missed that vital plot point."

"We could always watch it again."

He grimaces. "Highly unlikely . . . anyway, there's something I wanted to talk to you about, now that the kids aren't around." He's using his business tone of voice, which means it's work-related.

"Okay. What's up?"

"This isn't easy to say."

Uh-oh. "What's wrong?"

"I—this *really* isn't easy to say."

He's giving me a strange look, and I'm starting to get a little worried. "Just spit it out, sweetie. Whatever it is—"

"No. You don't understand. It's the *saying* that's hard. It's hard to *say*. Can't. Can't get the—"

And now he's breathing funny. Big, in-and-out gulps, like he can't get enough air. But—

But Cassius doesn't *need* air.

His face is turning red. Veins are pulsing on his skin. His eyes are bulging and he's clutching at his chest. If I didn't know better I'd swear he was having a heart attack.

"Jaaaaaaace," he gasps. "You have to—have to—"

I don't know what to do. "Charles! Lucinda!" I scream. "Call nine-one-one!"

Charles wanders into the room. He looks at his father with no expression on his face at all. "Nine-one-one? What is that, some kind of code?"

I rip open Cassius's shirt, trying to see if there's some kind of wound, but all I see is skin. Skin that's more flushed than usual—

Skin that starts to smoke.

I draw back in horror. I stare at my husband's face as he mouths his final words in a guttural hiss. *"Save meeeeeeeee . . ."*

There's the flash and *whoof!* of something catching fire very quickly. For one frozen instant, I see a statue where my husband was sitting, a perfect reproduction made of white-gray ash.

Then it dissolves, into powder so fine it's almost a vapor. It hangs in the air for a second and then starts to settle, ever so slowly, on the couch and the floor. And me.

I scream.

The scream pulls me back, back to Yomi and the blank gray concrete wall. Before the numbness can set in again, I blurt out the escape word I found in the programmer's file. It yanks my soul through the interface and into my own body with a shudder. I cross my arms, gasping, and try to pull myself together. "Only a dream," I tell myself. "Only a dream, only a dream." I do my best to believe it.

Charlie's soul is still at the interface point, his body as lifeless as a statue. I glance at the workstation's monitor, not terribly surprised to see it portraying a demon lying flat on its back with a dinosaurian Charlie sitting casually on its chest. He's picking his teeth with a long, pointy spike, which I realize is one of the *Oni*'s horns.

"Was that you?" Charlie asks, looking around. "Something just came flying past like a bat out of . . . well, you know. It was sort of Valchek-shaped."

I key in the command to draw Charlie out. His image vanishes from the screen and his eyes snap open. "Well, that was a thrill," he says. "Get what you were after?"

"Pretty sure I found the pire kids. Can't prove it, though."

Charlie stands up, picks up his fedora as gently as he would a kitten. "Can we get them out?"

"Oh, we're gonna get them out. Just don't know how yet."

He settles the hat on his head, snugs it down so the brim is exactly where he likes it. "Okay, then."

"What, you're not going to point out all the glaring flaws in the plan I don't have?"

"Nah. You'll think of something." He grins at me. "I just hope it involves coming back and doing this again. That was *fun*."

I swear to God he's whistling as we break back out of the building.

Back at the hotel, we fill Eisfanger in on what happened and what we've learned. "Okaaaay," he says when we're done. I'm standing, Charlie's on the bed leaning against the backboard with his feet up, and Eisfanger's perched on the room's one chair. "Can I ask a question here?"

"Shoot," I say.

"Why is it that every time I work on a case with you it always spirals into some kind of overblown hyperweirdness? Can't you just catch run-of-the-mill bad guys for a change? You know, a charm counterfeiter or a blood-bank robber or something? Something *ordinary*?"

I resist the urge to laugh in his face. "Eisfanger, the

very fact that you can reel off two examples like that as *ordinary* means you and I are always going to have very different standards of weirdness."

"So this is the new normal for you?"

"No, this is weirdness *cubed* for me. At this point, I've had so many bizarrities thrown at me I feel like I should celebrate Christmas with a freak show. But hey—if I can deal, you should have no problem."

He sighs. "Yeah, fine. Let's take this one revelation at a time, all right?" He leans forward and holds up a large, pale finger. "One. The Yakuza—a worldwide criminal organization—now have their own afterlife."

"Pretty much."

"Two. Said afterlife is being populated with residents of Yomi—the Asian version of Hell."

"Yeah."

"Three. This afterlife is being powered by the souls of the kidnapped pire children."

"Near as I can figure."

"Four. While in astral form, you had some kind of dream or vision featuring Cassius—the third one you've had. And right at the start of it, you heard the phrase *Yog-Sothoth*. Right?"

"Right."

He leans back and frowns. "I don't recognize the words, but they have that sound to them. That *unearthly* sound."

"I know," I say. "High Power Level Craft?"

"Maybe. If anyone would know, Gretch would."

"Then I guess I better give her a call."

I call but get her voicemail—she no doubt has her well-manicured hands full with running the Agency right now. I leave her a long and detailed message and tell her to call me back as soon as she can.

"So," says Charlie. He's taken his jacket off and is

fiddling with a mother-of-pearl button on his suspenders. "Looks like we're staging an assault on Hell, huh?"

"Don't get your hopes up," I say. "We're *way* out of our league here. The entire NSA might be outclassed in this situation. I have a real bad feeling about who or what this Yog-Sothoth is going to turn out to be, and it's not going to have a lot to do with sushi."

For a second Eisfanger looks even more confused, then he shakes it off and moves on. "Okay, well, what *is* our plan? Sit here and eat room service until Isamu sics the local cops on us again? Or that Triad warlord finds out where we are and tries to grab us? Or—"

I cut him off. "We gather our allies. We pool our resources. We analyze the situation and strategize."

"Yeah," Charlie says. "*Then* we storm Hell."

Eisfanger closes his eyes and groans. "You know, I'm even wishing you still had the use of your *gun*," he mutters. "At this point it's no more ridiculous than any other aspect of the situation . . ."

My phone rings. I grab it and answer, hoping it's Gretch. It isn't—it's Stoker. "Jace. How's the investigation going?"

"I've found them."

"Does Hemo have them?"

"In a manner of speaking. They're in Yomi."

I expect him to demand details, but he surprises me. "I know. We need to meet."

"What? You *know*? What *else* do you know?"

"Not over the phone. Meet me aboard a ship called the *Orca,* at the old Coal Harbor marina. Half an hour." He hangs up.

"That was Stoker," I tell Charlie and Eisfanger. "He wants to meet." I tell them where and when.

"I know where that is," Charlie says. "Foot of the park.

Used to be swanky, once upon a time. These days it's abandoned and fenced off."

"Well, according to Stoker there's at least one vessel still there."

"Then I guess it's where we're going, isn't it?" Charlie stands up, slips on his jacket. "Gathering allies and all that."

"Yeah." But it's not Stoker I'm worried about finding; it's Tanaka. If we're going up against the Yakuza, I can think of worse things than having a thrope samurai at my side—but I have no idea how to get in touch with him.

I'll worry about that later. I don't want to deal with more than one case of testosterone poisoning at a time, anyway; Charlie's bad enough.

"Let's go."

There's a major street called Georgia that cuts right through downtown. A long time ago, back when the city planners thought a second bridge across the inlet was the best way to link North Vancouver with Vancouver proper, Georgia Street ran all the way through Stanley Park itself. After the residents of the park made it clear they wouldn't allow any such bridge to be built, Georgia was redirected to the north, where it led to the mouth of the tunnel that became the compromise.

I can see the tunnel now, a hundred yards or so east of where I'm standing. A continuous line of vehicles thunders into its brightly lit maw, a hungry mouth mindlessly swallowing hundreds of tons of brightly painted metal every hour. Hard to believe that less than fifty yards to the west is a primeval rain forest populated with savage packs of thropes and criminal gangs.

But at the moment, my attention is focused to the north, to a stretch of rotting boardwalk and pilings that line a rocky shore. The remains of several boats are scattered among the boulders; a few have been turned into make-shift shelters. The weather's turned cold and damp, though it isn't raining yet. The sun's invisible, somewhere behind the gray of the sky.

There's only one vessel in the harbor, about twenty feet from shore. Half submerged and listing sharply to starboard, it's an old fishing boat that seems to be held together with rust and seagull droppings. The name ORCA is barely visible on its prow.

Charlie sighs. "I'm gonna ruin this suit," he growls. "You know you're not supposed to get wool wet, right?"

"Then stop drowning sheep," I say. I'm scanning the ship with binoculars, trying to spot Stoker. The only move-ment I see is two gulls fighting over the remains of a grease-stained paper bag.

"There's some kind of walkway," Eisfanger points out. "Those logs aren't just random. Somebody's lashed them together at the ends, probably anchored them, too—I can see chain wrapped around one."

Technically, Damon shouldn't be here; I should have made him stay back at the hotel, like the other times. But I want us all to stick together, for a reason I'd rather not admit to myself—that I'm still spooked by that dream about Cassius. "I see it," I say. "Guess we're taking that or swimming. Hope it isn't booby-trapped."

We decide the best approach is to send Damon across in half-were form first—as a thrope he's more sure-footed, and his enhanced senses will help him scope out the boat. He'll signal to Charlie and me if everything's okay or not, and then we'll either join him or I'll go ahead alone and Charlie will approach from the water for an ambush attack.

Damon shifts into half-were form, the cracks and gur-gles of his transformation masked by traffic noise. He pads across the beach silently, leaping from rock to rock and avoiding the gravel, then nimbly makes his way onto the first log. From there he has more than one choice; he takes his time, testing each log by putting a little weight on it. He has to backtrack only once.

He gets to the last one and pauses, swaying back and forth slightly, his muzzle in the air and his ears cocked straight up. He sniffs, he listens. After a long moment, he crouches down and springs aboard, his claws scrabbling a little on the tilted deck.

When he disappears into the wheelhouse, I start to get nervous. He's just doing a thorough job, but I really wish we had some comm gear right about now. One of those Morse code headsets thropes use in the field—okay, I don't know Morse code, but I bet Charlie does.

A long minute passes. I told Eisfanger I'd give him two. When his head reappears from the shadows of the wheelhouse, I let myself breathe again. He gives us the all-clear signal.

We make our way over the logs. They're fairly secure, but you have to be cautious; some are tethered so that they bob and roll when you put your weight on them, while others don't. I took careful notice of the route Eisfanger took, and we retrace it exactly.

When we get to the boat, Eisfanger extends a hairy white paw and helps me aboard. Charlie vaults over a second later, landing on the rusting deck with an audible *thump.*

Stoker's below, Eisfanger signs. *Want me to come with you?*

"No," I answer. "Stay up here and keep an eye out. If anything or anyone shows up, signal us—thump on the deck with your foot."

He nods. Charlie and I make our way into the cabin, where there's an open hatch. I can see a dim but steady glow from it, illuminating metal rungs leading down.

"Me first," Charlie growls. He's pushy that way.

He climbs down. I follow. The air is cold and wet and smells like fish that died a hundred years ago. The hatch leads into a small cabin belowdecks, just big enough for a tiny kitchen and bunk beds. Most of the fixtures were ripped out a long time ago, but the rusting frame of one of the bunk beds is still bolted to the wall. Sitting on it, with an electric lantern at his feet, is Stoker. He's wearing combat boots, stained khaki pants, and a spotless white T-shirt, his brawny arms bare. He smiles up at me as we clamber down, finding our footing carefully on the inclined deck.

"Glad you could make it," he says. "Sorry about the cramped conditions, but the location seemed appropriate."

I have no idea what he's talking about. "I'll get over it. Tell me why we're here."

"Sure. I know who's behind all this."

"You mean besides Isamu?"

"Isamu's just the facilitator. The real mover behind all this is a lot older, a lot more powerful, and a lot nastier."

"The deity that's backing Hemo's move into the afterlife market?"

"Exactly. His name is—"

"Yog-Sothoth?"

Stoker blinks, then looks annoyed. "What? No. Who the hell is Yog-Sothoth?"

I sigh. "Never mind. Just a guess."

"The player here is a badass named Dagon. You familiar with the name?"

"Can't say that I am."

Stoker shakes his head. "Imagine a cross between King Kong and the ugliest fish you ever saw. Gigantic, scaly, toothy, with fins like the sails on a Chinese junk. Webbed fingers and toes, claws you could use as meat hooks for a dead elephant."

"Wait," I said. "Fish?"

"And that's just the physical description. This is an Ancient One we're talking about here, one of those beings that lives and breathes HPLC. The bottom of the ocean is just as comfortable an environment as dry land as far as this guppy is concerned, and it ignores little details like rapid decompression, too—laws of physics are for the *little* people."

"Like leprechauns?" says Charlie.

Stoker gives him a look. "Like everyone else on the planet that doesn't have reality-bending sorcery running through their veins."

"So *not* leprechauns."

"No," Stoker says. "Not leprechauns."

"Wait," I repeat. "Fish? This is all coming back to *fish* again?"

"What do you mean again?" Stoker asks.

"I ran into this crazy skeleton-monster thing that told me fish were angry at me. Which *almost* makes sense, now. But—" I shake my head. "I must be missing something. Skeletor made it sound like some kind of personal vendetta against me, and that doesn't track at all. For that matter, why is some ancient fish god involved in all this, anyway? The hereafter environment wasn't aquatic."

"Maybe they're planning on flooding it later," Charlie offers. "Wouldn't be hard to do, right? If the whole thing's a simulation anyway."

Stoker shrugs. "Maybe. Could be that Dagon was the only deity they could interest in their project. A god of fish is better than none."

I think about that. It doesn't seem right, somehow. "How'd you find this out?"

Stoker looks away. "Sorry. Some of my contacts would prefer to stay anonymous. Let's just say I know someone on the inside and leave it at that."

"Let's not. The inside of what? If you had someone at Hemo, you should have told me before this."

"I didn't say it was someone at Hemo."

"Then who?"

He grins. "Would you believe a little fish told me?"

"Not likely."

My phone vibrates in my pocket. I pull it out and see that it's Gretch. "Hold on, I have to take this. Gretch?"

"Sorry it took so long to get back to you. I have the information you requested." Her voice is brisk and curt, all business. She must be busy. "Yog-Sothoth. Also known as the Key and the Gate, the Beyond One, Opener of the Way, the Lurker at the Threshold, the All-in-One and the One-in-All. An Outer God, extremely powerful—though it's hard to say exactly *how* powerful. The cults that worship these entities all tend to claim that *their* Unspeakable Entity is the last word in Unholy Ghastliness, so deriving any objective data is difficult."

"Can you give me a ballpark figure, cosmically speaking?"

"Said to be more powerful than Azathoth."

"And Azathoth is . . . ?"

"Said to rule all time and space."

"Ah. I see what you mean about objective data."

"Yes. But beings of this scale are often described in contradictory terms. For instance, Yog-Sothoth is also said to *exist* throughout all time and space, but its followers frequently concentrate their efforts on trying to bring it into this dimension—so apparently it isn't quite as omnipresent as they claim."

"Right. So what sort of god is it, aside from contradictory?"

"It's primarily a god of information—knows all and sees all. That description, while probably exaggerated, holds at least some truth; cults that follow Yog-Sothoth are usually driven by the esoteric knowledge that can be obtained. It may not know everything, but it does have access to a great number of arcane secrets."

A god of information. Well, that makes more sense, considering the computer-simulation aspect. "Okay. Does Yogi-Bearsloth have any connection to a marine deity named Dagon?"

"Mmm. Not directly, no." For the first time, Gretch sounds hesitant. It's not like her to be unsure, but she's probably juggling a dozen high-profile situations right now. "I seem to recall there's some sort of link through family connections, but I can't recall the precise details at the moment. I'll do some more research and get back to you."

"Sure. Sooner would be better, though, okay? Things are starting to escalate here and I need as much information as I can get."

"Will do." She hangs up.

I turn back to Stoker. "Okay, so this Dagon—he's big, he's mean, he's waterproof. I get that. But what else can he do? What kind of sorcerous whammy can we expect him to throw our way?"

Stoker pushes himself to his feet. He's a big guy, and this is a small room; he seems to take up a third of it. "Dagon's an up-close-and-personal sort of deity. He won't sit back and hurl thunderbolts or change you into a frog—if you tick him off, you can expect an actual visit from him. A dripping-wet, rip-the-roof-off-your-house-at-three-AM kind of visit."

"I hear Arizona is nice this time of year," Charlie says.

"Good advice," says Stoker. "In fact, I may just follow it myself."

"Oh?" I say. "The mighty Impaler, heading for the hills at the first sign of an angry Outer God?"

"Damn straight," he says, and seems to mean it. I see

something in Stoker's eyes I've never seen before: fear. "Near as I can tell, this thing is unstoppable. I may be a killer, but I'm just a man. I'm done."

I feel strangely disappointed. Stoker's right, he is a killer—but until now he also seemed unkillable, a force of nature unto himself.

He isn't, of course. He's only human, just like me—and even though an entire planetful of supernatural beings haven't been able to beat him, that doesn't mean he doesn't have limitations. And he's smart enough to know that.

But I'm still disappointed.

"So that's it?" I say. "What about the kids? What about that baseball glove you sent me?"

"Forget about them," he says flatly. "There's nothing we can do but cut our losses and walk away. Sometimes you lose—that's a harsh truth, but it's one worth knowing. I do."

Charlie shakes his head. "Come on, Jace. Last train to Loserville is about to board, and this mook needs to be on it."

"Give me a moment, will you?" I ask Charlie. "Stoker and I need to talk alone."

Charlie shrugs. "Try not to hurt him too bad," he says. "I'll wait up on deck."

He clumps his way up the metal ladder. When he's gone I turn to Stoker and say, "There's something you're not telling me."

"Yeah? And what makes you think I'll tell you now?"

"Because I'm talking to you as one human being to another. I know what it's like to feel outnumbered and outgunned. Whatever's got you worried—*besides* the Codfather—you owe me, at the very least, a heads-up."

He studies my face. "Maybe I do," he admits. "But I still don't know if I should tell you." He sees the anger on my face and adds, "You don't understand. I'm not keeping this secret for selfish reasons. This is something you might not *want* to know, okay?"

"I already know lots of things I wish I didn't. One more won't make a difference."

"This might," he says.

And then he kisses me.

NINETEEN

To say I'm surprised is putting it mildly.

I pull back, smacking my head against the metal bulkhead. "What the *hell*?" I blurt.

Stoker shrugs. "I *said* you might not want to know."

"Yeah, but—what the *hell*?"

"Very eloquent. I'm glad you're taking this so well."

I resist the urge to knee him in the groin. "In what universe did you ever, *ever* think a romance between me and you might be possible? You're an *international terrorist*. You've committed *multiple homicides*. It's not only my *job* to send your sorry ass to prison, it's the only chance I'll ever have to go back to my own reality!" I realize I'm yelling. *"How does any of that add up to you and me together?"*

"Well, I've always been an optimist."

I glare at him. The knee to the groin is sounding better and better all the time. "Listen. I've wondered since the day I got here just how crazy you really are. Now I know. Whatever signals your twisted brain thinks it's been picking up from me, they're imaginary. You hear me? Not interested. Not now, not later, not if we both become pires and go to the moon and the Earth blows up and we're stuck in a little moon dome for the next thousand years. Not with a gallon jug of tequila. Not if you have your brain swapped with a twenty-year-old clone of Elvis Presley. *Are we clear?*"

"Not really. Who's Elvis Presley?"

"That's it. I'm taking you into custody. You think you can drag me into another country, use me to take down a Yakuza operation, then *kiss* me—thirty seconds after you've told me you're giving up? *Forget* it, sunshine—"

I'm interrupted in mid-rant, but not by Stoker. No, the sound that cuts me off is an unearthly, echoing roar, a booming, guttural howl that *isn't* coming from above us. It's coming through the hull itself, and originating somewhere below the waterline. That reverberating, profundo cry is being generated underwater, by something big and very, very unhappy.

"Oh, no," Stoker says.

"Time to go," I say, and scramble for the ladder.

"You hear that?" Charlie asks when I climb out of the hatch.

"They heard that in Seattle," I answer.

And then we see it, too.

A fin breaks the surface of the water, looking a lot like a sailfish—one of those big, spread-out things almost like a batwing, thin membranes stretched between long, sharp spines. But on a sailfish the fin covers its whole back; this thing sports his the way a punk rocker wears a mohawk, on top of his skull.

Most punk rockers are a lot prettier, too.

The head breaks the surface, then the shoulders. It looks like the Creature From the Black Lagoon's great-grandaddy. It just keeps on getting taller and taller, as if a skyscraper from an underwater city decided to go for a walk. Its skin is dark green, the scales the size of manhole covers. Its eyes are the dead black of a shark's, above two slits for nostrils and the mouth of a hungry piranha. It's got fins running down its back, the sides of its arms, and its legs. It smells like low-tide just before a thunderstorm, rotting seaweed and dead mollusks and ozone.

And then it looks down, right at me.

"Stoker?" I say with a very dry mouth. "Now might be a good time to not be in a boat."

No answer. I glance down—and see an empty cabin through the hatch. Somehow, Stoker's already left.

Dagon regards me with features so alien I have no idea what's going through his giant, fishy mind. Then he raises one immense, web-fingered hand over his head, and clenches it into a fist. Well, *that* seems pretty clear . . .

"Hold your breath," Charlie says, grabs me around the waist, and jumps. There's a single frozen instant when we're in midair and that enormous fist is hurtling down toward us like a scaly meteorite, and then we splash into the surf an instant before Dagon destroys the ship.

My ears are underwater when his fist smashes into the *Orca,* and it sounds like the world's biggest bass drum being hit with a swimming pool: a booming, crashing, splintering impact with a chaser of *sploosh.*

Charlie and I are sinking fast, but at least I've got air in my lungs. Charlie spins me around and mimes, very quickly, that he's going to the bottom and I should swim for it. I nod, he lets me go, and I strike out through the water, heading for the surface but at an angle; I want to put as much distance between me and Codzilla as I can before I come up for air.

Ever try to catch minnows in shallow water with your bare hands when you were a kid? Impossible, right? It's not just that the minnows are fast and slippery, it's that you're pushing them out of the way by disturbing the water, too. And that's exactly what happens as Dagon's huge, scaly paw plunges into the ocean ten feet from me; the water surges at the point of impact, and carries me with it. Luckily, it pushes me toward the shore instead of farther away.

I make another ten yards or so before my head breaks the surface. I don't bother looking behind me, just take a quick gulp of oxygen and dive back under, this time striking off to my left, parallel to the shore.

Sure enough, that massive mitt smacks into the water right about where I'd be if I'd gone straight. I ride the surge again, swimming with it, and then curve back toward the shore.

This time when I come up I'm beneath the remains of a rotting dock. I get behind a piling as quietly as I can, and peek out.

Dagon's looking around at the water like a kid hunting frogs in a pond. I'm glad he doesn't have a net on a pole—these godly types are good at the grandiose stuff, but it's always the fine details that bog them down. He didn't even bring a bucket to put me in.

I paddle backward slowly until I can feel rocks under my feet. Then I very carefully creep out of the water, keeping to the cover of the rotting dock. With any luck I can get enough distance from the shore to be safe—something tells me Dagon won't stray too far from an aquatic environment.

"Geez, what is it with me and the jumbo-size baddies lately?" I mutter under my breath. "If I keep attracting them they're going to start calling me Jace the Giant-Killer."

"I very much doubt even you could kill *that*," a voice says from the shadows. "But then, I once saw you banish an Elder God, so perhaps I'm wrong."

I recognize the voice, of course. "You weren't actually there for the banishing," I say in a low voice. "You were in the brig of a US aircraft carrier at the time."

Tanaka's crouched behind a jumble of logs. He glances in Dagon's direction, then motions me urgently to run. I dart across the beach, feeling horribly exposed, and throw myself down on the pebbly ground beside him.

"What are you doing here?" I say. I keep my voice down, but I doubt we're in danger of Dagon hearing us—it'd be like me being able to eavesdrop on an ant.

"Looking for trouble." He's wearing a loose black coat, black drawstring pants, and black sneakers; he looks more like a burglar than a ninja.

But then, he isn't a ninja—he's a samurai.

"Well, you've found it." I scan the beach, looking for Charlie. He'll be safe enough on the bottom unless he gets stepped on, and even then he'll probably just get smushed into the mud. I hope that doesn't happen; the last thing I need right now is to mount a marine salvage operation to retrieve my partner.

But I don't see him. He might be waiting for Dagon to leave, but that's not Charlie's style. Which means—

"Oh, no," I say to myself. "He wouldn't. He *couldn't.*"

I fumble for the small binoculars in my soggy pocket, pull them out, and scan the water around Dagon's legs. And sure enough, there's a very determined-looking golem in a very wet wool suit climbing the back of the monster's leg, pulling himself up by gripping the edges of scales.

I shake my head. "What does he think he's going to do? Climb high enough to poke him in the eye?"

Tanaka smiles. "He will do whatever is necessary to protect you. You inspire great loyalty, Jace Valchek."

"Yeah? Guess you missed that memo."

I know it's the wrong thing to say the second after I've said it. Tanaka's only reaction is a brief incline of his head—an acknowledgment of his guilt, an acceptance of my accusation. "Tanaka, I'm sorry. I—"

"No, Jace. You are correct. I betrayed you, and by doing so dishonored my family name. I must make amends—that is why I am here."

I abruptly realize the obvious. "You've been following me. Since the park."

"It seemed the best course to pursue. Isamu is a wary target, but I knew that sooner or later he would approach you directly. It is his nature."

I thought back. "So you saw the whole fight in the graveyard?"

"I did. You acquitted yourself admirably."

"It never crossed your mind I might need a little assistance in taking down a giant, chomp-crazy skeleton?"

"It did. Should you have ever appeared to be in any serious danger, I would have intervened. But you rarely seem to need assistance."

I accept the compliment grudgingly. "Yeah, well . . . so you know where Isamu is holed up now, right?"

"Yes."

"Then why are you here?"

He meets my eyes calmly. "Because my debt is to you. It occurred to me, in the course of my inquiries, that a greater threat to you than Isamu might be lurking. I see now that I was right."

Charlie's up to mid-thigh by now. Dagon hasn't noticed him, but his attention is on the shoreline, still looking for me. "What, this? This is no big deal—just your run-of-the-mill angry Ancient One, looking for a little trouble. Once I catch my breath I'm going to march out there and kick his ass."

"I believe that would require an elevator, at the very least."

I grin, despite myself. "Got one handy?"

"I have something better." He reaches behind him and draws his katana from the sheath slung on his back. I eye it dubiously. "No offense, Tanaka, but that thing's not going to be much more use than Charlie's *gladius*. Frankly, I don't see what could take that beastie down short of a cruise missile, and those don't even *exist* here."

"It's not the size of the weapon, Jace—it's how you use it."

"Yeah, like I haven't heard *that* one before—"

Charlie's made it to the small of Dagon's back, though *small* isn't a word I'd use to describe anything about the situation. I'm starting to worry. Charlie's as bad as me when it comes to being stubborn, and he doesn't know how to back down from a fight. This could wind up getting him killed.

And then the creature spots us.

"Uh-oh," I say.

Dagon roars. Okay, it's more like a high-pitched screech with bass undertones, but even that doesn't really convey the sound very well; let's just say it sounds like a recording of whale noises played backward at really high volume and leave it at that.

I don't have to tell Tanaka to run. We both bolt from cover and sprint away from the water, and I hear the splash of Dagon's first tremendous step behind us.

Now what? There's a busy street not far away, and buildings after that. I need cover, but not something Dagon can just smash; unlike King Kong and Fay Wray, I'm pretty sure my pursuer's intentions aren't amorous. He might just destroy anything that gets between him and me.

Stanley Park or the tunnel?

The tunnel's farther away. It's big enough to let semitrailers drive through it, but Dagon would be a tight fit—he'd have to squirm through like a snake. If nothing else, it would slow him down and maybe even trap him, giving the authorities a chance to bring in some heavy-duty sorcerous firepower. I just hope the Canadian military has something in their HPLC arsenal that can deal with a being like this.

But there's collateral damage to think about, too. Vehicles with people in them, going too fast to stop when a big scaly foot stomps down in the middle of the road. No, it can't be the tunnel.

That leaves the park. Tanaka's come to the same conclusion; he wolfs out as he runs, going to half-were form to boost his speed and strength. His clothes are baggy enough to contain him, but his sneakers burst and fall away in pieces.

Tanaka reaches cover first. He resheathes his sword and crouches, watching me. I can see how badly he wants to dart out, grab me and run back, but he doesn't. He knows I hate being rescued.

I make it to the trees one step ahead of Dagon—one giant step. No sooner am I under the canopy than I hear the enormous thump of his foot. So much for him not leaving the water.

I wonder if I can use the same hiding-beneath-the-foliage strategy I did with Gashadokuro, even though this guy's considerably bigger. I get my answer a second later, as Dagon grabs the old-growth spruce I've ducked under and rips it right out of the ground like a gardener yanking out a head-high weed. Dirt and loam shower over me as the root bundle rises up, and then Dagon tosses it aside. It flies a few hundred feet and lands in the harbor.

I keep running, deeper into the park. He can't uproot the whole rain forest—can he?

Tanaka lopes beside me. He could go full-wolf and just take off, but I know he won't. What I don't expect is what he does next: He stops at the base of a redwood and leaps up the trunk, catching a branch nimbly and pulling himself onto it. He turns back to me for a split second and gives me a very formal nod of his wolf's head.

Then he starts to climb, springing from branch to branch, using his claws as nimbly as a jungle cat. I know what he must be planning.

"Tanaka, *no!*" I shout, but it's no good.

Dagon decides there's no point in ripping trees out of the ground when he can just swat them out of his way; he's around the same height they are, but apparently a lot stronger. The sound of timber cracking and crashing is deafening as he bulls his way forward. I run to the left, using the same tactics I employed underwater, and then stop when I'm out of the path of destruction.

Through a break in the canopy I can just see Dagon's head and shoulders. And then, working his way around the monster's neck, my partner appears. He's moving away from the head and toward the edge of the shoulder, still gripping the scales but only holding on with one hand; he cocks his other arm back like a major-league pitcher winding up for a fastball. Even though I can't see it, I know what's he's about to throw: a steel-cored, silver-coated ball bearing, several ounces of metal Charlie can hurl with deadly force and accuracy.

Which he does. Right through Dagon's eardrum.

I understand his strategy now. If it walks, it has a sense of balance, and that sense of balance is regulated by delicate mechanisms located inside the inner ear—in most animals, anyway.

The ones that breathe air. And aren't a hundred feet tall. Or owe their existence to supernatural forces that sneer at little things like physics.

It's still a good plan, and if it works it'll bring Dagon crashing to the ground like one of the trees he just knocked down—but it doesn't. It must hurt like hell, though, because his whole body shudders violently, and then Dagon lets loose with a roar that makes his previous bellows sound like whimpering.

Two things occur while this is happening, almost simultaneously. First, Charlie gets shaken loose and goes flying into the trees. I'm not too worried—they're mainly spruce and pine, with plenty of thick foliage between the peak and the ground to break his fall. He's survived much worse.

Second, as Dagon starts his roar, Tanaka springs from the top of the redwood, katana held in his jaws. His leap is perfectly timed and executed, taking him exactly where he intends to be.

Through Dagon's gaping, fanged jaws.

"No," I whisper.

It must take a lot to surprise a god. I swear Dagon's huge, jet-black eyes get a little wider. He does his best to cough the unexpected morsel out, but Tanaka's got claws on all four limbs to keep him anchored. Even gods don't have armored throats—not on the inside, anyway.

With the exception of silver or decapitation, it's hard to kill a thrope. They can survive drowning, burning, disemboweling, and just about every poison known. I never considered adding being swallowed alive to the list, but once you've gotten past the perils of chewing, all you have to worry about is being digested. Ugly way to go, feeling your flesh being slowly dissolved until the acid eats through your spinal column and separates what's left of your skull from your body.

Unless you use your claws to stop your descent partway down. Then you can do some damage of your own . . . especially if you've been smart enough to bring your own scalpel with you.

I start to think that maybe Tanaka will be okay. That maybe he can actually survive this.

Dagon roars again; this time there's more pain in it than fury. He's not used to his snacks biting back. But then, Tanaka is more like a nasty virus than a meal, a bad case of food poisoning with a lethal agenda. I can just imagine him in there, chopping though the soft flesh of the gullet, escaping into the thoracic cavity where he can wreak some real havoc . . .

Dagon claws at his own chest. Scales rip loose and fly through the air like fishy Frisbees. "Awwww," I say. "Got a little indigestion, big guy? Should have stuck with that all-seafood diet."

I hear heavy footsteps behind me and turn to see Charlie rushing toward me. His suit is wet and ripped in many places, and he's got a few branches sticking out of him, but other than that he looks okay. "What'd I miss?" he growls.

"Just the appetizer," I say. "Main course is coming right up."

Dagon seems to have forgotten all about me. He's pounding on his own torso like someone trying to get a stuck candy bar out of a vending machine. I wonder which way he's going to fall when he finally keels over.

But that doesn't happen. I'm forgetting that Dagon is, after all, more than a giant, two-legged amphibian—he's a deity, an otherworldly being from a different dimension with different rules. If explosive decompression can't kill him from the inside, what can one thrope with a sword do?

Just enough to save my life.

In the end, Dagon places both his hands flat against his chest and utters something—actual words, though they sound nothing like any language I've ever heard—and his whole body glows with an eldritch blue light. He drops his hands to his sides, opens his mouth, and exhales a small puff of black vapor.

I watch it disperse in the breeze. *Sayonara*, Tanaka.

I almost expect Dagon to spit out the katana as an afterthought, but that doesn't happen. Instead, the monster turns back to the ocean and strides into it, not looking back. In a minute he's completely submerged, gone like he was never here.

And so is Tanaka.

TWENTY

Charlie and I leave before the local cops show up. Lots of rubberneckers pull over to gawk, but everybody's attention is focused on the not-so-jolly Green Giant; Charlie might have been spotted, but I doubt anyone noticed me at all.

Except Tanaka.

"We must have hurt him some," Charlie says as we walk through the lobby of the Clarion. "Either that, or that blue zap he used took a lot out of him. Either way, we got the job done—"

I give him a look that could cut glass. "We got the *job* done? We lost one of our own today, Charlie. That's not an accomplishment, it's a major screwup."

"I know. I'm sorry—"

"Sorry? What have *you* got to be sorry about? That Tanaka was the one who got to sacrifice himself for my sake, instead of you?"

Charlie doesn't answer.

We've reached the elevator doors. I punch the UP button with my thumb. "That stupid, selfish *bastard*. So goddamn concerned with his *honor* he went and got himself *killed* for it."

Charlie doesn't say a word.

"I mean, what the hell *is* honor, anyway? A million different things to a million different people, and none of them understands any of the others. It's not a word, it's an excuse—people make it mean whatever they *want* it to mean."

Charlie stays silent. I push the button again, harder.

"You know what it meant to Tanaka? It meant he had to live up to some impossible ideal—one he probably didn't even fully understand himself—and when he couldn't, he had to pay for not being perfect. With his *life*."

I jab savagely at the button several more times. "What about *my* life, huh? Screw my honor, what about the huge load of *guilt* he just added to the never-ending fun ride that makes up my day-to-day existence? *What is with this goddamn fucking elevator?*"

I punch the UP key, with my fist this time. That hurts so much I decide to do it again. And again. And again.

The fourth punch hits the solid, sand-packed resistance of a golem's open palm, as Charlie keeps me from breaking every bone in my hand by putting his in the way. The elevator doors start opening around punch three, but I'm way past caring. I get a brief glimpse out of the corner of my eye of a pair of wide-eyed tourists, who stand completely still while the crazy woman screams and attacks the wall. They're still standing there when the doors slide shut, a moment later.

Charlie's gotten in front of me by then, and I'm hitting his chest instead of the elevator panel. It's a lot like working out with a heavy bag at the gym. Charlie just stands there and takes it, hands at his sides, face expressionless. His eyes are closed.

He waits until I've run out of steam and I'm panting like a racehorse. "You done?"

"I—*huh, huh*—I guess."

He opens his eyes. "Good. Break any bones?"

"Don't think so."

"Too bad. Would have helped with the guilt."

I glare. "Not funny."

"Not trying to be. Only two ways to deal with pain. You and Tanaka both seem to like the first."

I slump against the wall and cross my arms. "Swallow it whole. Beat ourselves up from the inside."

"Yeah. Never turns out well, but when you've got a talent for destruction to begin with? One-way ticket to Doomsville."

I look at him and raise an eyebrow. "Doomsville?"

"I try to stay hip. It's why I'm so popular with the kids."

"Yeah, you and the monster that sleeps in their closet."

"Hey, I know that guy. He's not all bad."

"What's the second way?"

Charlie straightens his tie meticulously. "Pass it along to someone else. Someone who deserves it more than you do."

"Like Isamu?"

"Like Isamu. And his stooges at Hemo. And anyone else involved in their dirty little business."

I manage half a smile. "Think it's too late for me to change tactics?"

Charlie shrugs. "Better them than me." He goes to press the elevator button, frowns at the wreckage dangling from the wall, and says, "Maybe we should take the stairs."

I sit on my hotel bed and think about Tanaka.

It's funny. There's some part of you that never lets go of an ex-lover. No matter how brief it was or how long ago, there's always a little corner of your mind that wonders *what if*. What if I would have stayed with him, what if we had met earlier or later or under different circumstances. And even past that, to what if we eventually wind up together, sometime in the future.

But when that person dies, that's not possible anymore. And that little part of you, that little piece of hopeful fantasy, it dies, too.

Tanaka didn't deserve what happened to him. He was put in a place where it was impossible to do the right thing, and he was someone who couldn't live with himself after doing the wrong thing. He was a good man in a flawed world, just trying to do his best. I owe him my life.

"Good-bye, Tanaka," I whisper. "Honor is yours, once more. Whatever that means."

Too much has happened, too fast.

Most people, when that happens, throw their hands in the air and moan about how unlucky they are or how unfair the universe is. More philosophical types will mutter aphorisms like *When it rains it pours,* and the stoic ones will just put their heads down and try to slog through.

Me, I start asking questions.

I believe in coincidence in the same way I believe in quantum physics or chaos theory. It's observable phenomena. I may not understand exactly why events are grouping together, but I know that they are. Incidents are happening together, ergo: Co-Incidents.

First the attack of the bargain-basement skeleton. Followed closely by Isamu banning me from his designer Heaven, Stoker making the worst-timed pass in the history of relationships, and Dagon mistaking me for Tokyo. Bookended by Tanaka's death.

Too many things, happening too fast.

Somebody's playing me. I can feel their fingers plucking my strings, making me run one way, making me run another. Look at Jace. See Jace run. See Jace jump through hoops. Look out, Jace! That hoop is on fire!

See Jace start to figure things out.

I'm holed up in my hotel room with my laptop. Charlie's

slumped in a chair, fedora over his eyes, catching a few *zzz*s. Eisfanger's in his own room, working on some kind of protective enchantment—because of the Dagon attack he's now acting more nervous than usual.

I'm doing a little mythology research, myself. Not a lot of stuff about Elder Gods on the Net—it's all restricted material, classified for high-level government use only—but there's plenty on the more mundane spirits, including a long and detailed list of Kami. I do a visual search on temple imagery, looking for one thing in particular, and when I find it I read everything the site has to say. The links it provides to other pages prove illuminating, too.

When I'm done I call Gretch. "Hey, Boss Lady. Got a minute?"

"If it's important." She sounds tense.

"You heard about Dagon's little rampage?"

"It's international news. The media, as usual, is rife with speculation; popular opinion is leaning heavily toward a rogue shaman and an invocation stolen from a government facility."

"He was there for me." I give her a quick summary of my day so far.

"I see." She sighs. "I suppose you still require the information you requested earlier?"

"It would help, Gretch. A lot."

"Very well. You're not really cleared for this level of disclosure, but as acting director I can waive that. Dagon is connected to Yog-Sothoth; in fact, he's Yog-Sothoth's offspring."

I nod, even though Gretch can't see it. "So maybe this is a family affair. Who's the Unspeakable Horror slash Mommy?"

Gretch hesitates, then says, "Shub-Niggurath."

And now it all starts to come together. Shub-Niggurath

is the Big Bad the pires made a deal with at the end of World War II, the one that let pires reproduce. Makes sense; Shubby's a fertility god, after all. And a fertility god—or goddess—always has a brood of her own.

"That's how Isamu is getting away with this," I say. "Good old-fashioned nepotism. Family connections. Mom's got herself a nice little sideline business in another dimension, and Dad decides he'd like to do the same. Junior's more than happy to help out the folks, because who doesn't like getting out in the fresh air and stomping around for a while? And—somehow—the old Yakuza thug managed to insert himself into the mix."

"That's a pretty big leap, Jace. For one thing, these other-dimensional beings don't relate to one another the way normal families do; Yog-Sothoth, Dagon, and Shub-Niggurath may all be bitter enemies."

"I thought you said they didn't relate to each other the way normal families do."

She ignores that. "Also, we have no proof of anyone other than Dagon being involved. A cryptic message in a dream is not precisely hard evidence."

"It was a message from Cassius, Gretch. I know it was. You know where he is and what he's doing, right? Tell me that you know for sure I'm wrong."

A long pause. "I can't," she admits. "Not for certain."

"Then I'm going to operate on the assumption that I'm right."

"Don't you always? No, don't answer that. Very well, the Yakuza are collaborating with not one, not two, but three of the most powerful entities we know of—one of whom tried to kill you. How do you plan to proceed?"

"I figured I'd charm them with my winning personality and dazzling wit."

"Excellent. Would you prefer cremation, a closed-coffin ceremony, or burial at sea?"

I think back to that pathetic little puff of black smoke that escaped from Dagon's mouth. "Oh, I wouldn't worry too much about details. Those tend to take care of themselves . . ."

I know exactly where to go. I brief Eisfanger and Charlie first, and Damon has some very helpful suggestions. Charlie thinks my plan is far-fetched, dangerous, and probably a waste of time, but he doesn't have anything to offer as an alternative.

Then we all go out for sushi.

Charlie doesn't eat, of course, so he just sits there looking bored and playing with a pair of chopsticks. Eisfanger's never had sushi before, so I spend most of the meal teaching him all the little rituals: mixing the soy sauce and wasabi, folding the slender paper envelope the chopsticks were packaged in into a rest for them, filling everyone's teacup but your own.

It's a good feed, though I eat most of it. I order some to go as well, and then we leave the restaurant and walk down the street to Blood Alley.

"What if he's not there?" Eisfanger whispers.

"Then I'll wait." I hold up the plastic container with the sushi inside. "He'll show up, sooner or later. That's how these things work, right?"

"You're the expert," Charlie says. "Oh, no, wait. You're the other thing. The one that's the opposite of that."

"I'm not a newbie anymore, Charlie. I'm getting the hang of this."

"Yeah, that's what the guy on the bicycle said just before he turned onto the freeway."

"Stop worrying. I'll have you two as backup, right?"

Charlie sighs and nods. Eisfanger swallows and says, "Sure, sure. Absolutely."

I leave them at the mouth of the alley and walk down

to the temple. I almost expect it to be gone, like one of those mysterious secondhand stores that only stick around long enough to sell you a monkey's paw and then disappear before the warranty expires.

But it's still there. I stop in front of one of the statues and study it critically. Now that I know what it represents, I can recognize the pointed ears, the long, bushy tail. I open the container of sushi, take out a small bundle of fried bean curd and rice, and place it carefully at the fox's feet. I repeat this with each of the statues, and then go inside.

The temple is empty. I go up to the shrine at the front and light some incense. Then I drop into a comfortable position on the floor, and wait.

I don't have to wait long. The old pire monk I talked to last time limps in, smiling benevolently. "Ah! You have returned. Was your quest successful?"

I smile at him. "Which one? I have so many I lose track."

"I believe you were seeking assistance for your weapon."

"Oh, that. Nah. Turns out I do just fine without it. How's the leg?"

"Still tender—" He stops. His eyes twinkle. That's the thing about tricksters; as much fun as they have fooling people, the part they really enjoy is when they can reveal how clever they've been. It's a trait, oddly enough, that they share with serial killers.

"I know how much you love fun and games," I say. "But every game has to end, right? So let's just lay our cards on the table. I know who—and what—you are. You're a *kitsune,* a trickster spirit. You often take the form of a fox, but you can pretty much look like anything you want: an old monk, a giant dumbass skeleton, or even a human sociopath. You noticed me when I got dragged into Yomi the first time, and you've been playing with me ever since."

The monk chuckles. "I see it would be foolish to waste

time denying these charges. Very well." Changes ripple through his appearance and in a moment the man who called himself Zevon stands there with a smirk on his face. "It's been a while since I ran into someone clever enough to make an interesting dance partner. Thank you."

"You really had me chasing my own tail for a while. Well done."

"You're not angry?" He sounds surprised. "I was expecting an eruption of the legendary Mount Valchek."

I smile. "Well, life's full of surprises, isn't it? It's what keeps it interesting."

He looks puzzled, then thoughtful, and finally he laughs. "Ha! It does, indeed! Jace Valchek, you are a *most* delightful human being."

"Oh, I'm a barrel of laughing monkeys."

"What gave me away, might I ask?"

"I'll answer that question if you answer one of mine."

He nods. "Certainly."

"Pacing. Things were happening a little too quickly, with a few too many coincidences thrown in: Dagon showing up right after Stoker told me about him. The dirty cops showing up at the graveyard. Stoker's kiss. Oh, and the whole 'fishies' thing was *entirely* too cute."

He shrugs, but looks pleased with himself. "You work with what you have. The sushi angle was too good to pass up."

"Of course it was. And you knew about Dagon and his folks because that's the kind of company you keep. You think of yourself as a professional trickster, but the truth is that it's really a part-time gig. You've still got your day job, right?"

Now he seems a little deflated. "Well, yes. But it's only temporary. I'm working on some great new material, and when it's ready—"

I roll my eyes. "Uh-huh. Listen, Seinfeld, you promised you'd answer a question of mine. Here goes: What was the deal you made with Stoker to get us out of Yomi?"

He shakes his head. "Sorry. You only get one question, and you already asked it. That little dig about my day job, remember?"

"What? Come on, that was rhetorical—"

"Rhetorical, shmetorical. If it's got a little upside-down fishhook over a dot at the end, it's a question. Asked and answered."

I sigh. "Okay, you got me. You win, you're clearly more devious than I'll ever be. But speaking of your day job . . ."

And now he looks a little nervous.

"You don't just hang around temples to Inari looking for people to screw with. You're one of her messengers, charged with doing her work. Correct?"

"Well, yes . . ."

"Oops, that was another question. Wasn't it?" I grin, and keep going. "And I'm thinking she may not be too happy with you goofing around when you're supposed to be on the job. You got away with it the first time I showed up because I didn't really know what I was doing. But not this time. I brought the offerings, I lit the incense, and I'm doing my best to put myself in a devout frame of mind. Because, hey, I think Inari and I will hit it off just fine; she's a goddess of warriors, after all."

"I told you, Inari won't get involved in the affairs of other gods—"

"I know what you told me. You also told me you liked biting off people's heads while masquerading as an over-size Halloween novelty."

"I was just kidding about that. Didn't you notice my whole skull was made of plastic? Including the teeth? I wasn't really going to chomp you, just nibble a bit. For fun."

I almost believe him—but, like all tricksters, he has a

tendency to take his jokes a little too far. "Sure. Point being, you've proven I can't take you at your word. Which means Inari and I need to have a little chat without you around. An honest and frank exchange of information."

He gives me his widest, most charming smile. "I'd love to help you out, but Inari's kind of busy this millennium, so check back in a thousand years or so and I'm sure I'll be able to fit you in—"

That's when I recite the phrase Eisfanger taught me. It's a simple shamanic invocation, one of the most basic things you can learn, and has only one function: to get the attention of the shrine's Kami.

Zevon goes pale. "Hold on. There's no need for that."

You need to say the phrase three times for full effectiveness, and according to Eisfanger there's no way Zevon can stop me once I've started. Against the rules. I give him my sweetest smile and say it again.

"All right, all right!" He holds up his hands imploringly. "I'm sorry, okay? All in good fun, nobody got hurt. No need to mention any of this to the Boss."

"Nobody got hurt? Tell that to my friend Tanaka."

"That wasn't my fault! Look, Dagon was coming after you anyway; I didn't tell him where you were, I just sort of made sure you were in the general vicinity. Better the beach than your hotel, right?"

He has a point. "I'll think about that. But I *am* going to talk to Inari. And you're going to do your best to convince her that she needs to help me—because that's the only thing that'll keep my mouth shut about your extracurricular activities. Understand?"

He studies me. For the briefest instant, something flickers across—no, *through*—his face. Something feral and deeply inhuman, a glimpse of his true nature. It doesn't look happy.

And then it's gone and he gives me an easygoing grin.

"Absolutely. No problem. You keep our little secret and I'll do my usual job of super-salesmanship. Now, what was it you wanted again? Something about bull pits?"

"Bullets. And that's going to have to wait—I've got bigger fish to fry. Really, really, big fish."

"You want Dagon off your back? Inari can probably swing that. He's not *really* a god, you know—I was exaggerating, back when I posed as Stoker. More godd*ish,* if you know what I mean. Gets a lot of street cred because of Mommy and Daddy; they're major players."

"I know. They're on the same level as Inari. And I don't want Dagon off my back; I want a sit-down."

I take a deep breath. "Inari, Yog-Sothoth . . . and me."

TWENTY-ONE

Zevon looks at me like I just told him Bugs Bunny was dead. "Are you out of your tiny human *mind*? You don't just arrange a meeting between gods like you're scheduling a conference call!"

"Why not? The corporate approach seems to be paying off for Isamu. If Yog-Sothoth will listen to him, he'll listen to me."

"You don't understand. Inari might—might—be willing to speak to you; she's very earthy sometimes, does the whole rubbing-elbows-with-the-little-people thing. But Yog-Sothoth is an *Outer God*. Most mortals can't even be in the same room without going a little crazy. And you want to have a *conversation* with him?"

"Then I'll deal with him through an intermediary. Inari has you—Yogi must have someone, too, right?"

"Well . . . he has been known to use avatars. Some of whom aren't *completely* homicidal."

"See? Now we're getting somewhere. Talk to your boss and set up a meet. And no more tricks, right?"

He gives me a reproachful look. "Please. When I'm representing Inari, I take my job *very* seriously—and Outer Gods have absolutely no sense of humor. I'll get back to you, but it might take a day or two. Gods have a different perspective on time."

And with that, he disappears. No puff of smoke or flash of light, just one second he's there and the next he's not. I take one last look around, close my eyes and try to project sincerity and good intentions; then I leave the shrine myself, to rejoin Charlie and Eisfanger.

And prepare.

This is the part that usually drives me nuts.

I can handle the long, boring stakeouts. I can deal with the emotional pressure, the long-term effects of violence, the actual danger. What I can't stand is that point when it's completely out of your hands, when you're waiting on someone else's decision to make or break your case. The control freak that lives in the back of my brain starts to go a little stir-crazy and makes me do things I otherwise wouldn't.

I go shopping.

I hardly ever do the retail-therapy thing. It's not that I don't like to shop, it's that I never have the time to do it properly. You know, wander from store to store, try things on, scrutinize prices and selection, look for bargains. My normal schedule means I hit the front door of the mall running, and exit the same way twenty minutes later with a shopping bag stuffed full of things that are mostly stretchy or baggy wash-and-wear basic black.

But here I am in a new city, with time to kill and a whole shopping district called Robson Street. Most of the stuff they sell is too pricey for me, but shopping is just as much about speculation as it is about buying anything. How would this look on me? Do I have anything that goes with these shoes? Who would I wear this for on a date?

For most men this would be slow torture, but Charlie's not most men. He may have the soul of a *T. rex,* but he's got an eye for fashion like a Paris designer. "What about this one?" I say, holding up a little black number. I already own several a lot like it, but I like to go with what I know.

"With your legs? Sure," Charlie says. "But that neckline is all wrong for your shape. Try this." He hands me a purple dress on a hanger.

I examine it critically, which is a waste of time; when it comes to style, Charlie's always right. But wasting time is exactly what we're trying to do. "I'll see if it fits," I say, heading for the change rooms.

"Don't take too long," he says. "I want to hit that Italian shop next." He may have great fashion sense, but Charlie's still a hunter at heart—one who's always hungry for the next trophy.

I'm down to my underwear when my phone rings. Unknown caller. I answer, hoping it's Zevon. "Hello?"

"Jace." It's Stoker's voice—but then again, it was last time, too. "Where have you been? I've been trying to get hold of you."

"Before I answer that, let me ask you a question. Where did we first meet?"

Stoker lives in a very paranoid world, so he plays along with no hesitation. "Outside a tent in the middle of Alaska. I was riding a blizzard bike and you were playing coroner."

Good enough. "I've been dealing with someone posing as you. Trickster spirit called a *kitsune*—he was probably screwing with my phone, too. I've got it straightened out now."

"Okay. Any progress on Hemo?"

"Quite a lot, actually."

"Then we should talk face-to-face."

"I'm not at the hotel right now. Where are you?"

"In the next cubicle."

I stop. Lower the phone. Look at the wall. "Stoker?"

"Hey, neighbor." His voice is muffled, but it's him. "How'd you like to come on over? Just put a fresh pot of coffee on."

"Give me a moment."

I get dressed in a hurry, throw open my door, then stalk over and yank open his. He's leaning against the wall, arms crossed, wearing torn jeans and a black leather jacket. "Sorry about the intrigue. Thought it was better we not be seen together."

I glance around, then step inside and close the door. "How'd you find me?"

"Let's not get bogged down in trivia, shall we? We've got important things to discuss."

He's right about that. I tell him what I've discovered since the last time we talked—Hemo, Hereafter 2.0, the pire kids in the Yomi facility, Dagon, the *kitsune*. He listens intently, nodding now and then like I'm confirming something he already suspected. "That's where we are now. I'm going to try to broker a deal."

"Using what as incentive? We don't have a lot to offer."

I give him a hard smile. "Speak for yourself. I've got something in mind."

"I believe you. Which is good, because I think negotiation is the only option we have at this point."

I think back to when the *kitsune* was posing as Stoker, and how he tried to convince me he was turning tail and running. I didn't believe it then, and I don't believe it now. "What, no bold plan involving a frontal assault and massive casualties? Just giving up without a fight?"

"I prefer strategy to suicide, thanks. And I didn't say anything about surrendering. I—" He breaks off and gives me a look I can't read. Like he's about to do something he's not sure about. I'm suddenly aware of how small the change cubicle is—a lot smaller than the cabin of the *Orca*.

But this isn't an imposter. This is the real deal. And the Stoker I know is capable of things a lot more lethal than a kiss.

He reads my body language in a glance, and shakes his head. "Relax. I'm not going to do anything stupid. Well, maybe I am, but I very much doubt it's what you expect."

I keep my guard up. A trained fighter can deliver a killing blow from a relaxed stance, and Stoker's been training his whole life. "Okay. Can't wait to hear your definition of stupidity."

"I've been doing a lot of thinking. About long-term goals—about what I've accomplished so far, and what needs to be done in the future."

He frowns, his eyes on something far away he can't quite see. "I realized a few things. One, that I was fighting a war I was never going to win; two, that I stopped trying to win a long time ago. And that—that's *insane*."

He takes a deep breath, lets it out. "But I'm not crazy. Not when I started out, and not now. I know that for a fact, because for a while I *was*—crazy, I mean. When I had the Shining Trapezohedron."

"Whatever happened to that?"

"I got rid of it. And when I did, that's when my head started to clear. I realized I needed a different approach, a new plan."

He shakes his head. "I know you think of me as a mass murderer, a serial killer, a terrorist. But that's not what I am. I'm a soldier. War is the only thing I've ever known, war against a world full of monsters."

"A war you can't win."

"I know that now. I do. So I'm calling a truce. No

more killing. That raid on the blood farm was my last military action. Time for a new strategy."

He's right; this isn't what I'd expect from him. "Which is?"

"Save my people. *Our* people."

I frown. "How? Don't get me wrong, I think it's great you've decided you can't kill each and every thrope and pire on the planet, but—"

"But it's *their* planet, now. Right?"

It's surprising how hard it is to admit that. "In a manner of speaking, yes."

"So let's go somewhere else."

"What?"

"You're from an alternate reality, another Earth. According to what I learned from Ahaseurus, there are an infinite number of others—some very different, some virtually identical. There has to be one out there that doesn't have pires or thropes or any kind of supernatural beings—but does have room for a million or so human beings looking for a fresh start. A new Earth. A new home."

I stare at him. "You want to relocate the entire human population to an alternate reality? That's . . ."

He studies my face. I can see the determination, and the hope, in his.

". . . not completely insane," I finish. "But hard to imagine. I don't know how you'd even find such a place, let alone generate the level of occult power it would take—"

"I know. I know. But it's *possible*. It could be done. Everything else is just details, willpower, and hard work. Not much different from how I've been living my whole life."

It's a lot to take in, but I can see that he's dead serious. I sigh. "That's a lot to process right now, and my head's already about to explode, what with the upcoming god-talks and all. Don't get me wrong, I think it's great you've found a more positive direction, but now is not the time."

"Understood. But I wanted you to know where I stand. It's important to me."

I meet his eyes. "I appreciate that."

"I might be able to help with the negotiations, too."

"What did you have in mind?"

"Always bargain from a position of strength. There's strength in numbers."

"Wow, two clichés for the price of none. You'll have to do better."

He shrugs. "Will this do?" He digs into the pocket of his jacket and pulls out a small black plastic vial. Hands it to me.

I open it. It's full of a dark gray, grainy powder that I instantly recognize. "Gunpowder?" I say. "Where did you get this?"

"Made it myself," he says. "Simple formula, actually. Surprised you haven't done the same."

Stoker has a definite talent for surprising me—but for once, it's a pleasant surprise. Maybe. "Any chance you'd be willing to trade recipes? I make a mean bundt cake."

"Trading's exactly what I had in mind. You let me sit in on the negotiations, I'll give you the gunpowder formula. I can even give you the name of a jeweler in China-town who might be able to crank out a few bullets before the big summit."

I stare at him. Hard. There are about a dozen different ways he could screw this up for me . . . but the worst he could manage in this situation is to ruin the negotiations, and I can't think of any reason he'd want to. The last time he tried to sic an Elder God on civilization he was, by his own admission, not in his right mind; at the moment he seems eminently sane.

But I just can't risk it.

"I can't," I say. "There's too much at stake. I'm sorry."

He shrugs. "About what I figured—but I had to try. Give my best to Charlie, will you?"

He reaches past me and opens the door. He's close enough that I can smell the leather of his jacket. "Wait. What are you going to do?"

"Me? Nothing. This one's down to you, slugger. Give 'em hell—no, wait, they already have that. Good luck, anyway—we'll talk more afterward."

I hesitate, then stand aside. He steps out, slipping on a pair of sunglasses at the same time, then ducks through the door to the changing area.

I follow, but he's already gone. I find Charlie sitting patiently on a couch thoughtfully provided by the store for suffering husbands and boyfriends; Stoker would have had to walk right past him.

"Well?" I say.

"Well what? That's the same outfit you were wearing when you went in."

I shake my head and sigh. Stoker has many skills, and selective invisibility seems to be one of them. "Never mind," I say. "Come on, we've got an errand to run."

"Where to?"

"Chinatown. I need to hit a few jewelers' shops."

I get the call six hours later.

"Hello, Jace," Zevon says when I answer. "I've arranged that little get-together you suggested."

"Where and when?"

"Uh-uh—not so fast. Rules and preconditions first."

"Go ahead."

"You won't, of course, being talking to Yog-Sothoth directly, though you will have the next best thing. You'll be dealing with one of his incarnations, a charming fellow known as Tawil At-U'mr. Inari herself has elected to be present, so I guess you caught her in a favorable mood.

"Tawil is to be addressed as the Most Ancient and Prolonged of Life. Inari is to be addressed as Inari Okami or Most Revered. You can refer to yourself any way you want.

"The meeting will take place at this address." I grab a pen and jot it down. "That's in the financial district. Conference room on the twenty-third floor, three o'clock sharp."

"What, not in a graveyard at midnight?"

Zevon sighs. "This is the big leagues, sweetheart; they can make *any*place scary. You can bring whoever you want, but they'll have to wait outside. Talks will be among you three and that's it."

"Anything else?"

"Be polite. Try not to stare. Make sure your will is up-to-date." He hangs up.

I bring Charlie and Eisfanger with me. Charlie's put on a new suit for the occasion, a purple so dark it's almost black, with little flecks of gray woven into the fabric. Black tie with a little silver sword tie pin. Gray suede shoes and fedora to match, with a thin black hatband.

"Pretty sharp," I say.

"You think?"

"You're making my eyeballs bleed just looking at you." I myself am wearing a very business-like black skirt and blazer over a white silk blouse. Low-heeled pumps, good for running in. No gun, no scythes—you don't go armed when you're trying to inspire trust, and against beings this powerful it would be pointless, anyway.

Eisfanger's in navy-blue pants, brown loafers, a clip-on tie, and a white shirt; it appears he forgot to wear antiperspirant today. Or maybe he did, and it just can't handle the load.

"You okay?" I ask him.

"Yeah. Sure. No problem."

"Take it easy. It's just a meeting, not the Apocalypse."

"Uh-huh. Right. No problem."

"Eisfanger, you won't even be in the room. You and Charlie are getting parked outside, remember? The only thing you have to do is sit down."

"I know. But—you're going to be diplomatic, right? Because these are *gods.*"

"Diplomacy is kind of the point."

"And don't sneeze. That could be seen as a sign of disrespect. That's all it takes, you know—gods can be very touchy. One little sneeze, and you know what happens next? *They* sneeze. But when a god sneezes, the effects are *very* different. One *Achoo!* from them and you're a used Kleenex in the waste basket of the cosmos."

"You have no idea how glad I am I have a trained shaman to explain these things to me."

He looks at me with pleading in his eyes. "Just—try not to be *you* for a while, okay?"

"Hey! I'm a little insulted, here."

"Sorry. Sorry."

I clap him on the shoulder. "It'll be fine, Damon. Or, you know, it won't. In which case I'm sure you'll be close enough to the epicenter that your death will be quick and painless."

Charlie drives. We don't talk much on the way there; I'm focusing on what I'm going to say, Charlie knows better than to interrupt my concentration, and Eisfanger's too overwhelmed to do anything but stare out the window and fret quietly to himself.

We park in an underground lot that looks a lot like Hemo's. We ride up in an elevator that's all brass fixtures and walnut paneling. We get out on the twenty-third floor, which is dedicated solely to the offices of a firm called Interfutures Trading. The receptionist is a brisk young thrope with an expensive haircut who checks his computer and directs us down a hall.

The place is decorated in the sort of bland corporate chic that suggests people with a lot of money who are too busy to worry about style: spot lighting, a few tasteful pieces of sculpture, a painting or two. Darkly polished hardwood flooring, large, heavy doors with brass handles set into walls painted an eggshell white.

There's a little waiting area just outside the conference room, with a few comfortable chairs, a low-slung glass table, and a nook with a coffeemaker. I pause outside the door. "Wish me luck," I say.

Eisfanger says, "Good luck, good luck." Charlie just gives me a nod and tugs on the brim of his hat.

I open the door and walk in.

I'm not fond of giving presentations, but I've done my share; working for the FBI, you get used to it. It's all about conveying information in the clearest way, minimizing problems and maximizing solutions. I know that sounds like mindless business jargon, but it's just shorthand for trying to figure out a plan without getting in one another's way. Even when everyone in the room has a different agenda, there's almost always some kind of common ground to stand on.

The ground I'm currently standing on is rocky, windswept, and uneven. It's shaped roughly like an oval the size of a two-car garage, and there's a large conference table of highly polished mahogany standing in the center of it.

Beyond the edges of the oval, there's nothing but black, empty space. Above and all around unfamiliar constellations glimmer, billions of miles away. I glance behind me and see that the door is still there, which is somewhat comforting. I resist the urge to step back through it, and close it instead.

There are two beings here with me, one at either end of the table. They're both standing; there are no chairs.

The one to my right must be Inari. My research tells me she can appear in many different forms—male, female, young, old, even in groups of three or five—but the one she's chosen today is that of a young Japanese woman. She's dressed in a flowing kimono of vermillion, her hair pinned back. She has a sickle in one hand, and a coiled whip hangs at her hip.

The other is just a man-shaped silhouette that looks like it's made of rippling, multicolored silk with lights behind it. No, more like a hundred flickering candles seen through a veil. Or maybe the aurora borealis trying to mate with a rainbow and a sunset at the same time . . .

I wrench my gaze away with an effort. Right. Don't look at Tawil At-U'mr for too long. "Hello," I say. I approach the table and stop, very carefully, at precisely the halfway point between the two. "I'm Jace Valchek."

There's a pause, and then Inari speaks first. "Welcome, Jace." Her voice is rich and soft at the same time. "I am here at your behest. Speak your mind, please."

"Thank you. I'm here because of an arrangement between Yog-Sothoth and a vampire named Isamu."

A voice issues forth from the humanoid kaleidoscope. *"The dealings of the gods are not your affair."*

When I answer, I try to keep my eyes fixed on a spot just to his left. "Respectfully, Most Ancient and Prolonged of Life, this is not just about gods. If it were, believe me, I wouldn't dream of interfering. But there are innocent children involved, children taken and used against their will. That *is* my affair."

"Yog-Sothoth knows all and sees all. These are not

your children. This is not your country. You have no reason to involve yourself."

"He is correct," Inari says. "How do you justify this?"

Oh, great. I've barely started and already I've got my own advocate ready to switch sides. "I don't," I say. "I'm not here to argue who is right and who is wrong. I'm more interested in practical matters—matters I believe Yog-Sothoth will also be keenly interested in."

"Your beliefs mean nothing. Yog-Sothoth does not care what lesser beings believe or feel. Yog-Sothoth dwells in eternity, where such things are meaningless."

"I misspoke. I *know* Yog-Sothoth will want to hear my proposal."

Tawil pauses. *"Proceed."*

I've got his attention. Now let's see if I can get his interest, too.

"First let me tell you what *I* want. *Destruction*." Always lead with a hook—and from what I've seen, if there's one thing that tends to whet an Elder God's appetite it's the possibility of some large-scale carnage. "I want Isamu's shiny new Happy Place, sometimes known as Hereafter Two-Point-Oh, demolished. Crushed, smashed, turned into cosmic smithereens. I want it *gone,* and all the souls it holds back where they belong."

Tawil doesn't mess around with the whole that's-a-tall-order-ma'am-I'll-have-to-take-it-up-with-management bullshit. For him, this is business-as-usual god stuff. *"What do you offer in return?"*

Here goes—time to lay my cards down and see if they're worth as much as I think they are. "The one and only thing Yog-Sothoth is really interested in: new information."

"Impossible. Yog-Sothoth sees all and knows all."

"Yeah. No offense, but—that's not strictly true, is it?"

I hold my breath and wait for the cosmic thunderbolt to turn me into a little wisp of black smoke.

"Truth is irrelevant. Knowledge is all. Yog-Sothoth knows and sees throughout all space and time; this shall not be disputed."

"Because it isn't true? So what, if truth is irrelevant?"

The silhouette's shifting glow gets brighter. I think I've just pissed him off . . .

"Hold!" Inari says. Her whip is in her hand, and it seems to be on fire. "This woman is here under my protection. You will *not* destroy her on a whim."

There's a long, tense moment of silence. The little voice inside my head is saying, *Well, as long as it's not on a whim . . .*

Finally, the glow subsides back to what it was. When Tawil speaks, there's no anger in his voice. *"Proceed."*

"Let's say—hypothetically—that Yog-Sothoth's reach isn't quite as all-reaching as he claims. Let's say that 'all time and space,' while technically accurate, refers to one specific universe. The *whole* universe, don't get me wrong . . . but both he and I know there's more than one out there."

I pause, waiting for a reaction. There isn't one from Tawil, or at least one I can read. Inari's smile seems a little wider, though.

"So let's say someone from one of those other universes visits this one. That person would bring a little bit of that place with her, encoded into the very essence of her being—her spiritual DNA, so to speak. Her experiences, her knowledge—every little thing she'd ever done or come into contact with in her own universe would have left psychic traces of its existence on her and in her. *And none of it would be known to Yog-Sothoth."*

I can't look at Tawil, so I look at Inari instead. She gives me a barely perceptible nod to go with her smile, and I start to think I might actually get away with this.

The key to catching subjects using a criminal profile

always boils down to one simple factor: What do they *need*? Killer or rapist, arsonist or thief, at the root of all serial offenders is a deep-seated compulsion to act the way they do. Often it's an outlet for rage or frustration, sometimes it's a sexual psychosis, occasionally it even comes down to boredom—but there's always some void that needs to be filled. Figuring out what that void is and how the subjects try to fill it will inevitably lead you to a place where they're vulnerable. I call it the lion-at-the-watering-hole approach . . . but the lion in this metaphor isn't the perp.

It's me.

"Proof of this offering would be required," Tawil intones.

I untie the cloth charm around my wrist that Eisfanger made for me. "Sure. Here's a taste." I toss it at the silhouette, where it promptly vanishes like I just threw it down a well. A little disrespectful, maybe, but I'm not getting anywhere near Tawil himself. He might just decide to swallow me the same way and save himself the trouble, Inari or not.

I wait. I honestly don't know if this will work. Cross-universe communication is difficult, but the NSA managed it; if Isamu has shamans on his payroll with access to HPLC, I might even be offering Yogi something he already has. I still don't know exactly what the Yakuza offered him in the first place, other than the chance to move from the cosmic IT department to management.

It seems to take forever. Gods, of course, don't experience time the way us mere humans do. For some reason I thought his decision would be more or less instantaneous, working on the assumption that power equals speed—but it could be just the opposite. It might take years for him to mull it over, years that mean nothing to an immortal. And of course, this being some sort of mystical realm, I wouldn't be allowed to do anything as mundane as die from starvation or dehydration. No, I'd get put on the metaphysical equivalent of hold, standing at this damn table as the decades grind past and I slowly lose my mind . . .

"Yog-Sothoth is undecided. You will both provide additional information to support your offerings."

"Both?" I say.

And suddenly, there's someone standing on the other side of the table, across from me.

Isamu.

TWENTY-TWO

Isamu looks at me with cold hatred in his eyes. I have no doubt that the one thing he wants to do right now more than anything is to rip my head off with his bare hands.

"I thought these talks were closed," I say mildly.

"Nothing is forbidden to the gods."

Sure. That's the thing about omnipotence, it makes you arrogant. Rules are what you make, not what you follow. I don't bother arguing the point. "Fine. I'll gladly concede the opportunity to have my competition make a counter-offer. But in order to bolster my own proposal, I need to bring in someone else as well."

"Proceed."

"Stoker?" I say loudly. "You can come in now."

For a moment there's nothing but silence, and I wonder if I've guessed wrong. Then the conference door opens and Stoker steps inside.

"Sorry I'm late," he says. "I miss anything important?"

He joins me at the table—closer to Inari than Tawil, I notice.

"Not much," I say. "Isamu is about to explain why his deal is better than mine. You're going to explain why he's wrong."

"Ah. I see." He stares at Isamu with a slight smile on his face, then turns and whispers to me. "How'd you know?"

"Eisfanger found the tracking charm you slipped on me in the change room. I knew you couldn't stay on the sidelines."

"So Charlie and Eisfanger—"

"Knew you were there the whole time. Believe me, if you'd tried to slip past them without me giving the go-ahead, you would have woken up with a concussion and a new pair of bracelets."

"Enough!" Isamu snaps. "*My* claim is the valid one. What can this pathetic mortal proffer that I cannot? Whatever she says she can deliver, I can do the same—as well as what I am *already* giving you."

"*She has offered knowledge of another realm. Her own universe.*"

"Nice," Stoker whispers. "What else do we have?"

"You do know you're whispering in front of an all-knowing being, don't you?"

"I can do the same!" Isamu says loudly.

My heart sinks. This is what I was afraid of.

"I have already given you a new realm of your own," Isamu says. "Not just to observe, but to rule! Is that not infinitely superior to secondhand knowledge from a single individual?"

"*It is not. All that enters your created domain is already known to me.*"

Isamu scowls. He's having a hard time understanding a being that's more interested in knowing than ruling. "Then I will acquire another such as her, or an artifact. Such things can be done."

"*Yog-Sothoth is not interested in vague promises. He desires only that which he does not possess.*"

Isamu's eyes flicker to Inari. I know what he's thinking:

If she weren't here, I'd give this infuriating human to you right now. "Surely an eternal being thinks of more than immediate gratification. Should you choose this woman over me, you would doing more than rejecting my project— you would be terminating an alliance. She has one thing to offer you, and her laughably short life span means she'll never have the chance to offer you another. I, though, am immortal, and an important member of a powerful and ancient organization. Can you not see that ultimately I am the better choice?"

It's a good argument. Tawil At-U'mr doesn't say anything for a moment, and I know I have to come up with a counterargument or I'm dead in the water. I turn to Stoker and whisper urgently. "We need more. Where'd you get the gunpowder recipe?"

"I stole it from Ahaseurus," he whispers back.

"How'd you know what it was? Or that I needed it?"

"I didn't know what it was, not then." He hesitates. "And I knew you needed it because I bugged your rooms. Technology, not magic."

Damn. I was hoping for a little extra cross-universe mojo, some kind of connection Stoker had made across the dimensional divide that we could throw in to sweeten the deal. My ace-in-the-hole just turned into a three of flubs.

"Any alliance is based on trust," Isamu says, his voice raised. "These two mutter and plot, while I make you an honest offer. They are not trustworthy."

"Sticks and stones, Isamu," I say.

"Her ally is an international terrorist—and no friend to you, either. It is known, in certain circles within the Japanese government, that he tried to bring an Elder God of his own to Earth. You know, of course, of Ghatanothoa?"

And now that sinking feeling in my gut goes right through the floor and into the yawning abyss below my feet. It never occurred to me that Isamu might be well connected enough to know the details of that operation.

"Ghatanothoa is known to me. He opposes Shub-Niggurath."

Who just happens to be Yog-Sothoth's mate.

I wait for imminent annihilation . . . but it never comes. And after a second, I realize why. None of this is news to Yogi; he already knows. *He knows everything.* Everything that *can* be known, that is—he can't know something that hasn't happened yet.

He just doesn't *care.*

He's a god, with a god's concerns. A hairless monkey tugging at the coattails of one of his associates—friend or enemy—means nothing to him. Yogi's not even really *here*—this avatar he's manifesting is just a sliver of his consciousness, a flicker of his attention. We're barely worth noticing. So why is he even bothering?

Because even gods have needs. And I know what Yog-Sothoth's are.

"While we're on the subject of reliability," I say, "let's not overlook your own failings, Isamu-san. You said once you would hunt me to the ends of the Earth—but I'm still here. You're big on threats, but kinda short on follow-through."

Isamu glares at me. "I have not forgotten what I promised you, Jace Valchek. It will yet come to pass—"

I interrupt him with a laugh. "Sure it will. You're all kimono and no katana, Isamu. Even that little stunt you tried to pull to block me from Hereafter Two-Point-Oh isn't going to work. When this is over, I'm going to bust you. Then you and I are going to have our own negotiation session, and I'll crack you like an egg. You'll roll over so fast you'll leave skid marks on the floor.

"The first thing I'm going to get from you is a way to neutralize that harmonics spell. Then I'm going to march right in to your little fake Heaven with a squad of NSA combat magicians and clear the place out—every single soul you co-opted is going back where it belongs, and that includes Roger—"

Isamu slams his hand down on the table hard enough to crack the wood. Even I jump a little. "No," he snaps. "*You will not.* You know nothing about me, Jace Valchek. My will is iron. You will never beat me, you will never cage me. Even if you did, a thousand years of torment would not be enough to bend my spirit. My word is unbreakable, my purpose unwavering."

He turns to Tawil At-U'mr, and doesn't flinch from the sight. "Know this, Most Ancient and Prolonged of Life. I am as unswerving in my aim as an arrow in flight. No punishment or inducement would alter that. This woman will suffer at my hands, and she will never set foot again in the domain I created for you. This I *swear.*"

I allow myself a smile. "He's telling the truth, Most Ancient and Prolonged of Life."

"*I know.*"

Tawil raises one shimmering hand, and points it at Isamu. "*Our bond is dissolved,*" he says, and vanishes.

Ever seen an ancient vampire Yakuza lord flabbergasted?

Me neither. I cross my arms and do my best to enjoy it.

"Impossible," Isamu whispers.

"Not so much," I say. "Want to know where you went wrong? 'Cause I'd love to tell you."

"There was no reason—no *reason*—"

"Oh, there was a big reason. Me. I was always the front-runner in this race, Isamu, you just never knew it. Your big mistake was in thinking that Yog-Sothoth wanted more power. Not true—he has all the power he wants. You neglected to consider his basic nature: He's a god of information. The only reason he was interested in your project in the first place was the chance—however small—that it might lead to new and interesting data.

"But access to someone like me trumped all that. That's always what it was about."

"But then why—"

"Why negotiate at all? Because he wanted to have his cross-dimensional cake and eat it, too. When you brought up the possibility that you might outlive me, Yog-Sothoth saw an opportunity. He couldn't just *take* me, not as long as I was under the protection of Inari Okami." I nod in deference to the goddess, who looks almost as pleased as I feel. "But if there was a chance that once I died my soul might be directed to a specific afterlife—you know, like the one he was Grand Poobah of—then he could gobble up my essence at his leisure. But you put the kibosh on that, didn't you?"

His eyes harden as he sees the trap I led him into.

"Kind of a variation on the old *Please don't throw me in that briar patch* strategy. No Hereafter Two-Point-Oh for poor old Jace . . . and you were so gung-ho at demonstrating your willpower, your absolute unwillingness to compromise, that you convinced your former partner the situation would never, ever change. Congratulations."

"You will pay for this humiliation," Isamu says quietly. "Both of you."

"Not right now we won't," I say. "Your project is being dismantled as we speak, and pretty soon you're going to have a whole bunch of unhappy demons and spirits on your hands as opposed to potential soldiers. Good luck keeping that contained."

"You believe you have won the game," Isamu says. "But there are still pieces in play. Do you think me so ill informed as to not know what Mr. Stoker was searching for?"

The kids. "They'll be released with all the other souls," I say. "That was part of the deal—"

"No. It was not. Tawil At-U'mr informed me as to the exact terms you were demanding, and you specified that the souls involved must be returned to where they belonged. But the souls of the pire children are not misplaced; they are still with their physical bodies, in a location within Yomi."

"You're bluffing."

"He is not," Inari says. "I am a goddess of fertility, among other things, and have an affinity for children. They reside where he has placed them."

"Can't *you* do something?" I ask. "You're a goddess, and they're only kids—"

Inari's eyes are sad, but she shakes her head. "I have already done much. To interfere further would not be appropriate. I am a goddess of fecundity, that of fields and that of women, it is true—but I am also very much a goddess of *warriors*."

She meets my eyes as she says this. I get the message, loud and clear.

"Stoker?" I say. "I think it's your turn at the bargaining table. Got anything our friend here might find persuasive?"

Isamu suddenly realizes that our neutral ground isn't so neutral anymore—and his ride has ditched him. No bodyguards, no preplanned escape routes, facing down two of his bitterest enemies and a goddess.

Isamu grins.

"Am I to understand the business of the gods is concluded?" he asks Inari politely.

"It is."

"And may I infer that any divine protection in place while that business was conducted is now withdrawn?"

Inari glances at me. It's probably the only time in my life that a goddess has asked *me* for approval. "I got this," I say. "I thank you for your help, Most Revered."

"Farewell, Jace Valchek." She pauses, and gives me a grin in return. "Kick his ass."

She vanishes, just like Tawil did. And Isamu leaps for Stoker's throat.

Two unarmed humans against a master vampire, one with centuries of murder under his belt. He thinks this'll be an easy kill.

He's wrong.

Isamu's been around longer, but he's spent most of his existence at the top of the food chain. Stoker started at the bottom and clawed his way up, link by link. Isamu's used to ordering assassinations; Stoker's used to carrying them out.

Isamu has supernatural speed, strength, and invulnerability on his side. Stoker has size—three hundred pounds of muscle, easy. All the speed in the world doesn't help you in midair . . . and when your opponent has already figured out what you're going to do and is ready for it, suddenly all those years of experience vanish in one cocky mistake.

Stoker doesn't try to dodge or grapple. He throws his elbow forward instead, meeting Isamu's considerable velocity with every ounce of that three-hundred-pound mass. He times it perfectly, catching Isamu in the middle of his windpipe.

Funny thing about pires. You can bounce a bazooka shell off their chests or break a pickax against their skulls, but their neck is their weak point. It usually takes silver or wood to kill a hemovore, but it's possible to decapitate one with nothing but steel if it's sharp enough; more pires die every year in auto accidents than impaling.

Stoker's elbow is strictly a blunt instrument, but it's one helluva shot all the same—it would have crushed the trachea of a human being like a cheap beer can. Isamu's body flips around, swiveling at the point of impact, and he slams down on the table on his back.

It's not a crippling blow, but it must hurt like hell. Enough that the shock and surprise of it freeze Isamu for all of an instant. A pire's inhuman reflexes make that instant a lot shorter than a human's, though—call it half a second.

All the time Stoker needs.

Did I say two unarmed humans? My mistake—and Isamu's. Having missed the conversation on etiquette, Stoker's brought a little insurance with him—as I strongly suspected he would. Looks like my three of flubs might turn out to be a trump card after all. He's got a short plastic tube jammed under Isamu's chin before the pire can even twitch.

"Don't move," Stoker growls. "You're a flinch away from six inches of sharpened teak, sitting on top of a cocked steel spring with a hair trigger. It'll ram that stake through your chin, your soft palate, and your cerebrum without even slowing down, and probably punch through the roof of your skull. You'll be a drooling idiot for all of a second or so, and then you'll be something the maid sweeps up."

Isamu's fangs have gotten a lot longer, and his eyes are that vivid scarlet a pire's eyes turn when they succumb to bloodlust. His hands seem to be trembling, but I think it's more out of suppressed rage than fear. He knows Stoker isn't bluffing.

"Jace?" Stoker says. "Do me a favor and retrieve the gentleman's cell phone, will you?"

I go through Isamu's pockets. Every nerve I have is on high alert, but Isamu doesn't try anything. Maybe that trembling is fear, after all.

"Got it," I say. "Let's see, who should we call . . . hey, I've got an idea. Let's ring up our old friend Mizagi at Hemo, shall we? I'm guessing he's on speed dial. Isamu?"

"Why should I cooperate with you? You will kill me regardless."

"No, we won't. I'm an agent of law enforcement, remember? Unlike you, I don't condone outright assassination. You play nice, I guarantee you'll survive this."

"Your associate is hardly on the side of the law."

"Maybe not," says Stoker, "but, like you, I understand the value of alliances. I don't care about your life at all, but I value Jace's trust. If she gives you her word, then I'll give her mine: Do what she asks, and I won't kill you."

"Awww," I say. "I'm misting up. Group hug? No? Then how about that number?"

"Two," he hisses.

"Thanks. Let's hope he's not out to lunch or something . . . hello, Mr. Miyagi? Jace Valchek. Yes, I imagine you are very busy at the moment, what with Hereafter Two-Point-Oh suddenly going offline. Do I have your attention? Listen very, very carefully, and don't interrupt.

"Here's what you're going to do. You're going to send a team of technicians into Yomi, and you're going to release the pire kids you're holding. You're going to take them out of Yomi and escort them to the front doors of your building. Then you're going to let them go. I'll have people watching, so they'd better all be present and healthy. Are we clear so far?

"Why should you do this? You know, I think your boss can explain it better than me." I hold the phone to Isamu's ear.

"Yes," he snarls. "Yes! Just do it, and do it now! Or I'll have your head atop a spike on my front gate!"

I take the phone back. "Okay? Terrific. Pleasure doing business with you—I look forward to our future dealings. Buh-bye." I snap the phone shut and meet Isamu's eyes. "Good boy. Now, what should we do with you?"

"Release me. I have kept my part of the bargain."

"Hold on there, speedy—I didn't say anything about releasing you. I said we wouldn't *kill* you, and we won't. Your freedom, on the other hand, is not on the table."

His eyes flicker from me to Stoker. The red in his eyes is fading, and his hands aren't shaking anymore. He's calming down and thinking, which isn't good.

I'm starting to realize we're in an untenable situation. At this precise moment Isamu's a hostage, but I have nothing to charge him with and he's got the local cops in his pocket, anyway. If Stoker's focus wanders for even a millisecond, Isamu's still capable of overpowering both of us. I need to get Charlie in here—

"On your feet," Stoker says. He grabs Isamu's shirt with his free hand and yanks him off the table, keeping the switchstake at his throat. "Time for a change of scenery."

"Good idea," I say. "Let's get him out of here, anyway."

Stoker turns Isamu around, marching him backward toward the door. He's keeping his hostage a little too close to his own jugular for my comfort, but if Stoker pushes him away he'll have to extend his arms, which makes them more vulnerable to any kind of attack or escape attempt—

And then Stoker does extend one of them. He lets go of Isamu's shirtfront and shoves him, hard. Isamu stumbles backward.

And right off the edge.

"Oops," Stoker says.

There's a high-pitched scream, fading as he falls. It changes to cursing in Japanese before it finally trails off.

I stare at Stoker. "You—"

"Didn't kill him."

"Right, the sudden stop at the end will. Not funny."

"Who says there's a stop?" Stoker takes two steps forward and peers down. "Looks more or less bottomless, to me. He might get kind of thirsty after a while, though. Or get a little too close to one of those stars."

"In a few million years or so."

He shrugs. "Hey, I don't know what the rules are in this place. Maybe he'll go into orbit around a nice little asteroid stocked with slow-moving, blood-filled wildlife."

"That he can see, but not feed on?"

"You don't make it easy to put a positive spin on things, do you?"

I shake my head. "All right, I guess that—technically—you didn't kill him. Now let's get out of here before that door disappears and we're stuck in the same boat."

"In a second." He turns and take another step, and I realize he's put himself between me and the door. And he's still armed.

I wonder if I can take him. I've got the training, but so does he. Plus size, weight, and a weapon. It doesn't look promising.

"There's something else, Jace. See, there's another deal I have to honor."

I nod. Shift into a comfortable stance. My best shot is to do the same thing he did to Isamu and throw him off the edge. It'll work if I can use his weight against him, but he'll be expecting that.

"You wanted to know how I convinced Zevon to let us out of Yomi. It was simple. All he wanted was whatever I was least willing to give up . . . so I made him a promise."

He tosses the switchstake over the edge. I don't take my eyes off him.

"I told him that once the children were safe, I'd surrender. To you."

He turns back to the door, grabs the handle. Looks back at me. "I know you probably don't believe me. But once you and Charlie have me in handcuffs, it'll start to sink in. You coming?"

EPILOGUE

It doesn't really hit me, not at first. Not when we cuff him, not during the ride back to the hotel with a stop at Hemo along the way, not when I get the phone call from Eisfanger telling me he can verify that seven pire kids just walked out of the Hemo building looking dazed but intact.

It's not until I call Gretch, with Charlie standing guard over Stoker in the next room, not until I officially report that Aristotle Stoker, aka the Impaler, is in my custody, that it starts to seem real.

"Be careful," Gretch says. "Just because he surrendered to you as part of a mystic contract doesn't mean he's willing to stay a prisoner."

"That's just it, Gretch. Maybe I'm the one who's crazy, but I believe him. He gave me this whole speech about changing what he's trying to accomplish, and it's beginning to sound like he means it."

"He's extremely good at manipulation, Jace. He could simply have been laying the groundwork for a false sense of trust he could exploit later."

"That's not going to happen. Charlie's watching him like—well, Charlie. Stoker tries anything, he won't get far."

"I'll start the necessary paperwork to bring him across. Vancouver may be a criminal haven, but the Canadian authorities do tend to respond promptly to anything re-lated to terrorism. We shouldn't have any problems taking him across the border."

"Good to know," I say. "While you're at it, there's a little favor I'd like to ask . . ."

But before I can leave, there are three things that need my attention. One I'm dreading and two I'm looking forward to, so I guess I'm ahead.

Eisfanger helps me with the first. It's a lot easier to trace someone's psychic essence when they aren't being masked by corporate shamans, and I find who I'm look-ing for beneath an underpass only a few blocks from Hemo's offices.

Street kids can smell a cop a mile away, but maybe his time as a captive has dulled his instincts. He's crouched barefoot on the concrete, sucking on an oversize bottle of Beefy Fizz through a straw—I guess it has enough blood in it to give a hemovore some nutrition. He doesn't look up until I'm a few feet away.

I stop and study him. "Hello, Wendell," I say.

He studies me right back. The look on his face is wary but not afraid. He appears to be around ten years old, with a child's slight body and shaggy blond hair. He's wearing torn jeans and a black T-shirt that's too big for him. The shirt has a beer logo on it. "Hey," he says. "How do you know my name?"

"I'm the one that got you released."

"Oh. Thanks, I guess. That was kind of messed up."

"I'll bet." I hesitate, but I have to know. "What was it like?"

"Not so bad, at first. They fed me, got me new clothes. Let me play some video games. But I guess they gave me drugs or something, because everything got all blurry and there was chanting and stuff. And then . . ." His eyes go blank, and then he blinks a few times very quickly and gives his head a little shake. "I don't know. I don't remember."

I can tell he's lying, but I don't push. If he wants to forget, that's fine by me. "I've got something for you," I say, and hand him the shopping bag I'm carrying.

He takes it—cautiously, like a wild animal you're trying to feed by hand—and then peers inside. He reaches in and pulls out his baseball glove.

The smile on his face is all too brief, but it makes everything I've gone through worth it. This is why I do my job, why I take the chances I do. For that one moment, all is right in my world: The good guys won, the bad guys suffered, justice triumphed.

"It missed you," I say.

"Thanks," he says. He tries to sound casual, trying to downplay it, not letting on how much it means to him. You can't appear to care too much about anything, when you live the way he does. If you do, someone will try to take it away.

Still, he must feel he owes me something, because he frowns for a second and then says, "It was my own fault."

"What was?"

"Getting snatched like that. I knew better. When something seems too good, too easy, it's always a scam. But I thought—I guess I thought I could scam *them*. People with money show up down here sometimes, you know? They think they know how everything works, but they don't. You can usually give them a sob story and get a few bucks, maybe more. I got greedy, that's all."

The worst part is that he doesn't sound bitter or sad, just thoughtful. He's fitting his new experiences into his worldview. Learning.

After all, that's what children do.

"It wasn't your fault," I say quietly. "None of it. I hope

you believe that, someday. For now, though, can you do me a favor?"

His eyes go flat. His survival instincts aren't that dull, after all. "What?"

"There's some money tucked inside that glove. Share it with the other kids who got taken, okay?"

He's already fishing out the roll of bills I stuffed into the thumb. "Yeah, sure."

He'll probably keep it all himself, but I don't have the time or the energy to hunt down the whole group. I tell myself that I'm wrong, that he'll diligently find all of them and give each one his or her share, and I'm going to keep telling myself that until I believe it.

And then I'm going to get drunk, and pass out in my own warm, safe bed, and try not to feel guilty as all hell.

Gretch is right about the Canadians' reaction. They're more than happy to assist in the capture of an international terrorist, less thrilled that it was done by an American working without an official government liaison, and downright nervous about the involvement of corrupt Vancouver police officers with the local branch of the Yakuza. Gretch does some admirable negotiating of her own, and when the dust settles the Canadians get to take a little public credit for the bust in exchange for getting Stoker into American custody.

But part of the deal is that this won't happen until we're already across the border. Until then we'll maintain a low profile, for security reasons. The Free Human Resistance is still out there, and they won't be too happy that we have their most prominent ex-member in our hands.

It's never as harrowing crossing a border when you're returning to your own country—not unless you're trying to smuggle something in, that is. All we have is an international fugitive, wanted worldwide for acts of mayhem, but at least we're armed with the proper paperwork.

I let Charlie and Eisfanger take Stoker across. I go alone, on foot, and about an hour before they do.

Officer Delta is working the counter for foot travelers today. What a coincidence. I wait my turn, and then walk up.

"Hi," I say.

Officer Delta looks at my visa and grunts. "Miss Valchek," he says. "I see you don't have any baggage."

"Oh, I've got plenty of baggage—mostly emotional. I thought I'd unload some of it here, actually. You okay with that?"

He frowns at me. "Why don't you have any baggage?"

"It's being brought across later, by my associate. He'll declare everything then. His name is Charlie Aleph."

Everything by the book. I wait. He studies my paperwork and says, "I can't let you in."

"Why not?"

"You're not a citizen. You arrived in America from somewhere else, then left the country. We have rules about that. If you want to reenter America, you'll have to apply to Immigration. Next."

I pretend to look shocked. "Oh, my. But this form I have here is a specific exemption." I point.

He picks it up, glances at it. "I don't know this form. You'll have to take it up with Immigration."

"I have to talk to someone else because of your ignorance?"

He gives me a hard look, but I see something else beneath it—glee. He's managed to provoke me into a confrontation, which is what he really wants. "Are you making trouble, ma'am?"

"No. I'm pointing out an error that you've made. My forms are in order, and I'd like to cross the border."

He tosses the paper down on the counter. "You don't get to tell me what to do. *I* tell *you* what to do. Now, unless you'd like to be strip-searched and to spend the next few hours in a windowless room, get your ass out of this office and back to wherever you came from."

"Uh-huh. I'd like to talk to your supervisor, please."

"No. You're dealing with me. If and when you decide to come back here and try again, you'll be dealing with me then, too. I've flagged your file. You think you can come in here and give *me* attitude? Lady, you picked the wrong guy."

"The only one doing any picking is you," I say. "And boy, did *you* make a mistake." I pull out my cell phone. "You know what? You don't need to get your supervisor. I'll call him myself." I hit a single button.

Officer Delta shakes his head. "That's it. You just bought yourself some time in detention." He signals to another officer in uniform, who stalks toward me.

"Yes, Captain Iota?" I say loudly.

The look on Officer Delta's face changes. He holds up a hand and the lem approaching us stops.

"Would you mind coming out to the front counter for a minute, please?" I say. "Thank you."

A door opens behind the counter. An ebony-hued enforcement lem in uniform walks out and stands just behind Officer Delta. "Agent Valchek," he says. "I understand the NSA has a problem. How can I help?"

"You can inform Officer Delta that I outrank him, for starters."

"Officer Delta?" Captain Iota says. "You heard that?"

"I . . . yes."

"Second, I'm invoking National Security Agency protocols for dealing with a possible threat. This office is now under my direct command until such time as I deem the threat has passed." I wave the other border guard over. "Handcuff Mr. Delta. Now."

The guard looks to the captain, who nods.

"Wait," Delta says, looking confused. "What's going on?"

"Shut up," I say pleasantly. "It's my turn to play. Escort Mr. Delta to a detention room, please. I'll be in shortly."

When I get back to Seattle, I feel a lot better.

It doesn't last.

I knew Yog-Sothoth was coming to collect on his part of the deal. I knew it wasn't going to be pleasant. What I didn't know was when, or how long it was going to last.

It happens while I'm asleep, which I suppose is a good thing—kind of like anesthesia before an operation. Unfortunately, my brain won't let me hide behind the comforting illusion that this is a dream; as soon as Tawil At-U'mr appears, I know exactly what's going on.

We're standing on the same rocky oval hanging in space, with alien constellations glinting in the blackness. There's no conference table this time—and no door. I'm naked, but not cold.

"It is time," the shimmering silhouette says. *"Look within me."*

I do.

I fall into the brightness. It swirls around me, through me, a cosmic wind blowing in the empty spaces between my atoms. It caresses every single part of my being and *knows* it, completely, totally, utterly. But there's more to it than that; it reaches out from me, throughout space and time, following some invisible network of connections to everything I've ever done, everyone I've ever met, every thought and memory and dream I've ever had. Jace Valchek, the boxed set—now with everything, including unreleased B-sides of adolescent fantasies and a rare demo version of her first kiss.

It should feel like an invasion, like something being stolen—but it doesn't. Because, unlike human beings with their own sets of experiences and prejudices, Yog-Sothoth doesn't judge any of it; he simply devours it all, adding it to the vast store of knowledge he already possesses.

But that's not to say it doesn't affect him. I get a feeling of—well, appreciation. All the good I've done and all the bad, all the things I regret and all the things I cherish; he appreciates it all. My life, if nothing else, is at least entertaining. A person could do worse.

And then he ebbs away, leaving me feeling not violated, but validated.

"Wow," I say. "That went a lot better than it could have." I look around, and realize two things.

One, I'm sitting in Cassius's office, looking at Cassius behind his desk. He's wearing a suit and seems very happy to see me.

Two, I'm still dreaming. I know this because I'm perched on Cassius's leather couch wearing nothing but an oversize T-shirt with a panda on it, just like when I was first brought over the dimensional divide.

"Jace!" Cassius says. He vaults over his desk and rushes to my side. "At last—I thought I'd never be able to reach you."

"Well, I'm here," I say. "Kind of. You know this is a dream, right?"

"It's more than that. I've been sending you messages for some time, but I wasn't sure how much of my communication was getting through."

"The dreams. That *was* you. They were kind of garbled."

"Cross-dimensional interference. For some reason the channel seems wide open now."

"Yeah, probably the aftereffects of divine bandwidth. Where *are* you?"

"In another reality. It's where Ahaseurus has been hiding. I thought I could track him down and capture him myself—but I was wrong."

"You went after Ahaseurus by yourself?"

"I'm his prisoner. Jace, you have to be careful. It's a trap—"

The door to Cassius's study flies open. There's a blinding white light on the other side, like we're on the surface of the sun. Cassius screams.

And then I wake up.

Read on for an excerpt from DD Barant's next book

UNDEAD TO THE WORLD

Coming soon from St. Martin's Paperbacks

The hours plod by. People come and go. I take orders, bring food, clear away empty plates. I catch Phil giving me dark looks more than once, though I have no idea what I've done to piss him off.

And I can't stop thinking about what happened last night.

It's not just the TV thing, either. It's that story Terrance told. I know he was just trying to spook me, but he did a good job. I keep fixating on that one little detail about the suicide's shoes dropping when the body goes limp. What if they were wearing boots? Gumboots might fall off, but anything with laces wouldn't. And how about beforehand, when the body was kicking and twitching— hell, a shoe could go flying, land in the bushes where no one would find it. Then you'd have a corpse with a shoe missing, and that would probably confuse the hell out of anyone investigating the case.

Except there *is* no case. Just a head case, named Jace. Who is losing the race to keep her sanity in place. Whee.

By the end of my shift I know I have to do something— anything—to get this out of my brain before it burrows in so deep it turns white and its eyes fall out. Unfortunately, about the only plan I can come up with is to give in and go see Old Man Longinus, who by all accounts is as receptive to visitors as an irritable whale is to a harpoon.

I go home first to walk Galahad and try to figure out my approach. "Hi, Mr. Longinus? I'm the local loon. I understand you're the local crank, and I was wondering if we could get together and maybe discuss mutual areas of interest."

Mmm. Needs work.

"Good afternoon, Mr. Longinus. A woman on TV with a sword informed me you have some answers, and I was hoping you might be willing to share them. No, I don't know what the questions are. Oh, that's down the street, under the big neon sign reading *Crazy Motel— Rubber Rooms available, free dry-cleaning of strait-jackets included*? Thank you *so* much, I'll be right back."

Big improvement. Should be tweaked a bit.

"MWAH-HA-HA-HA! My tin-foil hat pointed at your house! I like *frogs*! Would you like to floopa-floopa my gazinga-ding? No, sir, I am not phantasmagorical! Look, Ernest Hemingway eating a cupcake!"

Much better. Or at least more accurate.

I'm on our regular route, down to the end of the street and then through a little patch of woods next to the grocery store, so lost in thought I'm not really paying attention. That's how I wind up getting trapped.

"Hello, Jace," says a raspy voice.

I blink and look up. Father Stone stands in front of me. I'm not really sure what denomination he represents— the United Reformed Methodist Presbyterian Baptist Something, I think. He looks like a midget linebacker with a bad haircut and only seems to have one expression, like a robot that skimped on the options. That expression is supposed to be a friendly smile, but seems about as genuine as something assembled by a taxidermist. He never wears anything but solid black with a little white collar, and it wouldn't surprise me to learn he sleeps in the same outfit.

"Uh, hello, Father," I say. "I'm just out walking my dog." It's a lame and obvious thing to say, but the man makes me nervous. He doesn't blink often enough.

"I see," he says, smiling. "How have you been, Jace? How are *things*?" He puts just the barest emphasis on the last word, but it makes it sound like he's enquiring about a family of monsters living in my basement.

"Things are fine," I say inanely. *No, no, they're not. Things are moaning and squelching and waving their tentacles like a squid trying to signal a waitress. And those are just the ones in my basement, not my brain.*

"We haven't seen you in church lately," says a voice behind me. My eyes widen and my heart sinks. Never let them surround you.

"Oh, hi, Miss Selkirk," I say, turning. Miss Selkirk is a collection of wrinkles wrapped around a skeleton, with bright blue eyes and a mouth that wouldn't know what to do with a smile if one ever showed up—maybe she sold hers to Father Stone. That would explain a lot; it was probably a bad fit but he just jammed it in there anyway and now he can't get the damn thing to budge—

Shut *up*, brain.

"I've been . . . busy," I say. Actually, I've *never* been to Stone's church, but it seems unwise to bring that up now. They might insist on marching me down there for an inspection. "You know, with . . . stuff."

"Your soul is important," Miss Selkirk says. She's dressed in lime-green pants held up with an orange belt, purple-and-pink-striped blouse, white gloves, and a black hat with what appears to be a dead crow stuck in the band. "You should *take care* of it." She squints at me like a raccoon sizing up a garbage can.

"I do," I say. "I have it sent out and cleaned regularly."

Neither of them react to this little gem in the slightest. "Come by anytime," says Father Stone. Smiling.

"We'd love to have you," says Miss Selkirk. She sounds hungry.

"I'll think about it," I say. "But I just remembered—Galahad did his business back there and I forget to bring a plastic bag with me. Gotta go get one." I spin around and march away quickly, before one of them magically produces said item from under a hat or maybe a metal hatch in their chest.

I take Gally back home and consider my next move. I finally decide to just wing it—I'll march up to Longinus's house, knock on the door, and just talk to the guy. Feel him out. If nothing else, I can always invite him to church.

I change my clothes first. Not sure why. Stretchy black pants, sneakers, black top. Your basic breaking-and-entering outfit, though I have no intention of burgling the place—all I want is to have a conversation. I tell myself that, over and over, the whole way there.

Which doesn't take long. The Longinus place is on the edge of town, but Thropirelem isn't a big place—maybe a few hundred people, all told. Small towns are like islands, little pockets of habitation separated by plains or forests or mountains instead of water—but mostly just separated by distance. People say that distance has dwindled in the twenty-first century, shrunk by modern transportation and telecommunications into a single global village, but there are still plenty of places where you can expect to drive for an hour or more before you see another human face. That distance always has been—and always will be—a factor in how people who live there act and think; isolation always is.

Here that distance is mostly filled with wheat instead of water, vast rippling fields of pale yellow. The Longinus house perches at the edge of that grassy ocean like a rotting seaside warehouse, huge and ancient and dark. It's only three stories tall, but it seems taller. The wood is that rough gray that unpainted lumber turns into under the hot prairie sun, like petrified elephant hide. The windows are all shrouded by dark curtains, and the front porch has a tumbleweed stuck in one corner beside an old wooden chair; I can help but think about the Gallowsman.

I force myself to mount the creaking steps. The front door is a huge slab of oak with a panel of stained glass at head height. The designs worked into the glass are disturbing, but I'm not sure why; there's just something about the angles that seems subtly off, like an optical illusion you don't quite get.

And it's ajar.

Just a few inches, enough to show a narrow slit of darkness between the frame and door. I freeze with my hand up to knock, then rap gently on the glass. "Hello?" I say softly.

Stupid. What's the point in knocking and calling out if you do it quietly? I say in a louder voice, "Hello! Mr. Longinus?" and knock again, harder this time. Hard enough, in fact, that the door swings open wider.

Dark hallway. No sound. I see an old oval mirror in a silver frame on one wall, and faded wallpaper in some kind of floral pattern behind it. A shapeless dark coat hangs from a peg beside the door, and a worn pair of boots sit underneath it.

I take a step inside. My nerves are screaming at me to just turn around and leave, but some other part of my brain has taken over; I find myself checking the edges of the door, looking down for footprints, even glancing toward the ceiling at the cracked and dirty light fixture. My right hand keeps drifting toward my left shoulder, like I'm going to pull something out of a breast pocket.

No, not a pocket. A holster.

"Cut it out, Jace," I mutter. "You read too many police procedurals." I don't even own a gun, let alone a holster.

But apparently deep down inside I'm convinced I have cop DNA, because instead of leaving and closing the door behind me—or calling a real police officer—I move further down the hallway.

There's another door ajar at the end of the corridor.

When I peer through it, I see stairs leading down. Basement, of course. No trail of blood on the steps, but that would be overkill. Creepy old house, door open, basement. I'd have to be some kind of idiot to go down there, right?

I throw myself on the mercy of the court. About the only excuse I have is possible mental illness, which in retrospect is probably closer to an explanation than an excuse. Also convenient and less insulting.

Down I go. The staircase is well-lit and doesn't creak. The stairs go down and end at another door, which is kind of strange. This one looks like it was forged out of cast iron about two hundred years ago, and it's open, too. There's an orangey, flickering light coming from inside; I peer cautiously into the room.

I don't know what I expect to see, but it isn't this.

First impressions: big room, lots of black draperies hanging down. More candles than the bedroom of a teenage goth girl, all of them lit. Lots of cushions on the floor, but no other furniture except for a big-ass table at the far end of the room.

No, not a table. An altar.

That's what draws my attention and focuses it. Because the altar—a big chunk of square granite that looks as if it was carved right out of the bedrock—has a body on it. Male, dressed in a long black robe, with a face only an undertaker could love.

Old Man Longinus.

I don't hesitate. I walk forward and inspect the body. He's got a long, presumably ceremonial dagger sticking out of his chest, and no pulse. I don't touch anything else, not at first. Instead, I look around and try to figure out what happened.

That's when I notice the photos.

There are seven in all, and from the way three are positioned on the altar it looks as if Longinus was placing them in preparation for some sort of ritual when he was attacked. There are two more on the floor. I find the last one trapped beneath the body, the corner barely visible.

They're all of me.

Me in different emotional states—gesticulating in anger, weeping, laughing, even one where I seem to be having an orgasm.

"Double. You. Tee. *Eff*," I say.

I don't study the pics for long. They go in my pocket.

If there's one thing I've learned from police work research, it's that the person who discovers the body is often the perpetrator. That, plus me in house for no good reason plus pictures plus history of medical-grade wackiness equals Jace in jail. No way. I may be crazy, but I'm not stupid.

Okay, I may be crazy *and* stupid, but at least I try to alternate. And right now, I'm going to go with the crazy option and try to puzzle out what the hell went on here.

I look around. Candles are all really low—they've been burning for hours, which tells me the killer is long gone. No signs of a break-in or a struggle, so Longinus probably knew the person who murdered him. Whoever did it was fast, strong, and confident—the knife's buried up to the hilt, and looks like it punched right through the breastbone. You don't kill someone with a single thrust like that, from the front, unless you know exactly what you're doing. Maybe you've even done it before.

The body isn't restrained, and one leg is dangling off the side. Not a ritual posture, in other words. He might have been shoved backward and off his feet before the killing blow was delivered.

So he let someone in, someone he wasn't afraid of. He was in the middle of preparing his altar, and then he was abruptly attacked and killed, possibly with a weapon of opportunity.

The cushions bother me.

You don't just scatter a few throw pillows around a room like this to brighten it up. The pillows are there for people to sit—or, more likely, kneel—on while something vile and perverse happens on that altar.

The evidence seems conclusive. Longinus was running a sex club.

Why they picked me as their fetish object isn't clear, but maybe it was only Longinus himself who was fixated on me. I go searching for corroborating evidence, convinced I'll find a chest full of sex toys and illegal porn hidden behind one of the black draperies.

Not so much.